= THE =

BEST BAD THINGS

= THE =
BEST BAD
THINGS

KATRINA CARRASCO

MCD
FARRAR, STRAUS AND GIROUX
NEW YORK

MCD

Farrar, Straus and Giroux

175 Varick Street, New York 10014

Library of Congress Cataloging-in-Publication Data

Names: Carrasco, Katrina Marie, 1983– author.

Title: The best bad things / Katrina Carrasco.

Description: First edition. | New York : Farrar, Straus and Giroux, 2018.

Identifiers: LCCN 2017057595 | ISBN 9780374123697 (hardcover)

Subjects: LCSH: Women detectives—Fiction. | Undercover
operations—Fiction. | Opium trade—Fiction. | Smuggling—Fiction. |
Eighteen eighties—Fiction. | Washington (State)—Fiction. | GSAFD:
Mystery fiction.

Classification: LCC PS3603.A77437 C47 2018 | DDC 813/.6—dc23

LC record available at https://lccn.loc.gov/2017057595

Designed by Jonathan D. Lippincott

Our books may be purchased in bulk for promotional, educational, or business
use. Please contact your local bookseller or the Macmillan Corporate and
Premium Sales Department at 1-800-221-7945, extension 5442, or by e-mail at
MacmillanSpecialMarkets@macmillan.com.

www.mcdbooks.com • www.fsgbooks.com

Follow us on Twitter, Facebook, and Instagram at @mcdbooks

1   3   5   7   9   10   8   6   4   2

For my mamá, *and her fighter's heart*

= THE =
BEST BAD
THINGS

PROLOGUE

Hard recoil. Ringing. Bitter smoke and god damn it, the shot did not fall him. He's still coming, tiger-eyed, bloom of red spreading over his collarbone. Glass crunches under my boots. Shouts from the street and quick, there can be no trail, the plan to disappear the body can't work if I'm found with it. Trigger pull. Hardwired forearm reining in the kickback. He's still coming.

Shoulder to sternum, falling, hip to hip, carpet, knee to shin, glass sharp in one elbow, wet on my chest. He swipes for the gun, catches my neck. How the fuck is he still breathing with a hole in his lung. Knuckles twisted into throat gristle. Blood on his teeth, hissing in his inhales. Just go down.

He finds my fist, the iron locked inside it. His mouth so near mine its red dripping slicks my lips. More noise from the street but it's not in the hall yet, his hand crushing my jugular so dark spots clot the faraway ceiling, his too-close eyes. Keep hold of the pistol. Keep clear of the trigger. Think of the low body. Knees tight around his hips. Flesh memory: imprint of this position minus the gun. Memory of reaching up to pull him closer, liquid slippery between us. Surge to the left. Roll with bone gravity and come out on top.

Now his jaw unclenches. He knows it's over. When he looks at me, which face is he seeing, maybe all of those I've worn for him, overlaid in the darkening lens of his vision. I've made corpses before but never loved it. The stilling throb of pulse, the slowness in the eyes—they're wrong. Bodies belong in motion.

His hand falls from my throat, brushes my chest. Blood-thick breath. He says my name. I put the muzzle to his temple, gentle. I told you, I say. Don't call me that.

1

JANUARY 12, 1887

Last time Alma wore this shirt, she ended up in jail. The cotton still carries a cellblock tang of piss and mildew. Straw crackles on the sleeves. Ruddy blotches dot the shirt's collar—tobacco juice? No. The fight that landed her in lockup comes back clear: bone crush, jaw clench, freight-train heart. The marks are blood.

That was a damn good night.

Next to the shirt is a pair of socks, wadded into a bristling lump. Alma unknots the wool. Angles out a snub-nosed knife. When she tests it on her forearm, dark hairs gather on the blade like iron filings on a magnet.

Pins nip her scalp as she pulls them free. An auburn wig comes loose. She drops it onto the cot, where it curls among other castaway layers: oilcloth cape, green silk bodice, green silk skirt, lacy petticoat. A corset slumps gutted beside a sweat-ringed shift and cotton stockings. She chafes a damp rag across her cheeks, across her wrists and knuckles, stripping off a thick coat of cosmetic powder.

Wearing only her own skin and hair, she is unbound. Powerful. She can mold her form into any shape. But the nakedness also knocks her askew, kicks open an unlit pit. Who would stare back at her in a mirror when she has not arranged herself? Who is Alma when she stands naked and silent in a threadbare rented room?

Leave that thought. Be glad there is no looking glass here. Be glad for the smash and racket of the couple next door, the distraction of their fighting or fucking. The noise is an impetus: Put on a new costume. A new performance has begun.

To lacquer on manhood, Alma starts with the hands. Gentlemen wear rings. A workingman wears calluses. He leaves dirty fingerprints on newspapers, drops peanut shells in his path. His nails may or may not be bitten. In winter his knuckles crack with cold.

She shakes open a sackcloth bundle. Inside is a warped metal pipe, slick with grease, caked with ash. A sailor sold it to her from a dockside box of scraps. He said its explosion unmade a boiler room and nearly sent its ship to the bad place.

Only faint smears of French chalk remain between her fingers. Gripping the pipe, she twists her hands in opposite directions. Twists, so the pipe's grease grits into her skin and its metal ridges rouse the nerves of her palms.

Remember how to talk like Jack Camp. Rough voice. Tobacco-muddied tongue.

Grip, twist.

Remember how to move like Jack Camp. Hips first, cocksure. Twist.

Remember how to fight like Jack Camp—and at this, Alma smiles. This is her favorite thing. The red and sweat and swearing, the fire in her rib cage, the bend and crush of bodies. Muscles contracting. Sunbursts of pain. Nothing but the pummeling, the wild onrushing of life.

As Camp, she could be a thief, saying, *I was on a crew in the city. We ran small-time jobs—liquor, queered cash. Your place looked like easy pickings, and your boys sure as shit didn't put up much of a fight.*

She tosses the pipe aside. Curls her palms around the desk lamp. Its chimney funnels warm air onto her face as she inspects her fingers. They feel stronger. They feel sturdier. Soot and hairline scrapes form a blackened patchwork on her skin.

Alma pulls on the long woolen socks. Narrows her mouth, her eyes. No lace trimming softens men's smallclothes. The mold-soured shirt is rough against her armpits, rough against the bruised flesh of her throat. With each layer her breath comes faster. She hungers for heat, for movement and salt.

As Camp, she could be a gambler, saying, *He owes me fifty dollars. Skipped right out of a card game, the son of a bitch. I don't know who you are, mister, but if you're not prepared to front for him, I'll beat him again until he pays up.*

Knife into belt. Put out the lamp. Throw two jabs and a cross in the darkness just to feel the swing-snap of muscles under stiff oilcloth.

Dressed, armed, kindled to sweat, she slips out of her room.

The hall is lined with the fallen. Poppy-sick sailors and girls lie together, barely moving in the candlelight, all wreathed in bitter seed and smoke. She steps over more bodies on the stairs. A dice game. A whore earning a nickel. At the bottom a boy streaked with mud is hunched toward the wall, quietly vomiting. The midnight lobby, too, is crowded, but the manager's cubicle—where the hairless, sightless landlord keeps a child on the floor beside him to examine customers' coins—is empty. A man is crumpled against the door with his limp penis in one fist. As Alma steps over him, he grabs her trousers.

"Hands off, pal," she says, and kicks him in the ribs. Her gravelly voice and bitten-off inflection please her almost as much as the thump of her boot against his bones.

Outside, everything feels tight and shiny, crowded with energy. Frost gilds the thrumming boardwalk. Candy-colored lanterns light the crowded mouths of pleasure houses. A saloon rattles with shouts and a melodeon's groaning. At the corner, men are clotted around a brawl. The meaty slap of a punch fishhooks Alma's attention, but she turns up her collar and hustles past. The next street, darker, belongs to the wind. Icy brine fills her nose and mouth and ears. She walks with her shoulders up, hands flexing in her coat pockets, cap pulled low.

As Camp, she could go right for the heart of it, saying, *Word is you're moving tar. I want in on the work. I've spent time in the trade, and I'll be more use to you than your man here. I had him on his back in a minute flat.*

Green reek of kelp. Ship rigging rattles fifty feet out in the bay. She weaves through Lower Town, its shingles and piers coating the peninsula's shore like a barnacle cluster. The road is humped with piled wooden crates and construction gear. The foundry's furnaces suffuse the air with char.

Just past its smokestacks is the warehouse.

A tall plank box, it has barred, copper-paneled doors and high windows. It is on a private pier, close to Barnaby Sloan's boarding-house, and its entrance is frequently patrolled. All this, plus the deciding link: last night, she watched Sloan's man help carry a cartload of crates off the Victoria-based steamboat *Orion* and load them into the warehouse.

Opposite the foundry's coke shed is an unfinished building. In the shelter of its doorway Alma blinks ice off her lashes and strikes a match against new-caulked brickwork. As she lights a cigarette, her fingers flicker redly in the lower half of her vision, with the ware-house floating above, forty feet away.

She doesn't have to see the watchman before she approaches, but it would help to know which guard she'll face. Three take shifts at the door: a grizzled old-timer with long arms; a hulking man with a bad shoulder he tries to hide; and a boxy kid about her size. The youngster would put up a good fight. He keeps his hands near his midriff and moves light on the balls of his feet, so she can tell he's done time in the ring. The big man lumbers. She could fell him like a tree. It's the old fellow she worries about. A man like that might rely on his fists, but if his fists fail, he might switch to a pistol.

Pinkerton would love it if she was shot. It would be easier for him if the last trace of the Women's Bureau disappeared. No more cover-ups. No more embarrassments, like the time she swaggered into his private Chicago office and offered to work a case as a man, as Hannah sometimes did. Once Pinkerton recognized her, he was mortified. He cut in to say, "Unequivocally no, Miss Rosales." She hated him more for insisting on the "Miss" than for turning her down.

Yet here she is, investigating for Pinkerton while wearing Camp's clothes. Close to fulfilling the first part of the agency's instructions: find opium importers on the waterfront, trace chains to the top, and identify who's in charge. With his warehouse, his private pier, and his shipments from Victoria—the prime source of opium on the West Coast—Barnaby Sloan is looking like the perfect suspect.

The snow that fell briefly at sunset is coming back, thin sheets of flakes riding the wind off the strait. Alma's toes curl against the cold. Her pocket watch reads ten fifty.

Ten fifty is close enough.

Off the stoop, down the pier, and she's on private property. The three alibis crouch in her head, each trailing a skeleton story to be fleshed out in the moment. Her moves will depend on Sloan's, so she is still taking shape as she lopes toward the warehouse. She can be anyone. A gambler. A thief. An opium smuggler.

She flicks her cigarette into the water. Walks up to the doors like she owns the place. A chain is looped over the bar, held secure by a rusted padlock. The warehouse perimeter is night-shaded, vacant.

Pause in the pool of lamplight. Be visible from the neighboring docks, from the back of the pier, from the street. Lift the padlock and chain. Let go.

Clang.

Round one.

Whistling, Alma steps past the door to inspect a window. It's set two feet above her head. Not much of an outside ledge to grip, which will make for an awkward pull-up, with her elbows scraping the boards. She's reaching for it when a shadow flickers on her right.

"Nice setup you got here," she says, dropping her arm as she faces the watchman. It's the big fellow. Lucky break.

"Who the fuck are you?"

She lets him slam her shoulder blades against the wall. The breath bursts out of her. Tingling fills her arms, her emptied chest. The man's red hair is slicked back. His beard patchy. He smells like a bearskin rug: sour flesh, matted fur, the underside of boots.

"Who's asking?" she says.

"Get lost." His knuckles press into her breastbone, just above her binding cloth. "This is a private pier."

No skip in his voice, no wandering of his eyes. He sees nothing of a woman in her. She is Jack Camp, flawlessly.

"I ain't goin' nowhere," she says, grinning.

Muscles tight, she waits for the gut punch. When it comes, she wheezes, sags, drops to her knees and then her side; playing clumsy, groaning. The man shifts to better aim his kick, and the angle is right for her to snap her boot into his knee. He goes down hard and her fists are ready. Eye. Throat. Favored shoulder. Exhale with each blow.

Just as she expected, this giant is no fighter. She's barely worked up a sweat when the watchman's overstuffed arms flop onto the pier and his eyes roll white.

Too easy. And too quick. It's only ten fifty-five—not yet the eleven o'clock change of watch. The burst of heat from the fight is already seeping away: she imagines it leaving her in a red-sparked shower, like cigarette ashes peeling into the wind. She can't burn out yet.

To stay warm she shoves the big man's body against the wall. Standing on his back brings her twelve inches closer to the window. She chins up the remaining distance, but the warehouse interior is a deep trough of black. It could hold one crate of smuggled opium or one hundred. There's no proof yet.

Down again. Hands braced on boards. Boots muffled by the man's fleshy torso. From behind: footsteps.

"Son of a bitch."

It's an old man's voice, close to her shoulder. Maybe her luck has gone off. But maybe he won't go for his gun. Then the leather creak of a holster stirs a hiccup of dread. She hops from the body into gathering snow. The iced planks betray her. Boots slip-crunching, she stumbles backward into a yank on her jacket and a steel-tipped punch—

Drag, scrape. Knees on fire. Drag, scrape. Oh, Jesus. A wet cough wells up in Alma's throat and it tastes like blood.

Alive.

All right.

Buy time. Stay limp. Let limbs dangle, which is not easy when some of them must be hanging on by single tendons.

Drag, scrape.

Focus.

What's the damage?

Pulsing lower right rib. Hard hands in each armpit. Knees and jawbone stinging. General agony at the base of her skull. No bullet wounds, but check again—last time she was shot she didn't feel it at the entry point on her hip. That patch of flesh went numb, and instead she had the worst back spasms of her life. Until Hannah nudged the slug out with a knife tip. After that Alma recalibrated her pain scale.

Focus.

Think about location.

They are still outside. Cracking her eyes shows a sliver of blurry nightscape made up of yellow shadows. The ground bucks forward eagerly: plank boards, plank boards, granulated snow. They are no longer over water. She takes this as a good sign. If the men were going to kill her, they would've thrown her in the bay to bloat.

Her plan might have worked. They might be going to Sloan. The real game begins here. She knows how Sloan handles problems. Get on his crew, or he'll . . . No. There is no failing. Get on his crew.

Drag, scrape. She wants to pull away from the pinioning hands that send shocks through her neck and shoulders. Instead, as a diversion, she takes stock of the men towing her. A weaker grip on one arm and a holster's squeak near her left ear: the old-timer. The other man walks with a limp. Bulky thigh, bearskin stink: the huge watchman she was recently stepping on. As they move, the man has his revenge—his uneven gait echoes through their body chain so her knees bang against boards with his every other step.

A flight of stairs rises under her nose. They are going in. We are going in! She repeats this fierce internal shout over the jolting pain the steps ladder into her legs.

Warmth. Soft carpet. An embroidered patch of flowers passes under her face. So Sloan likes a bit of luxury. She coughs again, waiting for another clump of blooms on the blue rug, then lets copper-sweet spit dribble over her lips and chin.

"He's bleeding on the fucking runner," someone calls. An Irishman—a rarity in this town. Head down, Alma allows herself a private grin. She may have a new name to tie to Sloan's ring.

The men halt. Drop her to the floor. She lets out a groan that's not entirely for show.

"Shut up," the huge man says. His kick misses her throbbing rib by three inches, but the blow is still enough to puncture her breath.

Knocking above her. From inside the room comes a muffled voice.

"What?"

Now. Sober up. There is no failing. Alma stares at the carpet. It fills her field of vision with pure azure, like the morning sky. She thinks of waking, of moving, of life churning back into her numbed arms, her pulped knees and shins.

"Found a problem at Madison Wharf," the old-timer says.

Someone opens the door. A veil of firelight falls over the rug. Rough hands hoist her up—Don't flinch, damn it!—and the men haul her into the room and almost to standing. Blood rushes back into her legs in a needle-tipped tide. The air is scented with smoke: birchwood and a sweet tobacco note she starts to follow just as the old-timer speaks.

"He was trying to break into the warehouse," he says. "Beat the shit out of Conaway. He don't—"

Alma rears to life. Twists to kick at his knee. Still dizzy, she misses. The bigger man plows a fist into her stomach.

"Try that again and I'll shoot you," the old-timer says. Then, in a milder tone: "He don't look like none of Sloan's boys, but I brung him anywise."

No air.

She's got no air, and it's not just the punch. This isn't Sloan's place.

Her plan unravels and she comes apart a little, too, woozy, pooling with alarm.

A glossy pair of laced boots appears. Fine-cut black trousers. Her cap brim obscures the rest, and she can't lift her chin until she remembers how to breathe.

"You work for Sloan?"

This voice. She knows it.

Alma blinks away vertigo. She hangs between the men, lungs sucking into motion at last, so her own herky-jerk inhales fill her ears.

"You're going to tell me if you work for him," the man before her says, and she places the familiar smell: vanilla tobacco smoke. "If not Sloan, then whoever it was that sent you to nose around my warehouse. I'm busy; you're a bother. Quit wasting my time."

She does not have a strategy for this. As she cobbles one together, the man steps forward, grunts an order. Another punch to the stomach blots her mind with shadow. She wheezes, folding inward as far as she can strain with the two men wrenching her arms.

"Take off his cap," the man says. "So he can look me in the—"

Her cap flops onto the floor, leaving her damp forehead chilled. She doesn't look up. Maybe he won't recognize her.

The silence tells her he does.

She makes blank her face and raises her chin.

Nathaniel Wheeler stands three feet away. He is pale, staring, but even as she watches, he tucks away his shock-loosed corners: he closes his mouth, hardens his eyes. Brings a hand to his already-straight necktie and smooths it flat.

"Wait outside," he says to the men.

They don't obey at once, though the huge man's grip slackens.

"Put him down, and wait outside," Wheeler says again, louder.

Him. Wheeler has preserved her cover. Maybe her luck is back. The corners of her mind are busy mashing together fact and fiction. In ten seconds she'll have an alibi to suit this new geography.

The men at either side of her let go. One of them—the old bastard, she'd wager—shoves her forward. Her shredded knees drag over the carpet and she chokes down a gasp.

The hallway door closes. Wheeler comes to stand over her. She eases up into an unsteady crouch. He offers no help. As she levers herself to standing, her right ribs crunch into a knot of fire.

"Alma?" Wheeler says, when they are face-to-face. "Jesus Christ. What the hell are you doing?"

2

JANUARY 10, 1887
Two Days Earlier

The chophouse smells of burnt blood, butter, burgundy wine. Four tables share the lavish back room, where Alma is the only woman, though her plain gray dress and unadorned hair have drawn little attention. She spears a slice of veal, determined to eat despite the corset crushing her stomach.

"More potatoes?" Nathaniel Wheeler lifts the laden spoon, its knobbed handle flashing in his fingers. "You have a splendid appetite."

"Oh, yes, please," she says.

He is no shy eater himself. He has put away oysters, turtle soup, two sizable chops, boiled potatoes, string beans, a bottle of wine, and now a splash of liquor.

After he serves her, he swirls the tawny film at the bottom of his glass, a delicate motion for so robust a man.

"Take this whiskey, for example," he says. "It could not be made here. A distiller must have his own water, his own barley. You cannot transplant water from the Bailliemullich Burn."

"You miss home very much," she says.

"Aye. It's been twenty years." He wipes his hands with his white linen napkin, lays it alongside his plate. "Tell me about the colors of Queen's Park, in the autumn. When you were leaving."

His parched-blue gaze is distant. What does this wistful man have to do with opium? Perhaps he is nothing more than he claims: an importer of British and Canadian goods. Yet there are small oddities. The way his eyes narrow when she abruptly reaches into her handbag. That fighter's swagger in his walk, the way he holds his chin, both hint at a different temperament. When she called on him at his brass-and-varnish company offices, he apologized for the smoke next door, but Alma was almost certain the gunpowder smell was wafting from his shirt cuffs.

"The trees along Pollokshaws Road were gold shot with red, and on clear afternoons the moss caught the sun in emerald splendor," Alma says, catching herself on the word *emerald*, where her broad Scots accent almost falters. "Closer to town everything smelled of peat smoke and malt from the Loch Katrine distillery."

She is reaching for names and places and barely finding them. It has been almost twenty years since she lived in Glasgow, and her last trip to visit Uncle William was in the summer of 1880, back when the Women's Bureau was still in operation.

"The greenhouse at the Botanic Gardens," he says, "has it survived?"

"It has. When I left, they were showing orchids, brought all the way from the Merina Kingdom."

He sips at his drink. Smooths down his mustache with thumb and forefinger. At the start of the meal he had seemed agitated. Faintly angry. Now he is mellowed, contemplative, but it is not due to the alcohol—there is no slur in his voice, no slump in his posture. Another edge she was hoping for, blunted.

"You are kind to indulge me," he says, taking his hand from his face and smiling.

The expression makes him look younger, thirty rather than forty. He is handsome, in a rough-cut way; successful; a Scotsman. Someone she might not have lamented a match with, if her uncle had kept her pliant and bridled. Now the thought of marriage and its drudgeries makes her squirm. Her corset bones creak. God damn this costume. She is weighted with draperies, pinned with dead curls, forced to sit straight as a stick. Dressed in her own clothes, she could sprawl. Share Wheeler's fancy liquor. No one would expect Alma Rosales to mince on about leaves and flowers, and with not a drop to drink.

"Your company is a balm," he says. "This has been a trying week. Some trouble this afternoon, and then the trustees considering . . . But I won't bore you with all that again. Did you make your trip to the beach below Crow's Nest?"

Another swerve from the useful to the inane.

"I filled an entire hatbox with shells," she says. "It will break my heart to leave them when I repack. Though while I was there, a policeman was asking about some cargo that washed ashore. He spoke of smugglers. Is it true? Are there smugglers about, in such a fair town?"

Wheeler hesitates. Will he speak candidly? She leans forward, fingertips on the white-clothed table, every bit the piqued young innocent. But the room is not in her favor. It intrudes upon them: a man in the opposite corner bellows a laugh; a waiter appears with a silver tray of coffee, plum pudding, apple pie.

"There are plenty of rough men on the waterfront," Wheeler says, when the room settles back into its candlelit, velvet-curtained quiet. "Thieves. Charlatans. Those who would . . . mean you harm. Lark about on the beach all you like at midday. But when you're alone, you must keep to your lodgings after dark."

If Wheeler was a smuggler, and his ingénue companion showed an interest, would he not permit a hint of darkness to lure her closer? Alma has parried with crooks and robbers. Even the closest of them delights in his exploits, in recounting how a particularly intricate job was carried off. Yet Wheeler is dampened by her curiosity. He is frowning. He stirs cream into his coffee, pale eyes fixed on the filigreed spoon.

"I worry . . ." he says, then clears his throat. "If you are free tomorrow night, I hope you will join me again."

His voice has lost that momentary blur of emotion.

"That is, if your uncle does not appear and call you away to Tacoma."

"I've had no more news of his accident." Alma bites her lower lip. "My telegraphs have gone unanswered."

Wheeler reaches across the table, rests his fingers on her knuckles. It is the first time their skin has touched. Alma calls heat to her cheeks. After a few shallow breaths she lets her hand unfurl under his. Wheeler's gaze flickers. The thick vein at his throat is tapping faster.

"Come, hen," he says. "He will be fine. Let me take you to the pier we are building, I think you will enjoy seeing it."

She collects the pink roses he greeted her with, and he helps her to stand. His jacket smells of vanilla tobacco smoke. As she pulls on her gloves, he stays close beside her, warm, one hand hovering at the small of her back. An eager creature. Not her usual taste, bland as he is. But in the dark of the carriage he will be a hot mouth, she hopes. Maybe he will unlace her stays and let her breathe.

Outside, a fiendish wind sends clouds galloping past the moon. Union Wharf's lamps burn yellow against the blur of bay and sky. Men throng the doors of the Central Hotel across the road, a churn of suits and cigars and gem-topped stickpins. Wheeler pulls Alma's arm tighter into the crook of his elbow. She leans into him, ducking her head, letting him think she is shy about being seen together or nervous about their outing. In fact, she is hiding her face from the gentlemen at the Central. She is nearly done with Wheeler— he's not her opium smuggler, and it wouldn't do to have her next mark see the pair of them climbing into a carriage. Her vision is clipped by the brim of her hat: sidewalk planks glimmering with frost; her polished boots; the fine gray wool of Wheeler's coat sleeve.

At the corner he hails the waiting carriage. He hands Alma up into a cab lit by faceted lanterns. Wood paneling agleam. A plaid lap blanket folded neatly in one corner. She slides toward it, her skirts quick over the leather cushions. Wheeler takes a seat on the same bench, though he leaves a modest gap between them. She is growing impatient with these genteel maneuverings.

"Will the new pier serve trade for your railroad trust?" Alma asks, making her last attempt to steer their conversation in a more useful direction. Outside, the horses' shoes thump a drumbeat in the mud. "The South Port Townsend Line?"

She muddles the name despite having heard it more than a few times, waiting to see if Wheeler will correct her or become impatient. Instead, his reflection softens into a smile. He must think her very much the foolish girl she is playing: the untaught governess abroad for the first time. The wealthy man and the silly maid in a nightfall carriage. The wolf and the lamb. Alma stifles a yawn.

"I have not yet secured a place in the trust," he says. "If I do, my fortune in this town is assured."

He does not seem tired of repeating this. He likes to talk of money, of his fine imported woolens and liquors, of his waterfront warehouse and his commercial success.

"It's a delicate thing in these last few days of negotiations." He places his palm on the bench between them. "If I am successful and you have not been called away, we might celebrate together. The occasion would require the hiring of a yacht, or something just as decadent."

"Oh, a yacht!" Alma smiles at him. "I've never been on a yacht. Is it true you can sail to Canada from here?"

Her questions are becoming sloppy, almost too obvious. After three days of solicitous attention he has said nothing relating to opium, and she is taking shots in the dark.

He is closer now, his solid thigh an inch from hers on the quivering leather. In another private room, with another man, she might tear open his starched collar, press her body onto his. But Alma Macrae is apt to blush. Alma Macrae will not even take her gloves off as an invitation. So she tamps down her velocity, just as she tamped down her thirst for wine.

Wheeler is moving fast enough, anyhow. He sets his hand lightly on her knee. There is a fresh cut on his middle knuckle. Pink skin that might be the beginnings of a bruise. The iron-banded lanterns throw webbed shadows over the outstretched length of his arm, the sharp line of his nose, the sheen of his inner lip.

"Alma." His voice quiet, constricted. "May I kiss you?"

She clasps the flowers in her lap. The smell of pulped greenery and broken roses rises.

"Yes," she says.

His fingers tighten on her leg, neatly trimmed nails scritching over twill. He turns toward her, their limbs knocking with the motion of the carriage, and brings his other hand to her chin. Gentle, his thumb sweeps over the bone. This tenderness alarms her. He is no wolf after all; there is no abrupt pawing at her breasts, no

thrusting tongue. Alma has no experience with a man handling
her with care. She does not much care for it.

His mustache pricks her upper lip. As she opens her mouth, the
carriage hits a rut. Their teeth crack together. Wheeler pulls back
slightly.

"Never mind the railroad—you should join a trust for improving
the roadways," she quips, and he laughs, a husky chuckle.

"I will take that into consideration." He leans into her again,
runs his forefinger down the line of her throat. "This is not too fast?"

"No."

Three days of work, of shadowing him, wasted. He is no more
than a lonely man who longs for his old country; its water, its women.
But he has paid for her fine dinners. Sketched her a cameo of Port
Townsend. Now his palms are hot on her bodice. His clean-shaven
jaw smells of sweet clove balm. He pulls her closer, his dark brows
tilting inward. She lets the flowers fall from her lap.

3

JANUARY 12, 1887

How are you going to play it? The warehouse. The opium. Or: fogged carriage windows, smell of wet wool, his powerful fingers in your pinned-on hair. No. The railroad trust? What of Sloan's man sneaking? A traitor, somewhere. How are you going to play it, how are you—

Like this.

Alma leans on the chair beside her. The movement fires her inner right pectoral, already wrenched raw by Wheeler's men. She allows herself to flinch, her face to tighten with pain. Wheeler's gaze slides off her—is he squeamish?—and he walks away, to the sideboard behind his desk. The narrow table is massed with decanters. He pours a drink, yet no glass rattles. Nothing spills. Maybe he's not as shaken up as he seems. But there was that moment of recognition. Turmoil in his eyes.

"I can't even look at you in those clothes." He hunches over the liquor bottles, thickset shoulders bunched, knuckles white on the white marble.

"You must be surprised," she says.

In a hurry to keep him talking, Alma uses Camp's voice before she thinks better of it. At the sound his head twitches toward her, but he does not turn around. While he's looking away, she makes a quick scan of the office: sober blue wallpaper, hearth against the back wall spilling heat. An imposing desk at the room's center, its dark wood littered with a deep loam of papers. A second door in the far corner.

"I'm also very angry," he says. "I want to know what you're doing here, like that. I want to know now."

There's her free ride, over.

"I'm a detective," she says, and now she's committed to her cover story. "I was hired by one of your business partners."

Wheeler's long drink of whiskey hitches.

"You know I can't name names," she continues. "But my client wants to make sure you're not involved in anything illegal before cosigning with you on Judge Hamilton's railroad trust."

This is good. Close to the truth, in a way. Close to Wheeler's fears. Now all those dinner conversations, which she'd shucked aside as a waste of time, must be remembered. Wheeler's allies; his enemies. How joining the trust would cement his place among Port Townsend's property barons. Wheeler is not satisfied with merely owning an import company and its warehouse.

Of course, during their dinners, he neglected to mention his second warehouse, and how it's being used to move black-market tar.

Wheeler finishes his whiskey, pours another. He is of middle height, stocky; built like a prizefighter. In his private office he is stripped down to a tailored shirt and vest. Rolled-up sleeves reveal muscled forearms. His black hair, slicked back, is tinged silver behind his ears. Alma admires how he almost slipped past her. She'd classified him as a provincial businessman, one of any hundred found in the West, and a bore. In fact he is far more interesting. There's a keen mind in that fighter's body.

"A detective," he says, with a brittle snap of laughter. Then, shaking his head: "And no more Scottish than the Young Pretender."

"Maybe. And maybe you're more than an everyday businessman." She shifts her weight off her right knee, which is shot with pain and oozing, a warm drip down her shin inside her trousers. "I heard that warehouse is full of opium. Now I find it belongs to you."

Her voice wants to fall into rhythm with his, pick up scraps of his Scots accent. She allows it to dip into a brogue on certain words.

This will keep him off-balance. Keep him focused on reconciling the timid Glaswegian governess he courted and this new version of Alma—the bloodied scrapper, cap knocked off and bruised as a trampled apple.

"Opium's not illegal." Wheeler pushes away from the sideboard, makes a sneering survey of her. "You can buy a can at Sing Tai's for nine dollars."

"Unstamped opium is," Alma says, pleased that her guess about the warehouse's contents yielded an evasion, not a denial. "Either way, I'll be sure to include your knowledge of the going market price in my report."

Not even a twitch of his mustache. Despite her wandering accent he is recovering himself. He is becoming hard to read.

"What else will you be reporting?"

"It depends."

"Is this where I'm meant to get out my pocketbook?" he asks, clapping his glass on the sideboard.

"I'm not after a bribe," Alma says. "I'm after a job."

Now she needs a little luck. She'd had a plan for Sloan, who respects blood and money and the ability to extract both. Roughing up his guards might have given her enough currency to gain entrance to his organization. But she does not know what Wheeler respects. The way he's looking at her suggests he doesn't think much of detectives.

"I'll tell my client you're clean if you give me a place on your crew."

"You want to be a warehouse guard?" Wheeler raises an eyebrow as he rolls down one sleeve, then another. His fingers eclipse the tiny cuff buttons. "They make about ten dollars a week. You after that big money?"

"I'm sure you have work that pays more."

"You're not sure of anything." He carries his whiskey to the desk, a massive block of polished oak, its edges carved with trailing vines and tight clusters of grapes. His black leather chair creaks beneath him. "But you're going to haul your pack of lies, and anything else I say in here, to your *client* and use it to slander me."

Alma is not the only one wearing a mask. In the office Wheeler is sealed shut. He keeps his fists curled, his voice ironclad. Gone is the mannered gentleman who showed her around town. That Nathaniel Wheeler had life stirring in his eyes: mirth, homesickness, charm. Or was that a mask, too? It is difficult to pin down the wriggling truth of a man, to dissect what he lets slip from what slips out unbidden.

Alma readjusts her stance, painfully, inhaling hard, and this time Wheeler's pale gaze doesn't slide away. She is losing her advantage.

"You've seen my work," she says. "I surprised you, and I nearly took out two watchmen. I would have if that old bastard fought fair."

"All you've proven is that you're a problem."

Wheeler opens a desk drawer. He pulls out a black-lacquered Colt .45 and sets it on his papers, barrel pointed at Alma.

"Your men took my knife." She can't appear cowed by the gun, but she can't stand there much longer—her right knee is throbbing, the muscles of her thigh beginning to quiver as she holds it in place. "You're going to shoot me while I'm unarmed?"

"You ought not to have trespassed."

"I guess I wasn't listening when you warned me about the waterfront." She calls up his words from two nights before; puts back on the heavy brogue, the timid intonation she'd used while posing as a governess. "Nae place for a wee lass without a chaperone."

And there: a flicker across his face. A momentary confusion. That's going to be the way in, the way to get that heavy black barrel back in its drawer and get him on her side. She's got to be Alma in Camp's clothes.

This is not as easy as it sounds.

Start with the voice. Switching wholesale into the broad Scots she'd used as Alma Macrae is too much artifice. She must use her own voice with some of Camp's grit thrown in. She must rehinge her body. Loosen her mouth, her shoulders. Tuck her hips under her rib cage, a movement that sends twisting pain along her kneecap into her shin. Hardest of all is the mental shift: what will show in her eyes after she drops them to the carpet and concentrates.

"Can I sit down?" she says, and looks at Wheeler under lowered lashes.

"Don't fucking do that," he says.

This is the first time he's spoken so coarsely. He is off guard again.

"Maybe this is how I really talk." Alma grins, dried blood flaking on her chin. "You said you wanted to get to know me better."

Wheeler takes a sip of whiskey, keeps the glass at his lips even after his throat has stopped working. If he's hiding his mouth, he hasn't got control of it. She's getting to him. Maybe.

"Who hired you?" he says.

"I won't answer that."

"Yet you'll sell him a lie to work for me." Wheeler taps his tumbler on the desk, click, click, the glass sounding a high note, as if on the verge of cracking. "He wants me ruined, which is unpleasant but understandable. But what do you want?"

"He's shy about paying me. It happens a lot." Alma nods at her filthy clothes, at what Wheeler knows is under them. "I'm tired of it. Seems like I could make better money another way."

"I don't need the services of a woman," Wheeler says. "I do all my own bookkeeping, and while I might take a lady to dinner, I won't be accused of gauche hiring practices for taking a lady as a secretary."

Alma laughs. He holds up a hand to silence her.

"And you will not work for me like that," he says. "No. No, certainly not like that."

She needs to get him closer. She needs to pick at the little seam that appeared when she asked to sit down. To see her dressed in men's clothes gives Wheeler too much room to think. To stand beside her, smelling her skin, feeling the warmth of her body, will take that room away so she can break past his resistance. He finishes his drink, and there—that's how she'll draw him from behind his desk.

She locks her jaw. Growls an exhale. Without asking his leave she pushes off the chair and hobbles toward the sideboard, her right knee grinding.

"Excuse me, madam."

His choice of words, the real indignation in his voice, are amusing to a corner of Alma's mind—the corner not stunned by pain and the anger that pain calls up.

"You leave me to stand for ten minutes on a half-cracked leg, you owe me a fucking drink," she says.

This is too much of Camp. Her voice is too deep, too harsh. But the unsteadiness in her knee is worse than she expected. A patch of carpet, deep-piled, shifts under her boot. Don't fall. Almost there. Another determined step, rasp of chair legs behind her, and Alma is at the sideboard, tumbler in hand, when Wheeler grips her by the upper arm. Bonefire in her knee as he yanks her around. But now she can lean into the marble, decanters clinking with the impact of her hip. She can lean into Wheeler.

"Don't speak to me like that in my own offices," he says.

His face is inches from hers. In her work boots they are much of a height. He smells strongly of liquor, of sweetened tobacco. Spiced-clove aftershave. His fingers dig into the meat of her biceps. He has left the gun on his desk.

"I need a bit of whiskey," Alma says. "To clear the blood out of my mouth."

She lifts her right arm to draw the stopper. Wheeler holds her left immobile, but not with the punishing tightness of his first approach. His hand flexes, slackens, closes; signaling uncertainty more than it does a warning. His breath uneven. The tips of his ears red. His line of sight tangled in her shirt buttons where her binding cloth tamps down her breasts.

Yes. He likes her in Camp's clothes.

Here's something Alma has not seen in years. Not since the summer she first used the name Jack Camp. Heat seeping from the Chicago sewers. Borrowed clothes ready in a bundle under her boarding-school bed. Climbing over the rusted gate at midnight to where Ned waited, spark-eyed, so she caught the current and lit up like a filament. Brick stairs yellow under lanterns down to where men stomped, calling out bets in blackened voices as hats flew into the ring. Sweat and elbows all around her in the crowd; bodies banging against her clumsily bound breasts; in her gut, the fear of being unmasked warring with animal pleasure as the boxers in the pit dripped with blood. Later she threw her slouch cap on Ned's cot, popped free the buttons of her trousers, and at his open collar the pulse was jumping.

She remembers this. She is ablaze with remembering.

Wheeler's neck is flushed, too. She looks away from him toward the sideboard's spread. Pours out a nip. Whiskey washes over her tongue and she remembers the taste of his skin. His hip is so near hers that the ridge of his leather belt presses into her flesh. As she drinks, she finds his eyes again.

"You going to hold my arm all night?"

Wheeler flinches. What deep recess have her words reeled him up from?

"Some teetotaler." His hand drops to his side. "And that sad business about your uncle—all a lie, too, I take it?"

He does not step away, despite the harsh tone of his words. The space between them is alive with tension. Alma adjusts her right foot to ease her knee. At the movement Wheeler's eyes dart to her boot, then wander up along her bloodied trousers, her purpled knuckles. Now is the time to press him, when he's taut and wanting the better part of his judgment.

"You're not keen on me telling bad things to my client," she says. "And you're not going to shoot me. So take my offer, and put me on your crew."

"Stick to your detective work." He raises his chin, but his eyes keep slipping along the front of her shirt.

Her detective work requires her to find Port Townsend's top opium importer. Wheeler has the perfect setup: an unlisted warehouse on Madison Wharf and an import business to provide a constant flow of liquors and textiles from overseas, while untaxed tar creeps along for the ride. Then there was the wagonload of crates Sloan's man helped transfer from the Victoria steamer the night before, which led her to the Madison warehouse in the first place.

Sloan. Of course. The old-timer who dragged her into the office mentioned him, and it's clear he and Wheeler are not friends. The man she saw at the warehouse is working for both Sloan and Wheeler—and Wheeler may not know about that.

"Give me something I can sink my teeth into," she says, trying this new tack. "I'll take the dirty work your men can't handle. Anything. Hell, send me after Sloan."

Wheeler crowds into her, that fighter's grace lighting through his body as he grabs her collar. She tightens her grip on the tumbler, the closest thing to a weapon she's got. Its cut glass prints a spangling pain into her just-roughened palms and fingers.

"What do you know about Sloan?" he says, breath hot on her face.

Alma's heart is kicking fast, whiskey fizzing in her belly, in the big veins of her torso and thighs.

"I saw one of his men working in your warehouse," she says. "And I'm guessing you didn't invite him."

She swallows, moving the skin of her throat against his knuckles. He seems to realize, belatedly, that his hand is jabbing into her windpipe. He lets go. Steps back, mumbling an oath that sounds like an apology. Alma licks the insides of her teeth, pleased. She took a chance swing with this Sloan angle and hit a weak spot. Yet she is disappointed, too. She wants to brawl with Wheeler, call his blood out. Or pick up where they left off on that carriage ride and add fists and vinegar. But she has a deal to make.

"You want to know who it is, you give me a spot on your crew," she says, straightening her mangled collar. "And I don't mean guard duty."

Wheeler's breathing settles. He pulls his shoulders back, resets his body.

"It's heavy work." He pours whiskey into a fresh glass, waves the decanter at her legs. "I don't think you're in the condition to do it."

"I'll patch myself up," she says.

"Fine. Who is Sloan's man?"

"I get to work first. At least one shift."

He laughs—a thin chuckle, but it's the most he's given her all night. He even holds out the whiskey. She offers her glass and he tips some into it, fine amber-colored liquor, better by far than what she's willing to pay for.

"My men will keep you on a short lead," he says. "No problems. No second chances."

"Understood. I'll tell my client you're clean," she says. "I go by Jack Camp."

Wheeler does not move to shake her outstretched hand.

"What's your real name?" he says.

"Alma Macrae, if you go back far enough on the family tree."

"Your real name."

"While I'm working for you, my name's Camp," she says. "That's all the men will know, and all you need to."

Wheeler frowns. The corners of his eyes are red, recalling Alma to the late hour. Deep lines run along the sides of his mouth. Now that they've finished dancing, he looks tired. This gives him a certain softness, renders him human and more like her dinner companion—save for the gun waiting on his desk. He had to know that would give him away. Businessmen with clean hands pay others to wield weapons.

"Don't look so worried, boss." Alma raises her glass in a salute. "You're lucky to have me in your corner."

"Boss, is it?"

Wheeler takes his drink back to his gleaming desk. He puts his pistol in its drawer. Turns up the long-chimneyed lamp and shuffles through his papers.

"Be back here tomorrow night, at eight o'clock." He scribbles a note, tucks it under a ledger. "I'll have a job for you. And get your knife from Conaway. He'll be in the hall, brooding."

"Yes, sir," Alma says.

She finishes her drink, stops by the door to collect her cap from the carpet. Stooping sends hot wires through her ribs and knee, but it won't serve to show she's injured anymore. So she only grunts, quiet, and fixes her cap on low to hide her tearing eyes.

"I won't treat you like a lady," Wheeler says. "If you fuck me over, I will kill you."

Alma nods, solemn, but her insides are leaping. She's got a solid candidate. And other parts are leaping, too: blood and skin and electricity. I won't treat you like a lady, he says. Good. Don't.

4

JANUARY 13, 1887

In the dry-goods store women line up at the counter. Cooks and house girls from the hill stand beside matrons of Lower Town, their wash dresses cut from calico or dreary wool. Their baskets are piled with spools of thread, tinned fruit, paper packets stuffed with mother-of-pearl buttons. They whisper about the latest casualty on the waterfront, a man who drifted ashore under Quincy Wharf, shirtless, throat opened from ear to ear.

"He only had two fingers left on one hand," Alma's neighbor says. "What they did with the others we cannot know."

"Oh, my Lord." Alma's voice is shaped into a worn Southern drawl. She wears her shabbiest dress and a straw bonnet. Her skin is powdered into sickly pallor, and the sweet smell of French chalk tickles her nose.

The line moves forward. She hobbles to follow it. The bruises from her run-in with Wheeler's warehouse guards are ripened to full purple. Her eyes ache. After leaving his office she cased the place. Saw how the guarded door on Quincy worms into the corner building that houses Clyde Imports, wrapping all of Wheeler's business in a neat brick-walled parcel. Then she slept hard for a few hours and was up at dawn to scratch out a ciphered letter to the Pinkerton's agents. *Operative under deep cover*, she'd translated. *Contact must be limited and brief.*

Jingling from the shop's doorbell. The boy she sent to the post office tumbles in, crimson cheeked and smelling of brine. He holds an envelope.

"Thank you, dear," Alma tells him.

She places two pennies in his open palm, letting her pale-painted fingers tremble around the coins. Good. Her letter was posted, and here's a letter received.

At the counter she asks for a pound of sugar, still using the voice of a Savannah missus, and settles the letter under the loaf. Outside, low fog echoes with cart clamor, shouts of oyster vendors, hammer clang. Gulls and a tarry seawater stench signal the unseen bay. A man sweeps the Delmonico Hotel's front steps, where Alma dined with Wheeler. She keeps her chin tucked as she passes its glazed doors, her powdered face shadowed by her bonnet.

In each knot of pedestrians she considers stopping to read her letter. She does not. Even in this thick-drawn costume, she does not feel as concealed as she would like. Now that Camp is in play, she does not want to compromise his identity by switching disguises. Camp is known. Alma Macrae is known. And she must be invisible when she ascends to Upper Town.

A flight of brick stairs connects the waterfront to the wealthy neighborhood perched above. Alma's right knee, tightly bandaged, creaks as she climbs. She enters the fog. Cottony air sticks in her throat. Then: blue sky. Keen winter sunlight. The last few steps lead to a cobbled street bordered with lawns. All around are pastel dwellings, multistoried, with fine glazing on their ground-floor windows. A housebreaker's picnic.

She listens for footsteps. Waits for the prickling of her upper vertebrae that signals she is being followed. There is birdsong, the ships' bells below muted by fog. Solitude. On a bench by the stairs she pulls out the envelope.

Inside is a ten-dollar banknote wrapped around an embossed sheet of paper. A message is scrawled in green ink:

Thank you for the gift. Your kindness will be remembered. With gratitude, F.V.

The Pinkerton's agents have taken her bait. The cipher is working.

She drops the letter into wet grass, toeing it down until the paper is soaked, the ink a green smear. She tucks the money into her skirt pocket. The envelope, made out to J. Jones, needs more careful treatment: tearing away the stamp and the address, she stuffs these scraps into one boot, then kicks the crumpled envelope into a bush as voices drift up the stairs.

Two aproned women rise out of the mist. One holds a wicker basket; the other, a great spray of orange flowers. When they have walked uphill a ways, Alma stands from the bench. Recalls her instructions: First, go left on Jefferson until you pass the church. Then take a right on Polk, past another church, this one made of stone. Go left again on Clay.

As promised, here is the house.

It sits tucked into the corner of a broad square lot. Two stories, painted white and lemon yellow. Angles sharp as kitchen knives, with new copper edging the roof.

Alma passes the front walk, a span of bricks bordered by winter camellias, and continues on to the line of flagstones leading to the servants' entrance. She stops to fuss with her basket, using the pause to scan the vacant lawns and the neighbors' curtained windows. A flicker of cloth darkens the glass next door. With a small noise of interest, she approaches the back of the house.

Three raps bring a small woman in a starched apron. She is pink faced, spotless. Warm air scented with roasting poultry wafts from behind her. Alma's stomach burbles. The woman takes in her poor clothes, her pallid skin, and shuts the door to a meager crack.

"I've a pound of sugar for the mistress," Alma says.

"*Sucre?*"

"It came at an excellent price."

"*Bon. Bon, entrez.*" The woman drops her eyes from Alma's face and allows her inside.

The kitchen is stifling after her cold walk. She removes her bonnet, careful of her pinned-on hair. The woman hurries into a hallway. Alone, Alma tosses the bonnet and basket onto a counter. In the hearth a spitted chicken drips over flames. Fat pops and spatters. If the bird were already plated, she would tear off a chunk with her teeth. She prowls around, stops at a plate of glazed rolls cooling by the window. Alma eats one in huge bites, bruised jaw clicking, icing sticking on her fingers. When she licks at the sugar, her tongue lifts away talc, too. The French chalk smells sweet but tastes medicinal.

The woman returns to usher her through a passage full of dark furniture. There are no paintings on the pale walls, no carpets on the wooden floors. A large ebony crucifix is the only decoration.

"L'intérieur ici, s'il vous plaît."

The woman shows Alma into a parlor that, after the austere hall, feels lusciously inhabited. The windowless room is warmed by a hearth, its firelight gilding red-papered walls. Crimson roses spill over the lips of china bowls. Two yellow birds, fitted with tiny bells, hop and twinkle in a delicate cage. And a well-remembered smell sets Alma's heart thudding: jasmine and vetiver perfume. She closes her eyes.

Behind her, the door ticks shut. As if summoned by the sound, a tall woman rises out of a chair by the hearth.

"Delphine," Alma says, almost laughing, in part because it is so good to see her and in part because of what she sees. "What the devil are you wearing?"

The belle of San Francisco, famed for her beauty and bejeweled gowns, is swathed head to toe in black. Her dark hair is tied with somber ribbons. The pearl buttons on her dress have an inky sheen. Yet she is not wholly unadorned. Her dress is fashioned of velvet and silk—a wealthy woman's mourning clothes. Bits of gold sparkle at her wrists, her ears, her neck. Alma's gaze catches on these points of light. Even in widow's weeds, Delphine Beaumond is dazzling.

"I could ask the same." She dabs her eyes over Alma. "I hope you didn't bring in any fleas."

From anyone else the barb would not have stung. Alma regrets her shabby costume, her powdered face. She likes to be with Delphine while in Camp's clothes. Once she'd caught Delphine watching her as, dressed as Camp, she unloaded a stolen case of whiskey. Alma will never forget that look.

"You wanted discreet," Alma says.

She walks to the chair next to Delphine's and waits for her to sit. A pot of tea steams over a spirit lamp on the table between them. Cookies glitter on a silver dish. Alma bites into one without ceremony. Its insides are slick with a layer of marzipan. Her favorite.

"I assume from your late arrival that you've been making good use of your time."

Delphine's words are unhurried, delivered in a lush bayou drawl. Silk rustles as she pours a cup of tea. Her ruby ring burns a slow red arc as she takes a sip.

"I have." Alma wants to read the cookies as a good omen, a sign that Delphine remembers her tastes. Remembers her talents. This is Alma's chance for a promotion—a chance to show she's outgrown the San Francisco operation. But not if she's chosen the wrong man.

"Who is it, then?"

"Can I have a drumroll?"

"Don't be foolish, Rosales," Delphine says, but she is smiling, teeth white against her smooth brown skin. The enameled cross at her throat winks in the firelight.

"You're glad to see me," Alma says.

Heat blooms in her abdomen. The harsh welcome had her worried—more than worried, because there's bad news to deliver, too—but now she feels the old bond between them weaving back into being. She can still make Delphine laugh. And Delphine still calls out her rougher edges: Alma's voice drops in pitch, her shoulders widen, her thighs sprawl apart in the hot confines of her skirts. She notes these changes and does nothing to correct them. It is a relief, of a sort, to expand this way despite her clothing. To be in the company of someone who does not require her to wear so many masks.

"Of course I am," Delphine says. "Though you do look bloodless as a hant. You gave me a fright."

"I had to cover some bruises."

"Brawling again?"

"Always," Alma says, grinning. And then, because she can't wait any longer: "The man running your operation here is Nathaniel Wheeler."

Delphine blinks, but that is her only response. She has admirable control of her face.

"Are you sure?" she says.

Alma is not. But she wants to be. And she wants to prove she's now the best Delphine's got in Port Townsend. Delphine's assignment for her dovetailed nicely with Pinkerton's: find the man running the local opium trade. But Delphine is not interested in helping the law. She wants to know that her smuggling business is airtight under investigation.

"Yes," Alma says.

"Why?"

"I found three promising leads," Alma says. "Men moving just a little too much cash on the waterfront. Barnaby Sloan's got tar on him, but he's too busy mucking around in girls and sailors to give it his full attention. The railroad promoter Dom Kopp has deep pockets, but he's devoting them entirely to poker. And then there's Wheeler."

"What exactly do you have on him?"

Here's the sticky issue—where she has not followed instructions. Delphine does not like improvising, so Alma usually refrains from telling her when she cuts corners.

"I know he's got tar in his warehouse," she says.

"Have you seen the product?"

Alma pinches the bridge of her nose, for a moment regretting her haste to report. She could have waited a few days more, made certain. But she hates to wait. She hates to think of Delphine doubting her.

"No," she says.

"You're basing this on conjecture alone."

"He's got all the trappings," Alma says. "A cover imports business, linked to a back office for dirty work. An unlisted warehouse that's guarded like a vault."

Her mouth is dry. She looks down at her empty teacup blankly before remembering she must fill it herself. Delphine, as a rule, never serves others. She once smashed a champagne bottle onto the dining room floor when a guest asked her to refill his drink, then had him lick it up.

Alma pours tea, takes a stinging gulp. Until last night she was ready to pin Sloan as Delphine's man, despite his cathouse—a trade

Delphine won't touch. Now she thinks it's Wheeler. But she's not certain. She is starting to resent this grilling when Delphine could just come out and say yes or no. Not that Alma expected her to go easy.

"I'm sure it's Wheeler," Alma says. "He's up to something, and scared enough of blackmail to take me seriously. He thinks he's going to kill me."

"Well." Delphine picks up her tea, takes a delicate sip. "Let's hope you're right and he's not."

The amusement in her voice is an answer, at last. Yes. Wheeler is Delphine's deputy. Alma congratulates herself with another cookie, its sugar crust crackling sweet. She pictures Wheeler's desk, her boots on the glossy wood, a glass of his fancy whiskey in her hand. She sniffed him out. And she's first in line to replace him. She wonders what he'd do if she called him Nathaniel—Nate, even. What shape his face would twist into.

"Should I be worried?" Delphine says, one brow raised, dark eyes sparking.

"Not too worried," Alma says. "Wheeler runs a tight operation for you. He almost had me fooled, but Sloan gave him away—Sloan has a man on the sly at the Madison warehouse. I know him; I'll get him."

"Wheeler should get him."

"I haven't told him who Sloan's man is, yet. That's my bargaining chip to join his crew."

"This is not the time for games." Delphine leans back into the deep shadows of her chair. "Don't make new problems."

"I'm going to Wheeler's offices tonight," Alma says. "We'll take care of things."

"How did you do it?" Delphine says, her voice floating from the shadows. Firelight plays over the folds of her skirts, over her crossed ankles. She wears the same shoes she's always favored, polished boots with raised heels that add to her already majestic height.

"I never would have gotten to him as Camp," Alma says. "He seems likely to shoot first when a man causes trouble. I went after him as a governess. A Scottish governess—I got the idea when I heard him speaking, and thought I'd throw in a link to the old

country. Added some provincial innocence and an uncle connected
to the Northern Pacific, and he was paying for my dinner the first
night we met."

Alma recounts her initial shadowing of Wheeler, his attentions
to her as she played Alma Macrae, his concern with joining the railroad trust. Delphine, hidden in the shadows, absorbs everything
in silence.

"Poor Wheeler," she says, when Alma has finished. "He thought
he'd finally found a woman dull enough to live in ignorance of his
business."

"Poor Wheeler nothing," Alma says. "His boys put me through
the wringer when they caught me out."

"But you're all right?"

"I'm fantastic," Alma says, all teeth. "Now it's my turn."

"Almost."

This is a nasty word. She wishes she could see Delphine's face.
In the silence the fire snaps and the yellow birds chitter. Alma's
head twinges, at the bottom of her skull, where the warehouse
guard's gun left a walnut-size lump. She reaches up to rub the knotty
bruise.

"You've completed your investigation successfully," Delphine says. "I congratulate you. But there's a second part to this
assignment."

A twitch of irritation. Alma wants her promotion—Wheeler's
desk and office given to her—not another hoop to jump through.
And she wants Delphine to come out of the shadows. Come closer.
Delphine is keeping things all business, despite the last time
they saw each other. It's been six years but Alma hasn't forgotten
the sharpness of Delphine's nails, the gleaming skin of her long,
muscled thighs. Alma had hoped they might pick up where they
left off.

"Keep an eye on Wheeler," Delphine says. "He's been slow to
address problems lately: Sloan's man at the warehouse; two of my
shipments losing a few pounds en route to Tacoma. I will stop this
leak from the top down. Find out if Wheeler is still trustworthy, or
if he's found himself a new employer."

"So I can't tell him he works for me now? And we both work
for you?"

"He's still my deputy here." Delphine shifts in her chair. "Though I'm glad you're eager to prove you're more deserving of the post. Tell him who you are when you have to. Until then, see what you can see."

"The trick will be sticking close." Alma reaches for her tea, tamping down a grunt as her corset boning digs into her bruised ribs. "Then I can keep him off guard. He's awful bothered by the sight of me in trousers."

Delphine laughs, a high note of girlish delight.

"Don't have too much fun," she says. "Remember what I'm paying you for."

Alma shrugs, clatters her cup onto its saucer. As far as she's concerned, she's now getting paid to harass Wheeler. Boasting about him to Delphine is a pleasure.

"Speaking of trousers, I'd like to call on you in the proper clothes," Alma says. "Since the day you left, you've been on my mind."

A catch in her breath while she waits for an answer.

"How sentimental," Delphine says. "But if I tell you I've missed you, too, you'll be impossible to manage."

All the old spark and banter, all the old yearning comes flooding back. *Why did you wait so long to bring me here?* Alma wants to say, though she knows she was needed down in California. She put in years of work protecting Delphine's business in San Francisco: the biggest city on the West Coast, with a thriving black-market opium trade. Also home of the Families, who own the Canadian refineries that feed America's tar habit—and who supply Delphine directly, through a long-standing arrangement.

"You used to tell me all sorts of nice things," Alma says. "And I believe I still kept you satisfied."

Delphine uncrosses her ankles. Rustle of crinolines. The small nudge of one heel into carpet. Alma edges closer to standing, waiting for the invitation to approach the other woman's chair.

"I hear you left the city in a rush," Delphine says.

The room jabs into Alma with hard edges: her chair's wooden bones, red embers from the hearth, her corset's chilled seams. Here's the bad news, brought up sooner than she wanted. And caught off guard, at that—too tangled in the thought of Delphine's legs to think with any speed.

"And in something of a shambles," Delphine continues. "Deliveries not made. Borrowing cash and product from the dens in Chinatown."

"Yeah," Alma says. "There was a hitch with Lowry."

"Meaning?"

"Meaning I killed him."

Abruptly, Delphine sits forward into the firelight. Some bit of metal on her person glints, and Alma's hand twitches toward the knife in her pocket. She grips the velveteen armrest to cover her movement.

"You killed the Pinkerton's agent."

"He was going to ruin that part of the plan," Alma says. "He was going to come up here without me, and then where would we be?"

"You've been in town for a week." Delphine picks up her teacup, taps one nail against the china with icy little tings. "And I'm just hearing about this development?"

Killing Lowry was sloppy—the kind of risk taking that makes Delphine furious. Mad enough to withhold Alma's promotion, maybe. If discovered, Lowry's death might have brought the law down on Alma, preventing her travel north. It could have endangered the San Francisco operation, or called the Pinkerton's agents to Port Townsend too quickly, compromising the ring there. That's how Delphine will see it: all the potential fallout. But Lowry's body won't be found, not in Alma's hiding spot. Sloppy or not, killing him was worth the risk. That's how Alma sees it.

"I've got it under control," Alma says. "Why make you worry over nothing?"

Delphine rises from her chair. Alma starts to stand, too, but a wave of Delphine's hand—her bloodred ring glittering—is a clear message. *Stay.*

"I'm worried," Delphine says. "Reassure me."

"Pinkerton doesn't know Lowry's dead."

A drip of sweat tickles down the back of Alma's neck. She rubs it away. Remembers too late that her skin is coated with talc. Now the back of her neck might be exposed, a smear of olive flesh showing dark against the powder.

"I guessed that much." Delphine crosses the carpeted floor,

tugs the tasseled bellpull beside the birdcage. "You're trying my patience."

"I memorized Lowry's dossier." Alma twists in her chair so she can watch Delphine and the door at the back of the room, wondering who has been summoned, and why. "Among other interesting things it had a cipher and an address. I sent my first coded letter when I arrived. This morning the reply came. The agency thinks Lowry's up here, gone under deep cover—and they don't know about our little falling-out. They still think I'm acting as his assistant, sending correspondence for him so he doesn't risk exposure as a spy."

Footsteps in the hall. The knob turns, and the maid's pink, wrinkled face peers in.

"*Oui, madame?*" she says.

"*Mets le poulet dans un panier. Avec du pain sucré. Sois prêt à partir dans cinq minutes.*"

The woman nods, winks out of view. Alma's French is patchy, but she understands enough to know she's about to be dismissed. She doesn't want to leave Delphine angry.

"As long as I keep sending those ciphered letters, the Pinkerton's agents will think Lowry's alive," Alma says, once they're alone again. "They'll think he's up here investigating the tar trade, and I can feed them whatever information serves us best. This is better than the first plan—there's no agent getting in my way while I look after Wheeler and fix our leaky pipeline. We've got plenty of time to cover our tracks now."

Delphine remains beside the birdcage, watching the little creatures chirp and rustle. In the pause, Alma considers her, the way she harnesses all the light in the room to make luminous her jewelry and quick obsidian eyes. There had been a time when Alma was jealous, so viciously jealous, of Delphine—not of her beauty, but of her fixedness, her certainty. Delphine is always herself. She was lovely and fierce and brilliant the day Alma met her, and so many years later she has only grown into these traits. But she could never creep unseen into a boatyard or pass unnoticed among a smuggling crew. She is entirely too striking: tall, voluptuous, her skin rich golden brown.

Alma can be many things. She has learned to value this muta-
bility: how she can shift her compact body into many shapes, powder herself pale or let the sun darken her complexion. She loves to
see her costumes through other people's eyes. Delphine watching
her as Camp, cutting a deal over fenced diamonds in San Francisco.
Wheeler watching her as a governess, timid and wilting. Hannah
watching her as a rancher's daughter, flirting in rapid Spanish with
the Yuma vaqueros. Alma loves performance. What began as a
thrilling trick in a Chicago saloon has become a passion. And now
she's back onstage before her favorite audience—though it's hard
work to win Delphine's applause.

"If there are any other . . . developments, make sure I'm the first
to know." Delphine traces her fingernail along the birdcage's gold
wires. "This is not the only iron I have in the fire, and I need to
see what I'm dealing with at all times."

"I'll take care of Wheeler." Alma stands, slow, her body stiff in
all its bindings. "He's loyal to you, or he's a dead man."

"I decide on any punishments." Delphine's voice is sharp. "I
decide how they are doled out."

Alma clenches her jaw. It aches, deep in the bone, where she
fell hard after Wheeler's watchman downed her. She has her own
ideas about punishments and how to serve them.

"And, Rosales—be careful," Delphine says. "Nathaniel Wheeler
is a hard man. If you die, the cipher dies with you, and the Pinkerton's agents will come swarming up here ahead of schedule."

Alma hadn't thought of that. It's a notch in her favor—she's
indispensable—but also a liability.

"Have I ever let you down?" she says, lifting her chin.

Delphine is a head taller, though standing apart as they are, the
difference feels lessened. The gold cross at her throat catches the
firelight as she breathes, shining, dark, shining. Alma thinks of shipwrecks. How a lighthouse is a warning and an invitation, both.

"I have an appointment to keep." Delphine smooths the folds
of her dress. "You've been here too long already. The woman next
door will think I've taken you captive for some ghastly ritual."

"I wondered why the neighbor was keeping tabs on your
deliveries."

"She suspects me of voodoo." Delphine rolls her eyes. "And she's not the only one. I keep the place bleak as a nunnery, ruin my knees kneeling at church, and the backwoods creatures still chatter."

Port Townsend seems an uneasy perch for Delphine. As a dark-skinned woman with a fortune, she would be singular anywhere, but San Francisco's riot of faces and colors and languages provided a lively background into which she could disappear. Apart from its small Chinese community and a smattering of tribespeople, Port Townsend is white as a sheet. Alma misses the city's urban churn. And she's only been away a fortnight, while Delphine's been stuck up here in the wilderness for years. She must be bored. And lonely.

"Oh, for our glory days in the city," Alma says, though she is thinking of their nights.

"This is no San Francisco," Delphine says. "But the profits— they are *fine*."

"They'll stay that way. I guarantee it." Alma bows, despite her outfit, and lets herself into the hall.

5

JANUARY 25, 1887

TRANSCRIPT OF INTERVIEW WITH SAMUEL REED

WHEREUPON THE FOLLOWING PROCEEDINGS WERE
HAD IN THE JEFFERSON COUNTY JAIL, PORT TOWNSEND,
WASHINGTON TERRITORY, ON JANUARY 25, 1887.

LAWMEN PRESENT: CITY MARSHAL GEORGE FORRESTER,
OFFICER WAYLAN HUGHES

TRANSCRIPTION: EDWARD EDMONDS, ASSISTANT DEPUTY
COLLECTOR, U.S. CUSTOMHOUSE

OFFICER HUGHES: Have you been in town long?

MR REED: No.

OFFICER HUGHES: When did you arrive?

MR REED: A few months ago. Jesus. Can I have some coffee?

OFFICER HUGHES: In a bit. What brought you here?

MR REED: Nothing special. Looking for work.

MARSHAL FORRESTER: You gave your last place of residence as 2118 Grove Street, Chicago.

MR REED: Yeah. Yeah, that's right. Look, can't you draw that curtain? The light's in my eyes.

MARSHAL FORRESTER: That's the idea.

OFFICER HUGHES: Chicago, huh? You've come a mighty long way to look for work.

MR REED: I saw a Northern Pacific paper about jobs out West. Thought I'd try my luck.

MARSHAL FORRESTER: You hit the jackpot in Port Townsend?

MR REED: Doesn't look like it, does it?

MARSHAL FORRESTER: Don't take that tone with me, son.

MR REED: I'll be sweet as cream candy if you tell me why I'm in irons. And get me some coffee. Or hair of the dog. I can't hardly sit up straight.

OFFICER HUGHES: A few more questions first.

MR REED: Might have to puke . . .

MARSHAL FORRESTER: Wonderful.

OFFICER HUGHES: If you need a bucket, we'll get you one. Where are you staying in town?

MR REED: Wherever I can afford.

OFFICER HUGHES: And who's your employer?

MR REED: I don't want to say.

MARSHAL FORRESTER: You don't want to say.

MR REED: I don't want him to think I got him in trouble.

MARSHAL FORRESTER: That's a damn strange worry to have now.

MR REED: You don't know my boss.

OFFICER HUGHES: Leaving his name aside, what do you do for him?

MR REED: Uh, he's got me on the docks, mostly, with some other hands, working nights.

OFFICER HUGHES: And were you working last night?

MR REED: Yeah, I was . . . wait.

MARSHAL FORRESTER: Think of something?

MR REED: Is she why I'm here? Oh, Christ. I didn't—

MARSHAL FORRESTER: Jackson! God damn it. Jackson, get a bucket. Don't you dare—Aw, hell. These are new boots.

OFFICER HUGHES: Jackson, bring a mop, too. Sorry about your boots, sir.

MARSHAL FORRESTER: Smells like a god damn sewer.

MR REED: I told you I felt sick.

OFFICER HUGHES: Reed. You said she. She's why you're here. Who is she?

MR REED: (inaudible) . . . no. No.

MARSHAL FORRESTER: You better sober up quick, son, or I'll whip you into shape.

OFFICER HUGHES: Reed. Who's she?

MR REED: Oh, Christ . . . Her name's Sugar.

MARSHAL FORRESTER: Sugar?

MR REED: Yeah. Sugar Calhoun. She's done nothing good for me since the day I met her.

OFFICER HUGHES: How do you know Miss Calhoun? Or is it missus?

MR REED: Miss. She got hold of me when she came into town.

MARSHAL FORRESTER: You knew her already?

MR REED: We were in Chicago together. A while ago.

OFFICER HUGHES: You were lovers?

MR REED: (inaudible)

OFFICER HUGHES: What's that?

MR REED: I said that's none of your business.

MARSHAL FORRESTER: Everything is our business in here.

MR REED: I don't see what it's got to do with—

OFFICER HUGHES: These are simple questions, Sam. May I call you Sam?

MR REED: Nobody calls me that.

MARSHAL FORRESTER: Answer the questions.

MR REED: Can I have a drink? I feel awful sick. Water, anything . . .

MARSHAL FORRESTER: No.

OFFICER HUGHES: Just answer some questions, and we might be able to find a drink for you. Sir, we could probably find him a drink.

MARSHAL FORRESTER: Sure, I'll find him something.

MR REED: All right. All right! No need for that.

MARSHAL FORRESTER: Do as you're told.

OFFICER HUGHES: Walk us through when you got to town, when Miss Calhoun arrived, how she found you, and so on.

MR REED: I got here a few months ago, like I said. Early November? I don't know the day. Came in by boat from Seattle, which was a hardship. I get real sick in boats. So I came in, sick as a dog, and slept it off at a cheap place by the docks. The next morning I went to look for work. Found a spot on a loading crew.

MARSHAL FORRESTER: A loading crew where?

MR REED: On Union Wharf, by the freight warehouses. Sometimes we'd shift to Quincy.

OFFICER HUGHES: And you worked there for a while?

MR REED: Yeah. The job got me through that cold snap at New Year. A week, week and a half after that—

OFFICER HUGHES: A week after New Year?

MR REED: Yeah. I was finishing my shift and the foreman said I had a letter.

MARSHAL FORRESTER: Did you regularly get correspondence at the docks?

MR REED: What?

MARSHAL FORRESTER: Letters.

MR REED: No. I thought it was a mistake. No one knew where I was, or where I was working. I'd told some fellows in Seattle I was headed here, but they wouldn't write a letter.

OFFICER HUGHES: Who was it from?

MR REED: Sugar. She didn't sign it, but I'd recognize her hand anywhere. I had no idea she was in town.

OFFICER HUGHES: This wasn't a pleasant surprise?

MR REED: Pleasant? She sent me a piece of blackmail! That's why the blessed thing wasn't signed.

OFFICER HUGHES: What did the letter say?

MR REED: It was an invitation to meet her. An order, more like. If I didn't show, she said, she'd spill dirt on me from Chicago days. She said, if the sheriff didn't scare me, she knew plenty of men in Port Townsend who could sort me out.

MARSHAL FORRESTER: Do you have a record in Chicago, Reed?

MR REED: No.

MARSHAL FORRESTER: Oh yeah? Jackson! Jackson, run down to the post office and get a telegraph off to the Chicago bureau. Checking up on Samuel Reed, of that city, last known residence 2118 Grove Street.

OFFICER HUGHES: And get us some whiskey.

MR REED: You're wasting your time. I don't have a record.

OFFICER HUGHES: Sam, the letter. What happened after you got it?

MR REED: I said nobody calls me Sam.

MARSHAL FORRESTER: I don't care what anyone calls you. Do you understand this is a murder investigation? I can string you up in the courtyard and say you did it, and who's going to question me? Not Officer Hughes.

OFFICER HUGHES: Sir—

MR REED: That's not legal.

MARSHAL FORRESTER: Oh, now you know all about the law?

MR REED: That's not legal, and you care about things being legal. Why else would you have that fat fellow scratching away in the corner and keeping notes?

MARSHAL FORRESTER: He's the customhouse's man. Not my problem. Right now I care about being legal about as much as—

OFFICER HUGHES: Sir, I'd like to get back to the letter from Miss Calhoun.

MARSHAL FORRESTER: All right, Hughes. Go on, then.

OFFICER HUGHES: What happened after you got her letter?

MR REED: I went to meet her. She had me spooked. I'm trying to make a fresh start here. I didn't want any trouble.

OFFICER HUGHES: Where did you meet her?

MR REED: At her place of business.

MARSHAL FORRESTER: And what business is that?

MR REED: Some rooms on Water Street.

MARSHAL FORRESTER: A whorehouse?

MR REED: That's not what she'd call it.

OFFICER HUGHES: Is Miss Calhoun employed there?

MR REED: She runs the business. She rents rooms over a feedstore. The letter said to go to number four. She was waiting inside, looking just as good as she had back in the city. I wasn't glad to see her but she looked good, I can't say I didn't notice that. And the room all done up the way it was. Red carpet on the floor, red blankets on the cot, gold lamps.

MARSHAL FORRESTER: I bet what happened next is none of our business, too.

MR REED: You've got it wrong. She had me sit down, gave me a drink. Wanted to talk about home a little.

OFFICER HUGHES: Did she say how she'd found you?

MR REED: She'd been out with one of her girls and saw me loading a boat.

OFFICER HUGHES: What did she want?

MR REED: After some chitchat she got down to business. Said she needed a man for a few jobs, a man with talents, and wasn't it grand we were in the same town again. She gave me an address on Quincy and said I needed to get her a set of keys to the door.

MARSHAL FORRESTER: You used to be a safecracker, Reed? A hotel thief? What?

MR REED: I don't break the law anymore. I told you. I told her. But she reminded me of her pals here. She reminded me if I wasn't worried about the police, I ought to be worried about the men she knew who'd knife me in a tavern, or catch me at work and drown me in the bay.

OFFICER HUGHES: So this wasn't a friendly reunion.

MR REED: No. But she wasn't all threats. She gave me a bag with twenty dollars in it and said I'd get twice as much when I handed over the keys.

OFFICER HUGHES: Sixty dollars for a key job?

MR REED: A fortune.

OFFICER HUGHES: And you accepted.

MR REED: How could I turn that down? It's as much as I'd make in a month.

MARSHAL FORRESTER: You're a real son of a bitch, Reed. You take her money, do her jobs, and two weeks later, you kill her.

6

JANUARY 13, 1887

Alma takes the snow-dusted stairs to Wheeler's back office. Only this time she's walking, not being dragged. She likes the view better from up high.

Her knuckles crack against the door's cold wood. A creaking of locks, then Conaway is glaring down at her, his bruised eye black in the hallway's yellow light. His meaty hand coddles the ribs she dented with her boot the night before.

"Evening." Alma's spine is taut, her bound chest out. This posture puts a hitch in her breath where the men knocked her around, but she's not wilting. She wants him to know how little their blows meant.

"Don't you fucking talk to me," he says.

He lets her inside the hall—vanilla-sweet air, that plush blue carpet—but does not make way for her to pass.

"You want to take my knife again?" She shoves past him, aiming up at his bad shoulder. "So I can make you give it back?"

"Little piece of shit."

He grabs her by the collar, but Alma is ready, her knife out and nipping at the fat over his liver. She fists his shirtfront. Bars her forearm across his throat to plow him into the wall. Leaning up, she crowds her face toward his. He is sour with cheap tallow pomade and popping sweat.

"Touch me again and I'll do it," she says. "I owe you a few bruises but I'm happy to add interest."

Conaway's hoarse breaths, the way his body softens around her blade, have Alma eager to get to the main event. She wants to see Wheeler. She is restless to kick up the spark that flared between them. Delphine doesn't want her to have fun, but Delphine's not here, in this narrow hallway, with the whole cold night outside and Wheeler burning in his office.

"Fuck off, Camp."

Conaway's throat works against her forearm, his voice lowered in defeat. She sheathes her knife.

"Next time get out of the way when you let me in," she says.

What is he good for, exactly, this beefy cringer? If he's the best Wheeler can find, Wheeler's not looking hard enough. Alma walks away from the man toward the bend in the hall, filling the cramped space with her bandy swagger. She is taking notes for renovation. Replace Conaway with a fighter. Get rid of the bloodstained carpet. Keep the high-class liquor.

At the dogleg she slams into a man coming from the opposite direction. He is tall, with sandy hair, ruddy in the hands but pale faced.

"Sorry, excuse me," he says, pulling away from her and clutching his cap to his chest. A dark film coats his knuckles.

"What's the fucking hurry?" she says.

His eyes flick over her nervously as he angles his body aside. He smells of fresh sawdust. The smearing on his hands is not blood; from the strong whiff Alma catches, it is pine pitch, or varnish. He's a carpenter. Or a boatbuilder. And he's come to the back office—he's here on smuggling business. Alma makes note of his face before letting him by.

The man hustles down the hall, pulling on his cap. Conaway is taller than him by a few inches. As their forms eclipse the door, Alma imagines being that tall, having that much bone and muscle to sling around. The damage she could do with longer limbs. Champion brawlers, men like Sullivan and Dempsey, combine size with speed. But scrappers take you by surprise. She likes her advantage.

Wheeler's door is open. He sits at his desk in his shirtsleeves, hands busy in a mess of papers. There is ink on his fingers, whiskey in the glass beside him.

Before he sees her, Alma makes a sketch of the room, adding to her impressions from the previous night. A rectangular space with Wheeler's desk in the center, backlit by the fireplace. A shuttered armoire to her left. And a discreet corner door that faces Washington Street—a link to the Clyde Imports office. Convenient.

"Boss."

He looks up, and it is a distant glance—cold, uninterested. Disappointing.

"Shut the door," he says.

Alma lopes deeper into the room, playing Camp straight, all business, saving her slippage for when she needs to win a point. But Wheeler is already watching her more closely as she approaches. She realizes she does not have to loosen her mask at all: he is searching her for traces of the governess he knew, searching her face and torso, inspecting her clothing and the set of her hips. Here's your liability, Delphine—send a woman in man's clothes to Wheeler and he frays like a cheap pair of socks.

He locks his fists together before his chin. His movements are controlled, but Alma reads a tightening in them, a bearing down on some unwanted thing. *Get yourself together*, his hands say. She holds back a grin.

"What'll it be?" she says.

"I want the name of Sloan's man in my warehouse."

"That wasn't the deal." Alma shakes her head. "You said you'd have a job for me first."

"You're in my office. We're doing this my way." Wheeler unlaces his hands, pushes a scrap of paper across the desk. A line of text— an address. His fingers leave faint smears of ink on the paper. He might be sweating. "I want the man's name. Then I'll tell you what to do with that."

"I don't know what name he's using."

"Don't be coy. What does he look like?"

Alma pushes at the back of her cap so it slumps low on her forehead and hides her eyes. She needs a minute to think. Give up

Sloan's man and she gives up her leverage. Her last high card is Delphine's name, but once that's in play, Wheeler will be even more careful around her, and she needs him to lose his composure. If he's making mistakes, she can report them to Delphine, undermining him as deputy. And if Wheeler's involved in the tar thefts, he might let something slip about them, too.

"Take off your cap when you're in my office," he says. "Show some respect."

"Yes, sir."

She whips off the cap. Tucks it into her back pocket. Her eye twinges, the puffy skin around the socket alive to every current in the air. Wheeler's gaze catches on it, on her purpled jawline. There's that stutter she is hoping for—the momentary blankness on his face, the minute clench of his lips.

"You should see my leg," Alma says. She pushes a hand through her shorn hair to better showcase the bruises dappling her cheek.

"I don't want to see any god damn part of you."

"All right, boss."

Wheeler glowers at her, stiff shouldered, pugnacious. He's losing patience, but she makes no move toward his desk, toward the address perched on its polished edge.

"At Sloan's, they called him Pike," Alma says, working out this new angle as she speaks. "He's on your loading crew—I saw him carting crates from *Orion* to the Madison warehouse."

She can still invoke Delphine, if she must. But if Wheeler brings Pike in for questioning, there's much to be learned when Pike talks. It will show her Wheeler's methods. How far he's prepared to take such an inquisition. His questions will help her flesh out the extent of the Sloan problem, and how that figures into the missing tar. How Wheeler figures into the missing tar, maybe.

"I'd like to help bring him in," Alma says. "We have a score to settle."

"No."

"No? Remember, if I don't work for you, I work for your friend at the railroad trust," she says, and is not surprised when his pistol thumps onto the desk.

"Don't threaten me again," he says.

"He has brown hair." She ignores the gun. "Blue eyes. About three inches on me. Burn scars all down his left forearm and hand."

Wheeler takes a sip of whiskey, some change working over his face. Perhaps he expected her to bluff. But while her motive is fiction—she doesn't have a quarrel with Sloan's man, never even spoke to him—Pike's presence at the Madison warehouse is not. Poor bastard. He's about to have a rough night.

"Since you've held up your part of the bargain . . ." Wheeler sets aside his glass, points at the address. "Here's the job I have for you. Find a man called Beckett. Those are his lodgings. Don't ask for him outright. Don't call attention to yourself. He's about six foot two, sickly, thinning black hair worn short. He'll probably be drunk. He might be with a woman. Go knock him around."

"What's the objective?"

"He's an acquaintance gone sour, and he's talking about my business too much. I want him to stop talking. That's all you need to know."

Beckett sounds like just the man she needs to see. With some encouragement he'll give her all he knows about Wheeler and his business—his illegal business, because it's highly unlikely Beckett is talking about the quality of Clyde Imports' Scotch. But it makes no sense for Wheeler to trust her with this job. He wouldn't let her get dirt from Beckett and then walk away. The setup is a perfect death trap.

And she's given up Sloan's man. One less reason to keep her around.

Wheeler waves at the address she has not collected.

"Go get him," he says. "Or are you not so keen to fight for me after all? You said you'd be effective. You said I'd be lucky to have you in my corner."

"You remember conversations well."

"I like to watch people eat their words. Are you going to make yourself a liar?"

"I'd rather work on Pike," she says.

"I'd rather you didn't work for me at all, being a turncoat and a bloody sideshow freak besides," Wheeler says.

She wishes he would pick up his whiskey, stand from his chair, anything to force him to loosen up. But his hands are curled into a single fist. The great chunk of wooden desk sits between them. Without her edge she fires up, too; tucks her jaw and shifts her feet, so she's in the shadow of a fighting stance.

"I delivered him. I ought to get first blood," she says. "Not be kicking the shit out of some loudmouth drunk."

"Before I give you any sort of reward, you need to prove your loyalty." His teeth are bared. His neck flushed above his tight-buttoned collar. It reads as anger rather than eroding composure. "If I say bite, I expect you to come back with red teeth, do you understand me?"

If I had you in the ring, old man, you would be the one yelping, Alma thinks, and is surprised by the ferocity Wheeler calls out of her. The part of her not bristled and scowling is taken up with try-ing to understand how he does it, why she is so primed to respond to him. He's not the first son of a bitch to give her a hard time, that's sure, but she feels closer to doing something reckless. The toggling between female and male, between Alma and Jack, has her on un-certain ground: an undefined space between personas. For a mo-ment she's not playing a part or holding a pose, but just *being*; that sense she sometimes gets in Delphine's company of truly being seen. Yet with Wheeler there's danger in this visibility. With him it is a thrumming, high-wire walk. Exhilarating, dangerous, a comet burning across the night sky. She could do anything. With him. To him. Just as she is picking at some seam in him, he is doing the same to her.

"Is this Beckett job a trick?" she asks, watching his face. Some flicker, some twitch of cheek or eyelid, may answer her question. "Are you sending me there to die?"

"There are easier ways to get rid of you." He nudges the gun with a forefinger.

"I don't trust you," she says.

"The feeling's mutual."

I work for her, too. That's all she has to say. Then she can move about without waiting for a gunshot, for a knife in her back. But she will lose her cover before she's finished her job: before she's proven Wheeler's loyalty or treason. And he will know she took the coward's way out.

Alma reaches for the paper, at the same time glancing at the other ledgers and pages jumbled near at hand. Nothing she can identify quickly. She looks back to the address. The boardinghouse is on the south end of town, near the bones of the new pier and the scrap-heap shanties of Portuguese families. A lonely place. She and Wheeler spent nearly an hour there in his carriage, uninterrupted.

"When you say rough him up . . ."

"Have fun," Wheeler says. "If he loses teeth, so much the better."

He leans forward on his elbows. With Alma standing in arm's reach of the desk, this is the closest they've been all night.

"If things get out of hand and he loses more than teeth . . . Well." Now Wheeler's voice is evened out, confidential. "Get rid of the body. You can throw it in the bay between twelve and two thirty and the tide will take it out."

"I don't intend to kill him," Alma says.

"I am telling you what to do, just in case," Wheeler says. "Unless you want to get caught dragging around a dead man. And don't think you'd be able to pin it on me. Nobody knows you here, but I have lots of friends. You'll have a bad time of it in jail when they find out what you are. Marshal Forrester doesn't trouble himself to keep order in the lockup."

Alma has not been threatened this way before. Only one other man alive knows she switches between skirts and trousers: William Pinkerton, who, despite disapproving of the practice, has no incentive to menace someone on his payroll. She hates that Wheeler would goad her to be afraid of what she has trained herself to not think about—how some would punish her for daring to wear men's clothes. Camp is a fighter, his body bone-hard, wrapped tight in layers of cotton and bravado. No room for fear or softness.

Now she hopes Wheeler is double-crossing Delphine because she wants to pay him back in fear. Fear of pain. Of violation. She pictures standing behind him, holding his neck and her knife, feeling him breathe against the blade. Sneers at him as she pictures it. Before she can speak, he picks up his gun, cocks it, points it at her chest.

"Behave yourself," he says. "I can tell you right now I don't like employing loose cannons, and you're not making a good impression."

"I'll go after your man." Alma crowds the desk, its wood squeaking against the twill of her trousers. "But I don't like your talk about going after me. You think about it? Yeah? You want to come at me yourself?"

"I'd fuck you into next Sunday if I wanted." Wheeler rises, nudges the gun against her breastbone. "I was a few inches away from it in that carriage. But now that I've seen you like this, I've lost my appetite."

Yet he looks hungry. He is wholly focused on her, and that feeds her conviction she has some hold on him. The gun digs into her clothing. Into her skin. His hand is steady. His middle knuckles yellowed by the bruises she noticed on their carriage ride, when his fingers were creeping up her thigh.

"I'm working for you," she says. "That's it."

She does not back away. She waits for him to retreat first. But he does not drop his gaze or his pistol. He is breathing faster. She feels it in slight pressure changes of the muzzle against her chest.

"What do you want me to do with the woman?" she says.

He blinks, eyes narrowed.

"You said Beckett might be with a woman. Is she part of the problem, or not important?"

"Not important," Wheeler says.

"All right."

"Get out of here." He uncocks the pistol, lowers it.

Only after this does Alma pull on her cap. Her sternum aches. She is satisfied because she stayed longer at the scratch. She is satisfied because Wheeler is as drawn to her as she suspects—he needs a loaded gun to keep them apart.

Now the high color is draining from Wheeler's face. Circles of sweat darken the underarms of his shirt. Alma is sweating, too, as if she's just fought a bout. She is eager to see him again. To burn with the rage and want and curiosity he calls out of her. To grapple with their words or limbs. Fighting. Fucking. They could do anything.

"Have a good one," she says.

She leaves him standing behind his desk, grim faced, one inky hand curled around the dark grip of his pistol.

At its south end Port Townsend withers. The waterfront's bricked industry dwindles into squat clapboard houses. The golden sandstone cliff stoops down, leaning eastward until it overtakes Water Street and plunges into the bay. Sailor Town's ruckus fades, leaving lapping waves and the cries of night birds. Alma listens for footsteps among these muted sweeps of sound. There are none but her own, crunching in the ice-coated mud.

At the water's edge the sweat-and-outhouse stench of town gives way to seal dung and tide-line kelp. Frying onions and fire smoke drift from the shanties. One block ahead, just before the cliff meets the beach, sits a square building pocked with knots of candlelight. Beckett's boardinghouse.

Alma trudges through damp sand. She is freighted with protection against her misgivings: her knife, a set of brass knuckles in her pocket, a pistol strapped to her side under the cold oilcloth of her jacket. She stops before the wooden building and scans the path she just stamped across the landscape. A white shadow snags her gaze, but it is only a gull—alone, too, its pale wings skimming the wavelets.

Inside, the house is cold as the beach. A single candle gutters on a desk by the door. There is the bitter reek of a green-wood fire gone out. She stands with her hand on the knob, searching the low rectangular space for witnesses. A sleeping woman slumps in a chair. A ghost-pale, walleyed child sits among her skirts, gnawing on a chicken leg.

Alma holds a finger to her lips.

"No need to wake your mam," she whispers, easing closed the door.

The child does not cease its slippery chewing noises. Alma finds the ledger on the desk and squints at it in the meager light. At the top of the last page is a neat signature: *M. L. Beckett. Room 9.*

She climbs the stairs quietly, favoring her knee. The upper hall is lit by a lamp at its far end. Smells of turpentine and sulfur hint at a louse outbreak. Alma shakes off the echo of an old itch and counts the rooms until she reaches nine. The door is set unevenly, dark along its seams.

On her good knee, she woos the lock with her picks. No sounds or stirring in the rooms along the hall. In another breath the handle dips. Wary of rusted hinges, she shoves the door open and slips inside.

Gin. Stale vomit. Low cot bristling with limbs. Moon-hazed sky bluing the high window. Alma settles her breath. Lets her eyes adjust. When she can see with more certainty, she reexamines the bed. A tall man, alone. Thin back heaving under his shirt with each uneven breath. Nothing else in the room but a crooked washstand and a chair in the corner.

In two strides she is at the cot, one hand on Beckett's shoulder and the other unsheathing her knife. She flips him onto his back. Straddles his torso. Her ribs protest but she is heating up, eager for a fight.

"Don't make a fucking sound." She tucks her knife under his Adam's apple, her other hand clamped over his mouth. His lips rough against her palm. The upper half of his face looks familiar— the heavy-lidded eyes coming gummily open; the hard jut of his nose. She tilts her head a notch, recalling, and pins him down in her memory as his eyes settle on hers. He's friends with the rail-road man Dom Kopp. Kopp called him Max. Max borrowed money off him at the Cosmopolitan, to have another try at the gambling tables.

Beckett stares up at her, eyes widening, but slowly. He is stupefied with drink. This is a problem. A drunk man does not comprehend threats the same way a sober man might. He is unpredictable. He might shriek despite the blade at his throat, or start sobbing, or pass out entirely.

"You're going to get up and come outside with me," Alma says.

Beckett starts to shiver. Good. The danger of his situation has penetrated the gin fog in his brain. Or he's fixing to be sick again.

She sneers at him. Drunks remind her of her uncle and his rages. How he'd rail on about her father, that filthy Mexican who dared marry his sister, who dared teach Alma to speak a heathen tongue. He'd call her a half-breed, swear he'd beat her father's blood out of her. Drunks remind Alma how men can forfeit control of their bodies, of their minds. Yet in the morning they'll say, *It was not me, it was the claret. Forgive me. Forgive me.*

"If you shout when I let you go, I'll gut you," she says. "If you try to run on the stairs or knock on someone's door, I'll gut you. Nobody's awake. Nobody saw me come in. You'll be dead and I'll be gone in an instant."

All through this hushed set of instructions Alma has moved off Beckett and allowed him to stand, to get dressed. Now he waits, hands clasped before him. There is a dark bruise on his cheek, a raw split in his lip; marks she could not see with her fingers clapped over his mouth.

"Did Wheeler send you?" he says in a hoarse whisper.

"No."

Beckett seems inclined to cooperate, so she will get all she can with words before switching to her fists.

"I was sent by someone who wants to take Wheeler down," she says. "You need to tell me everything you know."

"Why don't we sit in here?" he asks, motioning toward the chair. There is an open bottle on the seat, a glass with flies crawling on its rim. Beside the chair a pool of vomit gleams.

"Outside." She motions toward the door with her knife. "You can have another drink once you've talked."

Beckett twitches, but he opens the door. He walks with his arms wrapped around his torso, so biddable that Alma again suspects a trap. Wheeler might have warned him she would be coming. He might only be playing drunk, waiting to try something on the stairs or on the dark beach.

They descend into the lobby without incident. Pass the sleeping woman and her child. Outside, Alma tucks her knife away. Beckett stops to glance back at the boardinghouse, and she nudges him on with her fist, once, twice. They walk until the bluff eclipses their faint shadows. High overhead, grasses whip the cliff face. Tears drip down Beckett's sunken jowls.

"I want to help." He is whispering, though there is now little need. "I want to serve Wheeler out for how he's treated me. But what if he hears I talked to you? He's already warned me not to cross him again."

Beckett gestures at his mouth, at the ridged cut on his lower lip. Alma thinks of Wheeler's bruised knuckles. So he went after Beckett himself. It must have been no contest, but she would have liked to have seen it. Seen Wheeler riled up and striking.

"I told you, no one saw me come," Alma says, the hot fizz of interest fading as Beckett hiccups on his tears. "No one will know I've been here. I just need your information on Wheeler."

"What will I get?" Beckett asks, lifting his wet chin.

"I brought money," Alma lies.

"Show it to me," he says, sharpening, getting suspicious.

"Not until I know you have something worth it." Alma points at a piece of driftwood. She wants Beckett sitting, so she is not the one who has to look up. "Tell me what the hell Wheeler is up to. My employer is concerned about his side business's legality."

"So you're from the railroad trust?" Beckett grins nastily, shouldering tears off his face in an abrupt movement that has Alma's hand in her coat, on her gun. "They'll never let Wheeler in once I talk to them. Everyone thinks he's so respectable, sinking a mint into public works, that new pier, but I know where he gets his money."

"Where."

"Give me the cash you brought first."

"I brought this." Alma pulls out her pistol. It sobers Beckett up a bit, his face working between fear and rancor. "Stick to Wheeler."

"I used to pass forged duties receipts for him," Beckett says. "I was an inspector for five years at the customhouse. Some of the forged receipts were for liquor and woolens for his import company—with my help, Clyde Imports dodged a nice lump of taxes each year. But the customhouse is happy to oblige businessmen that way, letting their duties go unpaid from time to time, as long as the staff gets a kickback."

The customhouse. Beckett was Wheeler's man there. Now Beckett is no longer a collector. If the Port Townsend setup is anything like San Francisco's—thick with corruption, with the collectors taking payoffs from every thief on the Barbary Coast—that's bad news for Beckett: a bribed customhouse man knows too much to be let off the payroll.

"Why'd you leave?" she asks.

"I was fired three weeks ago." His voice is tear-clotted, sniveling.

"For shirking my work, due to drink. My money's running out and Wheeler won't help me."

"Why should he?"

"Because I also made him a god damn fortune with opium imports."

Here's the meat of it: what Wheeler wants silenced. Beckett is talking about the business too much, but Beckett hasn't yet gotten the ear of the railroad trustees. So who is he talking to? His friend Dom Kopp, maybe.

"How much was he moving?" she says.

"Enough that I could build a couple mansions on the hill with the taxes he evaded," Beckett says. "Five years' worth of who knows how many hundred pounds a month, coming in from Victoria alongside his Clyde Imports goods. The opium money made his dodged liquor taxes look like pocket change. All that time I was the principal inspector. I was paid to not see opium on the boats, so I didn't."

Jesus. That's Delphine's main line. And this weeping man knows all about it. He should be dead, not getting a visit from a newly hired unknown like her. The sense of a net falling over Alma weighs heavier. She makes a sweep of the beach, of the low folds of the cliff face, waiting for the crack of bullets that will take them both out. Beckett stiffens, too, mirroring her unease. His skull shines through the stringy fall of his hair as he peers down the waterline.

"If you have proof, why are you sitting on it?" Alma says. "You don't need me or a railroad trust or anyone else to ruin Wheeler for you."

"I don't have proof." Beckett shakes his head. "I let pass an old sloop he used, then his new cutter. And steamer cargoes, when instructed. But I never saw anything. I never inspected his boats and cargoes, or their duty-paid stamps, too closely. That was the whole point. And I can't go to the law outright—I took my cut and let that tar into the country untaxed. I'd be in prison the minute I opened my mouth."

A splash in the surf jerks at Alma's attention. She wheels around, pistol raised. Empty beach. Curls of sand corkscrewing in the wind. Out in the water a bird flares gray wings. At her feet Beckett breathes fast and ragged. She scans the wrack-scattered shore again before turning back to him.

"I need something solid on Wheeler," she says, adjusting her finger on the pistol's trigger. "Not the allegation of an anonymous ex-collector that he moved a lot of opium."

"That's all I know," Beckett says. "Isn't it enough? I just used the word *smuggler* in my note to the police, and they moved on his boatbuilder quick enough."

"You gave Wheeler's name to the police?"

"No." He shrinks away from her, his staring eyes swollen with tears. "No, I only said they might find something interesting at Peterson's."

"Who?"

"Bill Peterson. He owns the yard on Tyler Street Wharf. He builds Wheeler's boats—builds them special, is the word."

Bill Peterson. The big man in the office hallway with varnish on his knuckles. No wonder he was so skittish—he'd just been visited by the cops. Alma hopes he knows how to keep his mouth shut. Beckett sure as hell doesn't. The man is talking himself into an early grave.

"Is there something interesting at Peterson's?" Alma says.

Beckett wipes his nose on his sleeve. Curls into himself, gangly arms folding around gangly legs. Shivering. He is closing off, his gaunt face twitching, not meeting Alma's eyes. Maybe he's finally realized she has no cash for him tonight. Or realized, too, that Wheeler can't pay him if Wheeler's in jail.

"I was just trying to spook him," Beckett says. "I want the money I'm owed."

"Give me more names," Alma says.

"I only ever communicated with Wheeler."

"What about Dom Kopp," she says. "You two have been spending time together at the gambling tables."

Beckett's shaking intensifies into jerky heaves. He leans forward. A gush of vomit splashes into the sand. Alma grits her teeth, her own stomach set to churning by the stench of bile.

"Kopp," she says, nudging the man's shinbone with her boot.

"I helped him bring in building materials," Beckett says, coughing. "Railroad ties, pig iron. I fixed it so he didn't have to pay duties. Now I'm in hard times, and I hoped he'd help me out, too."

"Did he bring in tar?"

"No." Beckett drags up his shirtfront, smears it over the wet-
ness on his chin.

"Who else," Alma says.

"I helped a lot of men out—"

"Who else connected to Wheeler's business."

"That's it."

Alma raises her pistol, sneering. Beckett puts his hands up.

"It's true!" he says. "God damn it! There are his two henchmen,
McManus and Benson, but everyone knows they work for him.
Other than that I don't know, I swear."

"You're lying."

Alma holsters her pistol and pulls out her knife. Beckett starts
to scramble off the driftwood. She twists a fist into his puke-
dampened shirt. Shoves him back down, ignoring the ache in her
shoulder and his whimper of pain.

"If Wheeler finds out I talked to you, he'll kill me," Beckett says,
sobbing into his knotted fingers. "He'll kill me and my girl."

"He's not going to find out." Alma holds her knife level with his
eyes. They are huge and bloodshot in the slice of steel. "Forget
about him. You're talking to me."

7

JANUARY 14, 1887

The cipher is growing familiar after several dispatches. It has two simple pieces, which is a tacit insult: evidently Pinkerton does not want to task her with something complex, like the Vigenère. Alma flips through the codebook, a worn, green-jacketed copy of Verne's *Eight Hundred Leagues on the Amazon*, until she finds the word *smuggler*. Page 112, line 36, word 10. Her mind scrolls through the alphabet as she applies the Caesar Six, then fits the letters to words in her little note about a friend's birthday.

Honeyed morning light falls over her hand as she writes, *Quite by coincidence, Lottie purchased*—The ink shines on the page as it dries. Someone is brawling upstairs: the distinct sound of a chair smashing. Never a quiet moment in this boardinghouse. But all is calm in Alma's room. Almost peaceful. She works without pause, running through the cipher in her head with each new word. A dull ache throbs over her rib cage. She puts a palm to her body, warming the bruised flesh, feeling the mewls of her empty stomach.

We devoured a boat-sized gingerbread—She laughs quietly at the line. It is rare to be fanciful. Rare, and a pleasure. The letter is loosely based off a real party. The Women's Bureau agents crowded into Hannah's apartment in the worst freeze of winter, huddling around the iron stove to share a bottle of applejack and admire Alma's new pearl-handled bowie knife.

Her missive to the Pinkerton's agents is nearly finished. A final word: 17, 20, 3, something starting with *k* . . .

A knock. Her pen skips across the neatly written page. Cursing, she picks up her pistol and pinches back the hammer. She points it at the door from her chair.

"What?" Her voice is roughened into Camp's. She is still wearing his clothes after her midnight visit to Beckett.

"He wants to see you."

"Who's he?" she says.

"God damn it, Camp." The voice is closer to the door's wood, pitched low. "*He* wants to see you."

Alma scrambles out of the chair. Scoops her papers under the blanket while kicking a petticoat under the cot. Wheeler has not contacted her at the boardinghouse before. She hasn't given him the address.

She unbolts the top latch, then the second one, her gun level with her eyes as she peers into the hallway. Conaway waits outside. He flinches when he sees the barrel.

"You're to report to his offices," he says. "Now."

"Shit." Alma stuffs the pistol into her belt. It's not yet eight o'clock. After being up with Beckett all night she should not be awake. She raises her hands, using the motion to check her skin for ink marks before feigning to rub sleep out of her eyes.

"What's the rush?" she says, though she doubts Conaway knows anything beyond his instructions.

The big man shrugs. Behind him, in the hall, there is an indistinct mumble, a long splatter. Some rum-blind drunk is pissing on the floorboards.

"I'm on my way," she says.

Conaway stands there heavily, his nose wrinkling as outhouse stink drifts along the corridor.

"Unless you're meant to drag me with you, get out of here," she says. "The boss wouldn't want us seen together if we don't have to be."

"Right."

He does not seem convinced, but Alma shuts the door in his face. Double bolts it. The room feels too hot. She wipes sweat off her palms before pulling back the blanket. Her letter to Pinkerton is ruined, slashed with a dark spray of ink. She will have to copy it fair again later.

Wheeler's summons troubles her. His knowledge of her boarding-house troubles her still more. He must have had her shadowed, something she never detected though she was looking out for such surveillance. And then ordering Conaway, the bumbling lout, to come fetch her. With this Wheeler is sending a message: all his men are not so inept. The caged feeling she had on the beach rises again—that Wheeler has some larger game, and she is being wedged into a corner. She twines her hands together. Cracks her knuckles one by one. What if he is turning on Delphine? What if Alma comes to the crisis point and gives Delphine's name, and it does nothing?

Stop it.

Alma unknots her hands. Flexes them steady. She folds up her papers. Presses them into the false bottom of one of her lady's shoes, then replaces the shoe in her suitcase, which she kicks under the cot. As she crouches over the chamber pot, bruised knee aching, she runs a hand along the binding cloth pinned over her breasts. It is tight enough.

Outside, her breath prickles with frost in her mouth, on her teeth, before drifting into air still blushed with sunrise. Wheeler's offices are three blocks away. She strides through the shadows of new waterfront buildings, all constructed in the modern style Port Townsend favors: high gables, square windows, painted scrollwork in ivory and yellow and robin's-egg blue. Her nerves rattling. Her pistol banging against sore ribs. Each time she turns a corner she slaps the wall beside her, the fresh bricks dripping red runoff into the street and leaving scratches on her palms.

Conaway is smoking on the back steps when she arrives.

"He's busy," Conaway says, opening the door. "Wait until he calls you."

"You told me to hurry."

"Now I'm telling you to wait," he says.

The familiar blue carpet. The hall's dogleg turn. At Wheeler's cherry-varnished door she leans against the wall. There are muted sounds inside, but no clear voices. A thump. Maybe someone else is getting a beating. For such a discreet operator, Wheeler sure is bringing in lots of bodies.

Her heel taps out a jagged rhythm on the carpet. She cleans her nails with the snubbed tip of her knife, blade gleaming against her thumb. She is working at a speck of dirt when a laugh comes clear from the office. A woman's laugh.

Alma slips the knife into her vest. She stills her foot, tilts her head toward the jamb.

Conaway clumps down the hall to peer around the corner.

"Get away from the door," he says, but his bite is blunted and he seems to know it.

She flicks her cap brim at him, insolent. The knob jiggles. She steps back, waiting for the door to open, for the woman to appear. It can't be Delphine. Unless there's some other game afoot for which Alma doesn't know the rules. This puts a sick twinge in her belly. She keeps her face empty, her hands in her pockets. Just a scruffy man lounging against the pale wallpaper. Ready for most anything.

A click. The door swings back to reveal a woman in a yellow muslin dress, cream skinned, gold haired, ample bodied. She holds a green velvet cloak. Her breasts overfill the gathered front of her gown. Alma's mouth opens.

"Don't be tiresome," the woman says over her shoulder. "That was never set down in writing."

"We'll discuss it later."

Alma can't see Wheeler, but from the sound of his voice he's at the back of the office, near the liquor board. She wouldn't be looking at him anyway. Her lips hitch into a crooked grin. She tilts her hips out.

"Ma'am," she says, wanting the woman's attention.

The woman glances at her, and the pout she was directing at Wheeler slides off her face, replaced with a coy smile. Her teeth are pale against carmined lips.

"And who are you?" she says.

"The name's Camp." Alma takes off her cap, presses it to her chest. "I'm mighty pleased to meet you."

"Mr. Camp, *enchantée*." She holds out one gloved hand. A painted fan dangles from her wrist. The air around her smells of honeysuckle and sex. Alma bends over her warm fingers, glad for the chance to hide her eyes. Is this Wheeler's wife? It seems unlikely when he took Alma out to so many dinners, made no secret of her on his arm. Alma kisses the offered glove, inhales its unmistakable scents, and is jealous, lust-shot, still buried in the shadow valley of the woman's bosom.

Footsteps. A low exhalation.

"Get into the office," Wheeler says from the doorway.

"Nathaniel Wheeler." The woman pulls her hand from Alma's and sets it on her hip. "I'm sure you are not speaking to me in that tone."

"No," he says. His collar is open. He is not wearing a jacket or tie. The hair at his temples curls out of its pomaded sweep. "You're on your way. Camp."

He crooks a finger at Alma, but she can't catch his eyes before he walks back into the depths of the room.

"I think I'm in trouble," she tells the woman, grinning, voice husky.

"Have you done something terrible?" The woman's fan quivers under her chin and her eyes flutter wide. Her lashes are darkened with charcoal. Thin rings of hazel surround huge pupils; she doesn't seem disoriented, and if it's not opium or drink, it might be belladonna. This is not a wife's trick. This is not a wife's dress. Wheeler might pay the woman for her time.

Alma has money, too.

"I'm a bad man," she says, taking a step closer.

"So are all his associates." The woman snaps her fan closed, traces its gilded side along her chin. "You'll have to show me why you're special."

Another step. Her nose full of sweet musk. Alma is the shorter of the two. She brings one arm up to brace herself against the wall, the warm round of the woman's bare shoulder brushing the underside of her sleeve. The tempting stretch of her neck inches from Alma's mouth.

"How about I show you a good time like you've never seen." She tilts her face up so her vision is filled with golden eyes, with golden curls.

"God damn it."

Wheeler is at the door again. Alma shifts her gaze to him. He is rigid, glaring, one hand clenched around the jamb. She hopes he's been standing there for a little while. Watching her lean into his company.

"I look forward to seeing much more of you, Mr. Camp." The woman slips out from under Alma's arm and draws on her green cloak, the velvet releasing another waft of honeysuckle blossoms. To Wheeler, she says, "I'll consider a price. It won't be cheap."

Inside the office Wheeler paces behind his desk, hands clasped at his back, dark brows lowered. The outline of the corner door is etched in sunlight. When he walks before it, the edges of his cotton shirt catch the glow. His jacket is crumpled on the floor by the liquor board. The room smells of the woman, of sweat and other drippings.

"What do you think you're doing?" he says after Alma closes the door.

"Just being friendly."

"You don't touch her," he says. "You don't get near her again."

"What's her name?" Alma tucks her cap into her pocket, flicks her tongue over her lower lip. "I could just eat her up."

Wheeler slams a fist onto his desk. The sound snaps through her, sets her skin tingling. She waits for him to shout, to unravel a notch, but instead he goes quiet. Goes locked down and hard with that maddening restraint of his. He flattens his hand against the wood, the gold ring on his middle finger clicking on impact.

"You didn't follow instructions," he says. "Last night."

Alma shifts her weight from one foot to another, thrown.

"I don't know what you mean," she says.

"I told you that if you went too far with Beckett, you were supposed to toss him in the bay, not leave him in bed."

"I didn't rough him up that bad," Alma says, thinking of the ex-collector, his greasy tears on the moonlit beach.

"'That bad'? That bloody bad?" Wheeler gives a wheeze of a laugh, shaking his head. "You leave the man with his tongue cut out and his head nearly severed off his neck, and then you stand here and tell me you didn't rough him up that bad? Jesus Christ."

"Now wait a god damn minute." Alma is starting to breathe faster despite bearing down hard on her lungs. "I didn't do that."

"I understand you want to move up in my organization." Wheeler comes to stand before her. There are nail marks on his neck, at his open collar. A smear of carmine on his left earlobe. "But you won't get far acting like a butcher."

"I didn't kill Beckett," Alma says.

"Oh, but you did."

For an instant, Wheeler's look of cold disapproval melts into amusement. Then, with the grim scowl back on his face, he collects his jacket from the floor. He shakes it out. Shrugs into it. Knots on his necktie. When he is buttoned up and presentable, his sweat-crimped hair smoothed down, he opens the door at the back of the room and waves Alma through.

She emerges, blinking, into the Clyde Imports office. It is a narrow space, half the size of Wheeler's private quarters, crowded with filing cabinets and framed price lists. At the front is a large glazed window. A woman stands before it. Alma squints at her, belatedly realizing a child is at her side.

"That's him," the woman says.

Alma's vision evens out. Her shoulders stiffen. Now she understands Wheeler's trap.

It is the woman from Beckett's boardinghouse. She wears the same brown dress. The same ghastly child clings to her hand.

"He's the one that came in late last night, skulking around, sir," the woman says.

Alma hears Wheeler come up behind her and does not struggle when he grabs her collar. He is good. He has got her good.

"He left with Mr. Beckett in the wee hours, and I did not see them return." The woman points at Alma, her voice rising. "This morning I went to check on a smell that poor man's neighbor was complaining of, and the Lord save us! I've never seen such a horror!"

"Thank you, ma'am," Wheeler says. "I may call on you again, if the marshal requests it."

"Good day, Mr. Wheeler."

The woman sweeps the hem of her dress along the floor in a

curtsy before dragging the child to the door. A burst of cart clatter and chattering fills the office. Then silence. Wheeler's knuckles are hard against the back of Alma's neck.

"So you see, it was you that killed Beckett—there are witnesses," he says.

He guides her back toward his office. Taps her side with his free hand, where her pistol hangs heavy at her ribs.

"Put the gun on my desk. That knife you carry, too."

Alma walks forward stiffly. She is impressed by Wheeler even as she wants to whirl around and savage him. There is the sense of wasted time—of wasted effort. He set this snare for her when he ought to be chasing Sloan and keeping better tabs on Delphine's product. Beckett knew too damn much and was too willing to talk about it, but nothing he said suggested Wheeler is turning away from Delphine. Everything she's seen points to a conscientious man: he keeps business quiet, stays respectable, sends men out to silence loose cannons like Beckett. He is good at his job. Ironfisted and decisive.

Except when it comes to her.

He has been too forgiving. He has given her too much time.

They cross the threshold into the back office. Alma's eyes are sun dazed, her vision haloed with afterglow. But there is a shadow beside Wheeler's desk.

Someone else is in the room.

She stares until the man comes into focus. He holds a silver pistol. He is Conaway's size, with meaty arms, a thick neck roped with muscle. Ruddy skin. Cropped beard along his lantern jaw.

Propelled by Wheeler, she walks up to the desk until the edge bites into her thighs. She takes her weapons from their holsters with deliberate movements: no need to spook the man holding a cocked Remington. Her pistol thumps solidly onto the wood. Her knife clatters. Without them she feels unanchored, unsteady, subject to a different, lesser kind of gravity.

"I warned you to throw him in the bay."

Wheeler shoves her forward so she loses her balance over the desk. She keeps her feet but only just. The other man is silent. He has small gray eyes.

"If you'd followed my instructions, you might not be where you are now."

"And just where is that?" she says.

"Fucked." Wheeler collects her weapons, putting them into a drawer and withdrawing his black-lacquered gun.

Alma holds her fists tight against her thighs. So he bested her. Fine. Maybe he wants her to say it. Impress his big friend.

"Enough with the games," she says. "What do you want?"

Wheeler nods at the other man, who sets down his gun and circles the desk toward her. She sees the metallic flash in his palm, but he is faster than a big man should be, the knife already at her throat even as he's twisting down her jacket to trap her arms behind her. There is a line of cold fire along her neck, a thread of heat dripping down her skin. The big man's pulse bangs against the back of her head. He's enjoying this, the bastard.

Wheeler is staring at her. His lips are pressed into a thin seam, his cheeks pallid. His eyes narrow.

He is forcing himself to watch.

This is no mere pissing contest—not if it's enough to make him wince. Alma's heart punches at her breastbone. Delphine warned her. Still, she didn't believe Wheeler would kill her. Until now. She is losing the fight to keep her breaths even.

"God damn it," she says, the words slicing the knife deeper into her skin.

She is not shaking, she is not shaking, she is steady as a rock, but what if Delphine's name does not save her. The man behind her pulls her closer and his erection jabs into the small of her back.

"Delphine," she says, blood coming faster over her throat. "I work for Delphine."

8

JANUARY 25, 1887

TRANSCRIPT OF INTERVIEW WITH SAMUEL REED

WHEREUPON THE FOLLOWING PROCEEDINGS
WERE HAD IN THE JEFFERSON COUNTY JAIL,
PORT TOWNSEND, WASHINGTON TERRITORY,
ON JANUARY 25, 1887.

LAWMEN PRESENT: CITY MARSHAL GEORGE FORRESTER,
OFFICER WAYLAN HUGHES

TRANSCRIPTION: EDWARD EDMONDS, ASSISTANT DEPUTY
COLLECTOR, U.S. CUSTOMHOUSE

MR REED: I didn't kill Sugar. I didn't kill anyone. I told you, I was working last night.

MARSHAL FORRESTER: For your mystery employer?

MR REED: I don't want him involved. I don't want to give you his name.

OFFICER HUGHES: That makes confirming your story difficult.

MARSHAL FORRESTER: Come on, Reed. You're usually on Union Wharf in the evening, loading boats. Two people described the man who put the body into a scow at Union: short, stocky, dark complexioned, gray cap and coat. That sounds just like you.

MR REED: Maybe I was wearing a different cap and coat.

MARSHAL FORRESTER: Maybe you'd better cut the crap and tell us why you killed Sugar Calhoun.

OFFICER HUGHES: Come in, Jackson. Set it . . . set it here.

MARSHAL FORRESTER: Did you telegraph Chicago?

OFFICER JACKSON: Yes, sir.

OFFICER HUGHES: Here's a drink, Sam. You want it, you just have to answer the question.

MR REED: I didn't kill her.

MARSHAL FORRESTER: That's not the right answer.

MR REED: I didn't . . . (inaudible)

MARSHAL FORRESTER: What?

MR REED: I put her in the boat.

MARSHAL FORRESTER: Really.

MR REED: But I didn't kill her. I swear I didn't. I was just loading the boat as I was told.

OFFICER HUGHES: By whom?

MR REED: If he finds out I ratted on him, he'll pay me back, in a bad way.

MARSHAL FORRESTER: That's not our problem. If you sleep with dogs, you wake up with lice. Isn't that how it goes, Hughes?

OFFICER HUGHES: Fleas.

MARSHAL FORRESTER: God damn fleas, then. You wake up with fleas.

MR REED: He'll know it was me who squawked.

OFFICER HUGHES: Sam. Have another drink, Sam.

MR REED: Oh, Christ.

MARSHAL FORRESTER: Who told you to load the boat?

MR REED: I'm never . . . Oh, Christ. His name's Barnaby Sloan.

OFFICER HUGHES: Barnaby Sloan? He's that fellow—

MARSHAL FORRESTER: Let the man tell it his way. Who's Barnaby Sloan?

MR REED: He's a big name on the waterfront. He runs a boarding-house near Quincy Wharf.

MARSHAL FORRESTER: What house?

MR REED: It's next to the empty lot at the corner of Water and Madison.

MARSHAL FORRESTER: He's a big name. Why? For running the house?

MR REED: He runs lots of things.

MARSHAL FORRESTER: You're going to need to be more specific.

MR REED: He has girls . . . a cathouse. Uh, there's talk on the wharves about men shanghaiing sailors. Some say they're his men, doing that. And dope. There's . . . there's talk of that.

OFFICER HUGHES: Opium?

MR REED: Can I have more whiskey?

MARSHAL FORRESTER: What's the talk of opium?

MR REED: (inaudible)

OFFICER HUGHES: Take as much as you want.

MR REED: Thanks . . . Some say he brings dope in. From Canada.

MARSHAL FORRESTER: I'll be damned.

OFFICER HUGHES: Have you seen him bring in opium?

MR REED: Uh . . .

MARSHAL FORRESTER: Answer the question.

MR REED: . . . Yes.

MARSHAL FORRESTER: Will you swear to that in court?

MR REED: No.

MARSHAL FORRESTER: You're telling an officer of the law, directly, that you will commit perjury?

MR REED: . . . No?

MARSHAL FORRESTER: Listen, you stupid son of—

OFFICER HUGHES: Sir. Sir, please. We can come back to this. But we ought to be talking about Miss Calhoun.

MARSHAL FORRESTER: Oh, you're damn right we will come back to this.

OFFICER HUGHES: Do you know why she was killed?

MR REED: No.

OFFICER HUGHES: Do you know any reason Barnaby Sloan would want her dead?

MR REED: They weren't friendly. She wouldn't cooperate with him. But I'm not saying he killed her.

MARSHAL FORRESTER: Better him killing her than you, right?

MR REED: I don't know who killed her, or why. All I know is Sloan told me to load a scow on Union Wharf, late.

OFFICER HUGHES: And then what.

MR REED: There were a few boxes and a bag. I was left to load them alone. The bag was terrible awkward. I got it up on my shoulder and an arm flopped out of the top. An arm! It fell right along my shirtfront.

OFFICER HUGHES: Sloan never had you load bodies before?

MR REED: No. Jesus, no. Like I said, there was talk he had . . . other things . . . in his crates, from time to time, but otherwise it was just the usual cargo.

MARSHAL FORRESTER: The usual cargo? Meaning what?

MR REED: . . . I don't know. I never asked.

MARSHAL FORRESTER: You said he's got you working nights on the docks.

MR REED: Yes.

MARSHAL FORRESTER: And you said he has a boardinghouse, girls, a shanghaiing operation, and dope.

MR REED: Yes?

MARSHAL FORRESTER: Any other businesses to add to his busy schedule?

MR REED: Uh. Not that I know of.

MARSHAL FORRESTER: Then I'll tell you what, son. Only one of Sloan's businesses requires you and a crew of men to load freight at night. Every night. And that's the opium smuggling. I think Sloan's usual cargo is crates and crates of opium.

MR REED: Well, I guess I . . . I assumed it was all goods for his boardinghouse.

OFFICER HUGHES: Would he really be so brazen about it? Loading all that out in the open?

MARSHAL FORRESTER: I don't know. But Mr. Reed here sure as hell does.

MR REED: No! No, I really don't.

OFFICER HUGHES: Let's stick to what you do know, Sam. Let's get back to the cargo Sloan had you load. There was a body in the bag . . .

MR REED: I had to see who was in there. I set the bag down, looked inside. The first thing I saw was long wavy hair. That turned my stomach, I can tell you. I almost stood up and walked away. Now I wish I had.

OFFICER HUGHES: Go on.

MR REED: Sorry. Sorry, I can just see her so clearly. She was wearing a green dress. She didn't have a scratch on her, but all her jewelry had been taken off. I'd never seen her without gold necklaces and pearls, even when . . . even when we'd been together. Alone. You take my meaning.

MARSHAL FORRESTER: Get yourself together.

OFFICER HUGHES: Did you take her all the way out of the bag?

MR REED: No. I'd pulled the bag down to her waist, and I picked her up like that. Carried her into the stern sheets. On my way back to Sloan's boardinghouse I ran into some of his men near Chain Locker saloon. I drank so much they left me there, and I woke up in my own mess outside the bar. I thought it was all a bad dream for a while, this morning. You know, like it didn't happen?

MARSHAL FORRESTER: Unfortunately for you, it did. Murder. That's a long life in prison, or a short drop on a rope.

MR REED: But I didn't kill her!

MARSHAL FORRESTER: I don't believe you.

MR REED: Damn it! I didn't—

OFFICER HUGHES: Settle down, Reed. Come on. Sit down.

MARSHAL FORRESTER: Even if you didn't kill her, you helped cover it up. So don't think you're out of the deep water. You want any sort of bargain, you'd better have a hell of a lot to say about Sloan.

MR REED: Sloan?

MARSHAL FORRESTER: His boat. His usual cargo. Maybe his bagged dead body. You don't want to swing? You better start talking about why he should.

MR REED: Talking . . . like what?

MARSHAL FORRESTER: When did you first meet him?

MR REED: A few days after I'd seen Sugar, and started casing that cannery for her.

OFFICER HUGHES: A cannery?

MR REED: That's what she wanted the keys to. On Quincy Wharf.

MARSHAL FORRESTER: You never got around to robbing it?

MR REED: No. She told me to case the cannery and get the keys copied. I wouldn't even know where to start with robbing it. Because I'm not a thief.

OFFICER HUGHES: You said you were afraid she'd turn you in.

MR REED: That was for older things. Things from our Chicago days. I was no angel but that's the whole reason I came West, to make a new start, clean slate, all that.

OFFICER HUGHES: Uh-huh.

MARSHAL FORRESTER: Get back to Sloan.

MR REED: The cannery was his building. She had me watching his building. Two days in to trying to find the door unguarded and his men collared me. I said I'd been hanging around because I was looking for work on the docks. Pretty sharp, right?

OFFICER HUGHES: Sure.

MR REED: Well, they thought so. They bought it. Said there was no work then but to check back the next day, when a few boats were due. And I figured, a paying gig, and what better excuse to figure out who held the keys so I could borrow them for a minute?

MARSHAL FORRESTER: Did you make it inside?

MR REED: Yes.

MARSHAL FORRESTER: What did you see?

MR REED: It was no cannery. There's some old equipment in there, but mostly shipping crates.

MARSHAL FORRESTER: There's that usual cargo again.

MR REED: It was all harmless stuff, in the open crates. Cigars, sailors' woolens. But I didn't get close to much. I wasn't at the cannery for long.

OFFICER HUGHES: What happened?

MR REED: This.

OFFICER HUGHES: Good God.

MARSHAL FORRESTER: Who did that to you?

MR REED: Sloan. His boys caught me making a copy of the keys.

OFFICER HUGHES: He tortured you?

MR REED: He used a meat cleaver.

MARSHAL FORRESTER: Jesus Christ.

MR REED: I told him everything.

9

JANUARY 14, 1887

"Let he—let him go," Wheeler says.

He takes a half step toward Alma and the man holding her.

"Sir?"

"I said stop."

The razor edge slips out of Alma's skin. Her jacket falls away, freeing her arms, and she presses one sleeve against her neck, shaking with the thunder of her pulse, shaking but fighting hard not to show it. Her sleeve is hot over the back of her hand. Her neck throbs. Did that bastard nick a vein? Her sleeve is hot over her wrist bone.

"If I bleed out because of you—"

"You'll live," Wheeler says, though he is eyeing her chin, eyeing the heat blooming along her forearm. "Get a clean shirt out of the cabinet."

The big man moves around behind her, boots heavy on the carpet. When he comes back, he hands her a bundle of white. She packs the cloth against her neck, into the crease under her chin that burns with growing fierceness as her heart rate settles and the fissure of panic that buckled in her abdomen closes, fades away.

"Start talking," Wheeler says.

"Not with him in here." Alma jerks her head toward the man beside her, the motion tugging barbed wire across her throat. His gray eyes are pinched and wary. He fidgets with his red-smeared knife, and with his other hand adjusts his inseam.

"Why don't you go take care of that instead," she says. "You might have better luck."

"Sit down before you fall down, Camp."

Alma realizes she is listing to the right. She gropes into a chair. Blinks to focus her eyes, the small muscles of her face protesting. The room loses its light coat of fuzz. Then Wheeler is at her side, holding out a glass of whiskey. She drinks half. Pours the rest onto the shirt, shoving it up against her throat again before she has a chance to imagine the pain. Oh merciful Christ. The breaths leaving her are fast, raspy.

Behind her, the two men speak in low voices. Alma peels the shirt from her neck. A fist-size bloodstain, yellow with whiskey at its edges. Only a fist. She will be all right.

The door shuts. Wheeler walks around the desk to his chair, rests his hands on the leather. But he does not sit. He circles around again to lean against the carved wood. His face is drawn, the untamed curls from earlier springing out around his temples. The knot of his tie askew.

"Talk," he says. "Quietly."

Alma angles her upper body to make sure the other man is gone. The movement twists a grunt out of her.

"He's away," Wheeler says. "But not far. You're not leaving here until I'm sure of you, and if you don't walk out, you'll be carried."

"Delphine brought me up from San Francisco." Alma forces the words through the band of pain around her neck. "I'd been down there greasing wheels for the Families."

Wheeler's hands are clasped over one knee. The light on his ring quivers, almost imperceptibly, a tiny gold window into his thoughts. Turbulence rattles inside him despite his set jaw, his level voice.

"Brought you for what purpose," he says.

"An audit. She gave me nothing—I was supposed to find the product, then try and find her."

"She trusts me so little." His smile is parched of any amusement.

"You've been having troubles with product going missing," Alma says. "And there are more troubles on the way."

She will not tell him about the Pinkerton's agents: she does not want to make a slip about the other angle in her game. Delphine can pass along news about the law. Though Delphine does not often deign to explain things. Her magnetic eyes, her measured speech; people turn to her, they wait for her. It will be the same with Wheeler. He will have to turn and wait.

He slides off the desk, returns with a tumbler and the whiskey bottle. While he pours a golden skim into his cup, she holds hers out, too, her sleeve damp and red stained. She is pleased her arm is not shaking. It still hurts to breathe.

"You shouldn't have left Beckett for so long." When she swallows whiskey, her throat burns inside and out. "He was a powder keg, and he was looking hard for a match."

"You don't know a thing about the situation up here," Wheeler says. "The alliances. The bloody hoops there are to jump through."

"I didn't think you were the kind of man to make excuses."

A flash of teeth. The crack of his tumbler on the desktop. But he only glowers at her. If he is Delphine's loyal man—that Alma's still alive seems good proof of that—he can't lash out at her any longer. They are on equal footing. Alma lets that sink in, one eyebrow lifted.

"I'll keep calling you boss," she says, the mocking tone in her voice hampered by pain. "Since you like it."

Since it will remind him he is no longer her master.

"I want to hear all this from her." Wheeler leaves his drink on the desk and stalks toward the door.

Alma pushes up from her chair. The flurry of nerves has crackled out, leaving her steady on her feet. But without the fire of a crisis her throat tears into her attention. The cut is weakly leaking blood. She folds over a clean swath of shirt as the big man appears in the hall, towering over Wheeler.

"Watch him while I'm gone," Wheeler tells him.

"She'll want to see me," Alma says. She does not like the thought of Delphine and Wheeler, hemmed up in a room together, discussing her. She wants to hear them when they say her names.

He pulls an overcoat and a hat off the rack, not looking at her.

"She won't be happy you're so unkempt," Alma says. "You're supposed to be working, not entertaining women."

And, damn, who wouldn't keep that woman entertained for as long as possible? Alma lingers on her remembered scent, the silken flesh of her neck.

Wheeler puts a hand to his hastily done tie. The big man in the hall shakes his head. Taps a meaty earlobe. Wheeler wipes his own ear and curses at the carmine smeared on his fingers. At the open cabinet he hesitates with his hands on his collar. But with the other man standing there he can't be nice about changing in front of her: in his offices everyone knows her as Jack Camp. Alma watches him pointedly, hoping he'll feel her gaze and squirm under it. He unfastens his collar. Pulls his shirt over his head. The skin of his shoulders is pale, freckled, stretched over shifting muscles. A scar runs from the top of one scapula to disappear beneath the cloth of his undershirt. She follows the pearly line of it to the shadow of his spine, his spine to the muscled small of his back.

"Take me with you," she says. "I don't know where you're meeting her, but she won't want to make two trips."

Wheeler twists open a tin of pomade. He angles the mirrored cabinet door to better see himself, revealing the right half of his face to Alma. His jaw works as if he's chewing on a bit of gristle. He rakes a comb through his hair in sharp tugs.

"If she wants to see you, I will arrange it," he says.

"You're wasting time."

He meets her eyes in the mirror. In the metallic glass, in the privacy of his shadowed toilette, he has allowed himself to be angry. His eyebrows are lowered. He jerks the silk of his tie into complicated knots.

"I am owed an explanation," he says.

A new shirt, glossed hair, tie tucked into a black vest. Wheeler closes the cabinet, and his face is neatened, too, the carmine wiped from his ear and the anger cleared from his eyes.

"Don't let him touch anything," he tells the other man. "And don't knife him if you can help it. I may be some time."

Then he is gone. Alma peers across the dim room at the big fellow, who leans against the wall by the door. She wants to test him, pick at him like peeling a scab. See when he tells her to settle down.

Taking Wheeler's blood-splotched shirt, she walks behind the desk and sits in the leather chair. Sighs. Nothing from her watchman. She clumps her boots onto the cluttered desktop. His gray eyes narrow.

"You get mud on his papers and he won't like it." His voice is colored with a rustic twang—Missouri, or Kentucky, though by the sound of it he's been away for years.

"What's your name?" she asks.

"Don't see how that matters." He folds his broad arms over his broad chest.

"I'm Jack Camp," Alma says. "Soon to be working with Mr. Wheeler. So I'd like to get to know the help."

His beard splits into a gap-toothed grin.

"Boy, you won't last long, talking like that," he says.

"Maybe it's how I got my promotion," Alma says. "Having a big mouth."

She winks at the man, whose face closes like a clamshell.

"Now, that ain't funny," he says.

"Do you have any cards on you?" She pulls her boots from the desk. At the liquor board she pinches stoppers off glass bottles and sniffs their contents. He is letting her touch more things than Wheeler would like. This suggests laziness, or a tendency to not quite obey orders.

"I'm a mean hand at draw poker." She stoops to collect her jacket, tosses it over the back of a chair. "I'll throw down two dollars for the first game."

But he only stays by the door, arms folded, humming snatches of a song Alma doesn't recognize. She pours a tall glass of gin. Delphine and Wheeler, Delphine and Wheeler—where are they meeting? What are they saying about her? She feels the sting of a job improperly done: she was supposed to evaluate Wheeler and then make a second report, but he has ruined that plan. Delphine won't be expecting him—though, knowing her, she'll be ready nonetheless. Delphine will have something to offer Wheeler to keep him sweet. What that might be has Alma itching with curiosity.

She tips back the last of her gin.

"How about a throwing contest?" She waves her empty glass at the man. "You'll have to let me get my knife out, but I promise not to gut you."

"You're a noisy customer." As if prompted by her words, he unsheathes his own weapon. From a pocket he produces a pale lump and sets the blade to it. Curled shavings float to the carpet. Alma crosses half the space between them. He is whittling a bird, the neat fletching of a wing already marked and catching shadows.

"Get away from me," he says, his eyes flickering up from the wood.

"Cut me a couple holes." She tosses him the bloodied shirt. "From the back, where it's clean."

He shrugs. Pierces the cloth, the blade barely making a whisper. He keeps it sharp. Alma thrums with the strong thump of her pulse and is grateful for it. Not much more of that knife would have let all her blood out.

The man throws the shirt back. Dark fingerprints, smelling of pine, mark its cotton. She tears it into long strips. Binds them together. The cleanest scrap of cloth she saves to dash with whiskey and pack under the bandage, against her skin, where it burns like a brand.

Jaw locked, the bruise there aching, she prowls the room's back edges. The light filtering under the door grows bluer and harder as the sun climbs toward noon. This is tedious, this waiting. It breeds unease. What if Wheeler turns on Delphine after all? In a small room somewhere, where they are alone. Alma can't remember if he took his gun. Though Delphine is not without protection: one of her heeled boots conceals a stiletto blade, a weapon she's carried since her youth in New Orleans. It has a ruby in the hilt. She's let Alma see it, but never touch.

At Wheeler's desk Alma lifts up a ledger, scans a neat column of names and amounts. Her gun and knife are in the drawer by her hip. She feels them as a warm pulsing, a potential. There's a twist of wire in her vest pocket. The drawer's lock would open to it in five seconds. Another sheaf of papers, each signed at the bottom. A few lists that are too densely written to decipher. She picks one up, peering close, and maybe it's not just smaller handwriting—the lots of names and numerals read like gibberish. They read like code.

"Don't mess over there," the man calls. "God damn. Mucking around like a pup."

Now he stirs, her slothful guard. But he's only just pushed off the door when the varnished wood shakes with a double rap.

"Shit." He stuffs the whittled bird into his trouser pocket as he opens the door, his body blocking Alma's view. "Who are you?"

"I'm here for Camp."

Something about the voice is familiar. Alma tries to place the speaker as she kneels before the desk, wiggling the wire in the drawer's lock. A slip, a catch, and the wood slides out quietly, its insides smelling of gunpowder and cedar. She stands up, her knife tucked away and gun holstered before she's fully on her feet.

"I'm supposed to keep an eye on him," the big man is saying.

"Mr. Wheeler said to bring him. At once."

"Well, he's a fucking handful. Good luck."

He turns away from the door, motioning to Alma. A Chinese man in black silk stands in the hallway. His face is somber, with no flicker of warmth at the sight of her.

"You're no fun," she tells the big man, pushing the gutted, bloodied shirt into his hands as she passes. "I'll remember that."

He takes the shirt with a grunt, preoccupied with kicking his wood scraps into a pile that he stoops to collect. Not so careless, then. Though he should have been as neat with her; not let her rummage about, kept her in a chair.

She follows the Chinese man down the hall, rolling up her bloodied shirtsleeves. Her jacket hides the rusty streaks on her forearm. She folds up her stiff collar to conceal the bandage around her neck. Pulls her hat low on her forehead, so she is snug inside her dark clothes like a bivalve in its shell. When she takes the dogleg turn toward the door—no sign of Conaway—she comes up next to her companion.

"How's things, Joe?" she says, her voice hushed.

"I'm well." He is quiet, too. "You don't look so good."

"Rough morning."

Then they are at the door. Joe slips through first. Alma gives it a few beats before she lets herself out.

The midday air is glary, brittle with cold. It tears at her broken throat. Her eyes water. She ducks her chin. Squints around until she catches sight of Joe lighting a cigarette under a tailor's sign across the street. His eyes drift over Wheeler's doorstep. She descends to the plankboard walkway, sidestepping the high splash of a passing lumber cart.

Denim-jacketed workmen and drowsy sailors flow between them as Joe walks southwest, past the theater and its doorstop drunk, past the steaming washhouses that cluster against the cliff face. Alma lets him lead by thirty paces, trying to tally the years since she last saw him. Five, maybe five and a half. In that time Joe Hong has grown from a reedy kid into a solid young man. When there are gaps in the foot traffic she studies his broad shoulders. The long, regrown gloss of his queue. Back in the city, Joe used to visit Delphine's gilded Nob Hill home. Those rooms saw lavish dinner parties attended by businessmen and thieves, and from them Delphine ran San Francisco's most profitable fencing operation.

At the corner, Joe passes under the shadow of a construction crane, its latticed ironwork pitched high into the sunshine. A flat of bricks sways from its winch. The bundle rises, slows, jerks to a halt. Someone shouts. One of the ropes snaps apart with a gunshot of sound. Pedestrians scatter, Joe among them, a horse-drawn carriage caught among the fray. Alma darts backward. In the street the horses kick and squeal as bricks smash into the wooden sidewalk. Flying splinters, sweet-hay smell of dung, screaming; some fool has run under the horses' hooves. Alma looks beyond the fallen man's red frantic face, the frantic builders swarming, and finds Joe watching her from the far cross street. She pushes along porches and past gaping shopkeeps until she is beyond the growing crowd and once again trailing Joe's black-clad form.

The cliff cuts off the road, forcing them east, and he disappears around a corner. Alma stops to check her pocket watch. When she turns the same corner, she is in a narrow alley, Joe squatting against a clapboard wall. Two women snap sheets onto a drying line at the far end of the lane. Otherwise, they are alone. Joe holds out a hand, as if for change.

"Guess who I met on my way up from the city." Alma lights a cigarette, watching the women twenty feet away bend and reach, their bodies supple. "Your old pal Frank Elliot."

It had been on the last leg of her journey north, waiting on a wet

Seattle dock for the steamer to Port Townsend. Briny funk of sea-weed. Sting of pine. Her body wilting after five days of hard travel, boat, then train, then boat again. A man calling her name out of the rain—"Why, Miss Rosales!"—when no one should have known her there. Frank Elliot. A god damn nuisance, as usual.

"He's here?" Joe's teeth are bared.

"In Seattle," Alma says. "Seems he left the law in California and set up a brick business with his missus across the Sound."

Elliot worked the Chinatown beat, and he loved to use his night-stick on the locals. He went after Joe a few times. Nearly broke the kid's leg once, and cut off his braid when they met again. But for all his savageness Elliot would not take a bribe. He fancied him-self incorruptible. So Alma went for his wife. Loretta Elliot was a pretty thing: young and bored and hungry. She ran distraction on her husband while Alma's crew was working, and in return Alma showed her a good time. They tangled in a public garden once, their skirts hitched up, crush of violets at Loretta's back, her hips pulsing so the broken flowers breathed perfume.

"You ought to pay Elliot a visit," she says. "He's passing along my greetings to his wife, but you might have a different message to deliver. He's got no cop posse up here."

Joe spits at her feet. Tucks away his outstretched hand.

"Thanks for the tip," he says. "First door on the left."

She flicks away her cigarette at the door. The wood is weath-ered, the brass handle tarnished almost to black. It opens without resistance.

Inside: a narrow hall. Its walls and ceiling are papered violet. A trio of white roses nods in a slip of crystal. The cramped space with its prim decor reminds Alma of a hatbox. An expensive hatbox, not without its charms: Delphine is here. Alma smells her perfume. Wheeler is with her, his voice urgent and just this side of angry.

Be careful, boss. Take too harsh a tone with Delphine and she'll finish you. Alma's seen it. It happened to Carlisle. To Warner; to Finnegan, the one-eyed Irishman; to so many others in the San Francisco underworld.

Wheeler's voice comes from behind a door with hinges shaped to look like tiny people. Alma unrolls her shirt cuffs so they show, stained, at her wrists. Up close, the figures crawling along the hinges are cherubs, complete with wings. But there's nothing angelic about their grins.

"—just be in the way," Wheeler is saying. "Cause trouble."

Alma opens the door without knocking. A circular room, small, crowded with a sofa and cherrywood stools and a round table topped by a teapot. Delphine is perched on the sofa, straight-backed and elegant in her rich mourning clothes. She toys with a length of gold chain. Wheeler is seated across from her on a stool, his hair jet-black in the lamplight. A dish of tea on his knee. How like Delphine to pin him down with the lightest touch: two ounces of bone china forcing him to sit placidly and behave himself.

"Saying sweet things about me?" Alma leans against the door until it closes, cool wood pressing into her shoulder blades. "Nathaniel, you shouldn't have."

Wheeler's jaw twitches. His teeth are bared pale beneath his mustache.

"Hello, dear," Delphine tells her.

She steps deeper into the room to take Delphine's hand. Her glove smells of jasmine, its silk slick against Alma's lips. She again remembers the woman in the hallway that morning; her opulent skin, Wheeler's eyes flashing at the pair of them tight-locked and whispering. And now he's here to see her bow before Delphine.

Alma's body flares with heat. Wheeler is watching her. Delphine is watching her. And Delphine hasn't seen her in men's clothes since San Francisco days. Back when they were lovers. When Delphine's attention would often catch on Alma, so she felt the power in her own muscles, saw the beauty of her sinewed forearms in the mirror of Delphine's eyes. That mirror is on her again. She is aware of the strong slope of her shoulders. Aware of the way her bruises shape her face into harder angles and her bloodied cuffs frame her roughened hands. She lifts her chin, displays the damp bandage beneath.

"Really, Nathaniel," Delphine says, frowning at the bandage and then at him.

He does not bristle at his name from her the way he did when Alma used it.

"I thought she was with the law." He takes a sip of tea, thick fingers clasping paper-thin glass. "If you'd warned me otherwise . . ."

"You are both safe," Delphine says. "Which means you're both trustworthy, and that is of the first importance."

Alma keeps her chin high. Of course she's trustworthy. After the long night and morning, after the knife in her throat, to hear Delphine suggest otherwise is grating. There's no call to hold the Lowry incident over her like this.

Delphine twists the gold chain around her index finger, which is pointed at Wheeler.

"That seventy-five pounds of product," she says. "I want to know who took it."

"No one likes a leaky pipeline," Alma says.

Wheeler takes a sip of tea—choking down some choice words for her, she suspects.

"I'll give it my full attention," he tells Delphine after he swallows.

"Rosales will help," Delphine says.

Wheeler's eyes meet Alma's briefly. She grins, showing teeth.

"You can demonstrate how you run things up here," Delphine continues. "It's a different world from San Francisco."

"That is the truth," Wheeler says.

"And let Nell know I'll be coming for a visit tomorrow." As Delphine drizzles the chain into her lap, Alma follows its snaky length to a ruby pendant the size of a hazelnut. "I was supposed to see her this morning, but she was away. At your offices, I believe."

Wheeler's woman. She knows Delphine, too.

"Nell," Alma says, trying out the woman's name, how it rolls around her mouth. "She's gorgeous."

"I have told you to not be distracted so easily," Delphine says. She is in no mood for play. Her black eyes glitter up at Alma. The ruby disappears into the silken knot of her fist.

"Sorry." Alma bites back a smile.

"One more thing. Your premonitions about the law coming to town are not wrong," Delphine says to Wheeler. "We'll need someone to hang for all our sins."

"Were you prepared to hang me?" Wheeler sets his tea on the table.

"You know I would not want that," Delphine tells him. "Not when our future is so promising."

Words should not be enough to placate Wheeler, yet he is smoothing out, some color coming back to his livid cheeks. Alma does not like this gap in her knowledge: those long unseen minutes when it was Wheeler alone with Delphine, among the blushing pillows.

"I've heard your opinions," Delphine says. "But Rosales brings a fresh perspective. I directed her to find the man moving my product through the waterfront. She came to me with three leads: Barnaby Sloan, Dom Kopp, and you. Why did you go after the first two, Rosales?"

"Kopp's loaded. He claims it's the railroad's money, and that there's more where it came from." Alma stands wide legged. Hooks her thumbs into her belt loops. She is taking up the center of the room, the center of attention, and it pleases her. "He throws his cash around at the poker tables and likes to stage-whisper about bribes. He's so obviously stupid I thought it might be an act—playing the fool so he can get away with under-the-table business. But after a few hours of his company I realized he is, in fact, an idiot."

Wheeler makes a small noise of amusement, though his face is unmoved.

"Sloan's a different story. He's into the usual waterfront tricks: girls, beatings, knockout drops," Alma says. "But he's importing product. He uses it, sells it at his sailors' boardinghouse, and I doubt he's paying full price. He's also getting bolder—his men have been knifing fellows on the pier at nights. People are talking."

"How is he getting product?" Delphine says.

"I need to look into that." Alma doesn't say, *Maybe he's the one stealing it from your warehouses.* But the words hang in the air anyway. Delphine raises one fine eyebrow and looks at Wheeler, who is kneading his fists together, his gold ring liquid in the candlelight.

"This is the plan," Delphine says, after allowing Wheeler, briefly, to squirm. "We must plug the leak but also prepare for the law's arrival. Rosales has purchased us some time in that arena—and, through a bit of . . . improvising, has given us the chance to influence their investigation."

Alma bows, though she knows Delphine will find it irritating.

"Sloan will take the fall," Delphine says, standing. "He's already dirty handed, and competent enough to be a convincing villain. Prime him. Get him into a corner."

Wheeler stands, too. Delphine is taller than both of them. Her skin in the lamplight seems impossibly smooth. Alma wishes it were just her and Delphine in this little room, with its soft corners, its raw silks and drapings.

"I expect you two to work together," Delphine says.

Wheeler adjusts his shoulders, as if under a load. Alma catches his eye and smiles.

"No mischief, Rosales," Delphine tells her. "I know how you love it."

"Yes, ma'am."

"Then I leave things in your capable hands."

Delphine walks to the door, her perfumed body holding Alma's gaze. This twisting wrings fresh pain from her throat. She presses her palm into the bandage. The latch clicks shut.

"So," she says to Wheeler, who is mashing the felt of his hat brim in his fingers. "Now are you satisfied?"

"Hardly. *Rosales.*"

"You really thought I was with the law?" Alma wants to know where she slipped, where she fell too hard into the wrong habits. "No marshal in his right mind would hire me."

"It doesn't matter what I thought." He puts on his hat, his jacket. "We have our orders. Let's go."

"What did you get from Sloan's man?" she says, standing between him and the door. She doesn't mind following him around a bit, now that he knows they're working together. She wants to see the Port Townsend setup, meet its key people. Get her footing as incoming deputy.

"Enough justification to set fire to his sty of a boardinghouse."

Wheeler pushes past, shoulder hard against her chest. The rough contact jars her throat. Takes her by surprise. She exhales, mouth staying open, lip curling. So this is how it's going to be. If he wants to muscle her around, two can play that game. Delphine said to work together, but she didn't specify they had to do it nicely.

"Don't be coy." She throws his own words back at him. Adjusts the bandage on her neck as she turns around. "Was Pike the one taking our tar? Give me the details. Before we're out in the street and anyone can hear."

He drops his hand from the doorknob. Lifts his chin.

"Sloan's not behind the leak, though he was trying to get at our product with Pike," Wheeler says. "He wants to control Quincy Wharf. He thinks he's going to do it by blackmailing me into co-operation, or baiting me into an open war. And I'm free to amuse him—now that we are granted leave to fraternize."

The bitterness in his voice is not so carefully concealed.

"You don't like the way she runs things?"

Say it. Say you're not loyal. The shakier he is during their in-vestigation, the better Alma will look as the candidate to replace him. And if she can unseat Wheeler before they solve the leak, so much the better: she likes directing her own operations, and find-ing the mole will be faster if she's giving all the orders.

"I don't want you involved," Wheeler says. "That is the extent of my dissatisfaction."

"But, boss—you're meant to give me a tour of the town." Alma lets her eyes go wide, plaintive, then drops her voice a notch. "Take me under your wing. Work real close with me."

"Go clean yourself up." He waves at her neck, the crusting cuffs of her shirt. "You're a mess."

"I don't think you understand," Alma says, stepping closer.

Wheeler's right hand curls into a fist, but she won't flinch.

"You don't tell me what to do anymore," she says. "I'll play your sidekick when we're out in public, but I've worked for Delphine longer than you. That gives me seniority. Don't like it? Go com-plain. I'll wait."

Alma can almost hear him sizzling, can almost hear his sinews strain as he holds himself together. She reaches down, hand nick-ing his hip, and twists open the doorknob.

"After you, boss," she says.

10

JANUARY 14, 1887

Brittle sunshine. White sheets glaring on the line at the alley's end. When Alma squints against the brightness her neck tightens, too, her cut throat twinging. It's been a rough week. She is operating on too little sleep and not enough food, feeling every day of her twenty-nine years. In the windy alley, waiting for Wheeler to finish pulling on his leather gloves, she pushes against the creep of tiredness. Expands her rib cage. Unfolds her shoulders. Now's not the time to wilt—not when there's a fight stewing a few feet away.

"Don't smile," Wheeler says. "Don't touch me."

"You got it, boss."

Wheeler glowers at her, his hat brim slicing a hard line of shadow from cheekbone to jaw. He glances at the flapping sheets. They are unattended. The mouth of the alley, where Joe crouched, is empty save for paper trash rattling against the wall.

"Roll up your god damn sleeves," he says. "You look like a butcher's boy."

Alma takes her time, shrugging off her jacket and folding the shirt's bloodstained cotton over her forearms.

"Don't do a thing to call attention to yourself," he says.

"I can play a man better than you can."

Alma waits for him to lunge, to more than shove her—to really hit her, so she can hit back.

He only stares, pale eyes undecipherable, then stalks toward the street. His ability to throttle down is impressive. But he must have a boiling point. And when he goes, it will be a glory. She follows his brisk footsteps, glad to be moving, warming with anticipation.

On Tyler they turn toward the water, where the long stretch of wharf juts into the sun-glazed bay in a chain of plankboards. Beckett said Wheeler's boatbuilder keeps shop at the foot of this wharf. Alma lifts her chin, neck stinging, to peer out over passersby and into the bright wavelets. Near the water's edge lumber piles cast triangular shadows. There are dark coils of rope. A shingled roof nips into the horizon.

"No tour of your boatyard?" she says.

Wheeler grunts. Adjusts the knot in his sky-blue scarf and does not pause.

At the corner opposite the boatyard is a slovenly building. The United States Customhouse. It has crook-shuttered windows. Peeling clapboards. A crowd of men smoking on the doorstep. What she's seen inside is just as haphazard: no public waiting area, papers in piles on the floor, the leering clerk frowsy and reeking of gin. The house wears its corruption even more boldly than the San Francisco office, where deputies wallow in the pockets of dirty cops and smugglers, but at least there's an attempt to appear law-abiding.

"And your pals at the customhouse," she says, as they approach the intersection, cart clatter and conversations damping her voice. "When do I get to meet them?"

Wheeler's step hitches, so Alma nearly runs into him. His shoulders stiffen under his gray coat. He touches his hat at a well-dressed man who is just leaving the post office across the street.

"Wait here," Wheeler says.

She lets him get two steps ahead, then follows. Wheeler does not turn to check her: he won't cause a scene. Alma's interest surges. Any man who makes Wheeler cautious is a man she needs to know. Her boots crunch into the rough frozen mud of the road. A gang of kids tumbles out of the notions shop next to the post office, yelping and clutching fistfuls of taffy. Alma waits for them to run past, using the pause to check for blood on her sleeves and hands and pull her collar around her bandage. Neat enough. She ambles up behind Wheeler. His companion has a sallow complexion; a cropped beard brushed smooth; the somber, fine clothing of a rich man. He has been grieving. His eyes are pink at the corners, his mouth twisted.

"Judge Hamilton," Wheeler says. "Is everything all right?"

"Mr. Wheeler. I'm afraid not."

"Good afternoon, sir." Alma knuckles her cap at the man.

Wheeler links his hands behind his back, the leather squeaking, a single dark fist that only she can see.

"And who's this young fellow?" Hamilton dabs at his nose with a silk kerchief.

"My new clerk," Wheeler says. "Forgive his appearance. He was robbed in Tacoma on his journey into town."

A clerk? That's her cover? Alma would smirk if Wheeler were looking at her. But he is pointedly turned away.

"Those heathens," Hamilton says. "I'm sorry to hear it."

He holds out his hand, shakes Alma's firmly. There is a splotch of blood on her inner wrist that she did not see, but Hamilton is distracted, his gaze twitching between her and Wheeler.

"I hope you'll find Port Townsend a welcoming city," he says, "though it is an inauspicious day. We've had something of a tragedy."

"What's happened?" Wheeler takes off his hat, presses it to his chest.

"Not an hour ago—"

A greengrocer's handcart rattles past, its wheels shaking the board sidewalk. The man's singing chant—"Onions, potatoes, peas, and cabbage in brine!"—is hollered three times before he moves far enough away for his wailing voice to fade.

"Not an hour ago, Harrison Doyle was run down by a horse," Hamilton says.

Alma recognizes this name. She flips through connections, through faces. Nothing, nothing . . . In profile Wheeler is tight-drawn, silent, but makes no other show of emotion.

"It was a building accident. On Washington," Hamilton says. "He attempted to rescue a boy who ran toward the animal and was caught by its kicks. His wife is with him at home, with the physician."

Alma was there. With Joe. When the crane broke and the horses spooked. There was no boy near the horses. It's possible she missed the kid, in the clamor, in the sharp light and shadow of the winter street. Or there is spin being applied to the incident. She looks hard at Hamilton, at his tired face. His grief seems true enough.

"My God," Wheeler says. "Will he be all right?"

"The doctor is allowing no visitors," Hamilton says, shaking his head. "I tried to get in and was turned away. Poor Mrs. Doyle. I just sent a telegraph to their son in New York."

Alma's got it. Harrison Doyle is a banker, fat on old East Coast money and stocks. Money and stocks that are catnip to the railroad trustees. Trustees who are considering Wheeler's bid to join them— and Doyle is the man who is most opposed to allowing a foreigner upstart into an American enterprise. Wheeler telling Alma all this at one of their suppers, his brow ridged in the candlelight, his injury surprisingly bare.

And now Doyle is down. If he stays down, Wheeler's position is stronger. His success almost guaranteed.

"I must be off," Hamilton says. "I need to inform the other trustees, and my wife will be wanting to visit Mrs. Doyle. We'll talk."

He nods at Wheeler, then crosses the street toward the way they came, heading for the Upper Town stairs.

"Bad news," Alma says.

She watches Wheeler for a hint of satisfaction. He only puts his hat on with careful movements. Alma walks behind him through Water Street's crowds, which thicken and coarsen as they approach Sailor Town. Maids and errand boys are replaced with seamen, laborers, bleary gentlemen stumbling out of low doorways into the salt-laced brightness of early afternoon. They pass the oyster vendor at Adams Street, his clanging handbell, his buckets of ice and winking shells. The prickly sting of brine catches at Alma's stomach. At Quincy Street Wheeler turns west, toward his offices, but pauses on the corner, under the shade of a fruit shop's awning.

"Do you have a match?" he says.

He takes off his gloves. Pulls a cigar case from his jacket, its silver frame reflecting the blurred reds and greens of apples, the golden skins of pears.

Alma pinches the matchbox out of her vest pocket. The cup of her fingers guards the little flame. Wheeler inclines his head to puff life into the cigar. A sweet note of vanilla. Then the wind shifts, twists around them, bringing a waft of blood and offal from the butcher's shop across the road.

"You don't need to look so grim anymore." Alma keeps her voice low as she tucks the matches away. "Your fine friend the judge is long gone."

Wheeler licks cigar paper off his lower lip. Spits into the gutter.

"Do I look grim?" he says, and there, in his voice only, is the glitter of dark humor.

Alma grins.

"Did you arrange it?" she says.

Wheeler lets a column of smoke drift out of his mouth. Narrows his eyes. A man brushes past Alma toward the fruit shop, holding a sheaf of papers and a little tin pot. He pastes a bill onto the door-jamb, whistling, so close to them that Alma smells the bittersweetness of the glue. MACAULAY VS DOBBS, the bill says, OUR MAN VS TACOMA. A boxing match. Set for the coming Wednesday, at Chain Locker saloon. She studies the paper with interest while waiting for the man to move off.

"There was no kid," Alma says, when they're alone under the awning once more. "Joe and I saw it happen. A crane lost its load. Spooked the horses. How he ended up under them . . . Bad luck. Maybe something else."

"Are you suggesting he was pushed?" Wheeler tucks his gloves into his coat pocket.

"I'm suggesting that whoever told your friend about it added some embellishments."

Behind his fingers, behind his cigar, Wheeler's mouth is stretched almost into a smile. The green awning overhead flaps and trembles in the wind.

"Let's raise a glass to the man," he says. "To his speedy recovery."

"Whatever you like, boss," Alma says. "Though I hope you'll treat your poor injured clerk to the round, seeing as I was robbed and I can barely afford a coal fire on my wages."

"A desperate soul."

"Cold and hungry as you keep me," she says, as they cross Water Street. "You're a monster."

He is almost smiling again, the cigar clamped between his teeth, his hat brim blotting his eyes so she can't quite gauge how her humor is landing. She walks beside him, not a step behind. They pass the tall windows of Waterman & Katz, spice bottles and twill jackets and candles arrayed behind the glass. The merchant hovering in the next doorway calls to Wheeler, comes out into the crunchy mud to shake his hand. Wheeler promises a new crate of Brown's Four Crown Scotch by the following week. Alma keeps her fists in her pockets, keeps quiet. She doesn't look like a clerk in Camp's getup, but she can play any part Wheeler gives her. She won't be tripped.

Out onto the long, boot-shaped expanse of Quincy Wharf. Wheeler's brisk puffs of cigar smoke rising. He doesn't even glance at the old cannery, at its plank stoop where two of Sloan's men lounge reptilian in the sun. Opposite the cannery, a neat whitewashed boardinghouse. Then the narrow passage between buildings widens into a platform over the bay. On it, a triangle of buildings: the Chain Locker saloon; a freight warehouse; and on the bay side, in a prime loading spot, the tawny brick walls of Wheeler's own Clyde Imports. Sitting out front is the big man who knifed Alma that morning. He's back at whittling, his blade a quick glimmer in the shadows.

At their approach he hefts himself up. Shakes wood shavings off his buckskin jacket. Alma wants to get closer, wink at him, show him she's good friends with the boss. But Wheeler stops at the Chain Locker's low door, thirty yards from the Clyde Imports warehouse. She leaves the big man to his knife.

Inside, the saloon is dim, all latticed shadows. Close ceiling beams. Thick pillars. Smells of kelp and damp wood. The lanterns salvaged off some ancient hulk, their frames warped with salt. There are a few men at the tables, too early in the afternoon for a full house. Bills for the boxing match are tacked along the bar.

Wheeler stands at the counter, waiting for the keep.

"I was serious about you treating." Alma elbows up next to him. "I've got nothing on me."

He stubs his cigar into an ashy metal dish. Leaves the bar of his forearm lowered between their bodies. At the other end of the counter, some ten feet down, the keep polishes glasses. He sees them, he must see them, but he finishes one glass, picks up another.

"Why are we really here?" she says.

"A social call."

"The welcome's not too friendly."

A patron approaches the keep, who takes his time pouring the man's drink.

"No," Wheeler says.

"Where's your pal?" Alma says, flipping around to lean against the bar. "I'll help you find him."

"This should be the point when he's pouring us two whiskeys on the house."

The bartender is looking right at them but has coolly returned to polishing his cups. He is a whip-thin man of middle age, with dark blond hair. His nimble hands twist the glassware and rag together in a knot of cloth and light.

"Clay." Wheeler waves the man over, and though he is slow to attend, he drifts toward them at last.

"Mr. Wheeler," he says, without a trace of good feeling.

"Is there a problem?" Wheeler takes off his hat, undoes the buttons of his jacket.

"I'd say so."

Up close, the bartender's skin has that particular leathery sheen sailors acquire after years on the water. He has keen black eyes. A gold earring in his left ear. All he's missing are the tarred pigtail and duck trousers.

"You want to tell me what it is," Wheeler says, "so I can set things right?"

The barkeep's eyes flick over to Alma and settle on her face.

"He's fine," Wheeler says. "A new man of mine. Trustworthy."

"Like the rest of your boys?"

Alma catches sight of a ratty little fellow sidling close. She steps around Wheeler to confront him, slipping out her knife and feeding the haft into her shirt cuff.

"Back off," she tells him. "This ain't none of your business."

"Just wanting a nip," the man says, breath hot and oniony.

"You wait until we're done."

He scuttles off at the flash of steel in her palm, and she returns to the bar. The two men are speaking in bare undertones, with no one but Alma near enough to hear them.

"—and ask me for a favor," Clay is saying. He grips the polishing cloth in one thick-knuckled fist, leaning over the bar counter so his face is close to Wheeler's.

"If you don't explain yourself, I might get angry," Wheeler says, not budging an inch as the bartender growls.

"His jaw's near on broken," Clay says. "And he spit out two teeth. He's got nothing to do with your concerns. Tell that to your trustworthy boys."

Wheeler resets somehow. The angle of his chin drops a fraction, and without actually stepping back, without losing the hard set of his shoulders or his ready stance, he draws away. Gives the smallest bit of room to the bartender.

"I'll take care of it," Wheeler says.

"You will."

"I need you to arrange that meeting."

"I'm not going to put myself in that position," the bartender says.

"I'll advise you not to view this lightly," Wheeler says. "I won't ask twice."

All through this exchange Alma has toyed with the knife in her sleeve, nudging the blade into her palm just hard enough to feel sharpness but not hard enough to pierce. Parts of the men's conversation might as well be code, but she is learning plenty about Wheeler under pressure. Calm, quiet. A man who will leave you to drown, who will not return to toss a lifeline. It's not her style. Too restrained. But it works on the bartender. He sucks at his teeth, lets out a long sigh through his nose.

"I take your meaning," he says. "I'll do it."

He pulls two glasses from a leaning stack and fills them with whiskey. His hand is steady. His jaw tight. Alma thinks he means to toast with Wheeler, a gesture of reconciliation, but the barkeep pushes one of the tumblers toward her. Then he leaves them, moving to the other end of the bar, where a trio of men has gathered.

"You sure he didn't spike that," she says, nodding at the tumbler in Wheeler's hand.

"It's always a worry."

He takes a sip. There is no gleam of triumph in his eyes, none of that dark satisfaction he let show, just slightly, after news of Doyle's accident. With the barkeep otherwise occupied, Wheeler loosens his hold on himself in little ways: that slight working of his jaw, the wiggle of his right boot on the footrail.

Alma shoots back her liquor, forgetting her neck until the motion tears her cut open. She knuckles the bandage. Swallows past the pain. The lantern above the bar splits into a fan of little flames in her watering eyes.

"I'm in the dark here," she says. "And I don't like it. Meetings. Favors. I can't do my job if you don't keep me in on company business."

"I'll explain at my offices."

"And when are we going there?"

"Now." Wheeler leaves his glass half-finished, palms on his hat.

"I need some food," Alma says.

It's been hours since she ate anything—some crackers and salt cod in the early morning, as she worked on her letter to the Pinkerton's agents. The blood loss and hunger are taking their toll, and the whiskey is pulsing hot and fast into her chest, into her forehead.

Outside, dark to bright, too much flashing in and out of sunlight. A tight band draws across the back of Alma's skull, just above the raw spot from the old watchman's clobbering. She wants oysters from the vendor up the street, or bread and broth from the soup stall in front of the Cosmopolitan. But Wheeler heads toward the Clyde Imports warehouse, where the big man still sits whittling, tapping his foot and whistling an off-key tune.

"Sir." He stands when Wheeler approaches.

"Get McManus," Wheeler says. "I want him at my desk in twenty minutes."

McManus. One of Wheeler's known henchmen, as Beckett termed it, along with a fellow called Benson. Wheeler's top crew members. Maybe this big bastard is Benson.

"Howdy." Alma flicks her cap brim at him, shapes her voice into a mockery of his drawl. "Thanks for giving me my gear back."

The man frowns.

"I didn't give you shit," he says, his gray eyes darting to Wheeler.

Alma drops her knife fully into her palm, twists the blade so it reflects the sky. With her other hand she pulls open her jacket to display her loaded holster.

"I guess you're just such a useless watchman that I took it back right under your nose."

"Knock it off," Wheeler tells her, and to the man he says, "That's sloppy work, Benson. I expect better."

So this is him. Benson is good with a knife, though he doesn't look it. It follows that if he doesn't look that smart, he might just have a quick mind behind those dull gray eyes.

"Twenty minutes," Wheeler tells him again.

Then Wheeler and Alma are headed for his offices, at last, only two blocks from the water. They do not take the side door on Quincy Street. In the daylight it is drab and unremarkable, withdrawn from the street atop its trio of wooden steps. Wheeler instead turns the corner at Washington Street, unlocks the shuttered Clyde Imports door. The cold room smells of ink, parchment, the polished sourness of brass. The private inner office, by contrast, is fire warmed. Its hearth yellow and crackling. Its air laced with vanilla tobacco. Alma slumps into her usual chair before the desk, amused at how quickly the office has changed shape into something familiar.

"The Quincy door not good enough for you?" she says, rubbing at the bandage on her neck.

"I keep the businesses discrete," he says.

"And you find that works, in so small a town?"

"I find that people are happy to believe the best of those with money to lend."

Indoors, in his private space, his shoulders slump while he's taking off his hat and jacket. But Alma is watching him, and this relaxed guard, this real breath, is quickly replaced with his usual stolidity. He circles the desk.

"Jesus Christ," he says, glowering at the floor. "Come pick this up."

Benson left Wheeler's shirt, now in red tatters, in the wire wastebasket. The cloth is covered in pale wood shavings. A few of the wisps have absorbed Alma's blood and are tinged rosy as cherry blossoms.

"What do you expect me to do with it?" she says.

"It's your blood," he says. "That makes it your problem."

"You won't like how I clean."

"No doubt." He slides into his chair, starts flipping through his mess of papers.

Alma stoops to collect the basket. Pink shavings slip out of the wire frame and ghost over her fingers as she carries it to the hearth. Nudging aside the fireguard with her boot, she drops the laden basket into the flames. It crunches against kindling with a scatter of sparks. Wheeler cranes around at the noise.

"I said you wouldn't like it," she tells him.

He glares at her, silent, angrier than she expected. Oh, well.

"Now that we're all tidied up," she says, slapping wood off her palms as she walks back to her chair, "tell me about Sloan. From the company's perspective, since he's Delphine's first assignment."

"Don't say that name again." Wheeler is frowning at the bloody shavings that trail past his desk. "Only Nell and Joe know it. She goes by Sarah Powell here. Mrs. Sarah Powell, widow of Conrad Powell, a wealthy Englishman some ten years buried."

"Ten years! That explains the deathly getup, and how she gets away with wearing gold in mourning," Alma says. "She does love her jewels."

It's a beautiful piece of fiction—true to Delphine's genius at deftly covering every angle. After such a long time, even a devout widow may put on ornament again and not be perceived as vulgar. It explains Delphine's fortune, too: all her money looks less suspicious if she came to it through marriage. And the perished Englishman is another nice touch. The upper crust of Port Townsend will more easily swallow the notion of European decadence than they would the idea of a white American man taking Delphine as his wife.

There is a knock at the Quincy-side door. Wheeler looks up from the carpet. Readjusts his body in the leather chair.

"What?"

"Brought you some lunch, sir."

Alma hustles to the door. Conaway has his cap in one hand and a wrapped packet in the other. He steps back, blinks.

"You still here?" he says.

"Oh, I'll be around," Alma tells him, taking the packet. It is soft, seeping faint warmth. She brings it to her face and it smells of sweet yeast and ham and butter. "Get us some coffee, too, won't you."

Conaway hesitates, looking past her toward Wheeler.

"Go on," Wheeler tells him.

The big man nods, scrapes a bit, still looking between Alma and Wheeler when she closes the door on him. She carries the packet to her chair and unwraps a thick sandwich, the bread crusty and freshly baked.

"You probably don't want any," she says. "I was just handling the trash."

"Help yourself to some whiskey, too, while you're at it." Wheeler leans back in his chair, crosses his arms over his chest. "Don't neglect to smash the bottle once you've done."

The warm bread is dense under her teeth, the ham and butter richly salted. Swallowing big bites hurts her throat, her jaw, but she is ravenous.

"May I suggest starting with the silver decanter, as that's the bloody expensive stuff," he says as she eats. "Since you seem intent on destroying my office."

"Don't ask me to clean again, and your office will survive."

Alma wipes crumbs from her mouth with the back of her hand. Picks up the second half of the sandwich.

"Sloan," she says. "What do I need to know about him?"

Wheeler stands, goes to the liquor board. He picks up the silver-topped decanter. Trades it for another. Whiskey's clean, sharp scent cuts through the air, which has gone smoky and metallic as the wire wastebasket blackens in the hearth.

"He's been a blight on Quincy Wharf for two years now," Wheeler says, after a sip that washes the sharpest edge out of his voice. "Started as a boardinghouse master and has expanded his interests."

"Into tar?"

"Rumor has it."

"What did Pike say?"

"Pike was ready to accuse Sloan of anything, once Tom started on him." Wheeler pours more whiskey. "One of his claims was that Sloan has girls bringing in product. But until I see it, it's still a rumor. Not enough to take him down."

"So give him some," Alma says. "Give him enough rope to hang himself, and there's one of our problems solved: he'll swing for all our sins."

Wheeler turns around. Leans against the marble-topped board, considering her.

"I was hoping to kill him," he says. "This new directive puts a crimp in my plans."

Alma pauses, the last of her sandwich tucked into one cheek.

"A *crimp* in your plans?" she says around the food, one eyebrow lifting.

"Aye."

His face is blank, but his voice is wry. He did mean it as a joke. Alma licks butter off her lips. It's a shame she has to get Wheeler out of her way. There's so much about him to like.

"So let me guess," she says. "Your new plan involves Clay the barkeep's favor."

Wheeler sips at his whiskey, and by now she can read that as a tell—he likes to shield his face when he's surprised, or unsteady.

"Give me some credit," she says. "We went to him first for a reason, and right now our biggest worries sit with Barnaby Sloan."

"Malcolm Clay is a useful man." Wheeler brings his drink to his desk. "Between his bar and his sailors' boardinghouse, he keeps the waterfront's pulse. And keeps me informed of it."

"But today he was not in an informing mood."

"No."

"Can he get Sloan to cooperate?"

"I want him to host a meeting between us," he says. "Where I will get Sloan to cooperate."

"Don't do it at Chain Locker," Alma says. "That place is a death trap. We couldn't cover all the doors even if we pulled every man off warehouse duty."

"I won't have him in my offices."

"Take the offer to Sloan's house," Alma says. "Where he'll feel strong. More willing to make a deal, when he feels like he's able to push for advantages."

"Walking in there is a fool's errand," Wheeler says. "My men and I won't be welcome."

"I'll go."

Alma leans forward, sets her balled-up sandwich paper on the edge of the desk. It unwrinkles, slow, with little ticks of sound.

"He doesn't know I'm your man," she says. "That'll get me at least as far as his rooms upstairs."

"How do you know he has rooms upstairs?"

"I cased him. We didn't go for a carriage ride, though, so I hope you still feel special."

"If you were in his rooms, how is it that he doesn't know you?" Wheeler's voice is flat, even.

"He didn't see me," Alma says, annoyed that he ignored her jab. She stands up, needing to move around, to keep her body warm as she thinks.

"I'll take some product in." She paces from one edge of the desk to the other, a tight, six-foot-long orbit. "Just enough for bait."

"I don't keep it lying around," Wheeler says. "We only store it here if there's a holdup in Tacoma."

"When's the next shipment due?"

A pause. "Tonight," he says.

"So free some up. Enough for bait and to make a trade." Alma stops at the center of the desk, where her body is aligned with his, looking down on him. "I take some product, along with a token showing we're serious, and explain there are consequences to saying no."

"What kind of a token."

"Do you still have Pike's body?"

Wheeler's eyes narrow, his mouth twisting toward a grin. He understands what she's after. Doesn't think it's such a bad plan, by the dark current flickering over his face.

"Coffee, sir."

The door opens on Conaway. Metal flare of a canteen and two tin cups in his broad fists. A new man is beside him, small and pale in comparison. Alma is startled by his youth, and by his resemblance to Wheeler. They have the same thin mouth. The same black hair and ice-blue eyes. Is he Wheeler's brother? Their age difference seems too great: the man looks to be in his twenties. Father and son? That would be an interesting piece of knowledge for her mapping of the Port Townsend organization—and its weak spots.

Conaway clangs the tinware onto the desk, his every move noisy: boots hard on the carpet, the door clapping shut as he leaves.

"You wanted to see me?" The pale man has Wheeler's brogue, too, and a limp that favors his left leg. He takes off his cap. Gives Alma an unfriendly once-over.

"Pay another visit to Peterson, did you, Tommy?" Wheeler says.

Alma pours herself some coffee and carries it to the sideboard. This must be McManus, brought to the office by Benson's summons. Seeing him at Wheeler's desk takes away from the family likeness. They have similar coloring, a mirrored stern control over their faces, but Wheeler is hard-cut angles and planes while McManus's features have an unfinished look to them, as of clay not quite sculpted to completion.

"He was talking to the cops again," McManus says, his voice composed. "I thought I'd remind him who he answers to."

He shifts his gaze to Alma as she leans against the wall by the sideboard.

"Who's this?" McManus says.

"This is Camp. He's to be trusted."

A flash of displeasure tightens McManus's mouth and jaw. Alma swallows bitter coffee, gives him a nasty little grin. He turns toward her, hands fisted.

"Pay attention," Wheeler says, sharp. "What do you mean, 'again'?"

"They were at his yard all morning," McManus says. "Right after Beckett was found. When they left, I stopped by."

"Did they ask him about Beckett?" Wheeler says.

"Aye."

Wheeler glances at Alma, who shakes her head. She can't see a connection with what Beckett told her. Beckett's letter had linked Peterson to smugglers, but it was penned anonymously. There should be no link between the ex-collector and the boatbuilder. No link to draw the lawmen back to Peterson. They might only be grasping at straws—a tip-off about the boatyard's link to smugglers, then a butchered body turning up the next morning, doesn't look so good for Peterson—but now that Beckett is silenced, someone else might be talking.

"Peterson doesn't know him from Adam," Wheeler says.

"That's right," McManus says. "I made sure of it. He swore he hadn't said anything stupid, but they'd knocked him around a fair bit. I knocked him around some more."

"You knocked him around," Wheeler says, on his feet in an abrupt surge of motion that has McManus blinking in surprise. "No. I'll tell you what you did. You fucked me. I needed a favor today, and instead I got a lecture about how Peterson's missing teeth."

"That was the police." McManus stands up a notch taller. "I only hit him in the body."

A smart fighter, if not an agile one. Get a man on the torso so his bruises aren't visible under clothes and save your knuckles from the jawbones, the skull bones, that might slow them.

"I don't want excuses," Wheeler says. "You have bright ideas about keeping men quiet, you come clear them with me first."

"Yes, sir."

"Good." Wheeler sinks back into his chair, runs a palm over his pomaded hair. "Is *Orion*'s shipment ready?"

"Waiting at the refinery," McManus says, with another patently mistrustful glare at Alma. There is more venom in his eyes than before his scolding—he has been dressed down in her presence, and it's a mark against her. "Packed in the stamped trunks. Johnny Yee says the boats are all late with the storm."

"Take thirty pounds out of the shipment when it comes through and bring it in."

Wheeler unlocks a desk drawer and withdraws an unmarked envelope. McManus steps forward to take it, his left boot dragging just slightly over the carpet.

"That's thirty pounds." Alma sets her coffee on the sideboard. "Or how about an easier number: two cases. With all the tar gone missing lately I wonder if you know how to count."

McManus pauses, the envelope halfway into his inner jacket pocket, his shoulders stiff.

"Watch your mouth." Wheeler relocks the drawer. "Go on then, Tom."

McManus nods, not bothering to conceal his scowl as he puts on his cap and sees himself out. The door clicks shut.

"Am I not meant to give friendly reminders?" Alma says.

"Not if they involve you bleating about missing product."

Or if they involve Tom McManus. Wheeler jumped to his defense quick enough. Alma finishes her coffee, wipes her mouth on her sleeve.

"When I shook Beckett down, he said he'd tipped the cops onto Peterson's yard," Alma says.

"That's why I sent you to shut him up."

"But he said he did it anonymously."

"I know."

Alma strides to Wheeler's desk. She pours herself more coffee, then splashes some into his still-empty cup, spattering nearby papers. While he scoops up a handful of wet pages and shakes them out, swearing, she takes the hot tin cup to her seat.

"All right," she says. "We have coffee. We have privacy. Tell me everything about your operation: people, drop spots, merchants, payoffs. Customhouse paperwork. The missing tar, and where it disappeared. I ran the San Francisco deliveries—I know the ropes. Follow your god damn orders and demonstrate how you do things here."

"Don't you ever speak to me in that tone again." Wheeler drops the coffee-streaked papers onto the desk, his face bloodless.

"You want my respect, you earn it," Alma says. "I hear you've got near on two tons of tar moving through every month. That's impressive. Tell me how it moves. I'm all ears."

11

JANUARY 14, 1887

Again, that ghost howl: a foghorn, far off, fading. Still no sign of ship's lights. Then, like a match being struck on a distant street corner, a yellow glow flickers to life. Another. Drifting steadily nearer through the mist that blends Union Wharf's boards into bay into sky. Alma pulls her jacket tight against the damp, takes the flask the young man slouched beside her holds out.

"About time." She tongues low gin off the corners of her lips. "It's past ten."

"These Red Line cunts," Driscoll says, capping the flask. "Never made an early landing in their lives."

Passengers scattered across the wharf are stirring, standing from their steamer trunks, shaking condensation off their cloaks and hats. Boards creak under boots. Faces are blurred in the dim haze cast by lanterns strung along the pier, but Alma picks out Wheeler's men by their postures, by the positions they've taken. McManus stands with three hired longshoremen at the far pylons, smoking and checking the tags of their cargo with the aid of a hand lantern. Lyle and Folkstone slap their arms for warmth and share a packet of cocaine, taking snorts of the stuff and shaking their heads like wet dogs. Driscoll, next to her, is the boxy kid from the warehouse she never got to fight, and that's just as well—up close he's a bruiser, with thirty pounds on her and a youngster's reckless energy.

"Last month it was fog delays every time, sure." Driscoll's hands are shoved deep in his pockets, his body in constant motion, rocking from heels to toes and back again. "And then that hailstorm, Christ Jesus, we waited in that for a steamer, two hours late, whatever excuse they had Tom wasn't ready to hear it, oh, no, not with his girl waiting on him in town. Fucking hailstones the size of conkers, I had one hit me in the teeth and thought I'd lost the buggers."

He's nervous as hell and gabbing to match, Alma following the looping skeins of his sentences with interest. Driscoll is the one who let Sloan's man Pike get close to the crew and eventually into the warehouse. What Driscoll had to say about that incident sounded innocent enough: he seems far too in awe of Wheeler to steal from him. In the end, the kid's too friendly and talks too god damn much. Not ideal for a crewman. But he's strong. Seems loyal. And the dips and blurs of his thick Irish burr pull Alma back to Chicago. To the boys she spied on from her boarding school, imagining herself in their midst, jostling over marbles and cigarettes, wearing their tatty tweed vests and cropped trousers.

"McManus has a girl?" she says. "One he's not paying for? I don't believe it."

When she speaks, she has to make an effort to not fall into Driscoll's rhythm. The chameleon's danger: a tendency to mimic whoever's near. As Camp she uses a bland Western twang. He could be from anywhere west of the Mississippi, and the accent is common enough in California. Other patterns come easy, too—easy enough to throw her off and smear into Camp's low drawl. Driscoll's is one of them.

"All I know is her name's Mary." Driscoll grins at her as he scrubs fog droplets off his stubbled chin. "Conaway says she must be ugly, but I think she's a proper beauty. And rich. Maybe lives up high on the hill."

Orion is close now, three tiers of lanterns glossing the fog gold. As the *thrum-thrum-thrum* of her side-wheel grows to a roar, McManus limps across the pier. So he's got a secret woman. Might be interesting to find out what about her makes him shy. He approaches a waiting passenger. The man takes out his watch, shows the time to McManus while shaking his head.

Driscoll's teeth worry at a raw patch on his lip. He's going to crack open the opium shipment—on this run it's packed into steamer trunks, one hundred pounds each, tagged with recycled duties stamps through to Tacoma—and bring up the thirty pounds of tar that Alma will offer to Sloan. Driscoll's never done this part of the job. When there's product to extract, a crewman called Barker usually does it, Driscoll said, but Barker is laid up with a kidney stone. So tonight McManus has placed the responsibility on the younger man. Another way for him to earn some trust back, after the Pike problem. Driscoll's coat pockets bulge and shudder. He is making nervous fists there, in the dark confines of the wool.

"Don't fuck this up," Alma says, testing him.

If the kid gets too jittery, she will take the burlap sack and skeleton key he's got tucked into his belt and get the cases herself. That would add some fun to the evening. She wanted to see a shipment in progress—how the tar passes safe through Port Townsend's customs checkpoint, how the ride-along man is put into position for the trip to Tacoma—and after some negotiation with Wheeler she was introduced to the crew as McManus's new mate. That makes her an unofficial boss man.

"I'm grand, I'm grand." Driscoll flares an elbow at her, playful, not overstepping too much. "Only watched out for Barker a hundred times."

A wet slap as *Orion*'s lead tie-line lands on the planks, then the steamer nudges into the bumpers and the whole wharf shudders. The passengers have formed a straggling cluster, baggage at hand, and three crewmen hop off the side of the boat to draw it closer with more lines. They lead out a gangway to the top deck and throw out another to the lowest, for the loading crew.

"Ready?" Alma says.

Driscoll nods. They push out of their shallow alcove—thick air chilling Alma's back, her neck—and cross the wharf to join the little crowd of stevedores. In this sweat-soured circle the men converse quietly: "Evening, pal," someone says to Alma, and she returns the greeting, tips her hat at Folkstone, who reeks of smoked fish, Driscoll, behind her, is muttering about the fog, and Lyle replies in an undertone that the Red Line is a bunch of sods.

Their gangway is tied in. Alma and Driscoll are eased to the front of the group. It's so smoothly done that Alma is surprised to find herself first at the walkway, hustling down, the roped planks tilting uncertainly under her boots. She ducks into the storeroom, Driscoll warm behind her, and lets him pass as Folkstone enters the low compartment, then Lyle. The two men get to work carting out crates and boxes labeled for Port Townsend, while in the shadows at the back, Alma blocks the shallow window with her body and keeps her attention split between the storeroom's starboard door and Driscoll. The kid creeps among the Tacoma-tagged luggage, pulls free a large trunk, and fits the key into its padlock.

A shout outside. Lyle, arms full with a crate, flinches toward the door.

The shout again, and then Folkstone repeats it loudly from the doorway: "Step aside, quick. Quick, step aside."

Someone is coming down—someone not on Wheeler's crew, which means it's not Moore, the bribed customs inspector, either.

Driscoll pauses, his hands in the open trunk, his eyes wide. She nods at him to keep working. Straw scatters as he pulls out a case. Alma threads through the waist-high piles of cargo toward the gangway, hauls up the closest item marked P.T. It's a burlap sack of something heavy and formless, grain, or sand, and it shifts in a way that pulls hard on her shoulder.

An unfamiliar man ducks into the storage room, squirming around Lyle, who goes suddenly clumsy with the crate he's carrying, apologizing as he bumbles into the man. The stranger is doughy in the face and torso, with dense black hair and muttonchops. He's not a laborer, not with that build. Not with that peacoat, those pressed trousers. His shiny shoes make Alma's spit go sour.

"Give us a hand," she says, and heaves the sack at him.

He catches it with a grunt, staggering backward. Drops it hard to the floorboards. A few coins fall out of his pocket.

"I'm not here to cart things around," he says, brushing hay off his coat.

"You're in the way of those who are."

Alma lifts her chin. Her knife is a hard flatness against her bound rib cage; another blade waits in her boot. The man looks damn like a customhouse inspector—but he's not Moore, the ring's new friend in the customhouse after Max Beckett's ouster. Moore, who just last week received a five-hundred-dollar bonus for his sterling ability to turn a blind eye to opium shipments.

A grunted call comes down the gangway, passed from man to man.

"Ten minutes." Folkstone hollers the call into the hold, his hoarse voice too loud in the dim confines. He is staring at the intruder, a bewildered worry in his eyes. He and Lyle don't know this man—another red flag.

"I'm here to inspect this ship's cargo." The man holds out a printed card. "Edward Edmonds, U.S. Assistant Deputy Collector."

"I can't read," Alma says, ignoring the card. How much longer is Driscoll going to fuck around with the trunk, is one question. Another: How can she punch out a customhouse man and not cause trouble for Delphine? "All's I know is you're in my way and we have ten minutes to get this dunnage shifted."

"Then I'll start at the back," Edmonds says, shouldering past.

Alma falls away as if he's knocked her off-balance, her hip thumping into a slatted crate. She uses the surface to impel her back toward Edmonds.

"You don't manhandle me, lawman," she says, grabbing him by the lapel. She shoves him into a stack of crates with far more force than he used against her. The top lip of a crate catches him in the upper back and he wheezes, eyes wide, Alma's fist pressed into his fat-padded jaw.

"Inspect whatever you want, but apologize to me first." She thrusts his chin up with her knuckles. "I've had just about enough of being knocked around today."

The bruises on her face and hands fit this angle. And not all of her reaction is feigned: she is sore, her neck a low-grade aching; she's been battered about over the last few days and is only too ready to dole out a throttling. But this diversion, authentic as it feels, will only work if Folkstone or Lyle joins in. She can't look at them to see if they're catching on, but she prays one of them is quick enough to pick up on what she's playing at.

"I will have you arrested," Edmonds says.

His pale face is flushed, dark red at the ears and cheekbones, hot against Alma's hand. He is angry. But there is fear in his eyes, too: the fear of a soft fellow who stormed into a room full of workingmen and found his office did not protect him. This flash of coward's remorse sends a surge of viciousness through Alma. Her free hand is slipping into her vest when someone grabs her by the shoulder.

"Jesus! Easy now!"

Lyle is behind her, pulling her away from the collector, her fingertips just brushing the handle of her knife but coming away empty.

"I'm sorry, sir." Lyle moves between Alma and Edmonds, offering the collector a hand, which the other man slaps away. "Forgive him, he had a rough time with some union boys earlier. We're all on edge after they came at us."

Good thing Lyle is a ready man. Folkstone is still gaping by the doorway.

"He didn't mean nothing," Lyle adds lamely.

"I don't know if you're drunk, or just stupid." Saved from a beating, Edmonds is brave again. He stands up to his full height, straightening his lapel and sneering at Alma, who positions herself so that the collector is facing the door, not the hold. "But it's a good thing your fellows are here to restrain you before you land yourself in jail."

She glowers at him. Over his shoulder, in the shadows, Driscoll reemerges from the piled luggage and vaults through the back window to the deck. Alma covers the brief wandering of her eyes by spitting copiously at the collector's boots and wiping her mouth with her sleeve.

"All right," Lyle says. "Come on."

He tows her by the sleeve toward a large steamer trunk. They heft it up together, eyes locking over the top. Alma gives him a tiny, approving nod. His mouth twitches into a lopsided grin, just for a second, and then it's back to business as he counts, "One, two, three!" to lift the trunk onto the back of the first man on the gangway, one of the hired fellows, whose massive muscled plane of a body bears the weight up the steep ten feet to the dock.

While Edmonds pokes around with a hand lantern, Alma helps move the rest of the P.T.-tagged bags and crates out of the hold. Lyle leads her into the back, to the last few boxes marked for Port Townsend. Nothing marking Driscoll's efforts save a little straw on the deck. They cart out the boxes under the customhouse man's glare. She is sweating, moisture collecting at her temples, the cut at her neck prickling with a fierce itch. If Edmonds doesn't look too hard at the luggage with customs-cleared stamps, they will come through the night unscathed.

But this was supposed to be a routine operation, the same one that takes place every time a loaded Red Line boat touches in from Victoria en route to Tacoma. There was supposed to be a friendly inspector, who would idly peer at a box or two, have a smoke with the men, leave. No high stakes, no surprises. Just a chance for Alma to see things in motion, see how the product moves south. So is Edmonds's presence an accident, or was she was meant to blunder— set up by Wheeler to fail? No. Not this way. Not by endangering the supply line. The Victoria–Tacoma steamers are half the business's main artery, and to damage that would be suicide.

"Coming down!" the men shout along the gangway line.

The new passengers' gear is being stowed. Alma and Lyle stack crates and trunks, Folkstone mumbling as he carts dunnage in; he did not act fast or well in the crisis, and he won't meet their eyes. When Edmonds makes his way forward to inspect the new baggage, Alma steps back, kicking at the straw-dusted floor and scowling. Without a word to them, the collector pockets his notebook, turns up his collar, and leaves the hold.

"What the fuck was that about?" Lyle says, once the customhouse man has climbed the gangway and is out of earshot.

"I don't know," Alma tells him. "But he didn't linger too long among the goods, thank Christ."

"I've been working with this crew for near on a year," Lyle says. "Never seen hide nor hair of an unfriendly collection agent."

The side-wheel, muted while the boat was tied in, is picking up—slow, loud slaps against the water. Alma thinks again of the timing. It is bad. But it would have been worse if she were not there. If Barker was out, Driscoll in his place, and there was no extra man to think fast in the hold and buy two minutes more for Driscoll's extraction.

She leaves Lyle at the lower rail; he's the ride-along man, staying with the product until Tacoma to make the handoff to the middlemen there. Folkstone is close behind her as she climbs out of the hold, the fog thickening into rain, pent-up tension roping through her neck and shoulders and stiffening her joints. The hurt she was ready to put on Edmonds is bottled up inside her arms, her chest.

McManus and the hired stevedores are loading crates into the Clyde Imports wagon. Its horse is tied up at the foot of the pier, champing and snuffling, tossing its head morosely in its blinders. McManus does not look up from the rope he's tying off when Alma and Folkstone walk past, toward the freight warehouse that anchors the wharf. There is no sign of Driscoll.

At the landward side of the warehouse, where they're sheltered from the weather, Folkstone lights a cigarette. He takes a long draw, hands it to Alma. They smoke in silence as *Orion*, blocked from view by the building, signals twice, three times, and thunders away from the dock. The landed passengers haul their goods off into the night or stride into Hoop & Barrow, the wharf's saloon. Street noise trickles in to fill the void left by the side-wheeler's splashes. Shouts from Sailor Town dives, a man hollering a hymn as he pisses against Hoop & Barrow's wall. The everywhere tapping of rain. A fistfight spills out of the saloon and briefly distracts Alma from the mess at hand.

Then McManus's peculiar dragging gait, at last. He comes round the corner of the warehouse. As he approaches Alma and Folkstone, his face gleams paler than usual, streaked with rainwater.

"Get the horse," McManus says to Folkstone, his tone flat yet somehow conveying fault that encompasses Alma, too. She flicks away the cigarette, those unused wires of power tingling in her arms and thighs.

"Driscoll's with the cart," McManus continues. "We'll meet you at the warehouse."

"Yes, sir." Folkstone touches his forehead and starts down the pier.

This is the first time Alma has been alone with McManus. He stands angled from her, his face turned, putting distance between them though they are close enough to lock elbows. He did his part and told the men to mind her, but his posture, his tight mouth, signal his disapproval.

"The unloaded lot is safe, then," she says.

He nods.

"So is this business as usual?" She wishes Folkstone were here; anyone to witness her taking rank over McManus. He is Wheeler's favorite. And maybe Wheeler's blind spot. "Do you routinely have unknown inspectors barge in and go sniffing around the product?"

"He's new." McManus glares at her out of the corners of his eyes, then shifts his gaze toward the lights onshore, where crowds tumble along Water Street. Folkstone approaches, leading the steaming shadow of the cart horse.

"Don't make excuses."

Alma is pleased when McManus tenses, his jaw locking. It might save her a heap of trouble if he throws a swing at her now—she'd go right for his bad leg, get him out of order quick, and there's one less man for Wheeler to stand on as he stands in her way.

"I don't care if he got his badge this afternoon," she says. "Not sweetening the collectors is two-bit, amateur nonsense. Their bribes should be the first thing you look to. Their wives should be getting flowers. Their dogs should be getting marrowbones. Do you understand me?"

"Who the fuck do you think you are?"

Now she has McManus's full attention: his face in hers, clean-shaven, pale as milk, blue eyes blazing under the brim of his cap. Sour gin breath—he must keep a flask on him, though he seems steady as a rock.

"You didn't do a thing to help while he came down on us," she says, and neither of them looks up as the cart and horse rumble past, fifteen feet away, shaking the boards under their feet. "So I can see why you're upset with your performance. But if you take it out on me—if you stand here and insult me—you had better be prepared to put your money where your mouth is."

He does not move, does not blink, and she wonders if Wheeler did give him a private talking-to, for him to show such restraint.

"Go on." Alma lets her voice go almost soft. "Start something."

"No." McManus closes his eyes, his nostrils flaring. When he snaps them open again, his gaze is pointing at their feet. This is enough to reset the space between them, take some of the crackling tension away. "I was given orders."

"How convenient, to follow them now."

McManus grunts, flips his collar up to his ears, and ducks into the rain. Alma lets him lead the way down the dock, past Hoop & Barrow, past the shuttered tailor's shop at the pier's foot. On Water Street she leaves even more space between them, like a rope let to sag, and allows her attention to wander over passersby and bright windows. A gold sign across the road reads THE CAPTAIN'S. This is the dance hall where Nell works sometimes, according to Wheeler. He seemed cagey about sharing the name of the place, and she's not convinced he told the truth.

She stops to take out a cigarette in the light of the window. Behind the fogged glazing, dancers whirl on a square floor, girls in gay dresses, men in calico shirts and dented hats. A fiddle band sways on a raised platform. Alma searches the room for Nell's face, her golden hair. Nell works for Delphine, too—of course she does, she's devastating, and Delphine chooses only the best. Alma wants to know more about her. She wants to buy her a drink, slide her hand up that yellow skirt. Wet heat and honeysuckle.

The match burns down to her fingers, a hot nip of pain. She shakes it out. Walks on, the wires of her veins sparking, full of current with nowhere to go. McManus's dark blue coat, his limping gait—she latches on to them just as he turns off Water Street onto Quincy, toward the pier.

At the corner she finds him again. He is halfway to the water. Slowing to a stop under the last streetlamp. Then he takes off running, his awkward gait amplified by quickness. Out by the Clyde Imports warehouse a dark tangle of bodies seethes beside the horse cart.

"Shit."

Alma throws herself into a run, too, barreling past a pair of sailors who swear after her, so ready for a fight she is salivating. Onto the wharf boards and she's close enough to see Driscoll drop a man with a beauty of a head hook, Folkstone on his knees taking a kick to the stomach, curling in, McManus slowing ten feet from the fight to pull out a pistol and take measured aim at the man atop the cart. Just as the sound splits the night air open, Alma skids up behind the man kicking Folkstone and whips his jacket down, trapping his arms, yanking his body back so her knee slams into his kidney. The collision echoes into her pelvis, into the thick pulse collecting at the apex of her thighs. He goes limp, groaning, and she catches him up by the hair to smash a fist into his nose, hot crunch of bone and blood and her teeth are bared and another bucko slams her in the shoulder with a punch, she wheels on him ducks his wild swing and feeds him her fist, yeah, this is what she's been wanting, half of it, anyway, someone is screaming, the man is still standing and connects with her chest, lungfire, let it out, swing—

Another gunshot, so near it leaves her ears ringing, and the men on their feet are stumbling away, blood on the boards, sweat in her mouth, Driscoll grinning a wild red smile as he shakes out his fists.

The last thief falls out of the cart, hands locked around his strangely crooked knees. He is screaming. He writhes on the boards, and now it is Alma's crew and this lone man, Driscoll helping Folkstone to stand, Alma sucking in cold ocean air. McManus tucks his gun away. He limps over to where the man is flopping, lifts his eyes to Alma's, then rears back his good leg. His boot thunks into bone. The screaming stops.

12

JANUARY 15, 1887

"Edward Edmonds. In two days ago from . . . Missoula, by train through Tacoma, and took the government cutter from there, which is how we missed him." Wheeler tosses the stack of papers onto his desk. "Where the fuck is Missoula."

"Montana Territory," Alma says. "He's a cowboy in shiny shoes."

"He's a problem," Wheeler says. "There couldn't be a worse time for a new deputy collector to ride in from the wastelands."

McManus stands stiffly beside Alma. Wheeler has not offered either of them a chair, and McManus's left foot is trembling, lamp glow slipping over his waxed bootlaces. In the windowless rectangle of Wheeler's office it is always dusk—the light smoky, faintly golden. This morning the room still smells of blood. Blood and a faint sweetness, coming from the little twine-tied box at the edge of Wheeler's desk.

"Well, I can't send you, after you nearly mauled him." Wheeler looks up at Alma without raising his head from the note he's writing, his eyes sharp under lowered brows.

She shrugs, rubs the bruise on her collarbone left by last night's brawl.

"Tommy, give this to Moore." He holds the paper out; McManus limps forward and pockets it. "He'd better have a damn good explanation for his absence. And we'll have to find out what Edmonds wants. What will keep him friendly on our boats."

"What keeps Inspector Moore friendly?" Alma says. "Besides his extra cash."

Wheeler taps his pen, twice.

"We give him time with Nell Roberts," he says, and takes a sip of whiskey.

Alma rakes her teeth over her lower lip. She is itching to see Nell, her body primed by the brawl. It's a long-ingrained habit: fighting, then fucking. And today she woke hungry. Her cot a tangle of cloth and sweat, honeysuckle scent lingering from her dreams, her sex so tight and aching that half a minute's touch had her biting her pillow, her hitched breaths damped by cheap cotton batting.

"Anything else?" McManus says.

His foot is still unsteady. Wheeler can't see it from behind his desk, but Alma looks down pointedly. The trembling stops. Starts again.

"Were they all Sloan's boys?" Wheeler says, so McManus has to stand there, shaking, on his bad leg.

"Two were," he says. "A pair of others I didn't get a good look at, and I didn't know the last man."

"The one you shot the kneecaps off of?" Wheeler says, sharp.

McManus puts one hand on the chair in front of him. Leans forward, jaw clenched. Alma considers his limp and shakes her head. Doesn't like to see others walking proper, does he, the bastard.

"The problem with a signature move, Tommy, is that people start to know it was you that did it."

"I couldn't go in after Edmonds." McManus's face hasn't changed, but a strange note is in his voice—repentance, or appeal. "I had to do something."

Wheeler finishes his whiskey. He lets McManus stand there, bracing white-knuckled on the chair, for a few long breaths.

"Give that to Moore, lad," he says at last. "Then have a rest."

"I'm fine," McManus says, but his shoulders are high and stiff as he walks to the door, landing hard on his bad leg and unable to conceal his limp.

After the door closes, Alma sits in the chair he was just leaning on. She takes off her cap, drapes it over one thigh.

"Your signature move," she says. "Making people stand there when they're about to fall over?"

"It was good for him," Wheeler says. "It showed him he could stand, even if it hurt."

"Is he your son?"

Wheeler barks out a laugh, his eyebrows high and incredulous.

"Jesus Christ," he says. "My son? No."

"You treat him like it."

"He's worked for me eleven years."

McManus could still be the weak link: The man who'll shoot too soon, or move too slowly to intervene when needed. The man who allowed that seventy-five pounds of tar to go missing, or made it disappear himself.

"He fucked you with the Peterson beating, though, and now maybe he's fucked me," she says, liking how Wheeler bristles at her choice of words. "I've got to walk into Sloan's house in an hour, and Pike aside, one of our men just crippled one of his."

Alma goes to the sideboard, not so much because she's thirsty but because she's bored of sitting down. An uneasy truce has settled between her and Wheeler since their briefing yesterday, and though it's fun to banter about business, she won't let him get too comfortable. She rattles through glassware. Lifts the silver-topped decanter, the expensive stuff, and holds it to the lamplight. Picks up the gin. She wants Wheeler to watch her touch his things like she owns them.

"If you're going to help yourself, get me another," he says.

Alma pauses, gin bottle in hand, making it clear she's heard him. Then she finishes pouring her drink and stays at the sideboard, facing the blue wall.

"What's your plan for Edmonds?" she says, following a thin stain on the wallpaper up to the ceiling, where a penny-size crack splits the plaster.

"See what Moore has to say about him." Papers crackle; he is riffling through them again, always at it with pen and ink, keeping notes or marking ledgers in that alphanumeric system she has not yet deciphered. "Then use a carrot or a stick."

"In the city we had it pretty good," she says. "Most everyone in the customhouse was willing to be bought. But there was a deputy collector who would not cooperate. He didn't want money, girls, boys, tar. What to do?"

She turns around. Wheeler is watching her from under lowered brows. His empty tumbler sits on the edge of the desk, waiting.

"He got a little too drunk." She carries the gin bottle over to Wheeler's desk though she's never seen him touch the stuff; fills his whiskey-filmed cup deliberately. "And ended up on a slow boat to China."

"You had him shanghaied?"

"Crimps are good for something." A clink as she nudges his cup toward him with the decanter. "We should keep that in mind while dealing with Sloan's boys."

"I don't take gin," he says, not touching the muddled liquor.

"My mistake." Alma picks up the twine-tied box. She shakes it; inside, a dull shifting. "Any special messages for our new friend Mr. Sloan?"

"Tell him the Chain Locker meeting is off."

"How scintillating," Alma says.

She leans one hip against the desk, three feet from Wheeler's writing hand and the heavy lacquered pen he's rolling between thumb and forefinger. He sets the pen down.

"Ought I write him a poem instead?" he says.

He turns toward her but folds his arms over his chest. Opening his body, then closing it off. Picking up on her jokes but not letting any looseness come over his face. She can't read what he'll do next. There is the sense of circling—of a dare, or an invitation, that has been laid out. She will throw some bait. See if he bites.

"I bet I'll get Sloan on the line before you get Edmonds," she says, tapping the box.

"And what's the prize?"

"Time with Nell Roberts."

His eyes go hard. The line of his shoulders rises. Yeah. Come on, Wheeler.

"If you can give her time to Moore," she says, "you can dole it out otherwise. Right?"

"Not to you."

Now there's blood in the water. His hands move back to the desk, fisted. Alma shifts forward a notch. Ready to cause trouble. Ready to fight, if he throws a punch. Or engage in other sport. Her tongue ticks over her back left molars, where the teeth are sharp, the sensation satisfying.

"I'm not good enough to share your woman?"

The leather of his chair creaks.

"She is otherwise occupied," he says.

"I'll bet. More and more customhouse men to look after."

"You don't know what the fuck you're talking about," Wheeler says. "She's our forger. And she has better things to do than . . . entertain you."

"Forger?" Alma resets her stance; takes the tilt out of her hips, gives Wheeler some space. She'd pegged Nell as Delphine's sugar dish, set out to entice the various officials whose cooperation the business depends upon. Set out, perhaps, to entice Wheeler into obedience. But Nell is even more interesting. "And a body like that."

"She's a woman of many talents."

"I look forward to enjoying them." Alma pulls on her cap, winks at Wheeler. "Forgers have nimble hands. Don't you find?"

He stands up, a harsh scrape of chair legs over carpet. Neck red, mouth tight.

"Save it," Alma says. "I'll be back in an hour."

She walks to the door with the box, waiting for him to follow, collar her, start something, but then the brass knob is turning in her palm and she is in the bitter kerosene chill of the hallway and it's time to pay a visit to Barnaby Sloan.

Wheeler called it a sty, but Alma has seen far worse flophouses than Sloan's boarding quarters. A two-storied clapboard building, it is marked with a simple LODGINGS sign and a row of signal flags tacked to the lintel, spelling out for sailors what some of them might not be able to read in words. White paint edging mossy pine boards. The usual collection of men loafing on the steps. Inside, salvaged wood knocked together into a bar counter in one corner of the drowsy afternoon lobby. A few rooms; one open and full of cots doused in dust-glinting sunlight. At the back, by the stairs, a couple of hard cases. Caps low, lips fat with tobacco plugs. Eyes locked on Alma from the minute her feet cross the threshold. She walks straight toward them, the wooden box tucked under one arm, her pistol snug under the other.

"I'm here to see Sloan," she says.

"What's your business?" one of the men, wearing an ashy cap, says.

"That's between me and him."

"He don't want to see you." The other man tucks his hands in his pockets, his elbows flaring out. The posture looks lazy, relaxed, but Alma keeps part of her attention on his hidden fists, on what they might yank out and stab at her given an excuse.

"That's because he doesn't know who I am yet," she says. "Or what I'm offering."

"Chocolates?" The man nods at the box under Alma's arm. His face, too, is streaked with ash. A splotch by one ear. A pale smudge along his stubbled jaw, the skin there wrinkling as he grins. "Cigars?"

"You can suck on these if you like." She unpicks the twine, holds the opened box toward the men. Nestled in a red bed of cotton are a few of Pike's fingers. Thumb, pointer, and middle. Skin shiny with the burn scars that licked up along his left hand and arm.

"Jesus," the first man says.

The other takes his hands from his pockets—empty—and leans over the box, his gaze darting between the fingers and Alma's face. The white-blond hair at the crown of his head is thinning. He has the mottled coloring of a heavy drinker: veiny nose; eyes like hard-boiled eggs, yellow tingeing to blue at the centers, dull, bulbous. He doesn't look scared, but he knows who the fingers belong to, sure enough. She would bet on it.

"The rest of him is still intact," she tells the blond man, which is true, though the rest of him is also two days dead. "And to keep him that way, I'll need to see Sloan."

He tongues his tobacco, exchanges a wordless glance with his companion. Then he nods. Alma pushes the lid back on the box.

"Follow me," he says.

Up the stairs, him leading; the creaking of wood; a flimsy, over-used building. At the top landing they pass a party of sailors heading down, decked out in their shore rig, crisp whites and blues. The second floor is tighter, a walled maze. More rooms filled with beds, half of them occupied despite the hour. Several closed doors. She notes each bend and turn—red cloth caught in a hinge to mark a left; the narrow hall that leads to a glazed window, a dead end. Then they duck under a black velvet curtain into a dim room crammed with tables, stools stacked bottoms-up atop them so they resemble dead beetles, legs crooked into the air. A coatrack is bare save for a gray workman's jacket. Lamplight wavers in a little recessed alcove at the back of the room. Slow shadows on the wall. Wood scraping; a cough.

"Someone to see you," the man beside Alma calls.

Cramps in her stomach; a hot bristle of nerves. This is the riskiest part. Not walking deep into hostile territory. Not opening the box to show Pike's digits once more. Not what will follow if Sloan balks at her tar deal. This moment: when Sloan will see her, and perhaps see her too well. See how, layered in paint, and paste jewels, and green silk, she came into this room once before, three days ago.

Sloan steps out of the alcove, wiping his hands on a folded cloth. A tall man, slender, with dark blond hair. Thick brows set at a plaintive angle. He is dressed neatly in fitted trousers and a shirt cut from white cotton. Fresh blood is spotted on his cuffs.

After her quick once-over, Alma keeps her eyes locked on his. Waiting for a flicker of suspicion, or recognition. She tethers her breathing to her knife, solid at her ribs, and her gun, solid at her side. If things go sour, she can stick the man beside her, race back through the maze of hallways and be out on the street in thirty seconds.

"Who are you?" Sloan, now a few feet away, pauses beside the last of the tables. The cloth in his hands is smeared red.

Still focused on him, Alma reaches her hearing back toward the alcove, listening for breathing, dripping, any sign more people are back there than she thought. Nothing but the man beside her, wheezing slightly; the rustling of cloth as Sloan wipes at his thumb.

"My name's Camp," she says. "I'm here with a business proposal."

"A business proposal?" Sloan says.

His eyes narrow; he scans her face more closely. Breathe, even, knife, gun. Don't blink.

"You new in town, Camp?"

Alma doesn't flinch. The question seems innocuous enough. Stick to the plan.

"Something like new," she says. "I handle affairs for people you'd like to work with. And they've decided they'd like to work with you."

She takes the box from under her arm, slow, and holds it out to him. His attention shifts away from her face. He pries off the lid. Those mournful long brows twitch up, but the flat calm in his eyes is not disturbed. He shakes the box, dislodging the digits and soiled cotton. The index finger tumbles stiffly to the floor. At the bottom of the box is a half-pound can of opium. Its white paper label splotched with blood.

"You want a cut of the trade?" Alma says. "Talk to me."

Sloan takes the opium out and sets the box on a table, dropping his dirty handkerchief inside. He runs a nail along the seam between can and lid, peels off the paper. His eyes close as he sniffs the resin.

"What are the terms?" he says.

She's most of the way there. He's not looking at her, or the fingers, or the cotton—he's examining the can, turning it over in his hands, his eyes tracking over the Chinese characters.

"No more attacks on our property. Men or goods," she says. "No more of your rats in our storehouses, or blackmailing attempts. Same goes for us. In short, civility. In exchange you'll be linked into the pipeline. You'll buy some off us, at a discount, to sell as you like. I'll handle your supply."

Sloan smiles. He looks disarmingly sweet, a boyish wrinkle to his nose, a softness to his eyes. She's seen this smile before—it doesn't mean he's feeling favorable toward the partnership. But at least he doesn't seem particularly fixed on her. Maybe this plan will actually work.

He leans against the table edge. Sets the opium can at his hip.

"To tell the truth, I was hoping McManus would make this visit." Sloan folds his arms, his eyes catching on the blood flecked on his shirtsleeves. "Damn."

"Cold salt water," Alma says, nodding at the stains.

"I'd like to dredge McManus through cold salt water, but you'll serve."

Sloan doesn't move when he says this, but the man at Alma's side stiffens to attention. She has her gun out and on Sloan, putting three steps between her and the blond man so he can't lunge for the weapon, but Sloan is still leaning there, lazy, like a cat. Shit. She jumped too soon. And once guns are out, there's usually only one way to go. Down.

"Now, that's no way to take a deal," she says.

"I didn't say I wasn't taking the deal." Sloan unfolds himself from the table. Waves, languid, toward her pistol. "Put that away, and I'll send Loomis out. If he's making you nervous."

She could play it that way: skittish, uncertain, the disgruntled middleman dropped into a bad situation in which he must bear bloody gifts. It will only help her gain Sloan's confidence if she's a little soured on Wheeler. But that can't come right away. Sloan's first impression has to be of a solid organization—a safe bet to go in on. She has to be solid.

"I came here to talk to you," she says, gun still out. "So just the two of us suits me fine."

Sloan nods at Loomis, who backs away into the curtain until it swallows him whole. Alma waits until the black velvet is swinging, vacant, then angles herself so she can see Sloan and the empty doorway. She slides her pistol back in its holster. The alcove hovers in her line of sight, too, a flickering pocket of shadow over Sloan's shoulder. Someone's in there. She is certain.

"Do you want a cut or not?" she says.

Sloan pulls the stool he's standing next to off the table, then flips another. He sits and motions for Alma to do the same. She approaches the table slowly. The seats are made high—her feet don't touch the floor, a feeling she dislikes, while Sloan's long legs let him sit comfortably. She compromises by half sitting on the stool, her weight planted on the leg still tethered to the ground.

"Is Pike dead?" Sloan says, once they're both sitting down, the table's rough pine boards between them.

"Does it matter?"

He shrugs.

"Right," Alma says. "He'd have been part of the bargain, but it was suspected you wouldn't trade much for him."

"I find your use of pronouns—or, rather, lack thereof—interesting." Sloan steeples his fingers on the table. He wears no rings. Compared to Wheeler, he's not flash at all, save his neatly laundered clothing. When he speaks next, his voice drops into a stage whisper. "Are we not going to name him? Your company man?"

"You're dealing with me," she says. "And you know who I'm working for. So let's agree we have a mutual understanding."

"I want that starch-collared son of a bitch to admit what he's up to." Sloan picks up the opium can and pounds it on the table. "Lording it over the waterfront like his hands are clean as the Mother Mary's."

"I'm not in the naming business," Alma says. "I'm in the tar business. If you can get better product somewhere else, then do it. End of story."

Sloan drops the lead-seamed can. Then she hears it: a scuffling sound in the alcove. A ragged inhalation. She tilts her head toward the sound, eyes hard on Sloan. A jet of worry that he has one of his girls in there, one of the painted women he keeps in rooms over the foundry, mad with Spanish fly and drink. That her blood is on his cuffs. And atop the clench of dread, an overlay of memory: Sullivan's Alley, Chinatown, pale arms waving out of barred windows, some scabbed from caning, some from scratched insect bites; a girl, not eleven, painted red at the lips and staring. The side of the underworld she could never stomach. The one side for which she could not shake off her conscience, the young detective's voice saying, "Do something, for God's sake, do *something*."

"You said we were alone," Alma says, tamping down this rush of thought.

"Well. We were until he woke up."

Sloan slides off his stool, miming surprise—eyes wide, eyebrows high. At the alcove he stops, sighs. Alma is finding depth in her lungs again.

"My dear fellow," he says, into the recessed space. "You're a mess."

Alma watches the edge of the wall, where the alcove opens into the main room. There is movement in the lamplight; a grunt; boots scraping. Labored breathing. Then a hand slaps against the wall, at the brightest part of the alcove's lip. The fingers leave a red smear.

A man totters into view, and the sheer amount of blood on him makes Alma grimace. His shirt is intact but dark stains cascade down from his left shoulder and ribs, the cotton sticking to his thin chest, his hollow bowl of a stomach. Damp spatters at his groin. He shies away from Sloan. Flinches badly when he sees Alma. She does not recognize him as one of Wheeler's men. He has blunt features; black hair and olive coloring that's only a shade darker than her own; a triangle of freckles on the bridge of his nose.

"Your jacket's over there." Sloan points to the coatrack. "Put it on so you don't scare my lodgers."

The man picks his way toward them, his steps uncertain, occasionally bumping into tables and setting stacked stools rattling. He's got so much blood on his shirt it's a wonder he can stand at all. He stinks of stale piss. Just past their table, he stumbles on Pike's severed finger. He claps his red hand to his mouth. His eyes are wide and white and glassy.

"Do watch your step," Sloan says. "You're in no state to take a fall. Loomis is waiting outside; he'll sort you out."

"Yes, sir."

A hoarse whisper, nervous eyes, hands clumsy as he pulls down the coat and works it on over his gory shoulder, almost whimpering. Then he edges under the curtain and is gone.

"Was his collar too starched?" Alma says, as Sloan returns to the table.

"I needed him to tell me some things," he says. "So he did, and I took notes. Then he slept it off."

"Charming."

"Consider your own welcome, Camp. I've been pretty hospitable, seeing as you've pulled a gun on me and brought me a box of body parts. I don't want that to happen again—I don't want you to end up like him."

The threat in Sloan's words is completely absent in his tone, in the faint smile lighting over his face. She's fixed his angle. Whether it's an act or unfeigned, Sloan is presenting himself as a breaker. He has something to prove: toughness, stature, situation. That's where his priorities lie. He's not the kind of man she would go with if she were feeling out new middlemen in San Francisco. But as long as he can leave the posturing aside and move the product, that's all she needs to suit Delphine's purposes.

"Your concern for me is touching," Alma says.

"I hope so. You're my new partner," Sloan says. "What grade of tar am I buying?"

Perhaps because trotting out the butchered fellow didn't shake her up, or perhaps because they are getting into details, Sloan's demeanor is shifting. His eyes are more focused, but his hands go loose, tapping the brass can, then the tabletop.

"Aged permit Patna, Wah Hing brand," Alma says. "Sourced through Hong Kong and refined in Victoria with a guaranteed morphine content of five percent or less. Your buyers will be satisfied."

He picks at the peeling paper on the can, twice, before leaving it alone. He's not as careful with his tells, with his body, as Wheeler: his fidgeting is not for show. This deal is better than the one he's been trying for—rather than blackmail money, or uncontested use of Quincy Wharf, he's getting hooked directly into an opium pipeline.

"What about the price."

"Near tax-free," Alma says. "Five dollars a can versus ten. Sell it as you like—inland, to Portland and points beyond. Or in town. The profit's better in Portland, best in San Francisco, but then there's the trouble of getting it there."

"I've had luck with girls," he says. "They waltz onto steamers with the stuff sewn into their hems or tucked into their suitcases. But one girl can only carry so much, and I need mine here, working. Maybe if I hired a few more . . ."

"You ought to knock it off with that small-fry nonsense. If you get caught messing around, we won't help you."

"Where's your sense of adventure, Camp?" Sloan grins, that friendly, amused grin, as if they were discussing baseball or a summer picnic.

"I don't have one," Alma says. "It's what makes me a good contact. I'm on time and the product's as expected."

"Boring but useful?"

"Think of me that way," she says. "And add short-tempered. You miss a handoff and our deal is done."

Sloan stands up, holds out a hand.

"Tell me where and when," he says. "I want in."

Alma stands, too, only then realizing how stiff the leg she has been leaning on has become. How tense she's held her body in the long minutes after the injured man left.

"Have a pair of men ready to collect a crate on Union Wharf, Monday." She shakes his hand, his skin warm, chapped with calluses. "That's the seventeenth. At nine thirty in the evening, on the water side of Hoop and Barrow."

"They'll be there," he says.

"So will I. With thirty pounds of tar—we'll see how you do with that," she says. "Bring three hundred dollars. In United States Notes."

She walks to the curtained doorway, the hot surge of accomplishment tinged by misgiving that it was too easy, that Sloan was too willing to put the murders and moles and missing fingers in the past. But he is standing by the table, smiling, bobbling the opium can from palm to palm.

"That's a sample from your product. It'll make an even thirty." She lifts the curtain and sees the hallway, empty, dim, two lefts and a right to get back to the staircase and get the hell out of there. "It's a good smoke."

"Oh, I plan to test it," he says.

She ducks under the velvet. In the hall her ears are on high alert, her fingertips tingling, each dust mote and afternoon shadow pulling at her eyes. By the time she thumps down the stairs into the lobby—crowded now with sailors at the bar, a man singing at the piano—her skin is prickling with energy. She walked into Sloan's boardinghouse with Pike's fingers and came out with a deal. As long as he's true to his word and has his men ready on Union Wharf, the plan is set in motion. And she's likely won her bet with Wheeler. Back in an hour, for more, as she promised.

13

JANUARY 25, 1887

TRANSCRIPT OF INTERVIEW WITH SAMUEL REED

WHEREUPON THE FOLLOWING PROCEEDINGS WERE
HAD IN THE JEFFERSON COUNTY JAIL, PORT TOWNSEND,
WASHINGTON TERRITORY, ON JANUARY 25, 1887.

LAWMEN PRESENT: CITY MARSHAL GEORGE FORRESTER,
OFFICER WAYLAN HUGHES

TRANSCRIPTION: EDWARD EDMONDS, ASSISTANT DEPUTY
COLLECTOR, U.S. CUSTOMHOUSE

OFFICER HUGHES: Where were you when Sloan knifed you? At the cannery?

MR REED: No. His men took me to his boardinghouse.

MARSHAL FORRESTER: That's right in the middle of the waterfront. Somebody must have heard you screaming.

MR REED: If they did, they didn't come help.

OFFICER HUGHES: What did he want from you?

MR REED: He wanted to know why I was hanging around his property. Who sent me. He kept asking if I was working with the police, if Sugar was working with the police. There were other names, too . . . too many for me to remember, I didn't know any of them. I just wanted that damn thing out of my shoulder. Are you working for that railroad man, then? he kept asking. I told him I didn't know any railroad man. I told him about Sugar, everything I knew about her, and swore that was all. But he kept at it . . . my arm, my side, and . . . God help me.

OFFICER HUGHES: All right. All right.

MR REED: God help me.

OFFICER HUGHES: You just take a minute.

MR REED: (inaudible)

MARSHAL FORRESTER: What?

MR REED: You've got to . . . You've got to keep him away from me.

MARSHAL FORRESTER: We don't have to do anything, son.

OFFICER HUGHES: Look, Sam, if you keep talking, if you're cooperative, we'll keep an eye on you.

MR REED: An eye on me? He'll kill me.

OFFICER HUGHES: He can't hurt you once he's jailed.

MR REED: He'll kill me. Oh, Christ.

MARSHAL FORRESTER: Get back to the incident. What else did Sloan say?

MR REED: I . . . I don't know.

MARSHAL FORRESTER: I think you do.

OFFICER HUGHES: Have some more whiskey, Sam.

MR REED: He said . . . he said, welcome to his crew. He said, hadn't I wanted to work with him, the way I was nosing about . . . well, I'd get my wish. He told me not to try and run, or tell anyone. And he said I wouldn't be seeing Sugar anymore.

OFFICER HUGHES: Did he mean because he was going to kill her?

MR REED: I don't know. I took it as I wasn't supposed to finish her job. But I was starting to black out by then. I don't know if he was talking, or if it was me saying things.

MARSHAL FORRESTER: You passed out?

MR REED: Yes. When I woke up, there were voices, and so much blood on me I thought I was done for. But I got up. Sloan was there with another fellow. He looked like a hard case, that one. And there was . . . there was a finger on the floor between them.

A bloodied finger. I almost fainted again. Sloan told me to put my jacket on and leave.

MARSHAL FORRESTER: Why didn't you run? Come right to us, turn him in?

MR REED: Run? I could barely stand. And I was frightened. I'd . . . I'd messed myself, as well. I was ashamed to leave the house.

OFFICER HUGHES: You should have come to us.

MR REED: I couldn't. I couldn't. As soon as I left the room, there was a big man waiting for me in the hall, saying he was going to put me in a bed to rest up. I got to know him later, the bastard . . . His name was Loomis. Big great fat lump, damn his eyes.

MARSHAL FORRESTER: You're quick enough to name him, I see.

MR REED: It doesn't matter. He's dead.

OFFICER HUGHES: What?

MR REED: I'm finished, anyway, aren't I? I might as well tell you everything.

MARSHAL FORRESTER: Sit up straight. Did you kill Loomis?

MR REED: No. I didn't kill anyone. Please, you have to believe me. I'll tell you everything I know, but I didn't kill anyone. And when there were murders, there was nothing I could do to stop them. Nothing.

OFFICER HUGHES: Murders? Multiple murders?

MR REED: Sloan's a hard man.

MARSHAL FORRESTER: Let's go back to the start. Sloan told you to load the Calhoun woman's body into the boat. Now you allege he's committed multiple murders. Did he kill her?

OFFICER HUGHES: Or have reason to want her killed? You said you told him all about her, when he was torturing you. So he knew she'd wanted his cannery keys, at least.

MR REED: I don't . . . I mean, there were her girls.

OFFICER HUGHES: He's killed women before? Sir, we've never had reports—

MARSHAL FORRESTER: I've heard things.

MR REED: He didn't kill her girls. He wanted to use them.

OFFICER HUGHES: Use them?

MR REED: To carry dope in from Canada.

MARSHAL FORRESTER: Elaborate.

MR REED: He had some of his own girls already engaged in the trade, and he wanted to use Sugar's.

OFFICER HUGHES: How do you mean? What are these women doing?

MR REED: They go up to Victoria via steamboat, meet with his suppliers in Chinatown, pack a load of tins into the sleeves and skirts of their dresses, into the bottoms of their valises. Come back on the next boat and pass the stuff to Sloan.

MARSHAL FORRESTER: Women couldn't do that. They haven't the fortitude.

MR REED: I'd agree with you, if I hadn't seen the dope they brought back. But they're terrified of Sloan. He's got them opium-sick half the time, laying about and smoking with the boarding sailors.

MARSHAL FORRESTER: Wretched. Those damn Chinamen and their filth. There's none of it in the decent places with decent women.

OFFICER HUGHES: How much opium are the girls bringing in?

MR REED: I don't know how much each of them can carry. But it was tallied up in one of the house rooms. There were cases stacked in a closet, and whole crates in the cannery.

MARSHAL FORRESTER: Ah. So the usual cargo is crates and crates of opium, after all.

MR REED: Yes.

MARSHAL FORRESTER: Your story keeps changing, son. Why should we believe any of it?

MR REED: It's the truth.

MARSHAL FORRESTER: And it wasn't before?

MR REED: It's the truth now. I'm telling you everything I know now.

MARSHAL FORRESTER: I ought to beat you, see what version of the truth that rattles out of you.

OFFICER HUGHES: Sir—

MARSHAL FORRESTER: Right in the bad shoulder, huh? In the ribs? Right where he knifed you? What version of the truth will you tell me when you're bleeding all over your shirtfront?

MR REED: No, please—

OFFICER HUGHES: Leave him alone.

MARSHAL FORRESTER: You sit the hell down, Hughes.

MR REED: Stop. Stop, please. What else do you want to know? Please. I'll tell you. I'll tell you anything.

OFFICER HUGHES: Sir! Let him go.

MARSHAL FORRESTER: You don't come into my jail accused of murder and expect to be handled with kid gloves. And I'll remind you you're an officer under my jurisdiction, Hughes. I won't have you telling me what to do.

OFFICER HUGHES: There's no need to beat him. That's all I mean to say. He's talking plenty.

MR REED: Please.

MARSHAL FORRESTER: You would've shit your drawers seeing some of the things we got up to in the Arizona Territory. You young city cops have policing all wrong.

OFFICER HUGHES: I understand policing just fine, sir.

MARSHAL FORRESTER: (inaudible)

MR REED: I'll tell you the truth. I swear. From here on out, I'll tell you God's truth.

14

JANUARY 15, 1887

At Wheeler's offices she snaps Conaway a salute. The man blinks at her, the thick skin of his forehead wrinkling.

"Cheer the fuck up," Alma says.

In the blue hall she feels her own energy intensely, bottled as it is by the small space, by the low ceiling. By the layered dangers that pressed in on her: Sloan's boys, Sloan himself, the mangled little man in the alcove, the scents of blood and opium. Her success is pressing in on her. She wants to knock something loose. Punch. The thump of pelvic bones. And Wheeler is there, just there, on the inside of the varnished door.

She knocks. Doesn't wait for a call.

He's at his desk, where she left him. The gin she poured untouched. Another glass, drained, at his right hand. Papers spread in that mysterious patchwork.

Once the door is closed behind her, she says, "Sloan's in."

Wheeler sets down his pen, nods for her to go on.

"First handoff scheduled as planned." She advances into the room's smoky firelight. "Thirty pounds on Monday."

"He accepted the price?"

"He knew it was good," Alma says. "He knew the product was good, too—got the smell off it, and he was interested from then, though he wasn't playing it that way."

Wheeler isn't giving her much. No flash of approval, no sign that he's impressed. This gets under her skin, burrows into the itchy restlessness that's already squirming, making the balls of her feet bounce on the carpet, making her mouth prickle with saliva.

"So are you going to congratulate me, or what?"

"For doing your job?" He laughs, a sour downturn of his mouth, one eyebrow ticking upward.

"For winning our bet." She flips a chair around, straddles it to face his desk. "Unless you got Edmonds under control in the time I've been away."

"I never agreed to your little game."

"Consider this part of my education." Alma loops her arms around the chair back and rests her chin on her fists. "I just want to spend some time with our pretty forger. See how she handles finework."

The atmosphere between them charges, grows denser. Heat collecting at the seam of her trousers, her legs pressing wide against the chair back, the cutout in the wood there a window Wheeler's eyes drift toward, yank away from. His mouth is open. Come on. Come on.

"What could you even do with a woman?"

"Oh, there's plenty." Alma brings her hand to her lips, curls her tongue over one knuckle. Her skin tastes of ash, of salt. "I've never had any complaints."

His ears are red. His throat. He shifts in his chair, a tiny motion, but the creak of the leather gives him away.

"Get me a whiskey," he says, breaking their chain of vision and picking up a sheet of paper.

Alma's chair scrapes as she stands. Her boots thump over the carpet. It is good to move, good to lean over Wheeler and collect his empty glass—that clove-scented aftershave firing her blood, his ear near and pink and pulsing—good to shake her body loose as she crosses the room to the sideboard. Clink of glassware. Trickle of liquor.

She walks into the space beside his chair, their boots close, his shoulder warm as she bends over it to set the glass in front of him. He is still. His fingers are still, midword, a splotch of ink clotting on the page.

"Come on, Wheeler," she says, her mouth close to his ear. "You used to like me. More than like, if you think back to our carriage ride."

"A brief fit of nostalgia." He pushes her hand off the whiskey glass, his skin hot, grazing over hers. "You seemed stupid enough to be easy company."

"Now you know I'm not stupid."

She puts her arm along the back of his chair, feeling all the places where their bodies are almost touching: forearm to shoulder blades, bound breast to shoulder, mouth to pink-pulsing ear. Her breath moves the hairs at the back of his neck. He sets down his drink.

"And still, I see how you look at me," she says.

He does look up at her then, his jaw working, and she imagines herself in the prism of his vision: shorn hair dark over her eyes, bruises dappling her jaw, dirty vest streaked with tar from being dragged along the dock, the amber sharp of pine pitch scenting the air around her. She takes Jack Camp's image and twists it, twists her body into a woman's shape: shifts her feet so her thighs are parted, angles her bound chest forward. How she would stand if she were in the lewdest dress—something revealing, all indigo silk, made with seduction in mind—except she is in a man's dirty work clothes. She is being two things at once. Grinning hard like Camp, chin up like Camp. She is in the gray space between identities and he *sees* her and she is lit up, spark filled, starving.

Wheeler's breath speeds. His eyes track over her. One of his hands lifts, almost, off the desk, and while Alma is half watching it he brings it up again, fast, so that she tucks her jaw against the punch. But he instead grabs her collar, yanks her face down to his.

"Don't you play around with me," he says, his voice wet with whiskey. "I'll have nothing to do with your filthy—"

Alma lunges, crushes her mouth to his. Her opened throat stinging. She latches rough fingers around the back of his neck. Teeth hard, tongue hard, shoving into him, knee into the meat of his thigh, her hand dropping between their bodies to his groin, and under the warm rough tweed he is hard, she is growling with satisfaction.

A snap of pain on her cheek knocks her back, off-balance. She sprawls to the floor. Jarred tailbone, jarred elbows. Knees wide. The imprint of his fist flaring hot on her face. All fire, all glory.

"Oh, yeah." Her mouth slick with his saliva as she bites her lower lip.

Wheeler comes to his feet. Slams his hand on his desk.

"Touch me again, you're a dead man."

She scrambles up, grinning, chest rising and falling rapidly against her binding cloth. A thread of wet on her neck, leaking from the bandage; she has torn the knife wound. Wet on her collar. Wheeler straightens his tie. Knuckles white against flushed skin.

"Do you understand me?" he says.

"Yes, boss."

More of that, she wants more of that, it's the kind of moment she lives for, when anything could happen. She shifts her weight from foot to foot, breathing down her eagerness.

"Get out of here," Wheeler says. "You've done enough for one day."

"My day's just getting started."

There is too much space between them for her to see how this jab lands. He hunkers behind the desk, its solid dark wood a break-water, a fortification. His body sunk out of view. He's wound up at least as much as she is, and that's a good way to leave him. Kicked off-balance. Reeling for his dealings with Edmonds. If he can't fix the customhouse man, Alma will—and win another point over him. Then she can contact Delphine and tell her the score.

"Boss."

She knuckles her cap and pulls open the door without looking back.

Outside the light has lost its piercing purity and dimmed to the color of weak tea. Clouds shift past the haloed sun. On Water Street the wind threads through crowds of workmen, picking up their smell of smoke and sweaty denim and whipping it across Alma's face. She knots her collar up high over her opened throat. Stops at the fish market on Adams Street Wharf for hot chowder. The soup is thick with mussels and potato cubes and parsley. Under the makeshift stall's awning she and three other workmen hunch over their tin cups, shoulder to shoulder, slapping down pennies for another ladle of soup, another slice of rye bread. Alma works through three cups and two loaf heels, her appetite whetted by the chill breeze, by the sparring with Sloan and Wheeler. The man to her left keeps pace, and by the third cup they have grinned at each other in solidarity, but not spoken. She likes his face—the clear brown of his eyes, the clean line of his jaw. His strong thumbs.

"You win," he says, when she lays down a coin for a fourth cup.

Then he's off into the busy street. Alma chews on a rubbery bit of mollusk, waiting to see if he'll look back at her. At the corner, he does. She bites into her bread, eyes on his from thirty feet away, showing off her strong, straight teeth. Port Townsend isn't half bad. She'd like to see more of Delphine—she has to find a line to her, a way to safely pay more visits—but so far there have been more than enough ways to have a good time.

A crew of roustabouts jostles past, laughing, jingling their pockets to make the day's pay sing. She follows the broad muscles in their shoulders, hard under damp cotton shirts, as their solid bodies shoal up the wharf. And there. At the Cosmopolitan Hotel's door, as though wished into being: Delphine. Alma swallows a lukewarm glug of chowder, neck throbbing. Wipes her mouth on her sleeve.

Delphine's face is shaded by a black lace bonnet. Her black dress shimmers at the bust and shoulders. It is beaded with jet, or pearls— she is wearing a fortune. Her gloved hand rests delicately on her companion's forearm. The man's hat brim hides much of his face. It's not Wheeler. It's another white man, dressed as elegantly as Delphine. Wind ripples the mink collar of his coat against his cropped beard.

A horse cart rattles past, loaded high with barrels. Alma finds the pair again as they step off the hotel's gilded stoop. She cranes to see the man. Grins when she catches him in profile. Delphine is on the arm of Wheeler's wealthy friend Judge Hamilton.

Under the cold shelter of the awning, Alma drinks the last of her soup and tracks the two as they stroll along Adams Street toward the Upper Town stairs. Delphine carries herself as she always does: head high, splendid posture, smooth gait. Lovely. But the judge is interesting, too. He keeps a proper distance from Delphine, as a married man must, holding his arm out for her to depend upon. Yet when she speaks, the upper part of his body inclines toward her. His gaze is fixed on her face. He nods his head closer to hers.

Perhaps nothing other than a man being friendly with a beautiful woman, more solicitous than he might be with a plain one. But Alma has spent considerable time shadowing stray husbands—the only reliable work she could find on her own, after she was dismissed from the Women's Bureau—and something about the judge's demeanor trips the wire of her suspicion. Others seem to notice, too: sailors and gentlemen, ladies and maids, all of them white, look twice at Delphine on the judge's arm. A few sailors laugh. A blond woman in rose silk watches the pair pass, her face screwed up as if she just ate a lemon.

Alma wishes she were Delphine's escort, rather than the errant judge, so she could sneer at all the scandalized passersby. But Jack Camp can't be seen with Delphine. There can be no connection between Delphine and dirty waterfront business. It would even be dangerous to visit her again in that cheap straw-and-powder maid's getup, now that more people have seen Camp and could recognize Alma in disguise. Camp's clothes are a powerful signal—no one expects gender lines to be crossed in such a way—but it would only take one sharp-eyed onlooker to put Alma in a risky spot.

She finishes her soup, wipes her hands on her trousers. Her throat aches. Some of the shine is coming off the day. Everyone else can arrange a visit with Delphine. Hamilton. Wheeler. Nell Roberts. Everyone except her.

Wait—Nell Roberts.

Now there's an idea. A line to Delphine that doesn't involve switching back to women's costumes.

"Where can a man find some pretty company?" she asks the lumberman guzzling chowder at her right elbow.

"Hear there's some nice pieces at the French Hotel," he says.

"You been to The Captain's?"

"I ain't been there. But it looks a treat."

"I could use a treat," Alma says. "Hard week. And I do love dancing on a Saturday night."

———

The Captain's gold sign kicks in the wind, keeping time with the music spilling through the door. Alma shoves through the crowd of men loitering on the stoop. To one side of the door is a window, its glass lit from within by lamps and from without by the reflection of the sunset sky, all orange and crimson fire. Fiddles sweep to a crescendo. She hands a nickel to the doorman and enters the room to claps and whooping in salute to the band.

Inside, sweat and smoke vie with fruity perfumes for the air's top note. Gingham-wrapped dancers, curled hair wilting with damp, pull their partners to the bar. The women are rosy with exertion. A few have darker complexions and glossy black braids. Others have the blockish bodies of farmers' daughters. Nell Roberts is not among them.

At the bar Alma orders a gin and waits to see who will approach her—which kind of Port Townsend working girl will think Jack Camp is a good bet. She is cleaned up, feeling handsome in newly bought clothes. Her high-collared shirt smells of starch. The stiff denim of her jacket crackles at the collar and elbows. But the trousers are too loose in the groin. She is not yet used to the cut of them, the way they sit over the folded bulge of cloth she's put in place for the occasion.

"Care for a dance?"

A plump little woman cozies up to her. Brown hair, brown eyes, her face heart-shaped and dimpled. Full bosom spilling over the lacy front of her dress. Sweet with orange-blossom perfume. Alma breathes deep before the sweat and smoke close in again.

"Yes, ma'am, I would," she says.

"I'm Emma."

"Jack," Alma says. "You as thirsty as you are pretty, Emma?"

The woman's laugh is gurgling, catchy.

"What'll it be?"

"A whiskey," Emma says.

She knocks back the drink like it's dyed water, which it likely is. Alma buys her two more and sips at her gin while a new song is played and applauded. They haven't even gotten to dancing but the woman starts leaning into her anyhow, telling her about the new band and its magic fiddlers, her warm, soft body pressing into

Alma's ribs, floral scent rising from her braided hair. Alma puts an arm around Emma's bare shoulders. Her skin is dewy with sweat.

"We ought to dance eventually," Alma says, "but I'm happy just to conversate."

"Did you come in from a lumber camp?" Emma asks. "It gets lonely out there, I imagine."

"Do I look like a logger?"

Alma likes to know what people make of her. What pictures they construct from her presentation, her mannerisms. It's a trick she picked up from Hannah, practiced for so long it's now a habit. In a safe spot, get at the cracks, Hannah said; have someone else tell you what is missing, or too visible. That was in the Chicago house where the Women's Bureau agents gathered, and though she was speaking of disguise in general, she spent much of the time looking at Alma. Only the two of them knew the binding cloth, the roughened voice, the thrill and terror of slipping into a male shape.

Emma wiggles out from under Alma's arm. Makes a show of looking her up and down. Alma's side is chilled. She wants the woman to come back—wants that body connection, that orange-blossom perfume in her mouth.

"Well, I don't know," Emma says. "You do look strong enough. And your arm's about as solid as a rock. Not that I mind!"

"I'm not a logger. Can you guess what it is I do? From back over here." Alma holds her arm out, and Emma nestles into her obligingly.

"A stevedore."

"No."

"A lawman." Those dimples blooming into view.

"Hah! Close," Alma says. "I spent some time as a lawman."

"Something at the ironworks?"

All strongman jobs, steeped in sweat and blood and muscle. Alma pulls the other woman nearer, pleased.

"I was gonna buy you another drink if you guessed right, but I think I want that dance instead." Bending a little ways down—Emma is only a few inches shorter—Alma whispers in her ear, "You smell like summertime."

Emma laughs, pinkening in the cheeks. Heat pools in Alma's

belly. The woman's hitting her just right, all soft and sweet eyed and cuddling. Alma could ask her back to the boardinghouse. Something every man tries, most likely, but there's the chance Emma might say yes. The thirty dollars in gold coin Alma's got in her pockets ought to help her cause.

"Why, if it isn't Mr. Camp."

Ah. Alma was having such a good time she forgot this part of the plan. She grins, while under her arm, Emma's smile is wilting. She wheels the woman around with her.

Nell Roberts is poured into a deep-blue dress. Her hair piled into curls. Her breasts rising against the taffeta trim of her bodice with each breath.

"Miss Roberts," Alma says, dipping a bow.

Nell taps her fan under the painted curve of her mouth, which ticks upward at one corner. She did not give Alma her name at Wheeler's office, so she must know she was asked after.

"I don't think we've seen you at The Captain's before," Nell says. "Perhaps you'd like to join me at a private table?"

"I'm all yours."

Alma hasn't let go of her little dancer. Nell looks at the other woman and raises an eyebrow.

"You're beautiful," Alma tells Emma, quiet, and slips a ten-dollar coin into one hot palm. "I want that dance later."

Emma nods, not really smiling, but after she glances at the money, her face brightens.

"Shall we?" Alma says, offering Nell her arm.

Nell's fan flicks open in a flash of gold lace.

"I know how to walk just fine, Mr. Camp."

"Oh, no doubt," Alma says, and tucks her elbow back against her side.

Nell leads the way through the hall, along the edge of the dance floor. Men take off their hats, call good-evenings. Alma lets her gait take on a swagger. Across the polished floor, at a small table, Wheeler's man Benson is set down before a bottle. A clean checkered shirt strains over his thick shoulders. Alma nods at him, and he tips his glass toward her in response. At the back, a velvet rope cordons off three tables, each hung with curtains to keep it separate from the others. A woman and a man sit at the right-hand table, the woman's lacy dress shimmering as she pours the man a glass of wine. Nell gestures to the table on the left.

Alma hands her onto the cushioned bench, then sits across from her. The music is muted—the band plays facing the door—but the smells of the place are stronger, bottled up and oversweet. Nell peels off her gloves. Twists each wrist as she bares it to reveal the milky skin of her inner arms. She's used belladonna again, and her eyes are liquid and huge.

"I thought you were a bad man," she says, setting the gloves aside.

"I am," Alma says.

Nell has remembered her words from their brief encounter in Wheeler's hallway. It comes back to Alma, too. Carmine on Wheeler's earlobe. Musk on Nell's gloves as she left his office. The electric, filthy look he gave Alma when she leaned into the other woman against his blue-papered wall.

"Bad men don't give a girl ten dollars just for smiling at them," Nell says.

"I didn't want to hurt her feelings."

"You didn't want to hurt your chances." Nell is good at this, delivering a jab of truth while at the same time fingering an earring, calling attention to her neck, the thick curl bobbing at her jawline. "Believe me, I know you men are all the same."

"Miss Roberts, honey, I'd like to buy you a drink." Alma twitches her eyebrows up into a plaintive shape. "Get on your good side."

"All right." Nell leans back on the bench in an artful slump that deepens the shadows of her bosom. "Champagne. We keep it special."

She waves and a boy scurries over from his place beside the ropes. His piped jacket is tight in the shoulders and far too short in the cuffs, coming up two inches past his oversize, knobby wrists. He takes Nell's order and is off again.

"What brings you to town, Mr. Camp?"

"Jack," Alma says. She toys with the idea of a past that will rile Nell up, corrupter of schoolgirls or some other tawdry nonsense. But if Wheeler's drawn a party line with his clerk explanation, she'll stick to it. "I've been hired as a clerk."

"A clerk." Nell's laugh is high, breathy. "I don't believe that for a second. What's your excuse for those bruises—you got into a scuffle over the inkpot?"

"It may seem unlikely"—Alma tugs at the bandage under her collar—"but I think I'm up to the task."

"A capable man."

"You said it."

"I say a lot of things, Mr. Camp."

The boy returns with the champagne. Alma gives him five dollars—highway robbery, but not unexpected—then takes the bottle, the glasses.

"Jack," she says again, as the cork exits with a weak pop. She fills Nell's fizzing glass to the brim.

"I heard you the first time," Nell says, taking a sip. "We're not yet on a first-name basis."

Alma could do this dance all night. She spreads her arms over the back of the bench, taking up her whole side of the table. Sprawls her thighs wide. Trouser seam tight against the knob of cloth tucked into her smallclothes, a nudge of lust. Her eyes mapping the curves of Nell's breasts with no attempt to disguise her staring.

"Why were you in Nathaniel Wheeler's hall yesterday?" Nell lowers her voice to a whisper, almost lost in the music. "From the way he spoke to you, I half expected to never see you again."

Alma lets her eyes drift up. Nell's lips are parted, a delicate furrow between her dark blond eyebrows.

"That's business," she says, the champagne's syrupy sweetness coating her tongue. "I'd rather stick to pleasure."

The band wraps up another contra dance, floor and table shaking with the last whirled steps. There are whistles, laughter, a momentary lull. Then a single fiddle sends up a high note. The others join in on a waltz made up of long, wistful ribbons of sound.

"Would you dance with me?" Alma says.

"Because you asked nicely."

The slow music calls for a matching sway, which suits Alma just fine. She slides one hand down Nell's bare arm and interlaces their fingers. Draws her close. Her other hand on Nell's waist, curving corset bones warmed by body heat. Honeysuckle scent wafting off Nell's neck. The shelf of her corset lifting her breasts full and soft between them.

"I guess I ought to come clean," Alma says in an undertone. She keeps them near the corner booth with slight pressure at Nell's waist, so they are dancing in the shadows, ten feet of empty space all around them.

"I'm not a clerk," she says, mouth so close to the shell of Nell's ear that her lips just brush its edge. "I work for Delphine."

Nell stiffens, but she doesn't lose the thread of the dance. Her hips swaying, her skirts brushing the tops of Alma's boots. She bends her head away from Alma so they are face-to-face, blinks up through thick lashes—an expert at dancing gracefully with men of any height, flirting at any angle.

"Oh, my," she says.

"I hear you're our paperhanger." Alma walks her fingers from Nell's waist to her low back, drawing tighter the space between their bodies. "Sure would like to see some of your work. I bet you make a pretty banknote."

"I don't do money," Nell says. "Not anymore."

"Can you get her a message for me?" Alma says, coming to the point—the reason for her visit. Not that she's minded the distractions.

Nell's hazel eyes narrow.

"Why don't you tell her yourself," she says.

"I'm not supposed to visit her fancy house. I don't know where the hell Joe got off to, and Wheeler's not happy with me," Alma says, laying out the inner circle's names as currency. "Now, I'm not trying to make him happy with me. But that does put me in a fix when I need a favor."

"You think I'll do you a favor?"

"Honey, I came here to see you," Alma says. "You're doing me a favor just dancing with me."

Nell purses her lips. Lets Alma pull her closer.

"I heard you saw her today, and I was jealous." Alma nuzzles the little golden hairs that curl behind Nell's ear. "I wanted to see you again as soon as you left that hallway."

"You might not be a bad man, Mr. Camp, but you are a dangerous one," Nell says, a trace of color blushing along her throat. "Silver-tongued as a snake."

"I promise I won't bite."

The waltz is swirling to a close. Nell leans in. Warm breath on Alma's ear, on the bruised skin of her jaw. Her nipples tighten against the binding cloth.

"I keep a tailor's shop," Nell says, under the last wavering note. "And make her dresses. She comes to see me there. You should stop by sometime."

"Oh, I will." Alma unlatches their bodies. Sweeps a bow. It's not a meeting with Delphine, but it's halfway there—a safe place, and a willing liaison. A golden-eyed liaison, who smells like night-blooming flowers. Full hips, soft upper arms. Her whole body ripe as a peach.

"I've shamefully ignored the other gentlemen." Nell drains the last of her champagne, chin tipping to display the long column of her neck. "Stay awhile. Have another dance or two. Emma's waiting for you."

"Good night, Miss Roberts."

"Good night, Jack," Nell says.

Alma triple-checks her letter by candlelight, flipping through *Eight Hundred Leagues on the Amazon* as she scans for the encoded words. She writes, *Moving two tons per month via small boats, fallen girls.* "Fallen girls" is obtuse, but it's the best she can do with Verne's source text, which has a regrettable lack of words like *brothel* or *prostitute*.

Midnight wind howls outside the boardinghouse. Alma's sweaty shirt and trousers have chilled and cling to her in clammy discomfort.

Need some weeks more for setup, she writes. *Emergency contact only.*

She rubs her eyes. Rolls her neck to get at the tension there, but nothing pops or loosens. As she is tucking the letter into a blank envelope, something ticks against the window. In the cot Emma stirs. Sighs. The sound an echo of the last hour: Alma's excuses— *Sorry, honey, I had too much to drink, but I can do you good another way*—hot fingers in Alma's hair, at the back of her skull, holding her down. And after, letting Emma stay when it was better otherwise. Leaning against the wall with one hand in her trousers, staring at the sleeping woman's freckled breasts and sucking musk off her own fingers.

Alma puts the book away among the stack of others she keeps. Wedges the letter into the notch she's carved on the underside of her writing desk. Puff of breath, candle smoke, darkness. She eases onto the cot, still fully clothed. Curls her body around Emma's and inhales the salt-sweetness of the woman's skin.

15

JANUARY 16, 1887

Just inside Wheeler's door, Alma shakes rain off her cap. Dark patters to the carpet. Smoky air warms her wet skin as she shrugs out of her jacket, the cotton of her shirt letting off a waft of orange-blossom scent.

"Don't bother," Wheeler says.

He stands from behind the desk. His clothes are impeccably neat: cuffs buttoned and linked, smooth silk tie speared with a gleaming stickpin, silver belt buckle. He is arrayed against her, after their collision the day before. She takes this as a compliment. And as a challenge.

"We're going out," he says.

Behind him the fire pops and seethes as rain trickles down the chimney. Alma tugs her jacket back on, her cap, the cloth band cold against her forehead and the tops of her ears.

"Where to, boss?"

"An errand."

"Could you be more specific?" she says.

"Specifically, I regret that Sloan failed to kill you." He approaches, shoulders up, chin up, to collect his scarf and overcoat from the rack beside her. "But seeing as that's the case, you're still my problem, and I will do as I've been asked and show you around."

"Your boys couldn't have pulled off that deal." Alma leans against the door, its knob digging into the small of her back. "Sloan's got it out for McManus, and Benson wouldn't be quick enough to dance. You ought to be thanking me."

"Get out of the way."

"Say thank you."

Wheeler pauses, his hands midway through tying his bright blue scarf. He glares at her. Three feet between them, but he comes no closer.

"God give me patience." He finishes knotting his scarf with a snap of his wrist.

"What *is* she giving you?"

He cocks his head, silver hairs at his temples glinting in the lamplight.

"You're rolling over and taking things pretty easy," Alma says. "Showing a lot of patience. What is she giving you? What did you talk about, in that little room, before I showed up?"

"I'm to train you to be my replacement."

He pulls down his hat, slaps it against his thigh—an impatient gesture. Alma doesn't move from the door.

"What's in it for you?" she says.

"A promotion of my own."

Alma frowns and doesn't bother to hide it. This isn't supposed to be a win-win situation. She is supposed to be getting the better end of the deal. Wheeler is supposed to be demoted, once he falters, so he's working for her. And where is there for him to ascend? He already runs everything in Port Townsend. A jealous twinge, sourness at the back of her throat: Delphine is presenting herself as a widow. Delphine wouldn't take Wheeler as a husband. It would draw far too much attention. But she could. If it was beneficial enough.

Now Wheeler is the one grinning, a nasty, sharp-toothed lift of his upper lip.

"Did you think you were going to fuck me over?" he says.

"I was planning on it."

"Here's something else to keep in mind."

He crowds into her, finally, but she is too put out, too resentful, to snap at him and start a brawl. The doorknob grinds against her tailbone.

"If I don't move up, you don't move up." His breath hot, tobacco scented, on her face. "Those are my orders—straight from the source. So I'd put a fucking leash on your antics. I don't know what it is you're after, but making me angry won't do you a scrap of good."

God damn it. Yet this is not a trick on Delphine's part, not exactly. Alma made her own assumptions about the move from San Francisco and the competition for Wheeler's post. Delphine merely refrained from correcting them. Alma has to admit it was nicely done, the kind of neat maneuvering that's brought Delphine to the top. And Alma will still get what she wants: a position closer to Delphine, Wheeler's desk, control of the Port Townsend operations.

"It goes the other way, too." She sees the benefit of confirmation this time—though she'll make sure of the situation when she meets with Delphine, at Nell's. "If I don't move up, neither can you."

"That does seem to be the case. So we're both disappointed." Wheeler points at the door with his hat. "Move."

She steps aside. He opens the door and calls down to Driscoll that they're away. Then they are threading through the office, through Clyde Imports' chill dimness. Outside, hard rain hisses down. Mud slops onto her shins as they walk toward the waterfront. She watches the streets in a constant sweep, sidewalk to sidewalk, Wheeler's gray-coated shoulders centering each swath of vision. She's not yet sure what to do with him. How to ingest their new partnership, the knotting together of their fortunes. Clever, Delphine. Guaranteed cooperation. Yet while it won't serve Alma's ends in the organization to shake him up anymore, it has been fun. She's not sure she wants that game over.

"Ah Tong is a business partner," Wheeler says, as they turn a corner and walk toward a building hung with red signs. On the stoop men crouch out of the rain, smoking and chatting. "So no rough talk. Meaning, if you have any opinions about Chinamen, keep them to yourself."

Closer to the building, its front door hung with bright banners runneled with water. She can't read the calligraphy. But the men on the steps are speaking Taishanese, the tongue of San Francisco's Chinatown. Alma bends her ear to their voices, testing herself.

Without context, she only catches a few words—*Gee's vegetable garden*, *newspaper*—and wishes she'd found more time for afternoons with Zhu Kang, who taught her most of what she knows of the language. She would trade cans of tar for liquor, their little transactions done under the table, and he would grow flushed in the forehead and tease her about her pronunciation until their shared bottle was empty.

The wooden steps creak under Wheeler's boots. The gathered men go quiet, stand up, disperse into the street. Inside it's warm, the walls stocked with imported goods. Incense, chilies, bitter tea— that first breath takes Alma back to the city, its lanes and shortcuts. A young man sits at a wooden counter in the back. Wheeler crosses the room, ducking under low beams hung with samples of silk, bundles of dried garlic. Alma follows, taking time to inspect the shelves: sheaves of paper, bags of rice, a generous display of opium cans arranged by price. Some small-time names she doesn't recognize. Stacked atop them, Wah Hing and King Tye, brands from the organization's partner refineries. Then a sparing arrangement of Fook Lung, a premium line out of Hong Kong.

"I'm here to see Ah Tong," Wheeler says, taking off his hat.

"Good day, Mr. Wheeler." The young man's accent thickens the words. He is handsome, his skin pale against a black cotton smock as he leans into a bow. "I will tell him you have arrived."

He disappears behind a patterned curtain. A handful of small bronze weights are heaped on the counter beside a set of scales. Alma swirls them together with the tips of her fingers. Clicks and tings, smooth coolness. Wheeler's promotion nags at her. She wants to know what he's getting. Delphine's bed? Or a placement that will benefit the ring? Maybe a new outpost in Tacoma, where he said they're paying through the nose for some rich middleman to cart tar from the steamboat docks to the railroad depot. Tacoma is a weak spot, as Alma sees it: too much product moving through, not enough trusted people on the ground to move it.

"Where's this promotion taking you?" She pinches a weight, taps it against the counter.

"Up."

She huffs out a laugh, raises an eyebrow.

"No shit," she says.

Wheeler folds his arms across his chest. The lifted set of his chin, in profile, signals satisfaction. He's got her curious and he knows it.

"How about Edmonds?" she says, to take him down a notch. It can be a long and tricky business, getting a new collector in line— testing if he'll take bribes, or if he'll only be persuaded by blackmail. "Any progress there?"

"Yes, actually." He turns to her, his blue eyes dark in the ruddy lamplight. "Despite the inconvenience of your arrival, I remain good at my job."

The young man reappears, beckons them to follow. Alma steps through the curtain last, its textured cotton catching at her shoulders. At the end of the hall is a cramped room hot with brazier char. A writing desk in one corner. Three chairs arranged around an oval table. An elderly man standing beside it, his body soft in the middle under a black silk blouse.

"Thank you for your visit, Mr. Wheeler," he says, bowing. His accent is faint, more of a carefulness in pronunciation than an inflection on the words themselves. "Please, sit."

"This is Camp," Wheeler says, a flick of his hand indicating Alma while also instructing her, too, to take a seat. "He's part of the business now."

"Mr. Camp."

"*Jeen gawl hain gain awl ney,*" Alma says.

Wheeler stiffens beside her. Ah blinks, his mouth twitching toward a smile.

"*Ney gong hoy san wa?*" he says.

"*Nit awr. Hok gin. M'haul yee thu, ngoy yiaw maan maan gong.*"

"Speak English, god damn it," Wheeler says.

He is glowering at Alma. She lifts an eyebrow, a flicker of insolence only he is meant to see, while across the table Ah apologizes. Movement behind them, hot air shifting, and the young man comes into the room carrying a tray. He places teacups on the table; a glazed teapot; a bottle of whiskey and two tumblers; a plate of rice cakes, thick and glistening. Pours tea for Wheeler, then Alma, then Ah.

"I have a shipment coming over," Wheeler says.

The young man tilts up the bottle of whiskey. At Wheeler's nod, he pours two glasses and sets them before Alma and Wheeler, with the bottle standing between. Then he tucks the tray under his arm and leaves.

"In two days' time," Wheeler says, once the three of them are alone. "The landing will be at Cape George, at night, between eleven and one o'clock."

Alma's understanding of this meeting shifts. Ah is not set to handle a shipment of opium. He is the man who takes charge of Chinese brought over by the night boat from Victoria. This is one of the organization's side businesses, a profitable scheme given the number of men who want to enter the country but are barred by the Exclusion Act. McManus crews a special cutter—courtesy of Peterson's boatyard—that can hold fifty crates of tar or fifteen close-packed bodies. She lifts her teacup, glazed clay searing the pads of her fingers, hot water searing her lip. Bitter, pungent. An echo of the city that's not entirely pleasant.

"I will make arrangements," Ah says.

"Don't send them through Tacoma." Wheeler sips his whiskey, his steaming tea untouched. "With the troubles there they've got a close watch on the waterfront."

"Seattle has been better."

"Agreed."

Wheeler stands, sets his hat on the table as he finishes his whiskey. Alma tosses hers back in a single gulp.

"If Camp comes without me, in future, you're to follow his instructions as you would mine," Wheeler says. "He'll bring the papers tomorrow."

Ah bows to him, then to Alma. She and Wheeler leave the small room. The air of the hall is distinctly cooler. No sign of the young man at the counter. In the street the rain is turning to sleet. Thick drops sluice off Alma's cap brim as she and Wheeler walk south. Away from the bay. Past a sprawling tack store and stable, where the air is thick with ice, with water, smells of wet leather and hay.

"What did you say to that man?" Wheeler's voice is just audible over the rush of rain.

"He asked how well I speak Chinese," Alma says. "And I told him, well enough."

"That's a useful party trick."

Alma looks at him sidelong, amused.

"If you're trying to give me a compliment, I'd say you made it about halfway."

"Then I was far too kind," he says, the thinnest thread of humor in his voice.

He stops under the shelter of an awning, deserted but for a few trays of wilted greens, rain spattered on their leaves, their root smell rising into the air. From his coat pocket he withdraws a slim silver case. This is the first time she's seen him with cigarettes. She digs out her box of matches, strikes one, holds it up for him to lean in to. Her hands are perfect, completely transformed into a workingman's. Blunt nails rimmed with dirt. Bruised knuckles, raw scrapes. Over the flare of the tobacco Wheeler's eyes are close to hers, red-lit, watchful. She still makes him nervous. But this is as close as he's allowed her all morning.

"What are these papers I'm delivering?" She flicks the match into the mud.

"Travel certificates, for the Chinamen."

"Are they made by our own talented Miss Roberts?"

"I take care of it," Wheeler says, sharp.

"All right."

Alma holds out her hand, and to her surprise he passes her the cigarette instead of ignoring her. She takes a deep drag, gives it back. Lets her attention drift over the street. Gray blur of sleet, men hunched in drab coats, shivering horses. No one out except those who must be, the laborers and hungry boys and a few tribeswomen huddled on a covered cart, staring into the rain.

"Benson's at the Quincy warehouse," Wheeler says, tossing away the cigarette as he leaves the shelter of the awning. "He'll show you how things work there."

"Our excursion is already over?"

At the end of the block is the Upper Town staircase, which Alma climbed in her shabby disguise to see Delphine. Wheeler walks toward it, and the thought of him with Delphine skitters past again:

Wheeler striding toward the front door like a proper guest, his over-coat dripping onto the pink camellias, onto the red bricks; taking off his hat at the steps; taking off his jacket inside; taking off his tie, his obsidian cuff links, in Delphine's private parlor. Her per-fume in his nose.

"I'm afraid you can't come to my next appointment," he says, one hand on the railing. "It's for gentlemen only."

"Sounds boring."

"A bit. The food makes up for it."

The moment takes an unfamiliar shape: the rain a veil between them, Wheeler almost smiling, their conversation almost casual. Almost friendly. Alma touches her cap, glimpsing what things could be like, if she stopped jabbing and he stopped coiling up against her. Not as much sport that way. But maybe a better understanding.

"Come in tomorrow morning," he says.

She waits for him to climb the first flight of steps, then ambles off in the direction of Quincy Wharf, which takes her past the of-fice. Driscoll is posted at the side door. He is red at the cheeks and ears, his nose streaming. He stamps his feet.

"Christ, it's cold," he says, wiping his nose on his sleeve.

"Want me to bring you some coffee?"

"Would you?"

"Give me five dollars," Alma says, and laughs as he kicks a spray of icy water toward her.

"Go on, Camp."

Driscoll is back in good graces after his extraction of Sloan's tar. During Alma and McManus's postdelivery report to Wheeler, McManus made special note of the younger man's performance: ducking out the back, neatly replacing the trunk he'd opened. And Driscoll had spoken warmly of McManus while the crew waited for the night boat. They seem too different to be friends—one sealed off and seething, one quick to smile, restless, ready with jokes—but something is tying them together. Alma likes Driscoll just fine. She'll like him even better if it makes McManus jealous.

"I'm supposed to give something to Nell Roberts," she tells Driscoll. "Who is she and where do I find her?"

Benson can wait. The icy wharf, the Quincy warehouse's dim rows of liquor crates, sound like a chore. Alma has better things to be doing on this cold and free afternoon. Maybe Nell has news about Delphine. Or maybe she's just in the mood for company.

"You lucky bastard."

"Is she pretty?" Alma says, wanting to hear about Nell from the kid, wanting to see her through someone else's vision.

"Like a Christmas pudding." His brown eyes narrow, go hungry. "All sweet and soft."

"I'll give her your regards," Alma says, winking.

"She doesn't know me." Driscoll shakes his head. "I try to catch a word when she stops by the office. She works at The Captain's sometimes, but I've never gotten a dance with her. And she keeps a seamstress shop."

"Where's that?" Alma says. "The boss told me to be quick about it."

"At Tyler and Washington. It has a blue door."

"Good man."

She leaves him sleet-laced and shivering. Winds her way back toward Tyler Street, stopping at a flower store, stopping again to take off her cap and smooth down her hair in a druggist's window. ELIXIRS is written across the glass in gold script, and against the lettering her reflection is clearer. Straight dark hair falling over her forehead. Her left eye and jawline still faintly bruised. The clean bandage around her neck just showing over the high collar of her shirt. She looks like a tooth-and-nail brawler. She looks good.

A few more blocks and she's at the corner Joe led her to, two days before. At the front of the corner building is a blue door, with a little brass-plated sign beside it reading SEAMSTRESS, TAILORING, NEEDLEWORK. Nell's list of talents grows. And this is a clever cover for Delphine. She can come down to Lower Town as often as she likes if she's visiting her dressmaker. It's a classic setup. Hannah would have approved: she had been with Pinkerton's agency since the war, when the Women's Bureau got its start, and had met Union spy Elizabeth Van Lew, whose seamstress sewed secret correspondence from the North into the hems of Van Lew's gowns.

Alma keeps walking, following a hunch. Yes. Here is the alley where Joe stopped. The door with a tarnished handle that leads into a private home, where Delphine and Wheeler waited in a parlor. That was Nell's parlor. This entrance lines up with the blue door, in a straight shot through the building, suggesting Nell's home and business are connected.

Back around to the front. Her knock shakes water droplets along the bright blue wood. Footsteps sound within. The door opens a sliver. Inside is warm dimness, laced with honeysuckle perfume. A shawl-draped shoulder. A tumbled lock of hair on the rise of a collarbone.

"Miss Roberts." Alma takes off her cap, holds up a clutch of roses.

"Why, Mr. Camp."

Nell's eyes are not painted. She has not used drops, and her pupils are tiny against the daylight, showing hazel irises intensely green at their centers.

"Pardon the surprise," Alma says. "But it's urgent."

"Come in."

Nell is wearing a striped wash dress, not one of the stiff-bodiced gowns Alma has seen her in before. In the faded pink fabric Nell's body is softer, its curves less defined. At the high waist of the dress, fabric clings close to skin.

"I'm here on official business," Alma says.

The shop is tiny, barely eight by eight feet, with a beige chair by the door and a neat table topped with a sewing machine. The walls are papered in striped cream. A filigreed iron brazier glows in the corner opposite the chair.

Nell brings the bouquet to her nose, smiling. Her hair is bound loosely at her nape. She traces her fingers over the flowers, pulling back the petals to reveal the sprig of dill concealed at their center.

"Official business?" Nell says, one eyebrow lifting.

The set of her mouth, her wry glance, tell Alma she has read the message in the flowers: orange roses for fascination, dill for lust. An arrangement that verges on insulting in its forwardness. But Nell does not drop the flowers or hand them back: she takes them to the sewing table and lays them beside the gleaming machine.

"Papers for Ah Tong," Alma says.

"Oh. Those aren't quite ready."

"I'm happy to wait. I have the afternoon off. And the evening. All night."

"You can bring me saucy flowers as much as you like, Jack, but that doesn't mean they'll get you anywhere."

Nell locks the front bolt. Three steps take her across the room, skirts swishing, to the inner door behind the sewing table.

"I'll be right back," she says.

Alma steps forward, as if to walk after her.

"Sit down," Nell says. "You're in my home, and if you don't mind me, you won't be welcome anymore."

"Yes, ma'am."

Alma sinks onto the beige-cushioned chair. In the opposite corner a glass-faced cabinet is stocked with spools of colored thread, a rainbow behind etched panes. Her reflection in the glass is shaped by pleasing angles: broad lines of her shoulders, strong slopes of her thighs. She considers the inner door. Nell's living quarters, and a link to the alley where Joe first led her. Set up like Wheeler's offices: a respectable front, and a back end to conceal more unusual traffic. Yet at the center of this building is a bed, where Nell sleeps; a stove, where she warms her milk and puts tea on to boil.

"I wasn't expecting company."

Nell backs through the door, a wooden tray in her hands. She sets it on the edge of the sewing table: a little pot of beer, a few wedges of cheese, a green apple. Going out again, she returns with a sheaf of papers and a glowing lamp.

"I've done five of the six." She pulls a pair of spectacles from a drawer under the sewing machine. "I didn't think they were needed until tomorrow."

"They're not," Alma says. "I just wanted to see you today."

Nell waves the eyeglasses at the tray of food, their wire rims flashing in the lamplight. A smile tugging at her mouth.

"Eat, won't you?"

"I'm staying seated until you tell me otherwise." Alma's cap is on her knee, its rain-soaked twill dripping onto the carpet. "I'm not looking to break the rules."

"Oh, I don't believe that." Nell nudges the tray an inch toward

Alma, watching as she stands and picks up the beer, the apple. "You'll fit right in with the boys, all spit and steel. Like that McManus."

"Has the bastard given you trouble?"

"None of them dare to." Nell hooks on the spectacles, turns up the lamp wick. "They confine themselves to saying good evening and leering."

"Wheeler wasn't too happy about me coming here." Alma shines the apple on her sleeve, its skin squeaking over wet denim. As her teeth crunch into sweet flesh, she keeps her eyes on Nell. "He's got a jealous streak."

"Jealous?" Nell looks up from her papers, her pen lifted off the page.

"I don't think he trusts me to behave myself," Alma says, washing down the apple with a swig of beer.

"Do you mean to say he's watching out for my chastity?"

"You're his woman, aren't you?"

Nell laughs.

"Nathaniel and I have worked together for years," she says. "But Friday was the first time he ever took a . . . special interest."

"Huh."

The timing of Wheeler's pretty guest, his tangled responses to Alma in her various disguises, start to take on a new meaning. He had another woman—a plump, perfumed woman in muslin and lace—when Alma, hard-bodied in her dirty shirt and trousers, would see. Reminding her what he really wanted. Or trying to re-mind himself.

"I've taken a special interest, too," Alma says. The apple core is sticky in her hand, a thread of juice tickling its way down one knuckle.

"But I don't need a favor from you." Nell's eyes glint under low-ered lashes. "When I do, I'll let you know."

She leans across the space between them, holding out the empty crockery plate for the apple core. Under the high square collar of her dress her breasts are suggestions of movement. Alma puts down the fruit. Wipes her hand on her kerchief.

"I have my uses," she says. "Try me."

Nell smiles. Turns her attention back to the papers on her table, the quiet scratching of her pen resuming. The warmth of the brazier has started to dry Alma's hair, her trousers. The chair is softer than her boardinghouse cot. She props one elbow on the armrest, setting her chin on her fist. Lets her legs sprawl open. Nell's eyes track over the paper as her long fingers smooth flat the page. The lamplight catches in her golden hair.

"How did Delphine find you?" Alma says.

"I found her." Nell holds up the paper, squints at it against the lamp. "When I first got to town. I was sewing, a little, and between that and some pickpocketing when steamers came in, I did all right."

"Never would have figured you as a cutpurse. You're too pretty."

"I've rarely found that a disadvantage," Nell says. "One day on the docks I saw a beautiful woman in a blue cloak. Velvet. Expensive. I got twenty dollars in coin and a gold chain out of her pocket just as she caught me, quick as the dickens, not even looking. Fingers locked around my wrist. She said, 'Jack be nimble.' And then turned around and said, 'Oh! A girl.'"

"You do her accent well."

"I've known her four years."

"She caught me, too, in a sense," Alma says, rubbing at the bruise on her jaw; sore nerves over ridged bone. "She's like that. You can't get away, and you don't want to."

"Do you love her?"

"I love the money we make together." Alma sits up straighter. Runs a hand through her hair, which is stiff with sweat and knotted. The bump at the bottom of her skull finally subsiding. She let herself get far too comfortable, in this snug room, in this quiet company. And that comfort is no accident—with the food, and drink, and flirtation, Nell has quietly encouraged her to talk. The woman knows her business.

"It's nice to have a full wallet." Nell lowers her face to her work, her expression unreadable.

"I need to see her." Alma puts on her damp cap. "Can you have her meet me here, tomorrow?"

"I can try."

"I'll come back for those papers in the morning," Alma says. "You let me know then."

"What happened to your afternoon off?"

"You're busy. So I'm going to go hunt up a favor I can offer you."

"Next time bring me tuberose," Nell says, as Alma unbolts the door. "It's my favorite. Or caramels. The notions shop by the post office sells the sweetest things."

On Water Street the sun is already sloping low. Winter days here are shorter than down South, the light in a hurry to die. The notions shop's window sparkles with rain. Bright bolts of cloth in pinks and blues are stacked behind brass door fixtures, a heaped basket of peppermints, enameled lamps. Playing with fire, that one. When Nell was just a lush bloom in Wheeler's hallway, in The Captain's, it was easier to classify her: the sugar dish, a tempting diversion. Now she's shown the real range of her skills. Flashed her wits, her forger's talents. Asked for tuberose, the bloom of dangerous pleasure that's rumored to induce sexual climax with its scent alone. Alma is more tempted than before—oh, the thrill of the challenge— but dancing with Nell calls for some caution. The woman gets Alma talking too easy.

She stops for a meal at the Adams Street fish market. Hot chowder, rye bread. Takes her time walking along the peeling-clapboard waterfront.

By the time she arrives at the Quincy warehouse she is soaked through. Sniffling. Her front teeth ache with cold. The building is outlined by purpling eastern sky. CLYDE IMPORTS is stenciled onto the bricks above the door, the letters dimming with the twilight. Benson stands by the entrance, behind the curtain of rain streaming off the eaves to splash knee-high off the plankboards. His head is nearly level with the top of the doorframe. His whistling does not pause as Alma approaches.

"Pretty fucking happy about standing in the rain," she says, ducking through the little waterfalls coming off the roof.

"This is dry, far as I'm concerned."

His buckskin jacket is wet, ripe with animal stink. Curls of hair cling to his forehead and ears.

"You part whale?"

"Naw. Worked in lumber camps, then on the loading side, in the Sound."

He opens the door. Alma follows him into the muffled chill of the warehouse. A sloped ceiling, banded with rafters. Two wall lamps by the entrance. A muted violet glow falls through the barred window at the back of the rectangular space. Stacked crates all around, high as Alma's chest; scent of damp hay and pinewood. With the rain shut out it is quiet enough to hear the water lapping at the pylons below. There are tiny shifts in gravity as the tide threads through the wharf's foundations.

"Got your whiskeys over here." Benson advances into the warehouse, slapping a neat block of crates marked with customs paperwork, inked stamps, branded distillery seals. "Gin just there. Those are the domestic imports: bourbon, mostly."

At the midpoint of the room he rolls a handcart out of the way, lifts oilcloth from another hulking pile. Overhead a flutter of sound: a bird's nest in the rafters, white flick of wing tips, and a wisp of straw floats down.

"Here's a batch of woolens. There's a drip in the ceiling, so we put out the cloth."

"Who's *we*?"

"Barker's in here from time to time," Benson says. "And Lyle. McManus's crew, when they cart things in."

"Where do you store the fun stuff?"

"When we keep any back, it gets squirreled away at Madison."

"Why?"

"No tar—ever—in the Quincy warehouse." Benson pulls the oilcloth back over the crates. "That's orders from the boss. This is the official Clyde Imports building. The other warehouse, on Madison . . . it's not part of Clyde Imports. The boss never goes there. He doesn't like to be around the tar, you know."

"Seems like a good way to not get caught," Alma says. "And so, what do you do? Just stand around here looking after a bunch of bottles?"

"Not bad work," Benson says, either missing her jab or not bothered that she's called him lazy. "But see, the papers all pass through here. The boss keeps things linked on paper, coded-like, so when we do send something along to Madison, it's on Clyde Imports' books. And what doesn't stop through town, it gets listed, too."

"You got some papers I can see?"

Benson's boots fall heavy as he walks back to the door, takes down a bound packet ten sheets thick.

"The special entries all start with two three six," he says, handing her the papers. "Kept back two cases of the last batch; the rest was all Tacoma-bound. Those are the liquor shipments, the cases of burgundy and the new bourbon—real smooth stuff out of Kentucky—and those are tar, the whiskeys starting two three six, see, you get it?"

"A value match?" Alma says, scanning the page. Two different hands are on it: the neat script listing the product details and batch numbers, and rough X marks next to each line, signaling receipt. Wheeler's work, probably, with those careful numerals, then Benson's scrawls over the top.

"Near enough. Everything gets squared away at the office; this is just the paper trail."

"I fucking hate paperwork." Alma flips to the next page. "Makes my toes curl."

Benson hooks his thumbs through his belt loops, leans against the solid block of wool crates.

"Word is you're from down San Francisco way," he says.

"That's right."

"Big city."

"Lots of girls there." She hands back the packet. "I see you favor The Captain's for your daily dose of skirt."

"I like the band. Never could play anything worth a damn, myself."

Alma runs her fingers over the crest branded onto the crate beside her. When she looks up, Benson is watching her close, his gray eyes narrowed at her face. She hardens her jaw.

"What?" she says.

"You look like someone I used to know," he says, drawing back a touch and considering her more openly. "Man named Franklin, at the Spokane camp. Damn good faller. He your kin?"

"I've got nobody there, and I don't recognize the name."

"You come all this way alone?" Benson says. "No woman to keep you warm?"

"Better to travel light."

More fluttering above. The birds set up a burbling chirp. Alma taps a cigarette out of her case. The edge of her matchbox is damp. It takes three strikes to get a light going. Benson whistles up at the birds, mimicking their song, and they quiet down. He's a big man, a thick man; she thinks of the whittled bird he was working on in Wheeler's office, so tiny in his callused hands. Big, but with precision in those fingers.

"That clerk, at the beach," Alma says. "Beckett. That was your work."

"Ruined a good jacket. A good pair of pants." Benson shakes his head when she offers him the cigarette. "Don't see the need of making a mess like that. But the boss wanted it a certain way."

"Did you really almost take his head off?"

"I got in there," he says. "Far enough to hit the spine."

"God damn."

"Now, cutting the tongue out, that made my skin crawl." Benson's thick shoulders hitch up. "Never been asked to do that before, and hope I won't be again."

The Beckett setup becomes a little clearer. It was less a snare to keep Alma secure and more a way to distance Wheeler from the murder. Someone, maybe another customhouse man, had to know Wheeler was feuding with Beckett. Maybe there were bystanders when Wheeler bruised his knuckles on Beckett's teeth. But with the boardinghouse woman as an eyewitness, the collector's death could be squarely pinned on Jack Camp: a stranger, new in town, capable of unprecedented brutality. Camp is no longer a convenient scapegoat now that Alma and Wheeler are working together—but she suspects Wheeler never meant for that to happen.

She scratches her jaw, the lit tip of her cigarette ghosting warm along her cheek. Benson's two-day-old slice in her throat still seeping.

"Were you meant to come knife me instead?" she says. "The night you got Beckett?"

Benson nods, his shoulders still up. His posture almost bashful.

"That was the plan," he says.

"But the plan changed."

"Lucky for you." He grins. "Next time we're both at The Captain's, come set down and have a drink. We can have a go at that draw poker game you offered. I've put Barker and Driscoll off cards—cleaned them out too many times."

"Do I look like an easy mark?" Alma sucks down gritty smoke, exhales through a sneer that bares her canines.

"Hell, Camp, you look like you might knife me, given the chance." Benson scrubs his thick wrist over his beard. "Just trying to be friendly. I want to hear about San Francisco. Aimed to go there when I first came out West. But I never made it."

The nesting birds twitch in the rafters. A white drizzle of shit drops to the ground at Alma's feet, followed by a slower-floating tuft of straw.

"I could tell you stories," she says. "Wicked as you like."

She is thinking of Benson's blade at her neck, again; of his body, hard and eager, trapping hers against the office desk. Bloodlust, or something else. She is thinking of Wheeler's eyes as the blade bit into her neck, how they narrowed in minute recoil. Wheeler had not been bluffing. He'd planned to pin Beckett's murder on her and then shut her up for good.

16

JANUARY 17, 1887

Driscoll is on the office stoop again, still flushed with cold but drier now that the storm has blown over. He jumps off the steps. Jostles against Alma, his breath smelling of coffee, his tousled head bent toward hers.

"Did you see her?" he says, bouncing on the balls of his feet, all worked up.

"I did." Alma knocks him back playfully with an elbow.

"Christmas pudding. Right?"

"She knew your name," she says, grinning when Driscoll's eyes go wide, his chapped lips parting. "She said you were all spit and steel. You're in with a chance."

"No." He is lit up like a firecracker, cheeks bright, breath rising in rapid puffs into the winter air. "She knew my name?"

Alma climbs the stairs, slapping his shoulder on the way. He is young, and foolish, and ready to believe anything. Into the hall; around the dogleg the air grows warmer. Wheeler's door is cracked open, a line of light on the blue wall opposite. She looks for him at the desk, but he is standing by the hearth, where a robust yellow fire roars.

"Driscoll built it high this morning," he says.

His jacket is off, but he has not rolled up his shirtsleeves—not letting his guard down against her. He prods at the fire with a poker, his arm red in the glow.

"To match his spirits," Alma says.

"He'll temper into a useful man." Wheeler props the poker against the bricks, wipes his palms with a kerchief.

"McManus thinks so," Alma says. "If the kid had been on my crew and let Sloan's man get so close, I wouldn't stand at your desk defending him."

"I believe you'd throw your comrades into the pit."

"Don't get me wrong." She shucks her cap. "I like Driscoll. He brings some cheerfulness to the place."

"Do you find us otherwise dour? Humorless?"

"A wee bit." Alma lapses into full brogue as she hangs her jacket on the rack. "Could be a touch of the Calvinist in you—too many morns spent in the pews, weeping for a barley scone."

"That is uncanny." Wheeler sits in his chair, the leather creaking, and taps his fingers on the desk. "Benson tells me you didn't bother showing up until sundown."

"I was busy." She switches back to Jack's voice, pleased that he mentioned her chameleon's accent.

"Other important affairs to see to?"

"Now, come on," she says, pulling the oilcloth-wrapped packet of papers from her vest and tossing it onto his desk. "I saved you a trip."

He picks it up, unwraps the envelope. Inside are the certificates for Ah Tong. Six neat sheets, each stating the bearer's identity as a returning Chinese merchant and resident of the United States. Wheeler's brow knots. His eyes track up to hers, slow.

"Nell sends her best," she says.

"Why did she give you these?"

"I told her I work for Delphine," Alma says. "She knows she can trust me."

"You're giving that name away like candy."

"Only when I need something."

"Be careful about it," Wheeler says.

Alma slides into her usual seat, the hardwood chair that's nowhere near as comfortable as the one in Nell's shop. His admonition irritates her. Mostly because he's right. Also because the thing for which she traded Delphine's name—a meeting, brokered by

Nell—will not be happening. During their visit that morning, Nell passed along a message: Delphine is not at liberty to descend into Lower Town today. But Alma is not at liberty to wait around and play second fiddle to Wheeler—not until Delphine clarifies the terms of the promotion Alma's laboring for. After leaving Nell's, Alma sent a message of her own to Delphine, asking for a meeting in Upper Town that afternoon, on neutral ground. She will have to wear her maid's costume again. She is not certain Delphine will show.

"Don't tell me how to do my job," Alma says.

"I thought that's exactly what I'm supposed to be doing." Wheeler turns his attention back to the papers, his posture stiff. He flips through them, examining each sheet, smoothing them down in a pile as he reads.

"It's good work," she says.

"I have eyes." He sets the stack to one side of his desk. Leans back in his chair. "While you've been out entertaining yourself, I've dealt with Edmonds. He won't interfere again."

"What did you do?" Alma is impressed: Wheeler has locked down the customhouse man in two days. That's fast work for bribery; faster still for blackmail.

"I found his weak spot," he says. "They do breed eccentrics out in Missoula."

"That's all you'll give me?"

Alma's temples are beading with sweat. This is the first day she's left her neck unbandaged, and warm air on the already itchy skin sets it tingling.

"For now."

"Fine," she says, rolling up her sleeves. Wheeler can be as nice as he wants with his clothing; she would rather be comfortable. "Keep your secrets."

His eyes, his mouth, hint at a smile as he returns to his paperwork.

"Benson told me something curious." She hooks her right thumb into her belt and taps, slow, on the buckle. "He said you'd had him ready to come knife me, before you decided to send me after Beckett instead."

Wheeler lifts one eyebrow in silent question.

"I didn't think you'd do it, at first," she says. "I misread you."

"You've made other mistakes," he says. "Don't be too surprised."

And she's not, sitting there, across from him. He would have had her killed despite his interest because he puts business before pleasure. She is the lunger. She is the one who sees to her hungers first and other considerations after. Wheeler is in the habit of denial, like a man who's fasted for so long he no longer even looks at bread. But he's got to eat sometime.

Alma drags her chair closer to the desk, its legs scraping dully over the carpet. Slides a handful of papers away from the edge. Wheeler looks up as she sets her boots onto the corner of the wood.

"I moved your papers." Alma nods at the empty space she's muddying with her heels. "Didn't I?"

"You've got no manners at all," Wheeler says.

"I'm on my very best behavior." She fishes a tin of candied fruits from her pocket. "That woman, from Beckett's boardinghouse. You paid her to identify me—but you thought I'd be dead, not hanging around town as your *clerk*. Will she be a problem?"

"I took care of it, when I discovered who you work for," he says. "A few dollars more and the good woman found she had nothing to say to the police."

Efficient. Careful, as he always is. Delphine chose wisely when she recruited him. Chewing on a sugary pineapple chunk, Alma considers Wheeler, considers the marked change between them. The understanding. It is of a piece with the sense she had at the Upper Town stairs. A continuation, a day later, of that loosening, that tendency to banter. It doesn't provide the same excitement as careening into him did. But if it's a slow burn he's after, she can meet that speed. For now.

"Want some?" She holds up the fruit, not bothered about sharing after she's already eaten her favorites.

"What is it?"

"Sugared apricot." She shakes the metal container, peering inside. "Plums. And one more pineapple, but that's mine."

"I don't care for sweet things," Wheeler says.

"Good. More for me."

"Take this to Ah Tong." He folds the paper he's been writing on, stacks it with the others Nell doctored. The whole lot he tucks into an envelope, and that into a clean wrapping of waterproof cloth. "To him, not the boy who keeps the counter."

"What if he's not in?"

"Wait for him."

"I was just getting comfortable," she says, sighing as she hauls her boots off the desk.

"It's fifty dollars a paper." Wheeler holds up the packet. "Plus our cut for the passage: eighty dollars per man, with eleven men coming through. Eleven hundred eighty dollars altogether. Count it when he pays."

She does the math, the waterproof cloth slick against her fingers.

"They don't all get a paper?"

"Ah Tong handles that," he says. "For those who can afford it."

Alma shrugs, tucks the packet into her vest, snug against her shirt and the binding cloth beneath.

"Come back when you've finished," Wheeler says, while she pulls on her cold jacket. "Without dawdling until sundown. Sloan's product needs preparing, and I don't trust you with my money."

Out in the streets, her face and hands whipped numb by the wind. Ah Tong is at the counter in his fragrant shop. She gives him the papers. Collects his money, handing back five dollars of it for a tin of hard candies, a packet of tea, an ivory-handled fan, and some firecrackers, shiny with foil. The sweets are for herself, the rest are presents for Nell. Mostly because Alma wants to meet Wheeler's expectations about spending his cash.

She takes the goods to her boardinghouse and is back at the offices in less than half an hour—a speedy time for the errand, not that Wheeler's needling about her lateness means a thing. Driscoll is away; the door unattended. Inside, voices are raised enough to be heard in the long part of the hall. Alma steps carefully, keeping to the edges of the carpet where the floorboards don't squeak, trying to pluck words from the heated blur of conversation.

"—a god damn embarrassment. And I hear about it from Tacoma, three days later?" This is Wheeler, tight voiced, furious, as she edges around the bend in the hall. "Don't shake your bloody head at me. This has thrice happened on your watch."

Another batch of tar gone missing. It has to be.

"Someone on his crew is swapping out the lading bills." This in a brogue thickened with anger, a shade higher than Wheeler's voice but otherwise its mirror. McManus. "Then the contents match the bills when they get to Tacoma. But not the inventory later."

"Take a look at the papers. They're all straight from the boss." A deep drawl. So Benson's in the office, too. "Your boys are the ones with access to the hold. The ones doing the ride-along."

"Not on this shipment," McManus says. "Barker was out. Lyle went to Tacoma."

Well, damn. Here's McManus, bold as brass, accusing Benson and his crew of the tar thefts. But Benson sticks to the warehouse side of things. And McManus's accusation doesn't hold much water if his own crew usually handles the shipments: as Wheeler noted, this is the third time product's gone missing en route to Tacoma.

"Lyle's straight," Benson says. "And he's too damn smart to try and fuck me over."

"Maybe you're too stupid to see it."

"You watch your mouth, you gimpy little shit."

Alma steps through the doorway, hoping McManus and Benson will come to blows. Hoping Wheeler will cringe to have her hear his men arguing like this, like a pair of schoolboys. The two men face the desk, Benson's thick body shielding her from Wheeler's view. McManus's fists tight at his sides, fingers flexing, pulsing white. Benson's thumbs hooked into his belt. McManus is ready for a fight and Benson doesn't seem bothered by the prospect. He is a solid mountain of a man, with a good eight inches on McManus— and no bad knee.

"You might want to keep it down," she says.

McManus whips around, his face blazing. Benson moves slower. Over the rise of his thick gut Wheeler comes into view, scowling.

"Otherwise all of Port Townsend's going to know you think he's a gimpy little shit." She shrugs at Benson. "Not that I disagree."

McManus lunges at her and Alma flips her knife out into the space between them. The flicker of steel makes him falter.

"Put your fucking fists away, Tommy." Wheeler rises from behind his desk, and his gaze, too, snags on the blade. "God damn it. And that knife."

Benson chuckles, shaking his head. Alma keeps her eyes on McManus as he backs off, one step, another, uneven, then she slips her knife back into its sheath and comes to stand between the men. Close enough to feel the heat of their bodies. Close enough to feel McManus's anger, a disturbance in the air, a potential. He's been told twice not to fight with her, and the words must be fraying, mere threads holding back his teeth, his fury. She is drawn to such displays. She wants to hold match to powder, just to see what happens.

"We'll talk about this later," Wheeler says. "Get back to work."

"Didn't you want—" McManus starts.

"No. Camp will meet you at Hoop and Barrow. Have the product ready for him."

Benson touches his cap, heads out the door first. McManus is hesitant, his eyes shifting between Alma and Wheeler, his nostrils flaring.

"What are you waiting on?" Wheeler says, and finally, jaw tight, McManus nods and leaves the office.

Alma closes the door—she has a new appreciation of the hallway's acoustic powers—and walks up to the desk.

"Let me guess," she says. "Another leak in the pipeline."

Wheeler gives a stiff nod.

"How much?"

"Sixty pounds of Wah Hing. Missing between here and Tacoma." His hand, flattened on an open ledger, curls into a fist. "McManus and Benson both swear up and down their crew is not responsible. But someone took that god damn tar. Again."

Lyle is the obvious culprit—the ride-along fellow, alone with the shipment for hours, then tasked with the handoff to the Tacoma broker. Lyle is on Benson's crew. But Driscoll was alone and elbow deep in the open trunk of tar. Driscoll is on McManus's crew. And McManus seemed to be on the defensive, accusing Benson outright like he did.

"This is on top of the thirty pounds we borrowed for Sloan?" she says.

"Yes."

She waits to see if he'll blame this on her and her plan for locking Sloan in—altering the shipment to take the thirty pounds, and so opening the whole batch to tampering, to uneven numbers. From the way Wheeler's glaring at her, he wants to blame her. But he pops his thumb knuckle in the vise of his fingers and stays quiet.

"Are you going to tell her?" she says.

"I want time to fix it first."

"I understand that. I hate looking like I can't do my job."

"Did you get the money?" He is scowling, hard lines bracketing the sides of his mustache.

She drops Ah Tong's payment onto the desk.

"I needed five dollars," she says.

"Don't make that a habit." Wheeler counts the bills. "It will ruin my bookkeeping."

"God help us."

He looks up, his mouth stretched into a cold smile.

"I don't know if you can do this job," he says. "It's a lot of paperwork. A lot of record keeping. Your inattention to detail gives me pause."

"I'll hire a clerk."

"No. You'll learn how to do it properly." He tucks the money into a drawer, locks it. "But not today. William Peterson needs a checkup."

Another runabout. He's sending her to and fro like a hired boy. It's not very egalitarian of him, but it gives her time to move freely—time for things like taking her new coded dispatch to the post office in secret. Until Delphine tells Wheeler about the Pinkerton's angle, Alma doesn't want him or his boys to notice her letter-sending habits. And Wheeler is following his orders, in a way. Each of his errands lets her trace a new line he's laid around town, the spider-web of connections that make moving product possible, the business's allies and enemies and key locations. Now that she's got a better handle on the ring—and more product has gone missing, making a fresh trail—she's ready to plunge in earnest into her investigation. William Peterson is just the man she wants to see.

"I'm tired of running your errands," she says, but doesn't put much heat into the words.

"Oh? Would you rather do a light bit of filing? Alphabetize the list of Clyde Imports' distilleries? Sit down for a while. Collate invoices."

"Jesus," Alma says. "No wonder you drink so much."

"You know where his yard is." Wheeler's voice, almost edged with amusement, flattens again. He holds up a scrap of paper. "Give him this, so he knows he can speak to you. See if the police have been back to visit, or if he's had other problems. And do not touch him."

"Or it will upset Clay, our tetchy bartender."

"Yes."

"Are they related? Cousins or something." She tucks the paper into her vest pocket. "Why the concern?"

"They're lovers." Wheeler opens a green ledger, its pages dense with rows of numbers. "It's not mentioned."

"How not mentioned is it?" she says. "Peterson's primed for blackmail with that. And he came off a little meek, the time I saw him. Not likely to stand up to pressure—from the cops, for instance."

"It's not at all mentioned," he says. "And it is prime blackmail material. Which is why I know it, and why Peterson quietly builds my boats."

"We're in a dirty game." A brief surge of conscience that she clamps down on, ignores. "The cops were last there on Friday?"

"As far as we know."

"All right. Don't threaten me with filing that again," she says, pointing at the paperwork on his desk.

He laughs, and it's not a strained sound. But he closes his mouth quick. Lowers his brows. She leaves him to his ledgers, pleased to have gotten to him at all, even if it was through a joke and not something sharper.

There is still lightness in her step when she walks onto Peterson's yard. It's a neat square of plankboards on the water, with a small dry dock and a slatted ramp descending into the bay. A modest boathouse. A keel, some fifteen feet long, is laid out crosswise at the center of the yard. Peterson didn't build Wheeler's special cutter here—there's not the space for a boat that size.

A gangly youth, his face dappled with pockmarks, sets down

the toolbox he's hauling across the yard. He approaches Alma, wiping his hands on his trousers.

"Can I help you, sir?" Up close, the boy has a bruise on one cheekbone. He looks to be about fourteen.

"I'm looking for Peterson," Alma says.

The boy's eyes darken. A ball-peen hammer hangs from his belt, and his fingers twitch toward its wooden handle.

"You have an order with us?" he says.

"No, son, I don't." She nods at the hammer. "But I'm not here to push you around—I hear you've had enough of that the past few days."

"Where's the fucking lathe?"

The call comes from the boathouse doorway. A tall, sandy-haired man walks into view, squinting against the light, wiping his forehead with his cap. This is Peterson, the big fellow smelling of pitch she barreled into in Wheeler's hallway. He recognizes her, too, she's sure—his eyes widen and his hand goes tight around the chisel he's holding.

"What do you want?" he says.

Alma walks past the boy, past the skeleton keel. Peterson's had a rough time of it. A purple bruise shows livid under the blond stubble of his chin, to one side, near the hinge of his jaw. Yellowness blooms under the skin all the way up to his ear.

"Let's talk." She gestures toward the dim interior of the boathouse.

"I'm done talking."

There is no insolence in Peterson's voice, just a deep tiredness. Alma doesn't see a need to push him. He's not going to give any sparks. She takes Wheeler's paper from her vest, holds it out. When Peterson unfolds it, his face slackens.

"Not until the boss says so," she tells him.

Peterson closes his eyes. Exhales. When he opens them, he's looking across the yard at the boy.

"Go get some lunch, Sam," he says.

Alma follows Peterson into the building's fragrance of sawdust and sap. A hull fills the center of the room, pale brown and beautiful, its planks tight-locked as a puzzle and freshly sanded.

"You have other men working here?" she asks.

"No."

She takes a turn around the hull anyway, admiring its lines, checking the room's dim corners. They are alone. Back in front of Peterson, the outside world reduced to a square of light in the doorway, she pulls off her cap.

"Mr. Wheeler's sorry for what McManus did," she says, and this is a lie, but a harmless one. "And I'm just here to ask some questions. Have the police come back, since Friday?"

"No."

"Why would they ask you about Max Beckett?"

"I don't know."

"Were you and Beckett friends?"

"I never met him."

"That's hard to imagine—the customhouse is just across the wharf."

Peterson is shaking his head, his broad shoulders slumped.

So that's Wheeler's questions, asked. Now for her own. If Wheeler has the damning lock he claims on Peterson and Clay, the boatbuilder should be scared enough without McManus resorting to his fists. And the day McManus thrashed him—it's the same day the sixty pounds of tar went missing. The boat came in after the beating. Still, the timing is suspicious. Especially since McManus had a chance to extract more than two cases from *Orion* if he had his pal Driscoll's help. Alma didn't get a good look at the kid as he fled the lower deck.

"Are you keeping any odd boxes you'd like to show me?" she says.

Peterson, already pale, goes gray, his mouth unsteady.

"No," he says.

She doesn't believe him for a second. She walks another circuit of the room, following its square edges. Under a drape of sailcloth: a clutch of stained paintbrushes. At the back of a dusty cubby: jumbled treenails. Spare boards, spars, broken files fill other crannies. A splinter jabs deep into Alma's thumb as she runs a hand under a counter. She sucks at it, hot salt blood on her tongue, her eyes hard on the sweating, ashen carpenter.

"You're not telling me everything," she says after her search turns up nothing closer to tar than a crate of old paint cans. "Is McManus hiding something here?"

"No."

"Is that why he beat you?"

"No."

"Can you say anything other than 'no'?" she says, and the way he cringes away from her has her lip curling.

"I just want to do my job," he says. "I've always done good work for Mr. Wheeler."

"What is this you're building here?" She nods at the hull.

"A salmon dory." Peterson wipes his forehead with his mangled cap.

"For who?"

"A salmon fisherman."

Alma has to laugh. She licks the insides of her teeth, shaking her head. Peterson does not smile. He looks so tired, so beaten down. If McManus has scared him this well, it's unlikely her patter of questions is going to crack through that fear.

"You built Mr. Wheeler's cutter?"

"Yes, sir."

"It's a beautiful boat," she says, throwing him a bit of warmth, a bit of praise to draw out his craftsman's pride. But his face doesn't change—doesn't lift or loosen. He swallows hard.

"This yard is too small for that cutter," she says. "Do you have another?"

"Yes, sir. In Irondale, just down the bay a ways."

Irondale. Why does she know that name? It sounds with a clink of glass—no, a clink of coins. Poker tables: fold, call. "Call me Mr. Kopp." Kopp, the railroad promoter, saying, "I'm heading to Irondale." And he said it to Max Beckett.

"You sure you never met Max Beckett?" she says.

"Not that I know of."

A final angle. Since Wheeler told her not to use her fists, she'll go for something else that hurts.

"How about Malcolm Clay," she says. "You know him?"

Peterson blinks, tucks his hands into his pockets. His breathing speeds. His tells are as glaring as a lighthouse beacon, poor over-matched bastard.

"Clay?" he says. "The bartender? I drink at Chain Locker sometimes. Who doesn't."

"I don't," she says. "But maybe Beckett did. I ought to go see Clay and ask him."

At the door she stops, fixing on her cap against the sunlight flowing low over the rooftops of Upper Town.

"You sure you've got nothing else to tell me?"

Peterson, alone in the dimness, closes his eyes.

"No," he says.

The inside of the church smells of cold stone and wood varnish. Alma walks down the aisle toward the candle chapel, the rustle of her skirts a reminder to walk slow, to take the swagger out of her gait. Her skin heavy with powder. Her ears conjuring old rites in the echoes of her footsteps. Heel, toe. Droning Latin chains of sound. It's been years since she made the sign of the cross. If she blessed herself incorrectly at the back of the church, at least there is no one to see—it is Monday, midafternoon, and the pews are empty. Delphine stands alone at the bank of votives, a flickering taper in one ungloved hand.

"Let's not make a habit of this," she says, quiet, when Alma stops beside her.

"I don't plan on it," Alma says. "You know French chalk makes my head ache."

Delphine's perfume is a welcome distraction from the powder's sugary scent. Alma leans closer to her as she reaches for a taper. Candlelight plays on the long column of Delphine's neck, her skin cinnamon brown against a dark lace collar.

"What is so urgent?"

"I wanted to see you." Alma crosses herself again, trying out another sequence of movements and deciding she had it right the first time.

"Rosales. I already stand out too much for my liking, and I can't encourage suspicious visitors," Delphine says. "I shouldn't have to explain the consequences of us being seen together, and how little wanting to see each other justifies the risk."

A mutual wanting. Alma lights the taper. Holds it to a votive until flame leaps.

"What are the terms of my promotion?"

"The terms?" Delphine is facing forward, hands clasped, as if in prayer. Her voice pitched so low it is barely a whisper.

"Wheeler says he's training me to be his replacement."

"Yes."

"He says if he doesn't move up, I don't move up."

Now Delphine looks at her, a sideways glance, one eyebrow quirking. A red-and-gold patch of light from the stained-glass windows gilds the sharp line of her jaw, the full curve of her lips. She is smiling.

"Don't be greedy," she says. "Everyone deserves a reward for a job well done."

"He ought to be working for me," Alma says. "I can find the leak faster if I'm in charge, uncontested."

Delphine's mouth takes a harder shape.

"Did you bring me here to complain about having to cooperate with a partner?" she says.

"No. I asked to meet you because I'm tired of knowing half the information I need to know." Alma pinches out the flame on the taper's end. "I can't be efficient that way. What is your plan?"

Delphine takes up her lit taper, lays it against another candle's wick. In the pause Alma adjusts her dirty shawl, using the movement to glance behind them. All empty gleaming pews. No movement at the door. The confessional a latticed block of shadow against the near wall.

"You're being trained to do Nathaniel's job." Delphine shakes out the taper. "But not here. In Tacoma."

"Tacoma?"

The city where the organization's tar is unloaded and sent to dealers all over the country via railroad. Distribution central: the real heart of things.

"I'm sure by now he's filled you in on the situation there."

"The inefficient situation," Alma says. "I don't like middlemen."

"I agree. And I'm eager to hear all your ideas for improvements, once you've taken your new position as Tacoma deputy."

Delphine sifts through her reticule. Slides a handful of small coins into the wooden donation box. Alma drops a coin in, too, regretting her choice of meeting place. No food, no drink. Delphine not meeting her gaze full on, adding to the obscure sense that Alma is in trouble for something—a vague guilt cued by the massive wooden crucifix and the echoes of the Paternoster.

"You vetted the organization. You're tracking the missing product," Delphine says, draping her gloves over one wrist as she loops closed the laces of her purse. "And while you do so, I want you to learn from Nathaniel. You don't have much experience with . . . desk work."

Alma clasps her hands under her chin, trying not to laugh because Delphine is right. The powder is coming off between her fingers, the insides of her knuckles showing darker, pitch stained. This meeting was worth the risk—she is learning the purpose of Delphine's maneuvers—but she is eager to strip off the itchy cotton skirt, the cloying powder, and duck back into Camp's clothes.

"Once you've studied that part of the job, and the two of you have solved our problems here, you'll move up," Delphine says. "Organize our new Tacoma outpost. It's what you want: autonomy, legwork."

She makes the sign of the cross and steps toward the aisle, turning to Alma at last. Under her bonnet her dark hair is curled away from her face in thick braids. The windows' rainbow light is bright in her eyes, soft against the planes of her face. She looks younger in the parti-colored glow.

"I've had you in mind for this for some time," Delphine says. "William Pinkerton was a fool to throw you out into the street. But I thank him for delivering me such a talent."

Alma likes this promotion. She likes that Delphine planned this for her; that Delphine has been thinking about her in the long years they've been apart. She wants to reach up and stroke the other woman's cheek. But that door might be shut. They have not touched since Alma came to town.

"You'll be my chief deputy." Delphine's purse clinks with coins as she pulls on her gloves. "You can do the job as Camp, if you like. And perhaps, once you're settled, you could reach out to some of your old friends. The more women in my employ, the better."

"From the Women's Bureau?"

Delphine nods, smiling again. A hot shiver washes over Alma's skin. Here's an offer Delphine has never made before. William Pinkerton shuttered the women's division in 1884, after his father died; old man Pinkerton had seen the genius of female agents, but his son William had never liked the concept. Alma doesn't know what became of the other spies—after Hannah's death in Yuma and Alma's subsequent dismissal, she drifted away from her fellow agents, ashamed—but a few of them would like this work. The rougher women. The women who didn't mind breaking rules and didn't have much love for William. The idea of seeing them again, after almost ten years, is a thrill and a worry all at once.

"I want to make you happy, Rosales."

Alma shakes her head. She does love to hear the other woman say her name.

"You want to make me happy?" Alma steps closer, so she has to tilt her chin up to meet Delphine's eyes. "Because this all suits me fine. But I have a few other suggestions."

"Not in church, you don't."

Delphine sweeps past, jasmine perfume and flickering jewelry, her bootheels ringing on the stone floor.

"What's Wheeler getting, to make him happy?"

"Do not ask for me like this again, unless there's an emergency," Delphine says, over her shoulder. "The town is too small to risk discovery. Have Nathaniel send a message. Or Nell, since you've clearly made some inroads in that direction."

"No need to be jealous." Alma's not sure what to feel strongest between the stings of irritation and the tempting sense that Delphine is, finally, flirting with her. "Now that I know the terms, I'm all yours."

Hoop & Barrow is lit up like a slat lantern, candle glow streaming from its gappy clapboards. Rain glitters as it passes through these bands of light, riding sideways on a strong wind that numbs Alma's hands and feet despite her lined pockets, despite her woolen socks. Sparks crackle from a pair of chimneys that throw pine-scented smoke into the blow.

She sits just inside Hoop & Barrow's woodshed, which is sheltered from shore view by its three walls and set back from the wharf behind the saloon. Her seat is a beat-up, unmarked crate the size of a fat sheep, its wood peeling with splinters. It is worth $230, untaxed. In Tacoma it'll fetch $540. In San Francisco, it's worth almost triple the untaxed price. Twenty-nine and a half pounds of Wah Hing brand opium. Neatly packed and ready to hand over to Sloan.

Spare logs are arranged behind her boots, so if someone unwanted stops by, she's simply a man hunched in the shed, perched on the saloon's lumber pile to stay out of the wind.

She can't see Driscoll, but he is posted by the saloon's rear door, to run interference should a keeper come out to fetch kindling. Otherwise it's her and the gale and the crate, her hands too cold to even fumble with her watch and check the time. It should be near on nine thirty; she was only five minutes early, even though it feels like she's been sitting in the frigid shed for hours.

Her thoughts, ice slippery, keep sliding between Tacoma and Sloan's men and McManus. The Tacoma deal even more enticing the more she mulls over it. A job in the place she considers the supply chain's most important link, with a handpicked crew of the best women and men willing to do black-market work. This handoff the next step toward that prize. So where are Sloan's men? Where did McManus go after dropping off the product? Is his mystery woman a cover for another kind of sneaking? Will Sloan's men have the money neat and easy to count or try for a distraction with something amateur like a jumbled bag of cash? Is McManus the leak, or is she jumping onto a suspicion with too much certainty? She likes to trust her hunches, but she's not been flawless in Port Townsend: her first instinct, after vetting her three marks, was to pin Sloan as Delphine's deputy. Ever since Yuma there's been the nagging specter of what can happen when she runs in, guns blazing, only to find she's guessed wrong.

Boots on the boards, vibrations shaking up her shins before she can hear the footfalls. A man steps into the square frame of the woodshed's front. His eyes are narrowed under a sopping cap, his hands hidden in a tarpaulin jacket. Alma waits for the second man, the second set of footsteps. This one she recognizes: Loomis, the egg-eyed tough from Sloan's boardinghouse, lower lip still fat with tobacco, ruined nose dark red in the dim light.

"Evening, lads," she says, flexing life back into her hands in her pockets, the joints sticky. But if she's cold and slow, so are the men.

"Camp," Loomis says. "You have the tar?"

"You have the money?"

The first man takes his hands from his pockets—empty, pale in fingerless wool gloves—and reaches under his tarpaulin. He pulls out an envelope, waxed against the damp, and holds it out to Alma. She takes it. Undoes the flap. Inside are three notes stamped by the Citizens Bank of Oregon. She slides one out with a fingertip. It is signed for one hundred dollars. She closes the envelope and holds it up, her jaw tight.

"Deal's off," she says. "Those aren't United States Notes, and I don't take other currency from first-time customers."

"What do you fucking mean it's off," the man says, not taking the envelope.

"Get out of here," she says. "If you don't have the money how I want it, I've got nothing for you."

The man slaps the envelope aside. Its waxed white shape slides over the mossy boards. Neither man moves to retrieve it, which makes pretty clear the papers inside aren't worth shit. He reaches into his coat again, but Alma, still seated, has her gun out now, aimed square at his groin. This is going badly. Sloan either has no interest in this arrangement or he's testing her—testing to see if she knows her stuff or if she will be an easy mark. Alma doesn't like tests.

"Is this really how you want to kick off our new partnership?" she says to the man before her. "You: gelded. Me: closed for business."

"Here's the fucking money."

Loomis reaches under his coat, works an envelope out of his

vest. Alma holds it with one hand, her other still training the pistol at the first man, who's gone cheese colored and quiet. She almost drops the envelope—her cold fingers not quite closing around its sides—but gets it into her lap, where she can pry it open. Three bundles of United States Notes. She lifts one bundle out, counts ten tens, holds it to her nose. It is crisp and smells proper. That's the way she's learned to do it, after six years in the business. Fresh cash has a certain smell, a starchy paperiness with the tang of ink. Well-handled bills keep some of that scent, too, but should also smell of sweat, of dirt, of copper.

"Tell Sloan I want one hundred dollars extra next time." Alma fingers through the rest of the cash, tallying it to the expected total. "To make up for this shit."

"Where's the tar?" Loomis says.

"I'm sitting on it," she says. "And pick up your trash before you go. If someone finds three hundred in false notes behind Hoop and Barrow, it'll ruin this spot for good."

She keeps her gun out, tucks the cash into her vest. Standing from the crate is difficult. Her legs are stiff, and the sense of peeling away from all that product is tangible. But she pushes past the men—a breathless moment when they might grab her, might flick a blade into her side—then she is through their thick bodies and into the rain, a freezing sheet over her chin, her still-tender neck. She walks toward Hoop & Barrow, its lights and crowds and music. Footsteps behind her. Her spine tenses. She glances over her shoulder and it's Driscoll, gliding along fifteen paces behind. Her lungs fill a little more deeply. She takes the long way round Washington Street toward Wheeler's offices. Cash counted and stowed tight. One step closer to Tacoma. Satisfaction bubbling in her stomach.

17

JANUARY 18, 1887

"'You, gelded. Me, done with you cunts.'"

"He didn't say that."

"Oh, yes, he did. Cool as a fucking cucumber."

Alma sits on the carpet, her back against the blue wall. Greasy paper in her lap. A kidney pie dripping gravy down her fingers.

"You were too damn close if you heard that," she tells Driscoll, who is relating the handoff, with embellishments, to Conaway.

They are gathered in the hall, sharing a late breakfast and Driscoll's flask. Outside a light snow is falling. Wheeler is away at one of his gentlemen's meetings in Upper Town. Sloan's money has been counted, double-checked, and locked away. He paid in full for his first crate of company tar. Now all he has to do is smear it all over himself, and Delphine's trap is baited.

"I got nervous when they threw that envelope," Driscoll says, taking a nip of whiskey. "So I split the difference between the pub and the woodshed."

"Next time stay where you're meant to." Alma shoves the last of the pie into her mouth, buttery crust sticking to her lips. "Are there any more?"

"I got one for the boss," Conaway says.

"He's feasting on ham and soft-boiled eggs." Alma holds out her hand, not getting up. "Champagne. Caviar. Oysters on the half shell."

"I heard they have steaks four inches thick at the new club on the hill," Driscoll says.

"You excited about four inches?"

Conaway fends off the boy's swatted punch, chuckling, and hands Alma the pie. Its greasy paper wrapping is translucent in the light falling through the cracked door. She unwraps it and bites into the crust. A seep of warm beef and butter.

"Put my bet down this morning," Driscoll says, giving Conaway the flask. "It's at ten to two, Mac's favor."

"I've got a few dollars on the stranger, myself," Conaway says.

"Sneaky bastard!"

"If he wins, I'll be rolling in cash. Enough to try out that steak you're talking up."

"Might not be a bad bet," Alma says, around her mouthful of food. "The Tacoma man is undefeated."

The Macaulay-Dobbs match is set for the next evening, and the waterfront is alight with it: bets piling up in favor of Mac; rumors of men filtering in from Tacoma, looking for trouble.

"He's never fought Mac before," Conaway says. "Three times he's been invited, and this the first he's stepped to the scratch. I think he's shy."

"Oh, you go tell him so, John," Driscoll says, laughing. "Go tell that big strapping bastard he's shy."

"I might," Conaway says.

"The fuck you will," Alma says.

"I haven't seen a good set-to since '85, when Dempsey came to Portland to fight Campbell," Conaway says, shrugging off their jeers. "On an island in the river, all rain and sleet. The second match was something—a couple of local crimps, London Prize Ring rules, beating each other to ribbons. Three men were killed after that, one with a fucking crate. God's truth. Some bastard smashed it over his head, then stabbed him with one of the slats."

"Christ Jesus," Driscoll says.

"I was at the Goss-Allen championship, outside Cincinnati," Alma says. "In '76."

"You weren't," Conaway says.

"Waited in line for six hours to catch the train to the secret spot," she says. "By the time we got to the pitch there were bloody noses everywhere, swelling eyes. My pal lost a tooth."

Her memories of that day are hazy, blurred by adrenaline and thirst and a good dose of fear. She and Ned braved the chaos together. Alma was still new to men's clothes, with no fights of her own under her belt. That trip was the most dangerous thing she'd ever done. Sweating in her starched trousers on the long ride to Cincinnati, then jostling into the queue for the Louisville Short Line. She didn't drink anything for two days beforehand because once they boarded the Louisville train there would be nowhere safe to piss for hours.

"You're bloody old," Driscoll says, but not without jealousy. It was a classic match. Every sporting man knows the statistics, the big punches, how the fight was busted up halfway through by cops so the final rounds had to be moved to another farmer's field.

Alma finishes her beef pie, crinkles up the wrapper. She tilts her head back against the wall, listening to Driscoll and Conaway banter with half an ear, letting her eyes slide shut. She is warm and full. She wants something sweet to chase the buttery crusts. Sugared pineapple. Nell's caramels.

"Here's Mr. Wheeler," Driscoll whispers at her side, and she blinks, snapping awake, unaware she had been dozing.

"It's a fine fucking morning," Wheeler says at the dogleg, slapping snow off his hat.

Alma rubs the heel of her hand into her eyes, squinting up at him. When he catches sight of her, sprawled drowsy on the carpet and spackled with pie crumbs, his smile doesn't wrinkle. He nods at the three of them before walking back down the hall to his office. She looks at Driscoll and Conaway, both of them slack-jawed, then scrambles to her feet, brushing off her jacket.

Here's a sound she's never heard coming from Wheeler's offices: whistling. It's a song she knows from her days in Glasgow. "Brochan Lom," a lilting, cheerful tune.

"Where's the party?" she asks, leaning against the jamb.

"At A. J. Hamilton's." Wheeler is at the armoire, taking off his diamond cuff links. "I dined with him last night. And this morning. As of nine twenty, I, am on, the trust papers."

He punctuates this last sentence with sharp little jerks on his sleeve, rolling it up and back to sit just below his elbow. Alma notes the openness of the gesture—today, at least, he is prepared to un-peel a layer or two.

"So are you rich yet?" she says, amused. Readier to smile with her own promotion on the horizon.

"I'm already rich." He starts on the other sleeve. "Now I'm respectable."

"Think of us commoners when you're on the hill," she says. "Throw down a scrap of bread from time to time."

"Maybe on a Sunday. The day of charity." He slides into his chair. "Though I don't know if it's the Lord's work or the devil's, keeping you lot alive."

"Too good for us already."

Shaking her head, Alma comes into the office, closes the door behind her. Wheeler is watching her more carefully now, tracking her progress to the liquor board. She deliberately pours two whis-keys. Carries them to his desk and sets them at the edge, staying out of his space. A reassurance. An echo of the other day minus the aggression. *You can relax*, it says. *You can trust me.* Since it's not his post she's ascending to, there's no sense in trying to kick him out of it—and cooperating with him just might get the leak solved sooner. He's in a good mood, and it will be best to keep him that way. She wants to find out if he's uncovered anything about the missing tar. Despite Delphine's orders about working together, he has a habit of keeping things to himself. Not that Alma's telling him everything.

"Congratulations," she says, raising her tumbler.

"I hear Driscoll's been busy making you into legend since last night." He tips his own glass in her direction.

"I should have shot them," she says. "If we didn't need Sloan on the hook, I might have. Showing up to the handoff and pulling that shit."

"He's an amateur. It makes him unpredictable. He could go too far afield, and it will make the product a beast to track."

"Where is there to unload it locally?"

"Ah Tong knows to not buy anything from him." Wheeler sips

his whiskey, sets it aside to flip through some papers. He pauses, works out a square handbill. "This is a new spot, opened a few months ago. Run by a merchant called Sing Tai. Otherwise there are a few small dens set behind the laundries, owned by China-men. And a scabrous little hovel on the south end of town."

The bill is hand-lettered in English, with a lotus flower unfurl-ing at the top. *Tea. Silk. Opium. Fine Imports.* Along the bottom, tiny and intricate, a row of characters.

"Let me guess: you can read it, too," Wheeler says, nodding at the handbill.

Alma grins, tucks the paper into her vest pocket. She never learned to read the calligraphy, but Wheeler doesn't need to know that. He is bent over another sheet, marking long lines, writing beside them. She finishes her whiskey as he works.

"For your rounds." He slides the paper over the desk. It's a sketched map of town, with each location marked in clear script.

"The boys are all talking about the fight tomorrow." She sets her glass on the desk, leans back in her chair. "You ought to have them draw straws to see who's on duty; otherwise they might mutiny."

If he registers her suggestion of insubordination as she means him to—a reminder of the leak—he doesn't show it.

"Fulton's volunteered," he says. "He tells me he's too old for all that."

"And at Quincy?"

"Benson."

Wheeler's leather chair creaks as he reaches over the desk for his ashtray. Clips the end off a cigar. Alma works at a thread of beef caught in her back molars. Match flare, then bitter smoke, vanilla richness, drift over her.

"Who's your money on?" she says when he doesn't give her any-thing else about his two bickering crew leads.

"I haven't thrown in."

"You don't like the sport?"

It doesn't seem possible, not for a man who moves like a fighter. Who's formed like a fighter. Is he that much of a track-and-tally bookkeeper that he won't bet? And on a fight like this, that's been brewing for years.

"I don't like this Queensberry nonsense," he says. "Back in my day it wasn't over till your man didn't get up."

"I knew it," Alma says, warm with a rush of satisfaction and fellow feeling—she called him right at the start, ten days ago, when she first shadowed him in town. "I knew you were a pug, from the first time I saw you, leaving that theater."

Forget the leak for a minute. She wants to know which matches he's seen. How he fared in the ring. At his size, fifteen years before and a bit trimmer, he'd make a damn good middleweight.

"What was your punch?" she says. "Your favorite to throw?"

"Are you a boxing fan?" he says, with a peculiar grimace that seems halfway between a grin and a sneer, as if it could teeter into either in a second. "You do seem the sort who'd sneak into matches. Drinking and shouting with the fancy, for whatever thrill that seems to give you."

"Oh, I drank, and I shouted." Alma sits up straighter in her chair, squaring off her shoulders, taking up more space. "But I wasn't just betting. I saw those ropes from the inside out."

"You're lying." Wheeler loosens his tie. "They don't let women fight, not in any civilized places—that's a relic of the forties."

"I fought as Camp. Made up the name for my first match."

"Impossible."

"Not at the dives I went to," she says. "They wouldn't turn away a featherweight in a flannel shirt as long as he paid the fee."

Something about his tie, half-knotted; something about the way they are easily, naturally talking about her as Camp and Alma, at the same time, not as an oddity but simply a body, a fighting body; something about the set of Wheeler's face, that tight satisfaction from earlier edging into a different kind of keenness. Unsettled air between them. Fire in his eyes as he draws on his cigar. She imagines herself as he must be imagining her, dressed as Camp and in the ring: sweat on her breasts beneath the dirty undershirt; a good punch connecting, so that her nerves sing and her nipples tighten.

"Always brought a second who knew my ways," she says.

Alma leans forward in her chair, sits splay-kneed. Rests her elbows on her thighs. She drops her eyes to a callus on her palm, peeling back the whitened skin, then glances up at Wheeler to see how he's taking her story, her posture. He is still amused, but now his gaze is jerky; a minute, constant refocus from her open legs to her face.

She is pleased by his reaction. Pleased she can still keep him off-balance. Though power has nearly equalized between them, they are still fighting that unspoken, darkly currented fight between her hunger and his, between her jabs and whatever is holding him back from coming at her with his fists, with his mouth. He is deliberate, she's learned that. Apt to sit there and ruminate for a frustrating length of time.

"Usually walked out on my own," she says. "With some money in my pocket."

Now Wheeler laughs openly, a deep rumble.

"Go on, tell me another." He is in control of his voice, if not his wandering eyes.

"I could hand you your bollocks," she says, tumbling into his brogue, into the street-boy banter she learned to mimic in Glasgow. "You'd be supping on sowans for days till your jaw got back on right."

His face twitching between amusement and sharpness and something she can't read, a softer emotion that hovers around his eyes. It's not the wistfulness he displayed while getting to know her as Alma Macrae, but close to it. She watches him, waiting to see what he'll do, which mood will prevail, but then Conaway is knocking at the door, calling out there's a parcel for Mr. Wheeler.

The thread between them snaps. Wheeler lets out a mouthful of smoke. Alma opens the door. Conaway is waiting outside, a brown package the size of a bread box in his hands.

"Expecting something?" she asks Wheeler.

"In fact, I am."

She takes the box from Conaway. On the side that was pressed to his body is a neat row of canceled stamps. The box came Special Delivery. From Missoula, Montana Territory.

"Didn't know you had friends in cow country," she says, setting the box on Wheeler's desk.

"I do now," he says.

"After the dens—do you need me tonight?"

JANUARY 18, 1887   **197**

She is close enough that the lip of the desk pushes into her thighs. The phrasing, the set of her hips, are intentional. If they are easing back into their game, she will play it.

"No," he says, cigar at his mouth.

The muscles in his exposed forearm twitch. He is tensing his hand. Walking a fine edge, as she is.

"I have a meeting with the trustees." He taps ash into the glass tray. "Until late."

"And you're still keeping mum on the sixty-pound problem."

"Are you going to report me?"

"Not if you keep me informed," she says. "We're supposed to be working together."

"So I've been told," Wheeler says, with a half twitch of a grin. "Tom spoke to Lyle. He gave an exact account of the ride-along and handoff. There was a weather delay in Seattle, but Lyle claims it was otherwise an uneventful trip."

"Have you had problems with Lyle before?"

"I don't mingle with the second-tier crews. Tom finds him a solid man, generally. And he was not the ride-along when the other thefts happened."

"All right," she says. "See you in the morning. You know where to look for me if something comes up."

Out into the hall, past Driscoll on his own and shadowboxing. He goes red in the ears when she whistles, claps him on the shoulder, says, "You'll be the next Mac with that uppercut, kid." Out into the street, ground uncertain with ice. Wind on her bruises, on the bared slice of skin at her throat. Wheeler's map in her pocket, but she can go anywhere. Butter pie crusts, sugar chasers, rise out of the always-waiting appetites that keep her prowling. She turns southwest on Water Street toward Nell's shop. Nell is not as useful a liaison as Alma had hoped, but she has other charms. Alma stops to buy a stalk of tuberose tied with silk ribbon, then a paper bag of caramels. Snow drifts over her jaw as she walks, the paper bag crackling, the pink-tipped buds breathing honeyed musk. Cart wheels crunch through frozen mud. Boys crouch in alleyways, sharing cigarettes and shivering.

"Jack be nimble," Delphine had said, when she first found Nell.

A scene so near to how she first found Alma, seven years ago. Still reeling from Yuma, its body count on her bill. Not finding much in the detective line with her Pinkerton's agent's badge vanished. San Francisco all grit and edges, her rooms shrinking to a borrowed closet, shrinking to a stolen cot as money ran low and her dresses coarsened. Then meeting John Devine, who ran with a fencing crew, where everyone was slippery, playing three angles at once. A chance to visit the Nob Hill house where the queen of thieves was rumored to hold court. At the house trying to sell a paste necklace to a beautiful woman whose red lips were painted to match her red dress, and the woman saying in a luscious Southern drawl, "Oh, dear, you must be new at this."

That kicked off the wild days, stale bread and water one night, an invitation to a champagne feast the next. Quick-tongued and hungry in Delphine's bed. Then some betrayal brought the law to Nob Hill, policemen breaking down the gilded door. Delphine was not home. She had disappeared and was rumored to be dead. A long period of shock, Alma's days blurred with gin. Scraping by. Until, nearly a year later, the note: *Go to Zhu Kang's shop at North Point.* There, Zhu handing her a jangling box, telling her where to run it and for how much. "Who's behind this?" she asked, not wanting to hope but hoping. "*Geem nuey lhoo,*" he'd said. Then translated, "The golden lady." Delphine's nickname, for her warm-brown complexion, and for the filigreed ornaments that sparkled on her ears, her neck, her wrists.

At Nell's blue door she knocks. Tuberose pressed soft and fragrant against her bound chest. No footsteps; no movement in the narrow, curtained window. Alma tries once more. Unwraps a caramel to leaven her disappointment. Browned butter in her teeth as she loops the flowers' ribbon over the doorknob. The caramels she pockets for herself, then digs out Wheeler's map.

The closest den, from his reckoning, is the flophouse at the south end of town. Not far from the lodgings where Max Beckett breathed his last. Alma picks her way along the same ruined road, the same pebbly stretch of beach, all of it as bleak in the gray daylight as it was under the moon. A neat X on the paper indicates a low-roofed scrap-board shanty. Even upwind Alma can smell it from fifteen feet away: coal-fire char, cloying smoke, unwashed bodies laid out for hours to sweat and moan.

Inside, threadbare blankets line the floor; six of them, arranged side by side. Two white men, in denim jackets and peeling leather boots, occupy the spots along the far wall. Their faces and hands pallid. Despite the noisy brazier the room is freezing. Another white man, sinewy, face cragged, stands from beside the brazier and points her to a mat. Alma is used to the city dens, operated and mostly frequented by Chinese. Standing in this cold shack feels like a memory corrupted, as if she were hearing a familiar song in which the lyrics have changed.

"How much?" she says, not sitting down.

"A dollar a pipe."

"That's cheap. What kind is it?"

He scratches his ear. Scuffles about on a low shelf and hands her an open can, the paper label splotched with reuse, the dark lump inside smelling of cane sugar. Cut with molasses. The markings on the can are not from any refinery she knows, and in any case its contents are several substances removed from the original.

"You don't have anything else?"

"What's wrong with that?" The man has blackened gums, a toothless slur. "Lights up just fine."

"I'll bet."

Sloan's not been here. Not yet. Though it's doubtful this den's man would pay nine dollars a can even if Sloan did come selling. The thirdhand trash she's holding probably costs half that, with the recycled can and the cutting.

She hands him the tar. Shoulders back out into the snowy wind. The flakes are thickening as the day goes on, from the morning's icy dust to a fat whiteness. She opens her mouth as she walks back up the beach, breathing deep the clean cold air, catching clots of ice to melt on her tongue.

The shop that produced the handbill is at the opposite end of town. Tucked into a row of Chinese laundries, the sandstone cliff rising behind. Sing Tai's is done up in the style of Ah Tong's shop, though it is only half its size. The same red banners ripple in the wind, framing a window stocked with plucked-bare ducks and jarred spices. Inside, smells of chili paste and dried shrimp. Sing is doing brisk business—groups of men converse as they sort through piled silk shirts, share newspapers. The shop's opium is stacked by the front window. A dozen half-pound cans of Wah Hing anchor the display. Sloan's made his first sale.

"You carry Wah Hing," she says, taking a can up to the counter.

"Ah," the shopkeep says. "A discerning gentleman."

"How much?"

"Eleven dollars."

"That's a Portland price," she says.

"If you know the brand, you know it is worth the cost."

"Are you Sing Tai?"

He bows, and she sets the can on the wood before him.

"Where'd you buy that?" she says, nodding at the tar. Double-checking her proof for Wheeler. It's beautiful when a plan works out, and even more so when she gets to report that success.

"I have trusted suppliers, sir," he says.

"That's not what I asked you."

Sing's pleasant smile goes brittle at the edges. He lays both hands on the counter. The conversation around them quieting. They are the same height, and he meets Alma's eyes directly, coolly. He's not getting nervous as quick as she wants.

"You've been open a few months," she says. "So I can understand if you're still learning the ropes around here. But I'll tell you that a smuggling Chinaman doesn't have a snowball's chance in hell of avoiding the law. I'll have you shut down and cleaned out if you don't cooperate. Where'd you buy that."

Now the store is silent, save for the crinkling of a newspaper being closed.

"I purchased ten pounds at auction," he says, still standing tall. "In Seattle."

The swell of Alma's satisfaction is punctured, withers.

"For how much?" She's hoping to catch him in a lie if Sloan was here, after all, and left instruction to keep his presence quiet.

"One hundred dollars."

"You're telling me you bought Wah Hing for ten dollars a pound," she says, almost laughing. He must be lying, after all—and not lying well, either, by claiming he got the stuff at such an obscene discount. "Show me the receipt."

He kneels behind the counter, rummages. As he stands, he hands Alma a neat bill of sale, marked January 4, 1887. Ten pounds of Wah Hing, at ten dollars a pound. Stamped by the auction house. She stares at the paper, the various official seals, the embossed stationery.

"I was surprised by the price, myself," Sing says. "I took a risk in buying it; other merchants thought it was counterfeit. But I stand by the legality of my purchase. I also have documentation of my trip to the Seattle auction, sir, which I will take to the marshal in my defense, if you provoke me further. I will not be accused of smuggling."

Damn it. Sloan hasn't been here. Stranger still, the partner refinery only produces Wah Hing for Delphine, and Delphine doesn't sell to Seattle. Not at auction, especially—too much publicity—and never at such cut-rate prices. Wah Hing goes to Portland at eighteen dollars a pound; to San Francisco at twenty-two.

Sing's product didn't come from Sloan. And it was sold before the most recent theft. There's only one other source: it could be part of the forty-five pounds lost en route to Tacoma in December the previous year. Or it's fake.

"My apologies," Alma tells Sing, and counts out eleven dollars. "I spoke out of line. I'll take that can."

At the window display she inspects the can's paper label for signs of tampering. Behind her, conversations pick up again, too low and blurred to untangle. If the can has been doctored, it was flawlessly done, down to the die-cut stamps on its brass sides. She flips out her knife, slices along the seal. It smells like Wah Hing—sweet and pulpy, toasted-hazelnut richness. Looks all right, too: a solid dark lump. Pure Patna tar.

The flash of metal against glass draws her gaze to her shadow figure upon the pane, square can held at her ribs. Past her reflection, the dimming clouds, a crowd of men on the Seamen's Bethel stoop, builders carting lumber up from the sawmill to the opera house that's under construction on the next block. Close behind them, a familiar gait. Shoulders up. Dragging limp. It's McManus.

He walks toward Sing Tai's. Alma tucks her chin so her cap shadows her eyes, though the sunset glaring on the window should keep her masked enough. She slides the tar into her jacket pocket. Her exit from the store is timed to match when McManus is passing. He continues south, toward the Upper Town stairs, but as she watches from the corner of the building, he cuts into an alleyway that threads behind Sing Tai's.

Wheeler doesn't sell here. There's no reason for McManus to be paying a call.

She walks to the mouth of the alleyway. Narrow, all dim, all still, after it swallowed him. In between the buildings, out of the wind, the air smells of lye and steam, the pitchy smoke of pinewood fires. At the end of the short passage an old woman is elbow deep in a wash bucket. Hair tied back in a calico cloth. Face spotted and deeply lined. She works silently, stares right through Alma as if she were a ghost, her eyes wet and white clouded.

"*M'on, aah paw*," Alma says as she passes, and the woman's head tilts upward—not her eyes, but her ear.

"*M'on, lhain sang*," she says.

Leaving the woman to her washing—her wrinkled skin bright pink under the water—Alma follows the bend in the alley, now listening closely under the snaps of hanging laundry, under the hiss of steam that billows through slatted windows set just above her head.

"Not today. He needs help in the store."

It's a woman's voice, close by, quiet. Alma flattens herself against the wall and inches forward. This is a bad place to be sneaking. No corners to hide in, all the flapping sheets giving an illusion of space, of distance, but the alley is barely four feet across with no breaks in the walls. A few snowflakes drift through the narrow opening overhead. She edges into sight of a closed door. An escape route. Maybe.

"Pretend you're unwell. Anything."

Alma stiffens. McManus's voice is so close it sounds like he's whispering to her. She turns her head. Presses her cheek to the wall her shoulder blades are already pressed to, and peers through the thin gap between the next hanging sheet and the clapboards. Three feet away are McManus and a Chinese woman. She is young. Black hair in a glossy bun, bare throat pale against the gray silk of her jacket. Jade bracelets on her wrists.

"We are too busy," she says. "Sing will look for me."

McManus bends to press his mouth to her hands. Pushes aside her bracelets, her long sleeves, to kiss the blue-veined flesh of her inner forearms. So this is Mary. Not at all who Alma was expecting. And if she's in the alley behind Sing Tai's store, worried about a man called Sing looking for her, it's likely she's the shopkeep's relative. Maybe his wife. Bold, McManus.

"Tom. No."

"For God's sake." His voice is muffled against the swell of her breasts. "When? If not now, when?"

"Take me to Seattle," she says, her lips at his ear. Her bracelets clink as she drops her hand between their bodies to palm his groin. He groans, eyes closing, head tipping back onto the peeling wall.

"If we stay here—"

"Oh, God, Mary—"

"If Sing finds out—"

"I can't take you there," he says, arching into her touch. "Not now. Not when we're—oh, Christ."

Each hitch in their breathing sounding clear. Steam from the windows falling over Alma in a hot pall that chills once it hits her skin. Her body quickening even as she sneers to see McManus laid so bare. Even as she stacks the pieces together into an unsteady whole: McManus is bedding Sing Tai's wife; this links him to Sing's store, which is buying tar out of Seattle; McManus's crewmen usually do the ride-alongs to Tacoma on steamers that stop in Seattle; he's talking to Mary about running off to Seattle; and someone is operating out of Seattle and selling the business's custom-made tar on the cheap. None of this looks good for McManus.

Mary has her hand in his trousers now. His chin still lifted. Clinking jade. She nuzzles along his reddened neck, its thick jugular pulse. The movement tilts her head toward Alma. Mary gasps, her bracelets quieting, staring at the ground at Alma's feet. Shit. She's seen Alma's boots under the edge of the sheet.

McManus is flinching away from the woman, turning to follow

her gaze. Alma pushes away from the wall before he can see her face, but holds her ground. Squares her boots toward his shadow darkening the sheet. He thrusts back the cloth. Falters when he meets her eyes.

"Word to the wise, honey," she says to Mary, over his shoulder. "Find yourself a new ticket to Seattle, because I'm tearing this one up."

18

JANUARY 19, 1887

Another snowy morning, the streets gauzy with refracted light, building eaves festooned with crooked icicles. Alma pulls open the post office door. The air inside is warm, reeky with mildew, tallow, unwashed woolens. Two men wait ahead of her. A dingy grimness seeps from the plain planked walls, the green-shaded lamps with their deep coats of dust.

She doesn't make a habit of checking the post herself, not when any boy will do it for two pennies. But she wants to be quick about it. She wants to get to Wheeler's offices.

The door opens, a cold rush of wind on the back of her neck, then another. Three men crowd in behind her. She peers into the glazing at the counter, trying to make out faces in the reflection. Strangers. Not Sloan's men. Not McManus, though he likely isn't walking so well this morning.

"Anything for J. Jones?" she asks when it's her turn before the grille.

While she waits, she takes out a cigarette, her matchbox, so she can lean against the counter and look back at the line without simply gawping around. Over the flare of the match are seven faces. Still no one she knows.

"This came yesterday." The clerk slides an envelope under the grille. "Special Delivery."

The envelope crinkles as she shoves it into her vest. Her tongue ticks over her back teeth. There's no need for Pinkerton to send mail Special Delivery. Unless something is changing, and changing fast.

Out into the freezing street. The bright window display of the notions shop next door. A good place to stay unseen. In the back, at a tiered table of sweets, she rips open the envelope.

Too much delay; Prime orders move. Kennedy and Grove en route, arrival Jan. 23.

It is not signed. It is not coded. Alma reads it again. Counts off the days between now and then. She has to try twice before she can swallow, her throat is so tight. *Prime* is agency slang for the president of the United States. This assignment just hit the big time.

"Hello, Jack."

She looks up from the paper, queasy with the sugar pall rising from caramels and cream candy and chocolate hearts. Nell stands beside the sweets. A basket is hooked onto her forearm. She wears a ribboned bonnet. Her pale green wrap and darker green dress set off her eyes.

"Morning," Alma says, still stupid, still holding the letter in full view. She doesn't know Kennedy and Grove, but she's heard of them. They're new agents, no friends of hers. She needs men who will listen, who will wait in Tacoma or Seattle until she's ready for them to come to town.

Nell raises an eyebrow.

"I got your flowers," she says. "At least, I think they were yours."

"They were mine."

Nell sifts through a dish of caramels, her eyes on Alma's, her gloved fingers ghosting over the twisted paper wrappers.

"I wish I'd been there to accept them," Nell says.

"I've got to go." Alma folds up the letter, stuffs it into her jacket.

"Jack, I arranged that meeting—"

Alma leaves the candy display, its sugar haze, and is halfway to the door before she stops, processes the words that just passed between them. Nell is talking about Delphine. The meeting with Delphine. Alma just saw her, but the Pinkerton's agents' letter changes everything—the timeline Alma was operating on has just been cut down from weeks to days, and Delphine needs to know it. Alma takes off her cap. Rakes hard fingers through her hair.

"Sorry, honey," she says, returning to the corner, where Nell is selecting chocolates one by one. "Just got some hard news. I forgot where I was for a minute."

"Is everything all right?"

"Most like." Alma stands next to Nell, her honeysuckle scent sharp and green in contrast to that of the confections. She is only choosing candies with a pink stripe. "You going for the peppermint?"

"Rose," Nell says.

"I'll help."

They pick through the display, bodies close. Nell's fingers brushing over the back of Alma's hand more than once. Alma standing wide legged, and Nell stepping in toward her but looking down, coy. They drop wrapped candies into the basket until there's near on two pounds of chocolate piled up.

"That's some sweet tooth."

"A few of them are a gift." Nell winks. "But only a few."

"When should I be there?" Alma says, as the thick fabric of Nell's dress drags across her trousers at the knees. "For the meeting."

"Tomorrow. At three o'clock." Nell's hazel eyes glint through lowered lashes. She adjusts the wrap over her shoulders, a waft of perfume rising from the cloth. Leaves one arm outstretched into the candies, her inner elbow an inch away from Alma's hip. "If you want to stay for supper after, I'll make a cake."

"You'd do that for me?" Alma lays her hand on Nell's forearm, the milled-silk sleeve catching at her roughened finger pads.

"If you promise to be on your best behavior."

"I know how to be good," Alma says. She takes a candy from the basket. Unwraps it. Nell tilts up her chin. Pink lips, pink tongue. Breath warm on Alma's fingers, pulse warm in her throat, in her low belly.

"Don't be late," Nell says, after swallowing the chocolate. She reaches out to run her fingers down Alma's biceps. Alma stands up straighter, tensing her arm so her muscles go hard.

"Oh, I won't."

Nell walks to the counter, green skirts swishing, then out the door. Once she's gone, Alma picks up a handful of chocolates. Swaggers to the counter to pay, though by the time she steps out into the wind, the thrill of Nell's unexpected invitation, her unexpected interest, is wearing off. The candy she unwraps on the stoop is peppermint. She drops the wrapper into the mud, untwists another as she walks over the frozen street. The Pinkerton's agents' arrival is a problem. If she can't hold them off, and they come to town asking for Lowry, Alma's hasty decision to take him out could create the disaster Delphine fears. Though it's no secret Pinkerton is handling this investigation for the federal government—which is the one losing tax revenue to the smugglers, after all—President Cleveland's impatience means everyone will be sloppier, looking fast for answers. They'll find the same men she did: Kopp and Sloan. And Wheeler. And now Sloan knows Wheeler's moving the stuff. Sloan could bring down the ring. Jesus. Even thinking the words makes her grimace, licking chocolate off her teeth.

The sweets are gone by the time she reaches her boardinghouse. Up the ruined stairs, past the tableau of sprawled bodies on the steps, into the third-story hall. She checks her room is as she left it. Lock, books, double tie on her suitcase. Clean. She lights a candle, edges the flame along the letter until the whole page has withered into gray wisps of ash that pulse through the air. Suitcase heavy as she kicks it back under the bed, weighted with all her lady's things, silk and lace and dead hair. With her boot still pushed into the bag, she pauses, following the scent of an idea.

At her writing desk she takes out a sheet of paper, the Verne novel. Codes a hasty message that will be short enough to telegraph. They'll know it's urgent when it comes over the wire instead of through the post. She needs them to agree to wait in Tacoma. Just for a few extra days.

"You're in trouble," Conaway tells her when she comes up the stairs, wiping snow off her chin.

"Why?" She had to go to the post office again to make sure the telegraph got off correctly. But she hadn't seen anyone around; none of Sloan's men, none of Wheeler's.

"Driscoll heard you hadn't put money on the fight," he says. "So he borrowed five dollars from Mr. Wheeler and laid it on the Tacoma man, in your name."

Alma laughs, this is so far from a problem. She guesses Mc-Manus hasn't shown his face yet. It felt good to pummel him. To leave him wheezing in that alley, his frightened lover holding him in the sparse snowfall. Payback for the sneers he's been directing at her ever since they met. He has spit and fire, that's sure, but he's not a brawler; only one of his throws landed, on Alma's lower ribs. She was faster, stronger. Her only regret is punching the side of his bad knee. That was stupid—the hard knob of bone left her knuckles sore.

"Little bastard," she says. "But, hell, you and I might be raking in winnings while the others wail."

"That's true. They've all got their money on Mac, even Fulton." Conaway blinks away snow, chafes his reddened hands. "Well, not Benson. He's not keen on the pugs. Says he'd rather save his coins for dances at The Captain's."

"I do love a dance," Alma says. "But those are two different itches. Sometimes a man wants to hold a woman, and sometimes he wants to watch a pair of bruisers bleed each other."

"I know it."

"Have you got a woman, Conaway?"

"I've got a wife. Married six months ago."

"In it for the long haul!"

"She's a comfort." He tucks his hands into his jacket pockets. "Her name's Nan."

His smile, his bashful posture, look odd on so big a man. Alma imagines him after their scrap at the warehouse, sitting on the edge of a neat cot while a woman with gentle hands tips up his chin to examine his swollen eye, his pummeled throat, presses a cool rag to his orbital bone and tells him to sit still. The domestic scene appeals, briefly. She walks inside, brushing powdered-sugar snow off her sleeves.

Wheeler is not at his desk. The door to the Clyde Imports store-front is just barely ajar, a hairline crack of pale light outlining its seam. Quiet, she crosses the carpet, circling the desk to inspect the papers scattered over its top. She has still not discovered the system that allows him to make sense out of the mess. There are shipping dockets tucked under import receipts, ledger pages covered in that number-heavy cipher, a handbill for the coming opera house folded around an envelope elaborately stamped in Aberdeen, United Kingdom.

The light on the desk changes, so she knows not to flinch.

"If you're looking for something, it might be faster to ask." Wheeler's broad frame fills the back doorway, his arms folded over his chest.

"Letters from home?" She holds up the stamped envelope.

"No."

"You said to ask!"

He is almost smiling, an ease in his posture, his face. This is the closest he's come to matching how she first encountered him—a pleasant gentleman, if a touch solemn, apt to let his eyes go soft, to reminisce about the old country.

"How was your dinner?" she says.

"Productive." His voice pleased, his silver cuff links winking as he breathes. He nods at the mail she's holding. "Let that be and come in here."

In the Clyde Imports office he has the drawers of two filing cabinets open. He waves her over to the first, which is neatly lined with fat yellow envelopes.

"I keep the records together," he says. "Clyde Imports' along with the organization's, as Benson showed you with the Quincy paperwork. This system may change, but if you've not dealt with inventories and expense ledgers, you can start learning those, at least."

"Expense ledgers?" she says, not taking the envelope he holds out.

"This is part of the job. Tom knows it." Wheeler shoves the envelope into her stomach, and she grabs it away from him. "You might be blessed from on high, but if you can't do the practical side, there's those who can."

"The boring side."

"Call it what you like," he says. "Product doesn't move without money, and when accounts aren't squared away, money has a way of vanishing."

Alma didn't think this far ahead. She'd thought of Delphine. Of new grounds to tramp over. Of rain, and salt water, and a desk to rest her boots on. But the desk will be in Tacoma. And it will be more than a footstool—there's paperwork to be done on it, long periods of sitting still, less work for her fists and more for her fingers, tallying, writing, scratching away at columns of numbers. Good Christ. In the city she'd been all motion, all action: running deliveries; scaring merchants into deals that didn't serve their best interests; checking in on product at the docks, at the dens. The deputy job is starting to feel less like fun and more like work.

She turns the envelope around so she can read the writing across the front. Wheeler's neat, blocky script: *August 1886.*

"Next you're going to tell me I have to wear a suit." She makes this sound like a hardship, but she's not put off by the idea. She'd left a fine-cut number behind in Chicago, sold to a tailor's shop for ten dollars to help cover her train fare out West.

"You're a poor clerk, remember," Wheeler says. "When you're not covered in blood, you'll fit in just fine."

"You shine up nice," she says.

He brings a hand to his tie and smooths it straight. Does not move away.

"All the prices and duties, filed along with their shipments." He nods at the envelope in her hands. "And what we really paid, including bribes."

Alma folds open the stiff envelope, slides out the top sheet. Rows of inked points of origin and numbers. A bookkeeper's sweet dream. It makes her eyes glaze over.

"Fascinating." She tosses the open envelope onto a nearby end table, setting the lamp perched at its center asway. A few of the neatly ordered pages shake free and drift to the carpet.

"You're a worry," Wheeler says.

"I'm good at the ground work," she says. Delphine wants her to study this, but Alma's still thinking she'll hire someone. Nell could keep accounts well enough.

"You're good at making messes."

With a deep sigh she kneels to collect the fallen papers, then fits them back into the envelope without bothering to check the

order. Wheeler takes the packet from her and shuffles the contents
back into neatness.

"By the way," he says. "You owe me ten dollars."

"I didn't place that bet. And it was for five."

"It was placed in your name. Plus the five-dollar loan you took
out the day before yesterday." He grins, pale gleam of teeth, and
she is warming to him, to his willingness to spar. "See? The benefits of accounting."

"I don't have it." She makes a show of digging through her pockets, so his gaze is dragged down to her hips. "I'll bring it to the
fight."

"Who said I'm giving you the night off?"

"You going to try and stop me?" she says.

She hops onto the edge of the desk behind her, tapping her heel
against the wood paneling, getting restless, getting curious. He is
standing only a few feet away, one thumb rubbing over the edge of
the envelope in his hands, the toes of his shoes pointed toward her
even though his body is not.

But he moves off. Replaces the envelope in the cabinet and locks
the drawer. The keys jingle into his pocket. His jaw working, just
slightly, on the obscured side of his face.

The front bellpull sounds. Alma slides off the desk, startled, and
they both look toward the glazed window.

"What are you doing here?" Wheeler mutters.

Dom Kopp, the railroad man, stands outside in a garish white
coat, straightening his lapels and fiddling with his gem-topped
walking stick.

"Shit," Alma says. "He's seen me before. In a dress."

"Go back to the office," Wheeler says.

"No. I want to listen in." She holds her hand out. "The keys."

He hesitates for a bare second before pulling them out, then
gives the bunch to her by a long silver key. As he walks to the door,
she fits it into the filing cabinet, pulls out a fat stack of envelopes.
At the little desk in the corner, farthest from the light of the windows,
she empties an envelope onto the table. Fans the papers wide with
one hand and pulls her forelock low over her forehead with the
other.

"Good morning," Wheeler says as he opens the door.

"Are you Wheeler?" Kopp says.

"Yes, I am."

Wheeler's tone is cool. He does not stand aside from the door, and Kopp peers around him into the office, catching sight of Alma at the back but not lingering on her, his gaze moving on to the gleaming cabinetry, the fine brass fixtures on the walls. He is a slight man, shorter and narrower than Wheeler, with a fussy mustache and bristling blond hair.

"Good morning to you, Mr. Wheeler. My name is Kopp. I've come with a business inquiry."

"What kind of liquor are you in the market for?" Wheeler doesn't move. "Or is it woolens."

"Woolens? No. No, I am in the railroad business." Kopp is nervous, fidgety; he taps his stick on the sidewalk in rapid little thumps. "Representing the interests of the Northern Pacific here in Port Townsend. I'm surprised you have not heard of me."

"I stick to my own sphere of commerce, Mr. Kopp."

"Seeing as you just signed on to Judge Hamilton's trust, the railroad is your sphere of commerce, sir."

This news is only a day old, and Kopp doesn't sound too pleased about it. Snow collects on his white lapel. His rings glitter against the body of his walking stick, just below the bulbous yellow stone at its head.

"You've had more luck than I with that circle," he continues, craning to see around Wheeler again. "Hamilton is dead set on it being a private venture. Though the Northern Pacific would bring ample funding to the line. Might I come in?"

"You're welcome. Have a seat."

Wheeler waves at the square table closest to the door and takes the chair facing Alma. Kopp sits opposite, claps his hat onto the tabletop. He glances back at her, to where she is busy scribbling gibberish onto a neat sales receipt while keeping an eye on the two through the dark fall of her hair.

"This is . . . delicate business," Kopp says, quiet but not so quiet that she has to strain to make out his words. A man not practiced at being inconspicuous.

"My clerk is hard of hearing," Wheeler says. "Anything you have to say is between us."

"Well then. Ah. Well then. How to bring it up lightly?"

Kopp is a changed man from when she saw him at the Cosmopolitan. He was happy enough to lord it over poor friends and workingwomen, but now that he's faced with a well-to-do businessman, he is high-strung, nervous, repetitively clearing his throat. Wheeler folds his hands on the table. A solid presence as Kopp twitches.

"I heard you're the man to speak to about certain, ah, imported product."

"Liquor," Wheeler says.

"No, not your damned liquor," Kopp snaps.

Wheeler does not move, yet he seems to grow larger. Alma studies the set of his body. Decides he does it by filling his lungs deep and forward, so his rib cage and shoulders expand up and out.

"Speak to me like that again and I will call you to answer," Wheeler says.

Kopp, on the other side of the table, has gone pale, his cheeks pinched. But it's not fear. His lips are peeling back from his teeth, his eyebrows set in a hard line. He is furious.

"I'm here to do you a favor," he says. "The railroad is coming and they have tasked me with locating the best sites for new lines. Your little trust might be attractive to Northern Pacific stockholders— but your smuggling won't be. And that's where I come in. I don't want to crush a decent opportunity. I'm willing to work with you, to protect your business and keep it from the railroad's attention, if you cut me in on the profits."

"I have no idea what you're talking about," Wheeler says. "But you look absolutely unsteady. I must ask you to leave."

"I'll give you time to come to your senses, man." Kopp stands, snatching up his walking stick and hat. "I can offer you security. Don't be a fool."

"Good day, Mr. Kopp."

A final, white-lipped glare. The door slammed so hard the bell jangles. Wheeler watches Kopp stalk down the street, then stands, slow, and turns the lock.

"Wonderful." Alma sets down her pen. There is ink on her index finger, a long line tracing from the edge of her nail. "We have a new problem."

"This is Sloan's doing." Wheeler comes to the back of the office. When he sees the paper on her desk, deeply streaked with ink, he shakes his head and gives her a baleful stare. "What is the matter with you?"

"I was bored," she says, then surprises herself by going on, in a less needling tone. "It helps me think. Moving. And I couldn't walk around, so."

"Just! Just leave them there." He flattens a hand over the papers when she starts to stack them.

She looks up at him along the length of his sturdy arm. He is so often two things at once, with one face slipping close under the other, flashing to the surface in a breath, in a twitch of muscle. The fastidious merchant and the cold enforcer. The dour bookkeeper and the tight-grinned fighter. This duality calls to her. He is self-contained and controlled in ways that intrigue. But will he also be smart when his own men come into question?

"Conaway. Fulton. Driscoll. Benson," she says, looking up at him, watching the tightening of his jaw. "McManus. Those are the men who know you. What are the odds, the honest odds, that one of them is talking to someone he shouldn't be?"

"It's Sloan behind this. He's been meeting with Kopp."

She stares at him, hard, in silent question.

"It's one of the concerns I've been following," he says.

"And you were planning on telling me when?"

"When I was sure. Now there's proof enough, wouldn't you say?"

"Why would Sloan mess with us when he's just gotten cut into the trade?"

"Because he's uninformed," Wheeler says. "He thinks he can weasel his way in, undermine me, and reap the spoils. He doesn't know how things work—how we're supplied, and why."

The Families. Delphine's contacts in San Francisco and the source of her premium opium. The Families are rumored to hold vast wealth in Hong Kong, in Macao. One patriarch, in particular, is said to have a special connection with Delphine, maybe based off

an old favor from her fencing days, maybe off something else. Joe
Hong, one of this patriarch's younger sons, with Delphine for years
as a companion and translator but maybe also as a watchman, someone at her side ensuring the Families' interests are protected. Alma
doesn't know much more; she's not sure how much of what she does
know is true.

"So Sloan tips off Kopp; they pressure you into a deal. That's
bad." She stands, comes around the little table. "That doesn't answer our missing-product question, though. Unless Sloan and Kopp
also have a friend among your men."

"I've not yet found anything suggesting that," Wheeler says, lifting his chin.

"It's one of the concerns I've been following," she says. "And
I learned something very interesting yesterday, while you were meeting with your wealthy friends."

The memory of McManus and his woman fizzes in the air, nudging her to take a step closer, tilt her face toward Wheeler's exposed
neck. They are two feet apart. "Take me to Seattle," Mary had said
to McManus, as she slid her hand down the front of his body. Sing
Tai's Seattle-sourced tar.

"Have you heard anything linking Kopp or Sloan to Seattle?"
she says.

"No." The vein at Wheeler's throat tapping faster.

Damn.

"Wait," he says. "Of course. Kopp has been collecting pledges
of land there, for his railroad schemes. There and in Irondale, south
of town."

Irondale again. The location of Peterson's second boatyard.
McManus's second visit to keep the boatbuilder quiet. Everything
McManus does is starting to seem suspicious.

"There's been strange tar coming out of Seattle lately," Alma
says, getting warmer, craving movement as her theory gathers
weight, gathers velocity. As Wheeler leaves his mouth open, wet
flicker of tongue behind his canines. "Wah Hing, sold at half price
to Sing Tai at auction, in Seattle, two weeks ago."

"The missing product. From December."

"Has to be. We don't sell there."

"How much?"

"Ten pounds," she says. "It's not everything. But I think I know who's moving it."

Another step. This is as close as he's let her come since she lunged at him. And his hands are not in fists. If he's done holding back, she hopes he won't be gentle about it.

"Tommy?" he says as his eyes skip off hers, over her shoulder. He pulls away with a backward lean in his upper body.

McManus steadies himself against the doorjamb linking the offices. Frowning as he watches them. His face is pallid but unmarked because Alma, too, knows how to hide punches. It's under his clothes where he's pulped and purpling, ribs, sternum, the outside of his bad knee. She waits for him to speak, to fly out at her, but he ignores her entirely, keeping the weight off his bad leg.

"Stopped by Ah Tong's," he says. "Made sure he got the delivery all right."

"You don't look so good, lad," Wheeler tells him. "Everything square?"

"Eleven men, all accounted for." McManus is sweating, broad forehead beading with moisture, breathing not quite at ease. "But he'd had visitors."

"Of what sort."

"Sloan's men tried to sell him some Wah Hing. Twelve dollars a can."

"Greedy bastard," Alma says. Sloan's price is absurdly high, but at least he is attempting to sell. Their trap is closing.

McManus's eyes flick over to her. His mouth splits into a crooked sneer, showing pale, crowded teeth.

"I'm not fucking talking to you," he says.

"Give it a rest." Wheeler moves past him into the other room. "What did Ah Tong say to turn them down?"

"Not much. They broke his nose and two of his fingers."

Wheeler stops halfway to his desk.

"God damn it," he says.

"You sure you didn't help break them?" Alma walks toward the door, aiming to push past McManus, but he is following Wheeler toward the desk, his left boot dragging heavily.

"Fuck you."

"Remind him who he answers to," she persists, coming nearer. "Like you did with Peterson."

"Camp. Enough." Wheeler lowers himself into his chair.

"That Pike bastard wasn't the end of it." McManus angles his body so he is speaking only to Wheeler, his back to Alma. "The altered bills, the missing product—he's got another man in. I spoke to each of the crew last night, and they didn't give me much, but with more time—"

"You'll what?" Alma says, stepping forward so she is in McManus's space, and closer than he is to Wheeler's desk. "Siphon off more tar and take it Seattle? To fund your honeymoon?"

"Seattle?" Wheeler says, and the seed she planted earlier is rooting in, his face darkening.

"He's got a woman, and she wants to go there," Alma says, and beside her McManus goes rigid, his throat working. "Very persuasive, too. She didn't get on her knees, but—"

McManus's boot catches on the carpet as he lunges toward her. He stumbles, falls against the desk, his hand and hip thumping hard into wood.

"I'll rip your throat out," he says, and the look he gives her is pure murder, his blue eyes fierce and bloodshot against his waxen skin.

"Tommy—"

"He's trying to turn you against me," McManus says to Wheeler, breathing hard, brogue thickening as his voice grows urgent. "He's a fucking plant from Sloan. Mind how he turned up, keeking around the Madison spot just like Pike was—"

"Get a hold of yourself." Wheeler glares at him. "Are you drunk? Talking nonsense, falling down."

McManus closes his eyes. Shifts his body against the desk with stiff movements. Once his back is to Alma again, she doesn't bother to sneer.

"My leg's bad today," he says.

"Who's this woman?"

McManus shakes his head.

"Who's this fucking woman? And what does she want in Seattle?"

"She wants to get away from her husband," McManus says, quiet.

"Jesus Christ. As if there's not enough—"

Knocking at the office door. Wheeler calls out, sharp, and Driscoll enters.

"Brought the post." Driscoll's grin falters as he registers the brittle tension in the air, as he gets close enough to take in McManus's pallor, his pained slump against the desk. "All right, Tom?"

McManus nods, not looking at him.

"I can bring you some coffee. Sir, would you like some coffee? Camp?"

"No, lad," Wheeler says.

"Run and get us a packet of cocaine, would you," McManus says.

"And a gin nip?" Driscoll sets the mail on the edge of the desk. "Aye."

"Back in a tick," Driscoll says, and lets himself out.

"You've got that pup trained well," Alma says after the door closes. "And he's the one who let Pike into the Madison warehouse. Funny, that."

"Camp. Take this to Ah Tong with my apologies." Wheeler unlocks a desk drawer, pulls out some silver coins. He scribbles a note and folds it around the money, then tucks the square into an envelope. "I know a bonesetter if he needs one."

"You got it, boss," she says.

"Sit down, Tommy." Wheeler points at the chair opposite his. "You and I are going to have a chat."

19

JANUARY 7, 1887
Twelve Days Earlier

Eight o'clock and the crowd in the Cosmopolitan's gaming parlor burns with gaslight and gin. Black hats, black jackets in a smoky patchwork. Hothouse spots of color from the faro players' pink shirts. Onyx and diamond and gold cuff links glitter. Jewel-toned dresses. Fewer women are in the hotel than Alma expected, making her cover sparse, making her stand out more than she would like. But the five or six good-time girls roaming the room are blessedly garish, bosoms powdered, grins dripping with carmine. They draw more attention than Alma, even in her pink dress and finely curled chestnut wig.

One woman drapes herself over a man's shoulder, fingers loose his wallet as he fondles her breasts.

"Three queens." This from the man seated next to the fellow who's being robbed. As the table groans, curses, the woman lifts a discreet haul of paper notes out of the wallet and slips them into her skirt before dropping the wallet back in place.

"Three queens, gentlemen."

The winner rakes money toward himself in a clinking pile. He wears bristly blond sideburns and a vain man's mustache, curled, tumid with wax. An expensive brocade vest, deep blue. The gem topping his walking stick could mortgage a Nob Hill house in the city. He's been jolly all night, but now the color in his cheeks has

built up to a crimson blaze. Dom Kopp is in a damn fine mood, and
when he next goes to the bar for a refill, Alma will follow him.

"Evening, ma'am."

A tall man in a red cravat comes up beside her, places a warm
hand on her elbow. She stills the urge to flinch—in her pink taffeta she is toeing the line between lady and lady of the night, and
this is not the first bucko at the hotel to try to buy her company.

"Good evening to you, sir," she says.

His coat is not of good cloth; the rough cotton shows its seams
in the yellow light. He's not a real moneyed man, or a flash investor—
not like her lucky mark at the poker table, who's throwing down a
fistful of notes on the next hand.

"May I offer you some champagne?" The tall man holds out a
glass.

"Thank you, but no," Alma says. "I'm trying to understand how
the game works, and I don't want to be any more muddled than
I already am!"

She nods vaguely at the faro and poker tables, together, as if unaware they are separate contests.

"Well, I'd be happy to help you puzzle it out," the man says, his
hand still on her arm.

He launches into an explanation of poker geared toward a child's
understanding. Alma fixes on a faintly baffled expression—widens
her eyes, parts her lips, tilts her face up toward him but not so far
that she loses sight of Kopp, who is frowning at his table, tossing
away his cards in disgust—and makes small coos as the man explains how each hand bests the next.

Kopp taps his fingers on the felt, rings flashing. He's a railroad
man, she's heard; he's spoken of it at this hotel, and at the Central,
where she first saw him the previous night. A promoter with ties to
the Northern Pacific Railroad, he is in town to drum up excitement
about a local line—and secure some cash to help fund it. Yet other
rich fellows seem to regard him as faintly unsavory, and that is what
interests her. He greets old-money men—those in beaver coats and
subdued silks—with brassy familiarity, and they draw away, their
smiles strained. During her brief surveillance, he has asked three
men for pledges of land for the tracks. Two of those men turned him

down. Strange, when the whole Northwest has railroad fever, now that the Northern Pacific is fifty miles away from completing a direct transcontinental line to Puget Sound. Kopp has cash; he has connections to the coming railroad; and, still, something is making his rich acquaintances nervous. Alma hopes it's tar. Or at least a whiff of the black stuff: a link to those who sell it in town.

Her cravat-wearing companion is smiling down at her expectantly.

"I'm afraid I'm more confused than ever," she tells him.

Kopp is raking in more winnings. Collecting his glass, his money. Standing.

"Excuse me." She detaches herself from the man. "I think I left something at the bar."

He starts to follow her and she ignores him, slipping through the maze of coats and chairs, the warm press of bodies doused in a liberal assortment of colognes. By the time she's made her way to the other side of the room, he is no longer behind her, lost in the crowd. Kopp is at the well already, his legs not quite touching the ground from his perch on a velvet stool. She is aiming for the polished notch of open counter to his left when two people converge on him: a blond woman in a crimson dress, and a tall, sallow man with thinning hair slicked back, the black strands showing sharp against white scalp.

The woman lays her hand on Kopp's arm. He leans to her ear. His hand rises between them, chucks her chin playfully, skims the tops of her breasts when he drops it to his drink. Alma hangs back, waiting, aware she is not in a good place among the currents in the room: too far away from the bar to be waiting for a drink; too close to a faro table, whose men glance up at her curiously; on a bare patch of carpet in a bustling room where she is already standing out too much in the crowd. The three people at the bar are playing a silent drama: the woman has Kopp's attention, his smile, but the man on his right is leaning in, whispering, all but tugging on Kopp's sleeve.

"Damn it, man," Kopp says, loud enough that Alma catches it.

The woman raises an eyebrow, pouts. Wafts her fan beneath her chin, so the follow-me-lads curls hanging to her shoulders sway. Her jaw is sharp, her body lean. Not the type to snag Alma's attention— but her mouth, the low neckline of her dress, are intriguing.

Kopp says something to the woman, who snaps her fan shut and sweeps away. Alma counts to five and then approaches the bar.

"A sherry cobbler, please," she tells the bartender.

Kopp glances at her, but his gaze doesn't stick. As the barkeep muddles sugar into wine, Alma trains her ears on the conversation between Kopp, beside her, and his anxious comrade.

"You're wearing me out with your excuses, Max," Kopp is telling the man.

"I've tried—"

"You promise one thing, then another, but when do you deliver?"

Alma can't see Kopp's face, turned away as he is, but she can just make out the side of Max's. His eyes are watery. He blinks, slow, as Kopp talks at him. Gulps down his drink.

"You don't deliver, and I'll tell you why." Kopp drains most of his champagne, waves his glass at the barkeep while snapping his fingers. "You don't have the stuff to talk to that friend of yours and tell him you need the money."

"I need that money, you know I do," Max says, voice low and cracking.

"Then go light a fire under him. Tell him to stop stalling and get to work," Kopp says, not bothering to keep his voice down. "First September, then December—a whole lot of promises, and no results. And now he's still got cold feet, and you come to me and whine that you need money? Don't talk to me, sir. I've got money because I've got luck, and with luck on my side, I'm about ready to step over you and take myself straight to your reluctant friend and tell him if I don't see an immediate return on my investment, I'll report—"

"Don't! Come on, now, don't." Max has one hand on Kopp's sleeve.

Kopp shakes him off, picks up his glass, the last of his champagne catching the light in a fizzing slice of gold.

"I'm heading to Irondale tomorrow," he says. "When I get back, I expect good news."

"I'll talk to him," Max says.

Kopp sniffs, sips his drink. His friend looks between his own glass, empty, and Kopp's. The pile of cash Kopp has sitting within the curl of his arm, crossed by the polished length of his walking stick.

"Can you lend me a few dollars?" Max says. "For the tables?"

"Going to turn your fortunes around?"

"God willing."

"Here, you creature." Kopp dumps some change into the other man's long palm. "Spend it or save it, that's my last donation to your cause."

Max takes the money, pockets it greedily. He drifts to the center of the room, near where Alma was standing, and she can almost see the same currents she felt working upon him: he moves a touch toward the faro table at his hip, then starts toward the exit, then takes a half step toward the nearest poker game. She leaves him to his confusion. Scoots a hair closer to Kopp, so their sleeves are touching.

"Your luck is golden tonight," she says, waiting to see how best to play it—how best to calibrate her attentions to his appetites.

"You girls sure are on the prowl, aren't you," he says, glancing over at Alma and grinning. But he is already leaning toward her with his upper body—as much as he's willing to belittle her for it, he is game for the attention. His champagne-sugared breath on her face.

"I don't know what you mean," she says. "I was watching you at the poker and thought I'd congratulate you on your winnings."

"They have added up." Now he is turned toward her on his velvet stool, switching his drink from left hand to right. She waits for him to reach for her, but he is looking her up and down, his forehead wrinkling.

"A bit buttoned-up for a ladybird, aren't you?"

She looks down at her collar, the regrettable lack of bosom shown by her dress. Sees a way to keep Kopp's attention—a flash, hard-to-please type might take this bait.

"You don't like it?" she says. Then, dropping her voice, her chin, letting her cheeks color, she says, "I hoped it would be all right. I'm new."

"New?"

And that's done it. He is turned all the way toward her, his tweed-encased thighs parted. A twitch of interest at his mouth. A twitch of interest at his groin.

"I'll leave you for the other girls," she says.

He lets go of his drink entirely. That's a first.

"Hold on, sweetheart." His fingers settle at the crook of her arm, his thumb stroking over her inner elbow, where the skin under the pink taffeta is thin and soft. "Let me buy you a drink."

The bartender slides her cocktail onto the counter. She smiles at him, at Kopp, and Kopp tosses him a coin.

"That's on me," Kopp tells the man.

"Thank you," Alma says, and lets Kopp pull her closer, his knees nudging against the sides of her bodice. She bites her lip.

"What's your name?"

"Annabelle," she says.

"This really your first night, Annabelle?"

"Yes, sir."

"Call me Dom." He lifts her chin, his fingers warm, papery. "No, call me Mr. Kopp."

He picks up her cocktail, puts it in her hand.

"You drink that up, now," he says. "And then we'll find somewhere cozy to get to know each other better."

"All right, Mr. Kopp," she says, and smiles around a mouthful of crushed sugar and ice.

20

JANUARY 19, 1887

An hour to the fight and Chain Locker is wild. The storeroom is cleared for action, outfitted with a roped-off ring. There's already a press three-deep around it, every logger and dockhand suddenly turned expert on the size of the ring, on the height of the ropes, on the chosen referee, a fellow from Seattle and therefore suspected of a healthy bias against the Tacoma man, the two cities being long-time bitter rivals. Men stream back and forth through the jointed middle of the building, where a windy hall only a few feet long connects storeroom to saloon. A sour throng of bodies obscures the bar.

Alma and Driscoll shove through the crowd to a scrap of counter, holding their space with hard shoulders and elbows. She adds her voice to the general howl, clamoring for the attention of Clay or one of the two barmen he's hired for the night. He's going to make a fortune and so is his liquor supplier—Clyde Imports.

"Four whiskey doubles!"

Driscoll catches a bartender first and hollers the order, high color in his cheeks, high excitement in his eyes. The man slaps four tumblers onto the wood, drains the last of a bottle into them.

"We're never going to get them back in this mess," Alma shouts in Driscoll's ear. "Better drink them ourselves."

He gawps and she pushes two dimes into his hot palm.

"On me," she says.

The barkeep takes the coins. Alma scoops the glasses toward the little space of bar top they've carved out, hands one to Driscoll, and picks up another.

"Fuck Tacoma!" she roars, lifting the tumbler, and the men pressed around them holler back, gleeful baritone agreements, whistles, stamping on the floor. The electric sizzle of being plugged into a crowd—voices and muscles and hot cloth on hot skin—jangles through her as she shoots back the whiskey. It's vile, cheap trash but fiery as she needs, and after Driscoll empties his glass, they take up the others and clink them together, drain them in unison.

Now the night feels like a proper rager. She slings an arm over Driscoll's shoulders and they barrel back toward the storeroom. The crowd is thinner at the joint between the buildings. Ten feet below, the bay slaps against wharf pylons. Sunset stains the water reddish, an upward glow that glitters through gaps in the floorboards. Driscoll is laughing and warm against her side, jostling against skin worn raw by the edges of her binding cloth—a rasp of pain within the many layers of Camp's clothes, shirt, vest, and jacket. If the kid notices her bound chest, Alma is practiced with an excuse: sore ribs needing bandaging. But excuses, worries, all burn away with the whiskey and the approaching fight.

"You bastards," Conaway says when they return to him and Barker empty-handed.

"Can't carry nothing through all that," Alma says. "Go try it yourselves."

"Five cents a double?" Barker leans against the wall into the shadow of Conaway's bulk, takes a long pull from his flask. "I don't pay those kind of prices."

"You'll be at the bar howling like the rest when that runs out," Conaway tells him, nodding at the flask.

"Sure enough."

"I heard the Tacoma cunt's seven feet tall." Driscoll is restless, eyeballing the crowd, peering at the ring with its knotted ropes, its clean sweep of boards. "A beast."

"Mac'll have him," Barker says. "I've seen him fight three times. He's got dynamite in those fists."

With one ear on their chatter, Alma glances around the store-room. She's searching for Sloan or his boys. And a gray overcoat. She wants to see Wheeler. Will he show up with McManus, as the men are expecting, or alone? Either way, when Wheeler arrives, she will angle her way over to him. She wants to watch the fight while he is watching her.

Driscoll slumps onto her, giddy at some joke Barker made. He is heavy with muscle, smelling of whiskey and sweat.

"Fuck off, kid." She shrugs him away, laughing.

This company's all right. Not a bunch of hard cases, save for McManus. Delphine's San Francisco crew would knife you in the stomach while shaking your hand. Six years of knowing them, and she never lost the feeling of walking on thin ice. But the Port Townsend men are making this a soft landing. A few punches exchanged, a few nasty words, then a week later they stand together in a bar, bantering, jostling, passing around Barker's flask of gin.

A commotion at the doorway. Two men call out, "Make way," carrying in low stools for the fighters, sponge buckets slopping water. Space around the ring is filling, the crowd thickening to five deep at the middle of the ropes.

"You going to be able to see back here?" Conaway asks, smirking down at her.

"I could stand on you again and gain a foot," she shoots back, and he laughs, full throated, showing tobacco-laced teeth.

"You're a son of a bitch, Camp."

"I know."

Barker's flask is empty, a small catastrophe. He and Driscoll thread their way toward the jointed hall, their promises to bring back enough for everyone met with jeers. Then, in the doorway: McManus. He is grimacing, badly limping. And he's not alone. Two steps behind him, eyes shadowed by a dark hat, is Wheeler. Driscoll stops to greet them while Barker forges onward, disappears into the dim hall. Alma's tongue flicks against the backs of her teeth.

Look at me, she thinks, staring hard at Wheeler. Look at me.

Instead, he takes off his hat. Nods at Driscoll. He is far better dressed than most of the crowd, and enough men notice and clear the way that he moves in a little pocket of space, around to-

ward the opposite side of the ring from where Alma stands with
Conaway.

Now Conaway's height comes in handy. When Wheeler appears
ringside opposite, Alma waits for him to see the guardsman, who
is conspicuously redheaded, six inches taller than most of the men
around them. Wheeler's eyes track, catch. Drop to hers.

She raises her fingers to her cap. Twitches up one side of her
mouth.

He gives her the same curt nod he gave Driscoll. The bastard.

"There's the boss man," she tells Conaway. "I'm going to go say
good evening."

"I'm drinking your whiskey," he says.

She pushes through the crowd, snapping back at a few overeager
men who try to start trouble. As she nears the hall, a wave of sound
echoes through it. Cheers and clapping signal the arrival of a fighter.
On tiptoe she peers through shoulders toward the door, where a
burly man in a plain brown coat ducks into the room, flanked by
three other fellows. The floorboards jump with the welcome he's
given. It must be Mac, the local hero. He comes to the corner nearest Alma, shakes hands with a thickset man in denim—the referee.

It's fight time, and she's stuck in between her good viewing spot
and Wheeler, with a growing stream of men pushing through the
hall in the wake of Mac.

She muscles through the reeking crowd—an elbow to her side,
a cigarette end flaring too close to her left eye—and then is on the
other side of the corner, a lucky gap opening that she squirms
through to the ropes. She is ten feet from Wheeler, with a clear view
of him over a triangle of clean, freshly sanded boards.

Look at me, she thinks, and this time he does: he looks right at
her, eyes narrowed, a tight grin flickering there and away. She raises
her chin.

I'd have your bollocks, she mouths, silent.

One of his eyebrows lifts. It reads like an invitation.

She is sweating. The whiskey and Barker's gin are making her
feel bigger, stronger, like she could climb into the ring herself and
beat any son of a bitch who answered her challenge.

A chorus of boos, stamping. The crowd shifts, bodies pressing into Alma's as the Tacoma man and his party parade into the room. Dobbs is not seven feet tall as Driscoll claimed but up there, six-two at least, blond and sunbaked, his yellow beard bright against the brick red of his cheeks. The two fighters shake hands, as do their cornermen and umpires. The coin toss goes to Mac. He chooses the nearer side, positioning Dobbs at the back corner, where unfriendly faces are thick and growling. As challenger, Mac takes off his cap first and chucks it over the ropes. Dobbs follows suit—that same yellow hair, limp with sweat—and the fighters and their cornermen duck into the ring.

"Come on, boys," Alma shouts.

The cornermen tie their fighters' colors to the posts: blue and gold for Mac, and the Irish flag for Dobbs. The pugs strip off their jackets, their shirts, their boots. Dobbs is pale white under his shirt, broad chested, heavily muscled in the shoulders and sides. Mac, in the corner to her left, is a solid slab of a man. Black hair thick on his chest, on his forearms. He has the flattened nose of a bruiser, a muscle-roped neck, chunky knuckles.

"London rules," the referee calls from his spot outside the ring.

Alma hollers her approval, knocking elbows with the men beside her as she claps. No gloves. No timed rounds. None of that Queensberry nonsense, after all. The men will fight, barefisted, until they fall.

"Nothing below the belt, sirs," the referee says, raising his voice above the crowd noise. "No butting, no gouging. Right? Come up to the scratch."

Mac and Dobbs shuffle forward, shake hands. Alma is grinning, her bound ribs pressed hard against the knotted ring ropes. Her eyes latched to the fighters' bodies. Flanked by the umpires, the referee nods. Calls time.

Dobbs comes up fast, feints, throws a hard cross that Mac catches with his outer shoulder, rolls away from. Roaring in her ears, in her throat. Mac ducks away with the momentum of the dodge, comes back with a quick snap of a shovel hook to Dobbs's ribs, thick meat smack of bone into flesh. Dobbs grunts and brings his hands up as Mac, already reloading, shoots his elbow from his hip and out into a right hook that ought to take Dobbs's nose clean off except he's not there, he's danced back a step, and Mac is off-balance. Pressure at her back as latecomers crowd in from the bar, hips and fists digging into her. Mac recovers his fighting stance. The pugs circle. Settle in.

Jab, jab, hook from Dobbs, and the third punch connects, Mac's jaw snapping down at a painful angle, Alma flinching and shouting, her voice already raw. Mac staggers forward, unsteady but moving in the right direction—is he playing?—and, yes, part of that was a show because he delivers another powerhouse blow to Dobbs's midsection, just where Alma would aim for the kidney. Dobbs clenches in, dropping his face enough to catch Mac's jab to the nose. There is blood, at once, a gush of it, and a man at the far corner starts hollering more wildly than the rest: that's a fellow with a sharp bet on first blood.

Dobbs wipes his nose on his forearm, a smear of sweat and red, and Alma is lit up with the violence of it, with the hot proof of a man's life splashed on his skin. The referee will call a pause if he's a neat sort, a fastidious man, but he doesn't look it with his florid, thickly bearded face. Sure enough, he holds his place at the ropes while letting the men continue.

A true cross from Dobbs, who's bleeding all down his chest but not slowed, and Mac's left pectoral blooms pink then quickly purple, a fist-size stamp of glory. He returns with a sly jab to Dobbs's jaw and the Tacoma man is down, panting, on his knees. The timekeeper clangs his handbell. That's the round.

The men retreat to their corners. Dobbs's sponge bucket is immediately red tinged. Mac's head is doused in water as he refuses a sip of whiskey. Shouts and stamping so the building shakes. Alma stands firm among the tremors, grinning, fierce, ready. It's been two years since she went to a fight—a real matchup, not some basement mill with no form, no science—and these pugs know what they're about. It's an even contest. She hopes that will make it a bloody one.

With this occupying her thoughts, she looks away from Mac and at Wheeler. He is staring at her. His mouth open. His ears red.

The bell rings.

She throws her head back and howls into the low rafters.

In the second round Mac takes the advantage, knocking Dobbs off-kilter with a few good throws, his punches coming in tight, fast little bursts, one-two, one-two, one-two-three. Dobbs drops again and Alma pounds on the ropes before her, roaring, afire with the knockdown, afire because she knows without having to look that Wheeler is watching her. Blood spattered on the pine boards. Her nostrils flare. Copper sharp, copper sour. The fighters hunch, backs heaving, in their corners. The performance of the sport, blood like red paint, sweat like oil. Hot throb of the audience. Wheeler, and McManus with his woman in the alley, and the stripped-down bodies in the ring, all seethe into a thick pulse in Alma's low body; she wants to knock Wheeler back against the office's blue wall and take him in her mouth.

Mac carries his second-round momentum into the next, and the crowd is behind him all the way, living for their local man. He has dripping cuts on his brow and lip but moves with a dogged energy, a workman's perseverance, his punches still precise. And once more Dobbs falls; slower, this time, to get on his feet and to his corner.

Alma looks for Wheeler but he is bent toward McManus, listening to the younger man. She follows McManus's eyes to Mac's corner, and there is Loomis, Sloan's crimp, with two others she's seen at the boardinghouse. No Sloan, but there are too many men between them to be sure. Sloan's crew doesn't seem to be moving; they keep their spot behind Mac, and when the fourth round starts, she doesn't bother watching them. The whole waterfront is here, it feels like, and they're far enough away from Wheeler and McManus that trouble seems unlikely.

Mac opens with a solid hook to Dobbs's abused ribs—his torso already a welter of red and black—and Alma is shouting encouragement when, with a neat two-step, Dobbs darts in and twists, delivering a left hook directly to Mac's ear. Mac drops to the boards, falling badly, one arm tangled under him and his legs bent sharply at the knees. The air squeezes out of the room.

The referee ducks into the ring, checking the fallen man's eyes, slapping his cheeks. Mac is flopping, nonresponsive. It's a knockout for Dobbs. Muttering starts in the back, behind the Tacoma man's corner. The air, still charged, takes on a bitter tinge. An elbow clips Alma on the hip. Around her, men shift uneasily. The referee, not looking too calm himself, lifts Dobbs's hand, and the muttering spills into boos.

"You fucking bogtrotter!" a man yells from the hallway door, and then, in the back by Dobbs's corner, a yelp, a surge in the crowd.

The Tacoma man rips Mac's colors off the post. Then he and his corners hustle out of the ring, shoving through the six feet of crowd and into the hall, Dobbs still barefoot and shirtless. Better to catch pneumonia than be murdered.

Alma takes another shove to the back. Conaway—along with Driscoll and Barker, if they ever made it back to that spot—is pinned between Sloan's men and the brawl developing in the far corner. Wheeler and McManus, on the other side of the ring, aren't near any trouble. Yet. She is closest to the door. Someone knocks off her cap and it's lost in a churn of boots. An elbow digs into her ribs, just below her binding cloth; a reminder of her hidden body that grinds against the desire to fight, to start a clot of violence all her own. She can't see Wheeler anymore over the red faces, the jostling. In the far corner a crunch, a high scream. All right. Time to get out.

She pushes toward the door. Breathless crush in the bottleneck of the hallway, then she's in the saloon. The boards underfoot are dark. Men are flooding into the night more than they are returning to the counter for another round.

At the bar Clay sets a tumbler before her. If he recognizes her as an acquaintance of Wheeler's, he gives no sign of it.

"That was a god damn disappointment," she says. "Gin, double."

"Thought it might go longer," Clay says, his voice neutral.

"Mac should have taken it in the third round."

Alma pauses, her hand in her pocket, her teeth out and stinging in the cold air. Wheeler's come up next to her, still wearing his gray coat. He sets down his hat. She sets down a dime, close to his fist. His gold ring glints.

"That's the truth," she says. "What are you drinking, Mr. Wheeler? It's on me."

"A drop of the pure," he tells Clay.

"Dobbs was playing slow, that whole fight," she says when

Wheeler has a tumbler in hand. "Testing our man. Sneaky, but a good strategy."

"Seems like something you'd favor," he says. "The bait and switch."

"I hardly want to say it. But maybe our man just isn't that smart. Too easily fooled."

"That would be an unpopular opinion," Wheeler says. "I'd be careful with it."

They are standing close. Elbows almost touching. Facing the bar counter, not each other. Here, in the saloon, the codes between them are different. It's not Wheeler's office but a public space, and none but the two of them knows what is under Alma's clothes.

"Careful? I've been hungry for a scrap." She leans in closer, drops her voice, hot clove scent in her nose. "Maybe tonight's the night for one."

"Four rounds not enough for you?"

"Not hardly." She tosses back her drink, shrugs off her jacket and slings it on the counter. Letting him see how ready, how strong-bodied she is—not mere empty talk. "I'm just getting warmed up."

"Did you catch the moment when Mac could have had it?" he says. "In the third round."

"After the hook. But he backed off. Why?"

"Making a plan, maybe." Wheeler sips his whiskey. "But maybe he should have moved sooner. Taken what he wanted."

She lifts her left boot, deliberate. Props it on the rail. Edging into the space at the front of his body, the hem of his overcoat brushing past her knee. Giving him something to lean into. If he will. Her heartbeats fast and thick and fevered.

"They ought to have a rematch," she says.

He folds his arms on the bar top. Shifts his stance. There is pressure on her leg. A hard ridge warm against the outside of her thigh. She pushes back.

"Most definitely." Wheeler is keeping a straight face like a champion, tilting his whiskey tumbler forward and back so the liquid pulses.

Alma admires the line of muscle in his neck from collar to jaw, sharp-cut in the lamplight, his skin freshly shaved.

"Let's go," she says, quiet.

"Mr. Wheeler." It's McManus. Angling through a knot of men to stand at Wheeler's other side. Alma scowls at him. Wheeler pulls his body away from her leg. Tilts his head toward the other man. McManus speaks into his ear, too low for Alma to hear. She can't get a fix on McManus's mouth to piece-read it. Wheeler's eyes drift between his boots and the bar top as he listens, losing the ghost of a smile he had during his banter with her, his face turning grave.

"Where is he?" he says, setting his tumbler on the countertop.

A quick sharpening of his eyes on hers—an urgency there, a message she is not sure of—and McManus nods to the far-left corner of the bar. Barnaby Sloan stands under a lantern, its yellow light oily on his blond hair. Wheeler takes his hat and walks toward him. She can't grab at Wheeler, so she goes for McManus; he is following, but slower, and her fingers in his denim yank him to a stop.

"What's up?" she says.

"Let go," he says.

"Fuck you. What's going on?"

Wheeler reaches Sloan. They do not shake hands, Wheeler running the brim of his hat through his fingertips. They are ten feet from Alma. She doesn't like leaving him with Sloan—in the smoky dim there could be a knifing, a shot—but there is Clay, polishing a glass behind the bar at Sloan's back, and there is Conaway, hulking tall over both men, a solid slab of bone and muscle should Wheeler need backup. A thin scream wavers in from the storeroom, abruptly stops.

"Let go or I'll shoot you," McManus says, swinging close to hiss into her face.

"You jealous?" She doesn't loosen her hold on his sleeve. "You should be. The boss man likes me better."

McManus is sweating and steel eyed, his jacket rough in her fist, her pulse thumping hot in her neck. He darts a glance at Wheeler. His hand twitches toward his chest, toward the lump of his gun.

"None of that." Alma jerks him closer, the heavy weight of him bouncing into her shoulder. "You start a firefight in a crowded bar, you're stupider than I thought."

"I owe you a bullet," he says, breath sour on her face.

"Oh, no. You want to have a go with me again, you use your fists." She nods at the door, the cold darkness outside. "You'll lose, but you're always going to lose against me."

She glances back at Wheeler, who is still speaking to Sloan. Clay and Conaway still keeping watch. Someone smashes into her. She lets go of McManus's sleeve, fists ready, but it's only Driscoll, his hair mussed, his smile loose at the corners.

"They're tearing up a few Tacoma boys in there," he says, panting, nodding at the storeroom.

"Not now," she says, shoving him off.

He stumbles back, blinking, stupid with too much drink. There's another scream from the storeroom, closer to the jointed hall. A man falls through the doorway, jacketless, his shirt ripped open, a trickle of blood leaking teardrop-like from one eye.

McManus's attention is darting between her and Wheeler and the howling in the hallway. The math of it ticking over his face: the chance of something going bad while they're outside, dancing.

"Eleven years of hard work, and I take over in a week," Alma says, to help him make up his mind. He won't be much sport, bruised to hell and with his bad leg, but if he can't walk, he can't make deals in Seattle. "How does it feel?"

Now McManus isn't looking at the hall or Wheeler or the door. Just at her. He twists from the hip, sends a sly hook at Alma's chin. One knuckle grazes her jawbone and the fire is burning, hot in her teeth, hot in her gut as she delivers a quick snap to his stomach.

Driscoll shoulders between them.

"Christ Jesus, what's the matter with you?" he says, one hand on each of their chests as McManus coughs for air. "Save it for the Tacoma lads."

"Get out of the way." Alma knocks Driscoll's hand off her breast. Only three layers of cloth without her jacket, so she felt the heat of his palm. She bares her teeth.

"Camp—"

"This isn't your fight, Conall," McManus tells him, straightening up, still unsteady.

His posture, Driscoll's sideways lean, leave her an opening for a jab. She launches a beauty right into his throat. Gristle and bone under her finger-backs and McManus is choking again; she is laughing aloud.

Now McManus throws aside the protesting Driscoll, right into a group of dockmen. Space is tight. They are hemmed in by the dockmen—Driscoll skidding through their midst—and by a pocket of crowd, so Alma can't dodge away when McManus spits in her face, hot in her eyes, and follows with a bonecrusher to her sternum, right at the notch that presses bad into the diaphragm.

"Fuck," she says, blinded, and there is more screaming in the hall. The bar's crowd is shifting, uneasy, contracting away from her and McManus. In the blurred lantern light the men are a night-colored wave, eyes like far-off city lights, murmuring harshly. Crunch of glass. High whining.

Shaking her head, shaking clearer her eyes, she lunges at McManus, coming a quarter inch from smashing his nose—it bends, just slightly, under her lead knuckle—and they are turning. McManus trips and goes down. She sneers at his bad knee, at his clumsiness, waiting for him to stand, but he doesn't. He is staring. Crawling to his side. His focus is not on her.

"Get up," he says, and she wipes her eyes with her sleeve.

Down in the shadows of the floor he is holding a long thing, a dark thing: a leg. Her vision clicks into place with her thinking and she follows the leg up to a belt, up to a vest, up to a face. Driscoll's face.

"Get up," McManus says again. He's not talking to himself, as she first thought. He's talking to the boy, but Driscoll's eyes are wide, they are wide and frightened, and he does not get up.

Alma steps toward them, shouldering past a pitch-smeared mill worker, and her boot skids over the boards. She can't see the floor, can barely see Driscoll's face, and she wants to think she's stepped in spilled liquor, but McManus is still saying, "Get up," and his voice is ugly, cracking. Against the bar, four feet away, Sloan's man Loomis is watching her. He smiles. Wipes his ruined nose and his fingers are red, maybe, or maybe it's just a shadow from the splintering lanterns.

"Is this your work?" she asks him, and her knife is in her hand, haft warm with her body heat so it feels part of her palm.

"Conall," McManus says, at her knees.

She can't fight Sloan's man. She can't ruin the deal. Sloan purchased their tar with the promise of peace—mutual peace, with no more attacks on each other's men. But Loomis knifed Driscoll, maybe. And his rotted-out grin brings a roaring to her ears.

"Help the kid," she tells McManus, but when she steps over Driscoll's shoulder her gut surges—there is blood, behind him, under him, a dark scribbling laced with pieces of glass, and his eyes don't follow her movement. McManus sways to his feet, bad leg crooked, and now Loomis is not smiling, he is showing all the yolky whites of his eyes.

"He's mine," McManus says.

Alma crowds in front of him, growling.

"No," she says, looking away from Sloan's man to McManus's waxen face.

When she looks back, Loomis has his gun out, two feet away, the barrel gaping and terrible and pointed at her. McManus yanks at her shirt in time with a heart-stomping explosion. The room snaps sideways.

She can't breathe.

Driscoll's face is snow-colored next to hers.

21

JANUARY 25, 1887

TRANSCRIPT OF INTERVIEW WITH SAMUEL REED

WHEREUPON THE FOLLOWING PROCEEDINGS WERE HAD IN THE JEFFERSON COUNTY JAIL, PORT TOWNSEND, WASHINGTON TERRITORY, ON JANUARY 25, 1887.

LAWMEN PRESENT: CITY MARSHAL GEORGE FORRESTER, OFFICER WAYLAN HUGHES

TRANSCRIPTION: EDWARD EDMONDS, ASSISTANT DEPUTY COLLECTOR, U.S. CUSTOMHOUSE

OFFICER HUGHES: That's all we're asking for, Sam. The truth. So let's start fresh. From the day . . . from that day Sloan attacked you. After you woke up, his man, Loomis, took you to a room in the house? What happened then?

MR REED: I slept for a long time. Maybe half a day. Someone brought me some soup and bread, a little vial of Figg's Tincture for the pain.

OFFICER HUGHES: And once you were up again?

MR REED: Loomis was waiting for me in the hall. He said we were going to go to work.

MARSHAL FORRESTER: This was the next morning?

MR REED: No, it was the middle of the night. It was snowing. We went out to the cannery, and on the way Loomis gave me a gun. I didn't want it. I was seeing double with the pain. He took me to a room inside the cannery.

OFFICER HUGHES: What was in the room?

MARSHAL FORRESTER: Opium?

MR REED: There were men chained to the walls. At least ten of them, maybe more? It was dark. The fellow closest to me had bare feet. It must have been awful, in the cold . . .

MARSHAL FORRESTER: Who were these men? Were they Chinese?

MR REED: No. No Chinese, not that I could see. Later Loomis told me they were men Sloan's crimps had picked up, promised to the captain of an incoming boat.

OFFICER HUGHES: Shanghaied.

MARSHAL FORRESTER: You'll see it a lot round here. Tacoma's got it worse.

OFFICER HUGHES: How is this possible? Every vice on the waterfront is happening under Sloan's watch, and we've got nothing on him.

MARSHAL FORRESTER: Like I said, I've heard things.

MR REED: Then why are you giving me such a bad time?

MARSHAL FORRESTER: You speak when you're spoken to.

OFFICER HUGHES: We should send men to arrest Sloan. If we wait too long, he'll notice Reed is missing. He'll get suspicious. Maybe run.

MARSHAL FORRESTER: I want the full story. And I want to be there to collar the bastard.

MR REED: He'll know by now you picked me up. He'll know I'm talking—

OFFICER HUGHES: More reason to act—

MARSHAL FORRESTER: I'm going to be the one to arrest Sloan, once I have all the facts. This is going to be the police bust of the decade. It's got shanghaiing, girls, opium . . . Everyone will be watching. It's not the time for us to make a mistake.

MR REED: Just let me out before he comes in—

OFFICER HUGHES: A woman was killed. I'm more interested in solving that crime than the publicity.

MARSHAL FORRESTER: You're pretty damn green when it comes to police work, Hughes.

OFFICER HUGHES: I served for six years in Peoria, sir.

MARSHAL FORRESTER: And you've served for three months in Port Townsend. We do things differently here. There are a lot of concerned citizens to consider.

OFFICER HUGHES: Jackson can at least get some men together—

MARSHAL FORRESTER: Sit down. You sit down until we get the whole story.

OFFICER HUGHES: Sir—

MARSHAL FORRESTER: That's an order.

OFFICER HUGHES: Yes, sir.

MR REED: Please. Let me out, then get Sloan. Don't bother with the cannery—those men are long gone, and there won't be dope either. Sloan just sent off a big shipment last night.

MARSHAL FORRESTER: Well, I'll be.

OFFICER HUGHES: Wait a minute. Something's not adding up. Why would Sloan want Miss Calhoun's girls to be his mules if he was shipping out crates of the stuff already?

MR REED: He wanted to move more dope, I guess.

MARSHAL FORRESTER: You guess.

MR REED: All I know is that Sloan wanted to use Sugar's girls. She said no, he left her alone. Would have kept leaving her alone, except she sent me to the cannery to copy the keys . . . and I got caught.

MARSHAL FORRESTER: You never found out why she had you casing Sloan's cannery?

MR REED: I did.

OFFICER HUGHES: And? How?

MR REED: I saw Sugar. One more time, before last night.

MARSHAL FORRESTER: You said you couldn't get away from Sloan, or his men. How'd you manage a visit with her?

MR REED: It was the night of that boxing match. Everyone cleared out to go watch it—Sloan, Loomis, the other men. They posted me at the cannery. It's on Quincy Wharf, same as Chain Locker. Sloan swore he'd gut me if I tried to run off. I started to creep away about a hundred times, but I was too frightened to leave the wharf.

MARSHAL FORRESTER: Twenty feet from freedom, and you couldn't find the nerve.

MR REED: Leave me alone, won't you.

MARSHAL FORRESTER: Not a chance in hell, son.

OFFICER HUGHES: And Miss Calhoun? Did you go to her that night?

MR REED: She passed by on Water Street. I was on the cannery steps, smoking. She called my name.

OFFICER HUGHES: She was alone?

MR REED: Yes. She seemed frightened—when she walked up to me she had her derringer out, ready at her hip.

MARSHAL FORRESTER: A woman's intuition. She might have saved her own life if she took yours, then.

MR REED: Damn you.

OFFICER HUGHES: Just tell us what she said, Sam.

MR REED: She asked if I was Sloan's man, now. I told her I was, but not by choice. I said it was her own fault that I was working for a criminal. She said she was sorry, that she wasn't trying to get me into trouble, that she only wanted the cannery keys to give to the police, anonymously.

OFFICER HUGHES: Anonymously? Why?

MR REED: She said she'd come to the police once, to lodge a complaint about Sloan, but instead of receiving assistance she was threatened with arrest herself, for keeping a bawdy house.

OFFICER HUGHES: Sir?

MARSHAL FORRESTER: I'll have to look into that. I don't know who was on duty, or why she didn't just pay the fine, like the other women do. But why was she after Sloan?

MR REED: Because he'd threatened her. She was afraid of him. She'd heard rumors of dope and kidnapped men in his cannery, and she hoped exposing him would land him in jail.

OFFICER HUGHES: We turned her away. She might still be alive, but we turned her away.

MARSHAL FORRESTER: They all have to pay the fine, Hughes.

MR REED: That night, at the cannery, she asked for my help again. I was on Sloan's crew, she said, and I could help her bring him down.

MARSHAL FORRESTER: You didn't agree? That ought to have suited you just fine, based on how he'd treated you.

MR REED: I told her it was a bad idea. Sloan would kill us both . . . We were arguing when the boxing match ended. There was gunfire inside the saloon. Men brawling outside, fifty feet away. Sugar left in a hurry.

OFFICER HUGHES: Did Sloan know why she wanted the cannery keys? Did he know Sugar was trying to have him arrested?

MR REED: I didn't say a thing about that night, but Sloan had suspected her from the start. He had asked me if she was working with the police, when he first caught me, and was . . . was hurting me. He was wary of everyone. He thought a lot of people were after him—even some of his own men.

OFFICER HUGHES: So Sloan had cause to kill Miss Calhoun after all. He killed her and had you load her body into the scow.

MR REED: Yes.

MARSHAL FORRESTER: I'm going to get him.

MR REED: Oh, I hope you do.

22

JANUARY 19, 1887

Breathe and it's hot ash burning, lungs bellowing, wires of pain lacing her shoulder tight, her teeth tight. Her left deltoid a blazing mash. Boots pounding into wood at her ear. Gunpowder in her mouth.

"Back off! God damn you."

Glass bursting behind her, so close she squeezes her eyes against the shards, a cold rain on her face.

Grunts, swearing. Coming from her or another, she can't tell. Roll over, get up. Her left hand doesn't exist. Her left elbow. Get up, Rosales. No. Camp. Get up, Camp.

"He glassed Conall, I'll break his fucking—"

"Shut up. Go outside. Now."

A shadow looms over her closed eyes. She cracks them open, careful of glass caught on her lids, and Conaway is upside-down, stunned.

"Help him."

She can't see Wheeler, but this is his voice. Past Conaway is a ring of faces. Blood needles back into her limbs, kicked fast by fear. She puts her right hand, still in a fist around her knife, to her chest— her left hand ghostly, not where it should be—and her shirt is hot and slippy. Sickness. If the bullet tore an artery, she might die here, in this shithole town, drained of her own dark matter. She breathes deep. Smells blood. Gunpowder. Whiskey.

"Let's see how bad, Camp."

Conaway puts his hands on her shirtfront as if to tear it open. She wrenches away.

"Get off me," she says.

She angles her knife at him. Scrabbles her boots against the wood. They don't stick enough to act as leverage. Don't panic. Get up.

Fear, sickness. She needs to move fast, needs to keep herself mobile in this seething crowd. The staring circle of others wavers. The lantern above the bar splits into two lanterns, four, more. Then Wheeler is standing over her, his gray coat brushing her jaw, his mouth at Conaway's ear, and they hoist her up with their arms around her low ribs, her shirt still buttoned on, the movement tearing at her shoulder and she's going to vomit. It hurts so much more than she remembers, but she won't go down like this, god damn it.

"Damn it! Easy." She's saying that aloud, there's a belt cutting into her armpit, sharp leather biting into skin, an extra jacket packed over her shoulder and it's Driscoll's lined denim and it's bloody and they are outside in the snow, flakes glowing honey-gold as they swarm around the streetlamps. Stumbling, limbs locked with Conaway's. He bears most of her weight. Cold on her face. Cold on her chest. Nothing on her left hand.

A blur of buildings, the men muttering over her slumped head, the office stairs snowy, so familiar to the night she was first dragged in that she laughs, but it comes out as a cough that shakes fire out of her shoulder and down into her lungs.

"Get Nell Roberts," Wheeler says, and Barker is standing there, cap to chest.

"No!" Alma twists in Conaway's grip. "No. Not her."

Nell can't see her like this, she can't see her as Camp peeled open and showing her cloth underpinnings like this, the breasts she's done so well hiding, the way Nell looked at her when they were dancing, when she ate candy out of Alma's hand—she was promised cake, she was promised time alone with all that soft skin.

"Who would you rather?" Wheeler says in her ear, harsh.

And there's no one else. It can't be Conaway. It can't be Barker or McManus. Driscoll is gone. There's no one else.

The blue hall. The blue carpet. Wheeler never uses the Quincy door—he's in a hurry.

They prop her against the office wall, Wheeler leaning into her, warm and good smelling after rancid Conaway, who has a wife— how can she stand him? Wheeler's hip pressed against hers to keep her upright. This is not how the night was supposed to run—or it is, but it's wrung out, crumpled. It's hard to stand, but this is the smart thing to do, keep the blood away from her shoulder and where she needs it, in her heart and in her head. *Buck up, kid*, Hannah would say, laughing. Hannah would tell the story of the operative who was shot in the arm and tied her limb to a lintel, letting gravity act as a tourniquet while she fainted, until she could recover enough to see to the wound.

"Jesus, he's bleeding," Conaway says, lighting a lamp, shaking out the match. "Sir, your coat—"

She closes her eyes to focus. Each inhale a wheeze she hears high in her throat. Wheeler undoes the belt at her arm socket and yanks it tighter. Pain jolt. Buckle click.

"Let Nell in when she comes. Let only Nell in."

Conaway hustling to the door, footsteps shaking the floorboards. Blink hard and there is Wheeler's face, close.

"Oh, Christ," she says.

"What the fuck were you thinking?"

"It's McManus," she says. "He's the thief."

His hand on her chin, hard, tips her lolling head up.

"The both of you, drunk and brawling like fools." His face pale, a dark strand of hair knocked loose from the rest to fall over his forehead. "Half the waterfront there and you pick a fight with Sloan's man when you know, you know, you have to leave him be."

McManus started it, she wants to say, but that would sound like an excuse. And it's not true. McManus is the thief. That is true. Her arm gnaws away at her concentration.

"I'll deal with Tom," Wheeler says, and Alma doesn't know what she's thinking and what she's said aloud. She blinks down at her bloodstained sleeve, vision splintered.

"Is it bad?" she says.

A shadow in his eyes; a pause in his breath.

"I don't know yet." His fingers loosen, thumb tracing the front notch of her jaw.

"Driscoll," she says, remembering his face, and it's too close to Yuma now, Hannah's voice in her head, "Make sure we're out before you move," passing a bottle around on the hill behind the safe house, piss-reek of sagebrush, horseflies thick in the summer night, "Make sure," Hannah had said, but Alma got impatient for action, for gunfire, the smoke clearing so she saw—

Gut heave and she curls sideways, away from Wheeler, the steak dinner she ate before the fight and the gin she pounded down during ripping out of her, the busted muscles at her shoulder tearing with each jerky coil-in of her body.

"What is going on?"

"He's been shot. Maybe more."

"Oh, God, his shirt—"

Bile tang and iron blood. She is hauled upright, Wheeler rough in his handling, but then a softer touch on her cheek, a cloth wiping her mouth. Gold hair, sweet perfume. Nell. Still in her green dress.

"Mind the belt," Wheeler says.

Silver glint of scissors up her sleeve. The stained cotton peeling away.

"Oh, Jack."

"Is that the only wound?"

Nell unbuttoning her collar, soft fingers on the underside of her chin. Alma slides to one side evasively. The wall slippery against her back. No knives of pain apart from her arm and Wheeler, you son of a bitch, did you say that just so Nell would strip off the shirt and see the bindings? He keeps her in place with his knee, his side.

"Son of a bitch."

"Shh," Nell says. "Let's get this off."

Nell works down the buttons, a line of touch from sternum to navel, pulling open the shirt as she goes. Smile worried, but warm. Golden curls at her ears asway.

"Let Wheeler do the rest," Alma tells her, but Nell peels off the sticky cotton.

Alma is folded away from the wall and onto Wheeler. Fingers on the back of her neck. His twill vest rasping against the skin of her stomach, bare and cold below her binding cloth.

"I can stand just fine," she says, stupid.

Wheeler laughs, short, a huff of sound that pushes his belly against hers.

"Shut up, would you," he says.

Nell saw. She saw the binding. Wheeler made sure of it. Made sure Alma's game with Nell was up. Even though he liked to hear about it, red ears, red throat. Doesn't he want to be in the office all three tangled, heat from the hearth and skin slick on the dark-wood desk and the leather chair creaking? Alma wants it. But not like this, with puke reeking on the carpet and her head going dim. Warm hands track around the pain in her shoulder.

"The bullet cut deep," Nell says beside her. "And there's glass. The bleeding is slowing, but you left it so long."

Maybe too long. Her vision fuzzed, her pulse sluggish. At least the bullet didn't stick. There will be no knife tip digging into her living meat.

"Can you fix it?"

"It needs stitching," Nell says. "And I'll have to get the glass out."

Alma buries her face in Wheeler's neck. He stiffens, his arm around her waist stiffens, she could bite him when they're this close, her nose below his ear, his pulse against her cheek. He deserves it.

"Here," Nell says.

Wheeler resettles her against the wall, pressing the edge of his body into hers. He holds up a cup brimming with whiskey. His vest splotched with dark stains. She gulps it quick.

"The good stuff," she says.

Nell is rummaging through a bag on the desk, ten feet away, her forest-green dress shimmering in the lamplight. She is threading a needle. She is pouring out another cup of liquor.

"I only keep the good stuff," Wheeler says.

"You did that on purpose," Alma says, quiet. "So she would see."

"I was being careful."

"Fuck you."

His eyes flinted with anger but he's hiding something again, like he does, something twitching at the edges of his mouth, in the movement of his eyebrows. Then he leans into her again. Pulls her against him. One hand splayed warm over her bare lower back, thumb fitting into the groove of her spine. His other hand worms between them to shove the starched collar of his shirt between her teeth.

"Hold on," Nell says, and then cold, pain, the whole world condensing into a bolt of fire in her deltoid. Brassy peat sting, ice dripping down her shoulder blade, wet along her binding cloth, disappearing on her nowhere lower arm.

It lasts for too long, needle piercing, fever, oh, Jesus, her jaw is trembling from grinding down onto cotton, but she is quiet save for the breaths hissing in and out of her nose, and that composure is good, Hannah taught her good, taught her well, it's been eight years since she died and Alma can still hear her voice, "Make sure before you move," when they said goodbye at the Yuma hotel not knowing it was the last goodbye. Red, hot, red, she is sweating, angry, gutsick, Conall and Hannah sound the same when whispered, hot, red.

"All right. Finished."

Wheeler takes his collar from her mouth, takes his hand from her back, his palm unsticking from her sweaty skin. The wall cold against her good shoulder, against the side of her forehead, the front of her body cold where it pressed into Wheeler's. Corkscrews of pain as Nell fishes out glass chips that dug deep through her shirt: back, armpit, upper rib. Fingers on her binding cloth, but they do not linger. Nell pours more whiskey onto a cloth and packs it against the side of Alma's shoulder, then wraps clean cloth around her arm. The belt left in place to thump against her ribs. Wheeler brings a clean shirt. Nell helps Alma into it, buttoning her up like a child.

"We'll go to my house," Nell says, pulling on her shawl at the door.

"No. I've called a hansom, to the boardinghouse."

"A boardinghouse? Freezing cold, with slop buckets stinking up the place?"

Wheeler steps away from Alma, raises an eyebrow. She nods; she can stand on her own. Just about.

"This is not your concern—" Wheeler says.

"I don't mind Nell's house." Alma elbows away from the wall, grunting. Words slurry. Legs rubber-boned as if she just stepped off a rough-water boat. "She's going to make me a cake."

Fingers dragging over blue paper. Her left arm thumping useless at her side. At the door and Wheeler's teeth are clenched, Nell is frowning, Conaway is on the other side of the wood and knocking, calling out, "Cab's here, sir."

"Money for the driver," Wheeler says, hand to Nell's. "And for some food."

In the hall and Nell guides her into the cold circle of Conaway's arm, his bearskin smell. Alma looks back at Wheeler, knot-browed in the doorway, his vest and sleeve stained, his body outlined with firelight.

"Is Loomis still alive?" she says.

He nods from the door.

"Is he going to stay that way?"

He shrugs.

"I want to be the one to do it," she says. "Wait for me—"

Conaway steers her around the dogleg turn and Wheeler is out of sight, Nell hurrying before them in a flurry of skirts and honeysuckle perfume, out onto the steps and toward the carriage waiting in the snow.

23

JANUARY 20, 1887

Alma rears awake, breath stinging, pulse hard. A purple wall. Sunlight behind a lace curtain. She moves to sit up, and a kicking pain reminds her of her shoulder. She is in Nell's bed, the sheets sweet with perfume, a knit blanket soft under her forearms.

She tries to shift her left shoulder—wheezes, fails. That deltoid is no good, full of barbs and splinters, her left arm dead. A moment of panic, grappling at the bandage, then finding her elbow and feeling her own touch, feeling it move down to her hand. The nerves in her arm can still be made to sing. She stares up at the pale wood slats of the ceiling, thinking of kneading the blanket's wool, little movements in her left fingers though they feel fattish, clumsy. She is still wearing Wheeler's shirt. Her own filthy trousers.

"Did I wake you?"

Alma dips her chin, exhaling hard, and there's Nell in the doorway. Wrapped in a shawl. Her face bare, her eyes tired.

"What time is it?"

"Two o'clock," Nell says. "Can you eat?"

"I might not try just yet. Something warm to drink?"

"I'll make coffee."

When Nell leaves the room, Alma starts the painful process of sitting up, wanting to wince and grimace when Nell is not there to witness, not there to see how she clutches at her right kneecap under the blanket, contracts her abdomen, breathes through the pain to pull herself upright, her left hand dragging over the wool. Its numbness alarms her. In the night she'd written it off as shock, blood loss, tourniquet choke, but it is still slow, still tingling. Her whole body hurts in a way it should not, an allover aching, but maybe this is the result of waiting an extra fifteen minutes to see to the wound: the cost of waiting for Nell and preserving her cover. Or maybe she's just getting old. When she was shot before, she was twenty—quicker to her feet, quicker to form new flesh over the wound.

She has her left hand in her lap, massaging the pin-filled littlest finger, when Nell comes back in with a tray. Rich dark scent, the sweetness of cream.

"Oh, no." Nell sets the coffee things on the bureau at the foot of the bed. "You should have waited."

Alma looks down, straining her eyes as low as they'll angle without her neck muscles pulling at her shoulder. Bright red pools on the cloth of Wheeler's shirt.

"Shit," she says.

"I'll change the bandage."

"It's fine. I can't feel it."

Something in her recoils from showing the binding cloth again.

"Come on." Nell drapes her shawl on the bedpost and sits beside Alma. Her eyes, in this light, are honey brown. A strand of hair sticks to her lower lip.

"You'll have to help me," Alma says, and here's another thing made no good—she's in Nell's house, in Nell's god damn bed, and she can barely sit up. Their game over now that Nell's seen too much of Jack Camp. "My arm's not working right."

Nell unbuttons the shirt. Air cool on her stomach, Nell's eyes on her shoulder, air cool on her back as they peel the cotton away and Nell bundles it onto the floor. Alma is bared to the waist, her binding cloth stiff with dried blood along her side. Fingers on her skin. Nell's weight shifting the mattress. A draft of cold air, a trickle of heat.

"I don't like how much you're bleeding," Nell says. "Hold still. I'm going to wrap it tighter."

A deep press of pain—Alma exhales hard through her nose—
and then little spasms as Nell winds a fresh length of cloth around
her shoulder, looping it over and under, her hands brushing the
bound side of Alma's left breast.

"I didn't want you to see me like this." Alma's voice, grooved
into Camp's deeper register, takes on an uncertain waver. How are
you going to play it? She wants to be Camp for Nell, but she is
peeled down to her own body, peeled down to woman skin.

"I'm not angry, Jack."

"Why are you calling me that?" she says, harsh.

Nell might be toying with her, to take everything in stride like
this. But maybe Nell guessed from the start. Maybe Delphine tipped
her off. And if she already knew, she still invited Alma over for
cake. If she already knew, she might still be game.

"It's your name." Nell scoots off the bed, dropping the bloody
bandage onto Wheeler's bloody shirt and bundling all the soiled
cotton together. "Unless you tell me otherwise."

Maybe waking up half-naked in Nell's bed is going to work out
right.

She comes back with clean hands, pink from scrubbing. Pours
coffee into a china cup, adds cream at Alma's nod.

It doesn't hurt to swallow. As the liquid drains down her throat,
her gut wakes. Wrenched empty the night before, it's now ready
for steak or pan biscuits or a whole pot of lamb stew.

"I could eat," Alma says. "Have you got anything?"

"There's a bakery a few doors down. I'll see if they have some
pies."

"You're an angel," Alma calls. The more they talk, the more her
voice is settling back into Camp's low drawl.

As soon as the front door sounds, she kicks down the blanket,
her trousers wretched against the clean sheets. The floorboards cold
under her bare feet. When she tries to stand, her knees buckle and
she hits the ground hard, right hip, right elbow, the impact jarring
a hot burst of blood from her shoulder into the bandage, the pain
jarring a yelp from her throat.

"God damn it."

Weak as a new colt, her legs uncooperative, her left arm useless, she fights her way up using the bedpost. That fifteen minutes of blood lost to keep her cover is not seeming like such a good trade now, when it's left her too shaky to stand, her head pounding, the punctured meat of her deltoid screaming.

Focus.

First: the toilet. All that whiskey's run through her and she'll take a bucket, a grass patch, anything near. Toward the door, walking crabwise to lean against the bed frame with her right hand, then staggering into the purple hall, pushing hard off the wall, palm dragging over the ridged paper with a trailing squeak. There's a ribbon of daylight: a little enclosure off the kitchen, two steps down to a dirt square fenced in with boards man-height. The air so cold it stings. Alma jolts down the stairs, learning the new way her body is moving, dead-weighted on the upper left, but her left leg sturdier than the right—some bad fall in the blurred night has beat her right knee and shin into shaking. There's no bucket here so she unbuttons her trousers clumsily, one-handed, works them down the same, says a prayer peppered with oaths as she lowers into a squat, her thighs unsteady. Sun on her bare back: a rarity. Icy air between her legs, hot splashing onto the dirt, onto her bunched trousers, but what can she do? It's taking everything to grip the lip of the top step and keep her balance.

Then levering up, piss-spattered but relieved, jouncing on her trousers, trying to use her left hand on the buttons but it's like a brick, all edges and heavy. Up the steps—up, damn it—and back into the kitchen, closing the door, the iron kettle on the stove seeping heat. The January page of a Wakefield's farmers' almanac pinned to one wall. A bowl of green apples on the table, weighing down a thin newspaper. Alma eats an apple in huge bites down to the seeds, spitting pith into her palm. The paper's main headline reads, "Macaulay-Dobbs Match Ends in Misery." No mention of Driscoll in the write-up; Alma's throat tightens when she realizes she's looking for his name.

A wave of sickness. Driscoll is dead. She knew this last night, but the knowledge was blurred by pain, by liquor. Now she *knows* it. The knowing is hard and sharp as a blade pressed into her midsection. Breathe too hard, push too hard against it, and something will burst. Blood, or tears. She fucked up again. Starting the fight with McManus that went so bad, so fast. And where is that bastard? Did he come back to the office? She remembers Wheeler, and Conaway. Nell. She remembers telling Wheeler that McManus is their thief, but she can't remember what Wheeler said.

Alma doesn't want to think of McManus, or Driscoll, or blood on the bar floor, so she pages slowly through the paper, reading all the vessel lists in the shipping news, the prices in sketched advertisements for shoes. On the third page is a large advertisement for Elliot & Co. Brickworks. The sunburst logo. The memory of Frank Elliot at the Seattle docks, smirking at her poor dress, asking if she'd given up on finding a man of her own after years of skulking after other women's wayward husbands. That son of a bitch. Joe's welcome to tear him to pieces. But Loretta Elliot comes to mind, next, along with Delphine's wish for a female-run operation in Tacoma. Elliot said Loretta was doing the brickworks' bookkeeping. She has a head for business, he'd said. Loretta was always fascinated by Alma's underworld ties, by the idea of slumming it with a bunch of smuggler lowlifes. If Frank Elliot was put out of the picture, Loretta might be worth bringing in.

Alma hobbles into the bedroom, blinking away vertigo. Ripples of unsteadiness run hot across her skin. She wraps the blanket around her upper body and leans against the wall by the window, the lace curtain brushing her cheek, her closed eyes.

Finally, the front latch rattles. Alma hopes for something hot: a meat pie, or a turnover, sugar-sprinkled and crisp from the oven. But when Nell comes into the doorway, her hands are empty. She is pale, her green shawl slipping off one shoulder.

"You all right?"

"Yes," Nell says. "The bakeshop was closed."

"That's a damn shame."

"I heard about Driscoll." Nell's wide eyes, her quick errand drawn long, start to make sense. "From the neighbor women. That poor boy."

Alma makes a fist so hard her knuckles pop. That blade of knowing back at her gut: Driscoll's face frozen next to hers, his glass-laced blood in thick spatters on the floor. It was nobody's fault, but she can say that a hundred times and it doesn't get any truer. She and McManus started that spark, that pocket of violence that swallowed Driscoll whole.

"He wasn't a child," Alma says. "He was drunk and stupid. If he'd been able to stand up on his own, that never would have happened."

"What a thing to say."

"I'll say worse if you keep talking about it."

Alma's shoulder hurts. Her neck. She is angry at the pulped slowness of her body, angry that she is still so dizzy, so dependent on the wall.

"I need to eat." She pushes away from the window, limps toward the kitchen. "I can barely stand, I'm so hungry."

"There's half a loaf in the breadbox," Nell says. "Some eggs."

"And my shirt?"

"It's soaking. To get the blood out."

"What am I supposed to do without it?" Alma says, sharp. "I don't have all day to sit around."

Nell stops in the kitchen doorway. Alma lurches past, the blanket wrapped around her shoulders catching at Nell's dress. She can't afford to lose a whole day. She needs to find out what happened with McManus. He disappeared too quick, and she doesn't trust him. Not that she can track him down in this state.

"You're difficult to love," Nell says.

"Nobody asked you to."

Alma sits down hard, the chair jarring her shoulder, not even trying to tear the loaf with her bad hand, just bringing the whole wheaten mass to her mouth and biting off a chunk.

"Fry me three eggs," she says, her mouth full of bread, not looking at Nell.

"Do it yourself."

When Alma looks up again, the doorway is empty.

She eats all the bread, though by halfway through she's not hungry anymore. It is dry and sticks in her throat. The coffee Nell brewed comes to mind. Leaving crumbs scattered on the table, Alma shoves to her feet, no better off for having eaten and sat down. Her left hand is tingling. She bangs it against the edge of the table twice, to knock some sense back into it. The pain is dull. Wrong.

Worry sets in once more. The gunshot wound's not that deep. It shouldn't be enough to cause such damage. Then there are her fists: fast, accurate. She is proud of her jabs, her head hooks, the speed of her strikes. A bad arm is a deadweight, a problem. She thinks of McManus and his bad leg. He is slow. He is ineffective. She does not want her wings clipped like that. And how does it look? A stab of vanity. She likes to watch her muscles shift in the mirror. The raised caps of her deltoids, the ripple of hardness under smooth skin. Now one is punctured. Her pride punctured, too.

Shrugging off the prickly wool of the blanket, she moves into the hallway, where cold air nips her bare skin.

Nell is mending by the bedroom window. Her needle catches sunlight in its short, sharp twists. Alma leans against the doorframe, the coffee she came in search of forgotten. The other woman's hair a gold swirl around her ears, around the edges of her neck. She really does look like Hannah in some lights. It's a confusion.

"Everything I say to you comes out wrong," Alma tells her.

Nell sighs. Lets the cloth she's holding sink into her lap. Her lips curve into a half smile.

"You didn't make the eggs, did you?" she says.

"No, ma'am."

"Your shoulder is bleeding again."

Nell comes out of her chair, walks across the squares of sunlight on the floor.

"I'll make the eggs," Nell says when they are standing close, her warm hands on Alma's bandages. "If you ask me nicely."

"What about the cake you promised? Can I still have that?"

Alma lifts her hand, slow. Trails the backs of her fingers along Nell's jaw, so light that their skins are barely touching. Nell's hands go quiet at her shoulder.

"I ought to wash your trousers," she says. "They're too filthy to wear to bed."

Either Nell is blushing or Alma's vision is darkening, both possible given the way her heart is speeding up. She drops her hand from Nell's cheek to the buttons of her trousers. One. Two, undone. Her fingers close to her sex, and it is tight, heating, drawing some of the pain out of her shoulder and draining it into a different kind of ache.

"This is about to be no fair." She's almost naked but moving like Camp, speaking like Camp just the same, and here is a new gray area in which to dwell. Quieter than what twists between her and Wheeler, softer than what links her to Delphine. "I'll have nothing on, but you have that dress."

Three buttons. The band of Alma's trousers droops around her hips. She looks up into Nell's eyes, the gold-flecked deepness of them. Nell has been drinking coffee; her breath smells of it, and sweet cream. She puts the tips of her fingers on Alma's bare stomach. Five points of fire, tracing a slow sweep across her low ribs, up to the raw underside of her binding cloth.

"Don't touch that." Alma's muscles clench. "It stays."

Nell shrugs, a little lift of one shoulder that moves her body closer.

"All right," she says.

"Keep doing the rest, though." Alma slides her hand up Nell's neck, the most of her she's touched openhanded, velvet flesh, hair soft on her knuckles. Pulls them together, slow, like they're moving through water, and puts her mouth to Nell's ear. "I've been thinking about you, honey. All the ways I'm going to please you."

A catch in Nell's breath. Soft press of her breasts against Alma's front. Alma tilts her head, sore neck muscles be damned, and tongues salt and heat from under Nell's ear.

"Jack—"

Soft hair in Alma's eyes, soft skin on her lips. She wants to hear Nell say her name again, loud, pleading. She wants Nell to take off her dress and show all the pinks and browns and shadows of her body, that honeysuckle musk scenting Wheeler's hallway on Alma's fingers, in her mouth.

She slides aside Nell's collar. Nuzzles under her clavicle as a knock sounds at the front of the house. The noise cracks them apart, Nell startling, her shoulders high.

"Oh, no." Alma holds the other woman close with her right hand at the small of her back, cursing her left arm as a no-good lump of shit. "Shop's closed."

"Wait," Nell says, pulling away as the knocking resumes. "It's Delphine."

24

JANUARY 20, 1887

"Delphine?" Alma's grip on her trousers falters, the front of her body cold where Nell had pressed against her.

"She's visiting today, like she promised," Nell says. "At three o'clock. Hurry, keep those on for now. Where's your jacket?"

Nell squeezes past Alma and into the purple-papered hall, calling out, "Just a moment," her slippers quick on the wood floors. Alma is lashed by Nell's closeness, by how it was ripped away. By Delphine's arrival: Alma's not ready for it. She buttons up her trousers with some trouble, not able to recall where she put her jacket. The blanket served earlier and it will have to serve now. Nell unbolts the front door, and sunlight pours warm into the hallway.

"Good afternoon, ma'am."

Alma wraps the blanket around her like a poncho, her shoulder stiff. She limps down the short hall. The light dims as Nell closes the door.

"Good afternoon, dear."

In the shop Delphine is taking off her gloves. She pauses, black crinkle of silk in one fist, when her eyes meet Alma's.

"Well," she says, her dark eyes unreadable. "I hope I'm not interrupting."

"A little bit." Alma is walking a fine line, her voice almost insolent.

"No, not at all," Nell rushes to say, and fusses with the beige chair in the corner. "Please, Mrs. Powell. Have a seat."

Delphine eases into the chair, gloves in her lap. Alma is watching the two women, hunting for a snag that shows the underpinnings of their relationship—it could be anything between them, loyalty or lust or pure servitude. Alma's seen Delphine inspire all of these things in men and women who did not at first seem susceptible. Felt some of each herself and not been sure why. She leans against the doorjamb. Spine of wood cold against her own, her eyes on the top button of Nell's dress, undone. A sneer wants to start on her lips. *I'm about to have her*, the sneer might say to Delphine, *so jump on in.*

"Make us some tea, would you?" Delphine says to Nell.

"Of course."

Nell hurries into the hall, her skirts brushing Alma's legs. As Nell clatters around in the kitchen, Delphine smiles at Alma. A warm smile, though her eyes are still guarded. Alma is wary—she has bad news to deliver—but they are alone in a private room again, at last, and Alma is stripped down to the skin. She is glad for Delphine to see her like this: those dark eyes on her, flickering over the blanket, the ridges of her exposed forearms, the line of muscle tracing down her stomach to the sagging band of her trousers. Alma has never felt so hard, so full of swagger and manhood, charged up by Nell's hands on her, by Nell's sighs.

"I thought I told you not to get distracted," Delphine says.

"I might be having fun," Alma says. "But that doesn't mean I'm dropping any balls."

Delphine laughs. Her face softens, but Alma doesn't know whether to trust it. She has to tell her about the Pinkerton's agents—about how things have gotten hot. How they're out of time. Damn it.

"And so saucy," Delphine says. "I've missed seeing you like this."

"I'll pay you a call anytime you like."

Alma peels away from the wall, takes three steps that bring her almost to stepping on Delphine's skirts. Her eyes on Alma's hips. One hand coming up to nudge her full lower lip, her ruby ring winking. Belatedly, Alma realizes her trousers are stiff with blood and sweat. Now that she's standing near Delphine, she hopes they don't reek of piss, too.

"I heard you were shot."

"News travels fast," Alma says, drawn closer as Delphine holds out her hand. Alma takes it: her warm palm, soft, the trace of her thumbnail over the calloused skin at the base of Alma's fingers.

"You love the fight, Rosales," Delphine says. "And I love that about you. But remember, you're still flesh and blood. When Nathaniel came to me with the news, I—"

Nell bustles in with a dish of chocolates.

"The kettle's on," she says, her cheeks pinkening as her gaze catches on Alma's and Delphine's hands, still interlocked.

"Wonderful." Delphine releases Alma's hand, something glinting in her eyes: mischief, or irritation. "I'm glad we had this chat arranged. After last night, I had to come check on . . . Jack."

Tell her about the Pinkerton's agents. Tell her, while she's flirtatious and almost smiling and might stay that way. But Nell is here, listening. Alma doesn't like how in Delphine's presence Nell dims a little, not so golden, not so enticing.

"Can I come to the house?" Alma says.

"I don't think so." Delphine nods at Alma's feet, planted wide for balance.

She looks down, and though she can't feel it, her left hand has started to shake.

"Jack, sit down." Nell rises, her light touch on Alma's elbow scratching the blanket against her skin.

Alma shrugs her off. The motion leaves her dizzy.

"Don't coddle me," she says.

At all costs she must stay standing. Delphine is watching her; Nell is close behind, warm, hovering. If Alma falters, it will feel like more than a physical shortcoming. She wants the two women to see her stand there, jaw set, bleeding but ready knuckled even though she's been kicked around.

"Take the day off," Delphine says. "You're only human. Let Nell see to you."

"They're coming," Alma says. She is busted up and reeling, but only she can handle the Pinkerton's agents—and she wants Delphine to know it. "Soon. We need to be ready."

Now she has Delphine's full, sober attention. Her dark eyes sharp. Her ring flashing as she drops her hand from her chin, curls it around her black gloves.

"Nell." Delphine doesn't say anything else, just nods at the inner rooms, and Nell bolts the front door and walks into the hall, pulling that door closed behind her. "I thought that was taken care of."

"It was," Alma says. "But we were meant to have friends on the case. Yesterday I found out they're not friends. Two new men, coming down from Colorado way. Due in Sunday."

"What are you going to do about it?"

"Thought I'd head them off in Tacoma. Ought to start getting to know the place, anyway."

This trip requires another disguise, of a sort. She must meet the Pinkerton's agents as Alma Rosales. Secretary to Daniel Lowry. Disgraced former agent scraping for any work she can get. Lowry's letter writer and link to the agency while he is undercover with the opium men.

"I thought we had more time," Delphine says. "Now you tell me we have three days."

"Or more. If I can persuade them to cool their heels in the Sound for a minute."

"Do try." Delphine stands, pulling on her gloves, tall in her heeled boots. "I have some social obligations to see to that will keep me away from Lower Town for a spell. I can't get mud on my skirts."

"What about that private call?" Alma lets the blanket slip to reveal her uninjured shoulder, its supple cap of muscle, the raised triangle of the tendons connecting her arm to her throat. "Sarah Powell's a busy woman. I wish she had more time for me."

Hot slide of Delphine's eyes down her right arm, skipping on the band of her trousers.

"She might if you'd get your job done," Delphine says. "I've been wanting to visit Tacoma."

Alma laughs.

"How long have you been using that name?"

"Sarah Powell." Delphine says the name with a dramatic flourish. "It's terribly boring, isn't it?"

"It doesn't suit you. The name. The clothes." All that somber cloth, the high choker of a collar. "I miss your old gowns. That red one. You wore it the night Finnegan died."

An evening of feasting, of excess: cigars, liquor, diamond-studded pistols, pretty company—the best bad things money can buy. The Nob Hill house a full-swing bandits' party, villains of all stripes on the stairs, in the corners, women draped in stolen jewels, men flashing stolen watches. Delphine's servants pouring bourbon like water, she watchful atop her smile, getting Finnegan and his friends stupid with drink so they would speak easy. Later, Alma smoking with Delphine on the balcony, feeling like a sparrow next to a phoenix in her drab wash dress, much patched, still living on bread and onions, still learning how to silence the part of her that yammered on like a policeman, listing her new comrades' sins: licentiousness, thievery, forgery, sodomy. Learning to listen as a new voice narrated the current of desire flowing toward Delphine like a sunset tide, the other woman so golden, so sharp-nailed and sure. She's a murderer and I don't care. She's a danger and I don't care. I don't care, I don't care. Just crack me open, Delphine. Just eat my heart out.

"I loved that dress," Delphine says, sighing. "Red has always been my favorite."

Seven years since that night. Seven years of money, of power, of freedom to rattle the bars of her body and take different shapes. Delphine never telling her to do otherwise. Delphine trusting her to get the job done, whatever the job might be. Now the prize of Tacoma, new conquests, new contests. If Alma can deliver on her promises.

"I'll keep Pinkerton's men busy," she says.

"Good." Delphine pulls a slip of paper from her reticule, sets it on the table beside Nell's sewing machine. Jasmine perfume rising from her skirts as she steps past Alma. "Take care, Rosales."

Delphine unbolts the door and slips through. In the seam of daylight, Joc stands beside an open carriage door, wearing a neat suit. Then Delphine pulls the door closed and the shop is dim, empty. Alma leans against the wall, unmoored, wanting Delphine back. Wanting, absurdly, to tell her she'd seen what happened to Finnegan that night: how, from a sliver of doorway, she'd watched him fall to his knees before Delphine, his single eye wet with tears, tearing his shirt open, and Delphine leaned down to kiss him, then shot him in the heart.

"She called you Rosales."

"How long were you listening?" Alma stops halfway to the table, halfway to that little scrap of paper Delphine left behind. She covers the motion with a stumble that ends up more real than feigned.

Nell comes into the room holding a wrapped parcel. She sets it on the sewing table, beside the lacquered machine, and puts the paper in her dress pocket. All the spit and fire that had held Alma up straight while Delphine was there is dredging away. It's hard to stand without support. Hard to look at Nell without seeing three gold-haired women in pink dresses.

"You're shaking," Nell says. "Come lie down."

The bread Alma wolfed down is climbing back up her throat, a sour pressure at the root of her tongue. Her left hand still not working.

"All right."

Nell is warm under her arm, warm along her right side. Maybe this will clear her head—salt skin under her mouth, heated breathing—but it's no good, she is too wrung out, too uneasy in her gullet, to pick up where they left off. She wants to be in charge, with clear eyes and sure fingers, not flop all over Nell like a rum-punched sailor. So she lets Nell lower her to the bed and undo her trouser buttons. Before, Nell's fingers on her body were like magnets, pulling all the blood and feeling to the surface of her skin. Now they are just fingers, gentle. She lifts her hips so Nell can pull down the filthy twill, leaving her in the binding cloth and a pair of yellowed men's drawers.

"I'll just close my eyes for a minute," Alma says, fisting the blanket to her chest.

Then it's quiet.

The smell wakes her. Onions and sage, mutton fat, pepper. She breathes deep. Opens her eyes to a shadowy bedroom. Lace curtains gilded rose gold. The day has burned down, leaving only a little waxy light. But Alma's shoulder has eased. And when she lifts her left hand, it obeys: its fingers open and close, flex into a fist, still tingling but regaining some of their dexterity.

She tries to sit up—fails, seized by a spasm under her bandage. Tries again in the crabbed fashion that worked earlier, hand to knee, stomach clenched, rolling up and swinging her legs to the floor. The room is cold and she feels it everywhere, at the scabbed edges of her binding cloth, seeping right through the thin cotton of her drawers.

"Nell?"

Perched on the side of the bed, Alma tests the muscles in her arm. She can raise her elbow a notch higher than she could that afternoon. Find more range of motion in the connected muscles of her neck. This is progress. She curls her left hand into a fist, pounds it against her thigh. A shadow fills the doorway.

"I made soup," Nell says.

"And I want to eat it."

Alma stands, finds her balance. She is steadier than before. Progress. She comes around the bed, keeping close to the post if she should need it. Nell watches from the door, eyes skittering down her body. Alma doesn't bother hiding her grin.

"I'll be better sport, now that I've rested," she says.

"Let's get some food in you first." Nell takes the blanket off the foot of the bed, drapes it over Alma's shoulders. "It's warmer in the kitchen, but not by much."

At the table Nell sets a steaming bowl before Alma, a new loaf of brown bread. The soup is golden, lobed with liquid fat and carrot rounds. Alma lifts the bowl to her mouth. Drinks broth and bites bread in alternate motions. The soup salty and rich. Chunks of meat butter-soft between her teeth. When the bowl is empty, she wipes her chin with the back of her hand and holds the bowl out for more.

"You like it?" Nell says, after she finishes her mouthful of bread.

"It's putting blood back in my veins."

Nell sets down her own spoon, stands to ladle more soup. Alma likes how the lamplight falls on Nell's hair, on the long paleness of her neck.

"Which is your real name?" Nell says, a spoonful of soup dripping between her mouth and bowl. "Camp? Or Rosales?"

"Pick your favorite," Alma says, twitching off the question out of habit.

Nell dabs at the fat glossing her chin. Some still glinting on the curved bow of her lower lip. A few minutes to rest, to let the food settle, and then Alma wants to finish what they started. With the warm flush of the soup her body is starting to heat again. She wants it to burn slow. Enjoy the spark, the hot coil.

"Forger, tailor, blue-ribbon cook." Alma licks her teeth, her eyes on Nell's. "How did you learn all your tricks?"

Nell laughs. Tucks a curl of hair behind her ear.

"My daddy was a schoolteacher. He taught me how to read, and how to write so fine." She folds her hands on the table, the bowl of soup within the circle of her arms. "I don't have much else to thank him for. I left home when I was fourteen. Worked my way toward the coast in lumber camps. Cooking some; there's the soup come in. Some washing and tailoring; there's the rest. But mostly keeping the men company. It was a hard time. I lost two babies. Left a third in Olympia, with a church."

She pauses. Nudges her spoon along the rim of her bowl. From the courtyard door, the sound of singing. The women back at their drying lines in the alley, two voices linked together, rising, dipping.

"That was ten years ago," Nell says. "My baby girl's ten years old, somewhere."

"What did you call her?" Alma says, because they're already talking about names. Because she has to say something—she can't just sit there watching Nell start to cry.

"Now, that's my secret." Nell blinks, flashes a tired smile.

Alma runs her hand through her hair. Leaves it cupped at the back of her skull and tests the movement of her neck, the sore left side biting into her attention. The blanket slides off her right shoulder. Nell's eyes catch on Alma's bare skin, on the muscle that ropes the underside of her arm.

"I'm getting sore, sitting here," Alma says.

"Back to bed with you."

Alma stands, rubs her left biceps. The touch pulls at her shoulder. Wrenching pain, but strength under the skin. Her body solid despite the abuse it has taken. She's not as steady as she'd like, but the alternative is waiting even longer to have Nell, and that's no alternative at all.

"Joining me?" Alma says at the doorway.

Nell's chair scrapes over the floorboards. Alma walks into the hall, into the bedroom, where everything is dusted with soft blue light. In ten minutes it will be full night. She throws the blanket off her shoulders, over the foot of the bed. Cold air. Stale blood tang on her binding cloth. Nell comes in as Alma is striking a match, her left hand good enough to hold the box, her right hand bruised and strong in the wavering flame.

"Take off your dress," she says as the lamp catches.

When she turns around, Nell is standing by the bed, her fingers on the third button of her collar, the lace frill of a chemise glinting in the seam. Her eyes autumn ivy-colored in the lamplight, latched on to Alma's. She crosses the space between them, floorboards ridged under her feet.

Five buttons. Alma stands near enough to feel Nell's warmth. The dress gapes open, over the rise of her breasts, over the thin boning of a workday corset. Alma stops Nell's fingers when they reach her waist. Leans up to her, breath passing between them, and then their mouths meet. Alma licks at the inside of Nell's lips, tongue curling, and slips her good hand into the open front of the dress. Catches the quick heave of Nell's breathing. She is thinking about Nell's thighs, the meat of them puckering under her fingertips, pressing into her neck.

Nell wraps one arm around Alma's waist, curls the other over her good shoulder, careful of her bindings. Lace chemise soft in Alma's palm. Pulling down so one pale breast spills over the corset. She bends to take the nipple in her mouth, and Nell's fingers flex, tighten, clutch Alma into place and she likes that, she likes having to remind herself to be gentle, how it makes her feel strong. Nell's skin smells of perfume—honeysuckle dabbed in the notch between her breasts—and sweat, sour and animal, the body she keeps wrapped under her clothes, the secret parts she is letting Alma stroke, take in mouthfuls.

Enough play. Alma's sore leg is shaking, her smallclothes damp. Nell undoes a few more buttons, hasty, before taking Alma's face in her hands and kissing her again. Nell is a little sharper now, and it is good: she nips at Alma's lower lip, at her tongue, and Alma growls low in her throat, hungry.

Nell kicks her dress aside. Her chemise sticks to her hips, her thighs, calling Alma to touch, all that soft skin only a slip away from her own. She hitches up the cloth, slow, and Nell's eyes go half-lidded and hazy. Then her palm is on skin, moving inward. Her thumb grazes damp hair. Nell shifts closer, parts her legs, tilts her hips. Her breaths edged with little blurs of sound. Alma drops one shoulder, ignoring the protests from the other, and curls her hand over Nell's sex, her middle three fingers finding wet heat, pushing into it.

"Jack, yes—"

"Oh, honey." Alma wants to pull Nell's mouth to hers, but her left arm is stiff, useless from the elbow, so she leans into Nell instead, fingers crooking, licking the side of her neck and grinding into her hip. It's not enough but it's something, sweet pressure to pulse into. Sweat collects between her shoulder blades, under the binding cloth, and Nell's hands are on the rise of her buttocks, circling around, hot at the front of her smallclothes, where her body is notched against Nell's hip bone.

"No." She bats Nell's fingers away, her clumsy left hand rougher than she intended.

"I want to touch you," Nell says, the words catching on a sharp inhale.

Alma shakes her head. She takes one of Nell's hands in the loose cage of her left. Pushes it to the corset ribbons dangling at the small of Nell's back.

"I can't work the laces," she says. "Take it off."

Nell hesitates, but Alma keeps her fingers moving, wet to the knuckles, and thumbs at the nub of flesh that crowns Nell's sex. Nell's eyes close. The sound she makes is good. Alma wants to hear it again.

"Take it off, Nell."

Her hips are rocking into Alma's touch. The pale ribbon whispers through each set of eyes. Nell unhooks the corset's busks, and
it falls open like a flower. She pulls off her chemise and is all bared
to Alma, her skin pearly in the lamplight, silvery lines on the skin
at her hips, on the skin under her navel, tracing toward the dark
thatch of hair where Alma's hand is still busy, still twisting. Alma
walks her backward to the bed. Drops to her knees and replaces
her thumb with her tongue. Nell moans. Hot musk in Alma's nose,
slickness on her tongue, oh, and it's good, her mouth dripping
spit, Nell's fingers in her hair, holding her down. Her breaths come
thick, fast, and god damn it, she can't wait any longer. She kneels
wider on the floor, the boards' seams biting into her knees. Pulls
her hand from the heat of Nell's body and works it under the band
of her smallclothes. Fingers wet with Nell's juices, Alma's tongue
pulsing in time with her touch, oh, yeah, it won't take much, her
body is wound tight as a watch spring.

"Let me see you," Nell says, breath hitched. "Let me see your
face."

No one has ever asked Alma for this. She doesn't know what she
looks like when she is mindless, pleasure-cleft. But she is close, too
close to stop her stroking, jaw tight, nose full of Nell's scent. So she
presses her cheek to Nell's thigh, and when the tremors hit she
clenches inward, groaning, hot slick flesh against her face, and it's
good, it's good, oh, God, it's good.

Nell is touching herself, fingers working inches from Alma's face.
Alma takes her hand from her smallclothes, works it back into Nell's
heat.

"Fuck on me, honey," she says, blinking away sweat to better
see all that quivering skin, Nell's eyes squeezed shut, her mouth
open.

For a long time after, they stay still, silent, bodies linked together, the quick beat of their breaths settling.

"Come into the bed," Nell says.

Alma licks the inside of Nell's thigh. Hoists herself up with her
right hand on the bedpost, her knees scraped and stinging. Her
shoulder burning fierce as it churns with fresh-stirred blood. She
folds her body, slow, next to Nell's. She is tired out. Grinning. Nell

curls onto Alma's good side, tracing her collarbone, the jut of her lower ribs. Her nails pale half-moons in the dimness.

Alma doesn't know when she falls asleep. She surfaces briefly to find the lamp out, the blanket pulled over them. Nell's arm a warm weight across her bound chest and bare stomach. She leaves it. Liking the feel of skin on skin.

25

JANUARY 21, 1887

Stepping through the back door of Nell's house into the sunshine, into the empty long alley. Alma's feet are heavy in her boots. Her whole body ballasted, yawing back to that warm bed, that lazy naked sprawling. But a fresh cloth binds her breasts. Her shirt is salted clean. Her left arm has come back to life, no more seeping bleeding, only a little slowness lingering in the pinkie finger, the outside of her wrist. Her right leg bruised but steadier. No excuses to stay, and lots of reasons to cleave back into the world.

Her shoulder aches. The left sleeve of her jacket hangs empty: Nell fitted her with a sling to protect her stitches, the cloth looped over her neck and forearm. This is good because it makes her look slow, even though her right arm's still fast. But it's bad because it's something to note about her body, and it's safest to be unremarkable: a small man in plain clothing, able to blend into most any street, into most any waterfront scene. Alma wants the sling off. Good or bad, it makes her feel soft. But she can't pick apart the knot one-handed.

At the end of the alley, Taylor swerves into a full-fledged street. The cart wheels are too rattling, the noontime sun too glaring on the bay. But by Water Street Alma is shedding the sense of respite, the huddled warmth, that grew up around her in Nell's house. She keeps the satisfaction, though—it makes her spine straight, tilts her chin up, edges her grin with teeth. Flashing the heat of the last day at every bucko who cares to look: I had a woman, and she was good.

The post office has a line out the door. Sticking to habit, Alma collars a boy across the street and says she'll give him two cents to collect her mail. She watches him from a notch between buildings, smoking, testing her shoulder. Rawness in the muscle, jagged pain, as if someone's drawing a serrated blade across her arm. How bad does it look? She hasn't unpeeled the bandage to see.

The boy waits in line, tapping his foot to some unknown tune, doffing his checkered cap at two house girls who don't even see him. Then he's in the building. A sick tingle in her gut. Sweat rising with an itch between her shoulder blades. She lost a whole day at Nell's when there aren't more than a handful of days to play with. If the Denver office hasn't confirmed her requested delay, there is real trouble. Not enough tar on Sloan's hands, not enough time to clean up the dirty footprints leading to him. Deep drag on the cigarette and her hand still smells of Nell's body; she was set to storm that castle for days but it just opened to her, open mouth, open thighs, god damn. They never did get around to the other cake.

This is her first time working with men out of the Colorado office. It's the Western headquarters. William Pinkerton makes a habit of frequenting the place. He is a stickler for the rules—not so much when he was younger, but now that he's in charge, it's everything by the letter: make a plan, run the plan, no cut corners. Boring. Men under his thumb might have the same philosophy. They might not like her last-minute scramble.

The boy tears out of the post office. Papers in his hands. Alma steps out of the shadows, and he leaps over a puddle, darts behind a cart to run to her. He gives her a plain white envelope and a telegraph, then takes his pennies. Alma stuffs the envelope into an inner vest pocket. The telegraph is dated January 19, the same day she sent her request over the wire.

Tacoma January 23 OK, it says. *Further instructions post.*

Alma crumples the paper into a ball as her lungs expand. The Pinkerton's agents will wait a few days, as she asked. Things might end up all right. Even her shoulder hurts a little less after that.

"You got a problem with the post office?"

Alma laughs. Drops her cigarette into the mud. Davy Benson is behind her—that deep, lazy drawl—and she takes her time turning around. She peers up at him, missing her cap, the brim that shades her eyes into inscrutability.

"Just wary of close spaces after that Chain Locker scrap," she says.

"I heard about it." Benson is holding a candy apple, caramel-glossed and bitten into, the inner flesh snowy white. "Hard luck."

"Not as hard as Driscoll's."

Benson whistles, shaking his head.

"He was just a pup," he says. "McManus isn't taking it so well. You seen him? Boss man's having trouble keeping him down."

Up to no good is he, the thieving bastard. He's had a whole day to cause new problems. Benson ought to be able to fill her in.

"I've been sleeping off the blood loss," Alma says. "I haven't seen anybody but the devil."

"Huh." Benson takes a huge bite of the apple, a crunch that leaves pale flecks of juice in his beard. "You know how to write?"

"I can scratch out a letter," Alma says. "Just sent one to a girl I know in Tacoma. Told her to get ready for me—I've been missing her."

"Might want to send something myself to a girl I know," Benson says, his mouth full of fruit and dark sugar. "Could you spell it out?"

"For a few dollars."

"I'll make you a trade," he says. "I'll whittle you something."

"I'm not in much need of a wood carving. But I'll trade for some talk."

Benson finishes the apple in two more bites. Shrugs.

"Why's McManus so interested in Seattle?" she says.

"Aw, he wants to take some tail there." Benson laughs. Chucks his wood-stuck apple core into the street, wipes his hand on his trousers. "Never did find out what poor girl he's hounding."

So most of the crew know about Mary. Still, McManus could be using her as a convenient screen, hiding the real reason for his interest in the town across the Sound. And Mary doesn't relate to which of Wheeler's men tipped off Kopp—her next question.

"A girl. Didn't know about her," she says. "McManus only mentioned a man called Kopp when I asked him about Seattle. Dom Kopp. Is he a partner of ours?"

She watches Benson's face closely for a flicker of anything—alarm, surprise, hesitation. His gray eyes are flat. His thick brows tilt together, but the expression seems pure perplexity.

"The railroad man?" he says.

"Don't know."

"He's not part of the business." Benson hooks his thumbs into his belt. "He's best known around here for spending money at the poker tables. Big bets, is the word. He's fixing to get robbed with that fancy walking stick of his, all gem and no stick, just about."

"All right," Alma says. "I'm obliged. Still trying to get my footing, with all these names and places."

Benson's a dead end, and she is moving on already, thinking about getting to her boardinghouse and deciphering the Pinkerton's agents' letter. Thinking about Wheeler. How he tried to ruin her chances with Nell. How he will be different with Driscoll dead and after all the ways their bodies touched the night of the fight. Her arm aches, her neck. Nell filled her up and drained her. Still. The game she's playing with Wheeler calls to her with all her names.

"What about my letter?" Benson says.

"I don't have any paper," she says. "Tell it to me next time you're at the office."

"I'll tell it to you now."

"You expect me to memorize it?"

"You might," he says. "Here goes. 'Dearest—'"

He leans down, his breath sugary.

"'—Rosales.'"

Her name drawn out and muddied by his drawl. It takes everything she's got to not flinch, to keep her face slack, listening. But her throat is locking. Her skin hot.

"'Don't speak to me again about Dom Kopp.'"

Her chest clenches.

"'Or I'll tell Wheeler, and all the boys, what you've got under those trousers.'"

How does he know? Not through Wheeler, if he thinks Wheeler

is in the dark. That leaves three people who do: Joe Hong, Delphine, and Nell. Joe and Delphine make no kind of sense. Neither does Nell, but Alma was out for hours at Nell's house, sleeping, bleeding. Time for Nell to do just about anything. The night past, after their sex, Nell left Alma in her bed and went to work at The Captain's, which Benson frequents. By then she knew Alma's body, knew her real name. But, Jesus. When they'd just been so close, drinking each other's sweat.

Focus.

Benson is still hunched toward her, the meat of his gut spilling over his belt. Expecting a reaction. Expecting her to be afraid.

"Don't tell Wheeler," she says, letting her voice crack a bit, seaming it with desperation. If Benson thinks this is a bargaining chip, it's the best one she can use—fool's gold, meaningless to her but shining in his eyes.

He laughs, a low chuckle pitted with filth. She doesn't flinch away from his breath on her face. It's a fine line to walk: Camp, still tough, but letting some worry seep through. Some fear. Not the fear Benson must think he's calling out; why is it men go for that first, the reminder of her sex, vulnerable, as though theirs is not? But other fears. Her promotion, perhaps endangered by the tear in her disguise. Nell turning on her. How? And why? And for what? Along with all this is the quick calculation of what Benson will reveal if strung along: who else he'll name after outing Kopp as his partner.

"I don't know what he'd do with you if he found out," Benson says. "He's a cold-blooded son of a bitch."

She knows what Wheeler would do: he'd send Benson to knife her in her sleep. Luckily they've moved past that reaction, on to more interesting ones, but now is not the time.

"What do you want?" she says.

"I've got a pair of lading bills I need swapped," he says.

Damn it. McManus was right, all along. He wasn't covering his own tracks—he was tracking Benson. He'd called this bastard out four days before and must have suspected sooner. McManus solved the puzzle before she could. That's hard to swallow. Where the fuck is he, anyway? Another gripe in the gut: Benson might have gotten him. Not that Tom needs help digging his own grave, it sounds like, after Driscoll's death. Alma almost admires that: McManus's single-minded determination to not let anyone be his friend.

"I don't touch the bills," she says.

"I know." Benson is scowling, getting impatient. "But the boss man wants you filling in while McManus isn't around. So I'm going to give you the bills, and you're going to fix them onto the new shipment that comes in tonight."

Keep him talking. He's close to giving it all away—who he's working with, how they're siphoning off the business's tar.

"Fix them how?"

"Simple swap," he says. "Change the labels so they're unloaded in Seattle instead of Tacoma."

Seattle. Things start sliding into place. Benson and Kopp, working together. Kopp must be trying to play both sides, making money off the stolen tar with one hand and hoping to make protection money off Wheeler with the other. Then there's Sing Tai buying Delphine's opium at auction in Seattle, and Benson routing more product to that same city, maybe to auction off again, or to sell another way. Who else is involved? An inside crewman? Someone who's done the job that Benson wants her to do now, getting at the crates while they're in the hold and swapping the lading bills. And then whoever's in Seattle receiving the stolen tar.

"Why Seattle?" Alma says, hoping for a name, though Benson's not likely to be that stupid.

"Because I said so." He drops his bass drawl still lower. It's clear enough so close to her ear. "I'll tell you, I don't knife women. But seeing as you're dressed like that, I don't think my rule signifies. I know you felt me once."

Get the papers, even though the urge to growl is rising. The urge to slide her knife into his throat, right under the Adam's apple. Payback for the thin scab he left on her neck. But those papers are the first part of his death warrant.

"Give me the bills," she says, sneering at him.

"Yes, ma—I mean, yes, sir."

She holds out her good hand for the envelope. Tucks it into the notch between her chest and arm sling, even that movement enough to wrench her wound.

"You say one wrong word and the deal's off," she says once the papers are secure.

"I'm not planning on saying a thing. But these kinds of secrets get expensive." Benson grins. "You better start thinking about other things you can offer me. In the future."

She leaves him whistling on the corner. His eyes on the sun-dazzled bay, his fingers tapping time on his hips.

Two blocks to her boardinghouse's blackened sign. She needs to see Wheeler, catch him up. But if Benson's blackmailing her into cooperation, he's not going to move just yet—he won't be an evolving threat until at least tomorrow, after the diverted opium reaches its destination. There is time to stop and decipher the letter. See what the Pinkerton's agents have in store.

Swerve into the smoky lobby. The manager in his cubicle, dressed in a dark felt suit that looks cut from an undertaker's tablecloth. His cataracts magnified behind thick glasses that are more for show than use, given how calcified his eyes are. The underfed child on a stool beside him. Alma drops coins into the kid's grit-laced palm.

"Four more days in number thirteen," she says.

"One dollar," the child tells the man, who nods.

Up the stairs. Each step jars pain into her shoulder. At the third-floor landing a new splatter on the wall that might be blood or shit, but she's not inclined to sniff and find out. She unlocks her room. Freezing cold and slop-bucket stink—Nell described it just right. Alma could have healed in here, but not as easy. Too easy, if Nell's the one who gave her up to Benson. She makes her usual sweep of the space, kneeling to check the lock's mechanism for scratches, for sloppy tampering. Clean. Nell's name calls up an echoed low-belly pulse, remembered pleasure, though it's marred by the sting of being sold out. She runs her hand over the stack of books to check their order. Clean. Benson came right to her and handed her leverage while thinking he bought some for himself. That is some satisfaction, warm in her gut as she crouches to pull out her gear and check the double tie. It's wrong.

Alma glances at the bolted door. The room is too small and spare to hide in, but she eyes each corner just the same.

Someone's been in here. Someone who took care to cover their tracks but couldn't replicate the special knot she uses on her luggage. They opened up her case. Saw the mix of women's and men's clothes, the twill vests folded onto pink skirts, the stockings under hemmed trousers.

It must have been Nell. She'd insisted on taking Alma home instead of to the rented lodgings on Water Street. Or maybe Nell and Benson. One to keep Alma confined, the other to visit the boardinghouse with time to snoop. Benson knows her room number. After all, he was meant to come and kill her in it the night the Beckett hit went down. Throat cut all the way to the spine.

Alma sifts one-handed through the suitcase. Everything is put back neatly enough, but the broken knot tells all. She reties it, slowed by her single hand, slowed by the thought of Nell turning on her, then replaces the bag under the bed. Sulfur flare; lamp-wick crackle. At the desk she pulls out the Pinkerton's agents' mail, rips the envelope, clumsy. Clean sheet of paper; inkpot and pen; the Verne book. Working through the cipher. The agents' letter takes shape. Tension in her neck unknotting as she decodes each new word. This is good news. Who to look for. Where to find them. What to say. Time and space to bargain. Everything can still come together as she wants.

Lamp flame to the original, blowing floating ash off the desk. Then a thick scribble of ink onto the deciphered copy, making it unreadable before committing it, too, to the fire. And last, the little onionskin telegraph, burning quick and bitter as a strand of hair. Distracted, Alma rubs her arm before she remembers how the muscle's pulped, hisses an inhale through her nose.

Now it's time for Wheeler. This means talking about Driscoll, likely, but her news about Benson should take front burner. She's got the mole with links to Kopp and Seattle. That's something right.

The walk to the office is quick, wind kicking at her back as though to push her along, chilling her shoulder into stiffness. Numb is good. At the back steps Conaway rises from a slump, his eyes and nose red with cold.

"Camp." His voice is clotted. He has been crying. "You all right?"

"Been better."

She jogs past him up the stairs, focusing on the bouncing in her shoulder, the sharp pain of it, rather than his melancholy. It hits her, though, once she's in the blue hall. The knee-high bump in the plaster that nudged her spine as she sat, three days before, with Conaway and Driscoll. Eating pies, laughing about bets they'd placed. She strides toward the dogleg turn. "He's seventeen," McManus said, when defending Driscoll in the office. Seventeen, talking about Christmas pudding. Like he'd never even had a girl. His arm over her shoulders; his hoarse laughter in her ear. That blade of guilt at her gut. Stop it, Rosales. You're old enough to fight, you're old enough to fall.

Two raps at the door and Wheeler calls out, "What?" The sound familiar, a constant, a thing to be expected. Boring, maybe. But maybe it's good to have some things to rely on.

"Afternoon, boss," she says inside.

Wheeler looks up—his face for a moment open, expectant—but he recovers just as quick, sets down his pen, motions her forward. She closes the door. Leans against it.

"I didn't look for you so soon," he says.

"You know me. Can't hardly sit still."

She walks to his desk. No play, no twisting Camp into Alma and back. The wind, the empty hall, have chilled her into a more solid shape. Wheeler could melt her a notch, but not today: his voice is muted, the fire in the hearth not leaking much heat. He eyes her warily. Does not move to stand.

"I saw Benson on the street." She is close to his chair, her voice shaded almost silent. "He's the mole. He's the one who outed you to Dom Kopp. The two of them are rerouting our tar to Seattle."

Wheeler's expression recalibrates, the darker fire clearing from his eyes. She has missed the puzzle of reading them. Now they are cold, ice blue, all business.

"How do you know?" he says, quiet, too.

"Someone told Benson about me," she says. "He knew to call me Rosales. He got real touchy when I mentioned Kopp. Said if I asked any more questions about Kopp, or if I didn't swap out these lading bills for him—"

She pulls the envelope out from her jacket, drops it onto the desk.

"—he said he'd tell you, and the whole crew, who Jack Camp really is."

Wheeler peels open the envelope, unfolding the papers and sifting through them. Shakes his head.

"One hundred twenty pounds to Seattle. One hundred twenty! He's getting bolder," he says. "Tom was right."

"I hear Tom's been wild," Alma says, not wanting to dwell on McManus's hunch being better than hers. Not looking forward to asking McManus for a favor: for his inside information on the loading crews and Benson's most likely accomplice among them. "After the fight."

"After Driscoll." Wheeler stops shuffling the bills. Lets out a long breath. "They were close."

"Did he get Loomis?"

"He wants to," Wheeler says. "But he can't. Not yet. Not while we need Sloan to keep selling our product. I gave Tom very clear instructions on the matter."

"So Benson and Kopp are working together. Going after their biggest haul. That's one problem. Sloan's another problem. Have you spoken to him, since the fight?"

"Yes. He claims Loomis had no part with Driscoll. Was just standing nearby." Wheeler rubs his forehead. A tired gesture he's not allowed himself before in front of her. "I thought our mole was feeding Sloan. Maybe he's not. Sloan's still keen on the next batch, and we must get it to him. It's King Tye coming in."

The King Tye brand will make a muddied trail of opium, so Sloan appears to be selling tar from several refineries—avoiding an inconvenient spotlight on the Wah Hing refinery, which supplies Delphine alone.

"What did Sloan want at Chain Locker?"

"He wanted me to ask him to dinner."

Alma laughs without smiling.

"A romantic soul," she says.

"He said if we're doing business, he wants the benefit of that." Wheeler glares up at her, hand falling away from his face. "The social benefit, as a gentleman invited to my home."

"Your home?"

"I don't sleep in this office. I have a house on the hill."

"Filled with ledgers. Gloomy portraits of your grandfathers."

"You'll have to live in wonder," he says. "There's no forthcoming invitation for you."

"I'm crushed. Devastated. *Désolée.*"

Wheeler waves her away, smirking. She doesn't move from the notch in his desk. Her fingernail clicks against her belt buckle. She never had a nice place in the city. Preferred the rough dives of the Barbary Coast, their porous shadow alleys good for going unseen. Still, she was welcome at Delphine's gilded doorway, in the polished halls of the women who used her detective services. Her invitation to Port Townsend's upper crust seems to have been lost in the mail. That exclusion, that confinement to the gutter, is starting to grate.

"Are you going to have him over?" she says.

"No. He's not popular with the city fathers, on account of his whores."

"And you need to be popular with the city fathers."

"I am popular with them." Wheeler finishes the film of whiskey in the glass beside him. "But it's an . . . evolving friendship. There's been a snag with the trust papers."

"I thought you'd signed already."

"I did. Then Harrison Doyle passed, at last," Wheeler says. "And his wife stepped up to claim a financial stake. Mayor Brooks is getting cold feet. Now it's complicated."

"Jesus. I'm out for a day and everything goes to hell."

"You helped it along." Wheeler sits back in his chair. "The way Tom told me, you two started that fight."

"It was an accident."

"You let Driscoll know that," Wheeler says. "He's in a pine box Peterson knocked up, waiting in the warehouse for Tom to get back so we can bury him."

"God damn it," Alma says. "You don't need to throw it at me like that."

She walks to the sideboard, pours a gin, the operation slower than usual with only one hand. She is tired, her arm aching. No heat at Wheeler's desk. He is as worn down as she's ever seen him and not bothering to put much of a mask over it. Driscoll might as well be lying on the floor between them. Frightened eyes. Red glass. Alma's hand is not steady. The stopper clicks hard against the lip of the decanter when she drops it into place.

"'For Tom to get back,'" she says, only then catching on that piece of the sentence. "Back from where?"

"I sent him to Victoria yesterday, to keep him from doing anything stupid."

"You sent him to—" Alma shakes her head. Now she can't grill McManus about the crews. Another delay when there are mere days left to work things out. "He could have been the mole."

"He's not." Wheeler glares at her. "He's meeting with Yee at the Wah Hing refinery to work out a new loading system. It will take a few days."

"Benson said you were looking for him."

"You've established Benson's apt to say anything that suits his purposes."

"I thought the same about McManus until this morning," she says. "I could have been right. Then what—the mole planning a new handoff method with our prime refiner?"

"Tom is clean."

"You never suspected him."

"He never gave me cause."

"Not even with Seattle? With his married Chinese girl?" Wires of pain in her deltoid as her shoulders tense, so she can't stand as straight as she wants. Her left hand, held against her chest by the sling, curling into a loose fist. "With his crew doing the ride-along on shipments that went missing? If that's not cause, you weren't looking at all."

Wheeler gets out of his chair, crosses half the space between them.

"Because I trust him," he says, low. "Do you understand what that means?"

Alma tips back her head to drain her gin. Grunts at the twinge this wrings in her neck. Not two days of being saddled with this injury and she is snapping at the bit, wanting her body back, its easy motion.

"It means you've gotten too close to someone," she says. "You trust them . . . you trust them and then they can fuck you. They can make mistakes."

She knows this. "Make sure we're out before you move," Hannah said. "Don't get impatient, kid." Of course Alma didn't listen. She made a mistake. Blood in Hannah's shorn gold hair, on the bow of her lip. Alma blinks away this image, slops more gin into her cup. The stopper clips the side of the crystal rim and drops onto the carpet.

"You make quite a few mistakes for someone with such a horror of them," Wheeler says.

Yes, I do, Alma wants to say, but the words would come out too bare. She downs her gin instead.

Wheeler collects the fallen stopper. Fluid bend and rise. That fighter's body. Though right now she wants his healthy muscles for her own more than she wants to touch them.

"You're happy to point out when I slip up," she says. "But certain people get off easier. I see how it is. After the fight you try to send me back to my boardinghouse to bleed out and freeze, and McManus gets a free vacation to Victoria."

"Do you know how Tom hurt his knee?"

Wheeler comes to the liquor board, places the stopper, soundless, in its decanter. Folds his arms over his chest. Two feet away but closed off. She is closed off, too, sweating thick and fast as if all the rest and food of yesterday are leaking out of her. Her arm throbbing. Her head.

"He tried to help me in a fight. Eleven years ago, back in Portland. He'd just come over from Oban with his brother, two lads looking to make a new start." That wistful flicker in Wheeler's eyes, then gone. "His brother was glassed, at a saloon near the river. He died. They were young. Driscoll's age, nearabouts. So if I give him space to calm himself and grieve, you don't fucking take that out of him."

"Fine. Play favorites."

She blinks, hard. No one's watched out for her like that since Hannah. How things could have been different with eleven years of someone to turn to. To trust. There's Delphine, but she's always been slipping away, one step ahead. Jasmine perfume. Golden-belled birds chirping.

"Alma."

She is drifting forward, hip sliding over the marble edge of the sideboard, crystal clinking. Blue wall blurred. Wheeler's hand around her right biceps, mooring her.

"I think you need to sit still a while longer," he says, close.

"There's no time." Alma shakes off his hand. "Benson needs trapping. Sloan."

She flattens her palm onto the cool marble, takes a wider stance. Once again she must stay standing. Stay composed. But god damn it, she's tired.

"You're going to charge after them when you can barely stand?" he says. "Or maybe fling yourself, fists out, in front of gunfire again. Jesus Christ."

"I've got to be on the boat tonight." She forces her eyes to focus on the filthy backs of her knuckles, seamed and stained against the white stone. "Benson's handing himself to us on a platter. Keep quiet, play scared, and he'll lead me right to his friends on the crew and in Seattle."

"I don't know if you'll manage."

She turns to Wheeler, sneering, but her face slackens. Nothing taunting in his eyes—they are solemn. Worried, even. The top button of his collar undone, showing a triangle of skin above the loose knot of his tie. "Please, call me Nathaniel," he'd said at their second dinner. He'd said, "I haven't heard a lass from home say my name in too many years." The more she sees of him, the more she thinks she glimpsed him best, and truest, when they first met.

"Do you want to plug the tar leak or not?" she says.

Wheeler's mouth twists into something like a smile.

"I see why she recommends you," he says. "And you're right about Benson. But the night boat is seven hours from now."

He nods at her left arm, tucked against her chest, her left jacket sleeve hanging empty.

"Take the time to rest."

It's not what she wants to do, but it's what she needs. Her head is a wreck, full of foamy water and splinters, the dull thump of pulse.

"We'll have him," she says. "Soon."

And what about Nell? Alma should share this new treachery, but it's embarrassing. All that swagger and bragging about having Nell, and it was just a trap. Alma doesn't want Wheeler to see her like that—the fly that buzzed right into the sugar dish. She needs to visit Nell again, privately, and find out what the hell she's playing at with Benson.

"There's an event tomorrow you should be at, if you can," Wheeler says. "A fund-raiser at the school. For the Seamen's Bethel— Sarah Powell's newest charity work, with Judge Hamilton."

That explains Alma's sighting of Delphine and the judge at the Cosmopolitan Hotel. But not how close Hamilton was standing to Delphine. How solicitous he was with her.

"Are you inviting me to Upper Town after all?" Alma turns toward Wheeler, keeping her hip in contact with the liquor board for balance. "I thought I wasn't welcome among the gentry."

He spins the gold ring on his left hand. Twists so the beveled face is toward his palm, twists so it's toward his knuckles, twists. Something about this request making him uneasy.

"Keep an eye on Hamilton, on the mayor, on that idiot Kopp, if he shows up," Wheeler says. "I want to know what they're saying. Especially if it's about the product. Or the railroad trust. Or me."

"So this is a personal favor."

He stops fiddling with the ring.

"No. It's for the good of the organization," he says. "And it's a favor to yourself—making sure you'll have a post to be promoted to."

So he doesn't know about Tacoma. Everyone still has their secrets: the things they're playing close to the vest.

"You don't move up, I don't move up," Alma says.

Deep inhale. Wring of pain in her shoulder as she leaves the sideboard, walks to Wheeler's desk. She tucks the envelope of lading bills into her vest. Seven hours of sleep better put some life back into her. She can't fade out just as things are getting interesting.

"The school's at Taylor and Clay," Wheeler says. "Be there at noon. Lots of sailors will come for the free food, I imagine, so no need to spruce up."

Alma salutes from the door, then lets her arm sweep down in a motion that takes in her whole body, new clothes already ruined, busted limbs, bruised to hell but standing.

"See you in class," she says.

Orion's hold smells of smoke and rotting straw. Alma breathes deep, her dinner of beef hash not quite settled in her stomach, her left arm shaking. She cut off the sling at the boardinghouse, wanting the limb free while she slept. Now a stabbing pain dogs her deltoid as she watches Lyle creep between the hull and the high-stacked baggage.

He lifts his hand lantern up to a crate. Taps it with his crowbar.

"This here's one," he says.

"Bound for Tacoma?"

"That's right."

Twenty feet away at the storeroom's front Barker and Folkstone count in unison, grunt as they lift a load.

"Take off the bill." Alma crouches beside Lyle, pulls Benson's envelope out of her vest.

Lyle twists to look at her, his dark eyes narrowed in the lantern's thin light. He's the crewman she suspects of helping Benson. He and Barker spend the most time with Benson at the Quincy warehouse. And while Barker was out sick when the last batch of tar went missing, Lyle was not—he was the ride-along man, alone with the product all the way down the Sound.

"Sir?"

"I said take it off. I've got a new bill for it and one more crate."

Lyle hesitates. Cold sweat trails down Alma's neck. She props her right forearm against the tar crate, leaning hard into the splintered wood.

"Come on," she says. "You know how this works. Yeah?"

"I don't touch the goods," Lyle says. "That's always been Barker's duty."

"Barker's occupied. And I've got orders to reroute two crates to Seattle."

None of this alters the set of Lyle's face: puzzlement, wariness. No flinching at the mention of Seattle. He sets down the crowbar and hand lantern, his upper body vanishing into shadow. The pale shape of his hand scratches at the bill and peels it off the wood. He holds it out to Alma. The underside of the paper is sticky with glue.

"Get the bill off that one while I fix this," she tells him. "And take four cases out of another crate—they're staying in town."

He's not acting the way she anticipated: no averting of the eyes, no bluster to displace suspicion. If he's not Benson's man, then it might be Barker. Or Folkstone, though he's the slowest of the bunch. Playing stupid is a skill, and Alma doesn't credit Folkstone with that sort of talent.

She pulls her arm off the crate. Smooths the Seattle bill into place with her palm. Water drips from the low ceiling, taps at her sleeve, her cap brim. She needs to swallow down the nausea for a few minutes more. Then it might pass.

Lyle gives her the second Tacoma bill. She shuffles sideways to replace it, straw crackling under her kneecaps. Lyle's thigh is inches from hers as he wedges the lid off a third crate, nails squeaking in the planks. He is warm; breathing quickly. Maybe gearing up to pull a knife on her, back here in the dark—a last-ditch effort to hide his guilt. He digs out four cases. Four solid clunks on the deck. Alma tosses him an empty burlap sack.

"You'll have to carry that up for me," she says. "I can't manage the weight with my arm banged up."

He whacks the lid back into place with his crowbar. Nods.

"Evening, sir."

"Evening, sir."

On the gangway, the stevedores are greeting the customs inspector: Edmonds is expected, and the dockworkers' calls confirm it is him and not some surprise guest. Alma hauls herself to standing. Lyle slides the crowbar into his belt, hefts the bulky sack over one shoulder.

"Hopefully our customs man has learned the ropes by now," she says as she walks to the front of the hold.

"Sure," Lyle says.

He is two steps behind, frowning. He doesn't like this business with the bills. Another notch against him as a suspect; it's unlikely he is Benson's inside man. But Alma swapped the bills like Benson wanted. He still thinks he's got her in a corner, and his next assignment might take her farther up the line—to his Seattle contacts.

"Evening, sir," Alma says to Edmonds at the storeroom door. A wave of dizziness blurs his pale face. Alma blinks, wiping her nose on her sleeve to buy time for her vision to refocus.

Edmonds's hands are in his pockets, his eyes skittish.

"I'm here to inspect this ship's cargo," he says, the words stiff. He doesn't even look at Lyle, who's standing there with a sixty-pound sack of opium on his back.

"And I don't aim to stop you," Alma says.

She leans against the hull, making room for Edmonds to pass. Wet planks cold against the back of her neck. Lyle glancing at her, mouth pinched, as Folkstone helps Barker lift a brass-striped steamer trunk.

"We'll wait till he's finished," she tells Lyle, trusting Wheeler's hold on Edmonds more than she trusts the crewman to walk away unattended with all that product. She'd rather carry the tar herself. But it's taking all she's got just to hold herself upright. Just keep standing for a few minutes more.

26

JANUARY 22, 1887

Eleven bells, twelve, from the two spires on Taylor Street. The Methodists' tower taller than the Catholics', where Alma and Delphine met. Alma leans against the cold stone of the Methodist church, smoking, set up to have a full view of the school across the road. The school's doors are closed, and as people arrive for the fund-raiser, they mingle uneasily in the street. The sailors, in their scrappy oilcloth ensembles, clump together, hands in pockets, shifty eyed. Gentlemen in frock coats and watered silk flow between them. Sometimes a woman in gray or pale taffeta linked to a man by the arm. Blue flowers in her hat, or misty netting on her bonnet.

No Delphine yet. At the far end of the road, by a gray house, Judge Hamilton and Wheeler walk together. Hamilton only half turned to Wheeler. Wheeler tapping his cigar ash out and away, so as not to drift onto the judge's boots. Keeping a step behind. Not such good friends, then. No wonder Wheeler's worried.

Dom Kopp is here, with his cheap flash and tenacity, wriggling into a new stream of Upper Town men each time Alma finds him in the crowd. His sallow cheeks red with cold, or excitement. His walking stick glinting like a beacon.

And a new face, still flushed from climbing the steps from Lower Town: Edward Edmonds. He was docile as a lamb the night before:

toeing a crate or two, then hurrying back up to the dock to report the boat cleared by customs. Alma delivered the four cases to the Madison warehouse, then staggered back to her rented room. She didn't have it in her to tick off the last stop on her list: she wanted to call at Nell's, pound on her door, but fell into a hard sleep instead.

Edmonds passes by and Alma flicks her cigarette into the mud. She trails him into the crowd, keeping his gray felt hat in view, her collar turned up against the rain. Her shoulder burns under its bandage, though her left hand is waking a little more each day. She flexes it with every step.

Huddled bodies, muted conversation, smells of wet wool and tar. Alma right behind Edmonds now, concealed by the press. He waves at a cluster of men in black coats—clerks, judging by their inky hands and gaudy stickpins, stabs at ostentatiousness—but continues toward the school. On its steps a woman in blue-striped silk stands next to another woman in an apron, who holds a handbell but does not ring it.

Edmonds pauses at the edge of the schoolyard. Looks back. Alma keeps her cap low over her eyes, using her lack of height to her advantage. The clerk is staring into the crowd and trying to cover it by lighting a cigarette, glancing at the two churches, picking ash off his lip. But he keeps sticking his eyes back to the same spot. She follows his line of sight, and it points directly to Wheeler, still speaking with Hamilton, their gray coats pale shadows under the dark boughs of a leafless maple.

A high voice, excitable, rises near her aching left shoulder. Dom Kopp. Alma angles sideways, grunting pardon to a group of uneasy sailors in their shoregoing best, and comes to a stop just outside the little circle around Kopp. Four gentlemen in furs and polished boots, Kopp himself in a tweed coat piped with gold thread at the collar and cuffs. Big gold buttons. The lower tip of his walking stick lashed with mud.

"The Seattle line is a guaranteed success," Kopp is saying, with no effort to be discreet, his nasal voice spiraling up into the low fog. "And I've started construction on a depot in Irondale, with twenty miles of right-of-way land already pledged. But the costs are high, as you might expect. The benefits, excellent, but the costs are high."

"I don't see the point of funding an Irondale spur," says a man collared in silver mink. "It will only impede a straight shot to us from the south."

"That's why Hamilton's trust is a better investment," another says. "His rail line would link us to Portland."

"Hamilton's trust be damned," Kopp says too loudly. "The Northern Pacific is coming to you, gentlemen. Routing through Portland will be an antiquated inconvenience, once the Stampede Pass tunnel is complete."

"A transcontinental link to our doorstep." This from a thickset man in a beaver coat. "That's what I'm betting on. Think of the money we'll make, getting wares directly from the East Coast, but with Northern Pacific's rates."

"That's precisely what I'm talking about, Mr. Weiss," Kopp says. "More money in your pockets. Port Townsend's bright future. But if commerce in this town is to thrive, we need infrastructure prepared for the new line's arrival. And something ought to be done about our less-savory inhabitants."

"We have clean streets," Weiss says. "Much to offer in the way of commercial business."

"Commercial business, yes," Kopp says. "I appreciate your healthy company, and those like it. But I'm speaking of the criminal element. Bawdy houses and crimps aside, there are the smugglers."

"Not uncommon along the coastal waters, surely."

"But here the smugglers include men of standing." Kopp's eyes narrow, and he surveys the crowded street, the gentlemen's finery among the clots of sailors, Wheeler and Hamilton still in conversation under the maple tree. "Men who might even be here today."

The men around him sniff, seem to withdraw a space, though they don't shift their feet. Alma's cigarette stings her fingertips, burned down to a mere stub as she listened. She drops it in the mud to hiss out beside her boot. Lights another under the shelter of her cupped palm.

"That's quite a charge to level, Mr. Kopp," the man standing beside Weiss says.

"Oh, I have names, and proof enough," Kopp says. "What I need are guarantees that other men in the town will stand up to the corruption."

"Monetary guarantees?" Weiss says stiffly.

"You'll reap them in kind when the Northern Pacific is stocking your warehouses."

Weiss glances at his companion.

"Who are you accusing, sir?" he says.

"He's here today." Kopp's sharp little nose twitches. "Among you."

Alma could step in now. Call Kopp over on some ruse, just to stop his mouth. But she wants to see how far he'll go—who he names. It's hard to believe he's talking about Wheeler. Benson is already feeding him product from the business. Kopp is expecting more money from Wheeler to protect the smuggling operation from the railroad. It doesn't follow that he'd compromise his bribe money, or his own supply chain, by selling Wheeler out.

"I won't stand here and gossip like a fishwife," the man with the mink collar says. "Gentlemen."

He nods curtly, walks off. A second man follows. Weiss and his companion move a little closer to Kopp, who preens under their attention.

"Meet me at the bar in the Delmonico," Kopp tells them. "After this affair. I don't think I need to remind you that this favor is not free."

How many men has Kopp made this offer to? If he's going the rounds at the gathering, it's best to shut him up. It's a risk: he might catch a flash of the girl she played for him under the dirt and stained denim and cigarette haze. But from what she's seen of him, he's a dull customer.

It is not such a great change, to go from invisible to eye-catching. She takes off her cap to wipe mist from her face. Settles it back on so it sits higher on her forehead, showing her eyes. A step to the left puts her in clear view of Kopp, in the space behind his two uneasy companions. She stares at him, unblinking, keeping her cigarette and its flaring spark of light near her mouth.

The first glance is dismissive, his gaze sliding over her soiled jacket, her dirty hands. The second glance lingers. She nods at him, slow. His face clenches. He shakes hands with Weiss, whose companion declines to do the same, a silent insult Kopp pretends to ignore. When he reaches Alma, he is frowning, sour.

"Who are you, and what do you want?"

His right hand, at his hip, is clenched around the loud expense of his walking stick. The big gem that declares him a better man, a wealthier man, than this battered fellow in rain-damp denim. She waits for his eyes to widen, for him to remember her as the clerk from Wheeler's offices. Or recognize her as Annabelle, now that they're standing close. But no such knowing lights his face.

"I've got a message for you." She lowers her voice so he has to lean in, scowling. Their eyes and shoulders level, though his posture droops limply under the thick tweed of his coat. "From a man I know you're keen to do business with."

"Who do you mean?" Kopp says.

"The man you're getting awful close to naming to your friends."

He goes pale. Then, with no sense of discretion, he looks directly at Wheeler.

"Don't stare," Alma says. What is he playing at? Maybe there's been a break between him and Benson. And if there hasn't, that will be a good place to start. Make a fracture.

Yes. She's got a plan. Wheeler's not going to like it. Oh, well.

"I gave him time," Kopp says. "I gave him a chance to avoid this. But I warned him I wouldn't wait forever."

A sailor bumps into her bad arm, apologizes. She shifts the joint, pushing against the soreness. Moves closer to Kopp.

"Benson said you were impatient," she says, her voice a low blur under the conversations around them. "He spoke to me privately. Said you were a bad partner."

"That mongrel." Quivering mustache, fist gripping his flashy stick. Finally dropping his voice into a low hiss. "He's been the disappointment. Promising cartloads of opium, but producing mere handfuls. I did all the work to set up a buyer for us, and he left me empty-handed more than once. An embarrassment. If I'd known Benson was supplied by Wheeler, I would have gone straight to the source sooner, but I only recently found out. I don't like dealing with second-tier men."

"Don't say the boss's name," she says. "He doesn't like dealing with second-tier men, either. That's why he's willing to link you in directly. He's decided to take your offer and cut Benson out. But that's if you keep quiet here, sir. If you burn this bridge, you can't cross over it come Monday."

She needs to give Kopp just enough reassurance of Wheeler's interest to keep him quiet, but not enough to make him cocky. Set a time limit on the negotiations. Make him think he's made inroads. And do it all so delicate, setting every snare she needs. It's tempting to ask him who his buyer is—Alma's jaw aches with holding back the words—but she can't scare him off.

"What's on Monday?" Kopp says, and though he is still sneering at her, there is interest thickening his voice, excitement in his sparse-lashed eyes.

"You're coming back to his offices," she says. "We'll have something concrete to offer you. If you bring five thousand dollars."

At the Cosmopolitan's gambling table he crowed about a Northern Pacific investor's gift: fifteen thousand dollars for his fledgling lines. He might have lost most of it by now—he's got a reputation for big bets, night after night, at poker—but even if he comes with a third of that, it will serve.

"That's too much," he says.

"What we're selling isn't cheap," she says. "It's more than product. It's a place in the chain. A place to make back your investment tenfold."

Only a fool would believe these numbers, but enough men outside the trade talk it up as easy riches, milk and honey, that someone like Kopp might buy them. He is considering it. His face crunched into a knot of concentration, ridges all down the sides of his nose.

"A hell of a lot more than the tiny sums Benson was filtering to you." She adds up the missing tar, splits it between Benson, Kopp, and the Seattle contact. "What, you were making one hundred, two hundred a month? Less? Sometimes nothing."

"Much less," Kopp says. "He said he was starting small, getting a supply line set up, but I've yet to see the profits I expected."

"The profits we can give you," she says. "Hundreds a week. Don't piss it away on blackmail. You were going to sell the boss's name to those men for a onetime fee. And then you'd have no supplier."

"A few hundred would have been more than Benson's made me so far."

A tinkling, tinnier than the church towers' clangs. The aproned woman on the school steps is shaking her handbell. Behind her, the double doors are open. The fund-raiser and its free lunch have commenced. The crowd shifts around Alma and Kopp, flowing toward the stairs.

"Monday." Alma exhales a long column of smoke. "Will you be there?"

Feverish eyes. Nervous hands choking up on his walking stick. She's got him.

"What time?"

"Eleven o'clock," she says. "At night. Come alone to the office. Knock three times."

This last bit she throws in as a jape, mocking him, but Kopp only nods tightly.

"The deal's off if you try and sell the boss's name again—here, or at that Delmonico meeting," she says. "Did you make that offer to anyone else?"

"No."

"Good," she says. "Tell those men at the Delmonico you had a change of heart."

"Yes. And I want—I want to see some opium when I visit."

Amateur. Alma hides her disdain behind a long draw on the cigarette.

"That's fine," she says. "Don't mention this to Benson. Do you have plans to see him between now and Monday?"

"We were going to meet in Irondale Tuesday," Kopp says.

"Keep that on the books, so he's not spooked. We'll talk before then."

Alma leaves Kopp fidgeting in the mud. It will be interesting to see what Wheeler wants to do with him when Kopp shows up with his cash. She has some ideas about that, too.

Wheeler and Hamilton have parted ways at last, Wheeler heading into the fund-raiser, passing under the roses and lilies garlanding the school's door. Alma walks up the path, letting herself be hustled along by the flow of eager sailors, intent on their hot coffee and lunch. The drowsy scent of daylilies sifts down at the top of the stairs. A snowfall of pollen, shaken loose by the tramping of boots, men's voices. Inside, the building is warm, sweet breezed as a greenhouse, a big open room set up with long tables. Flowers on the trestles and the walls. A throng of men at the back beside a spread of salads, cakes, silver coffee urns.

Alma steps out of the press as it flows toward the food. Delphine is here. Her black dress embroidered with glittering jet beads. She stands beside a wreath of pine and ribbon, in conversation with Judge Hamilton and two men Alma's not seen before. One of the men has hair the color of an old copper penny, a mustache long and bowed out in the Western style. The other wears a somber suit, charcoal gray and flawlessly tailored; a pale tie at his pale throat; a silver beard cropped neat.

She walks up to a sailor who's setting match to cigarette, ten feet from the foursome, and takes out one of her own.

"Can I get a light?" she says.

The man obliges. He is lean under his oilcloth coat. His knuckles are dark with tar, as are his hair and temples. Alma nods over her cigarette in thanks.

"Food looks good," the man observes.

"Uh-huh."

And then they can be silent, standing together in that linked space made by match and tobacco, the best way Alma's found to make friends in unfriendly places.

"I'd say you've outdone yourself, Mrs. Powell."

Hamilton hovers at Delphine's side. The other men lean in, too. The cowboy holding his cattleman's hat at his thigh, his gray-suited companion fingering a silver watch chain. Such is the allure of Delphine's body, her face: she draws people to her. Sometimes they come under a misapprehension. They see a brown-skinned woman and think they will have power over her. Or they see her body draped in riches and think they can help themselves to both. In San Francisco, Delphine was respected, revered by thieves and admired by the lawmen she paid off to protect her business. But she doesn't hold the same sway here. Alma watches the three men crowd around her, a pinch of unease in her chest.

"I hope this is the start of a wonderful enterprise," Delphine says, allowing the judge to lace her gloved hand through his elbow. "A service all the good workingmen in this town may benefit from."

"If they're at the bethel, they're not getting into liquor on Water Street." The cowboy's accent matches his handlebar mustache—the chaw-stained drawl of the Arizona Territory or its neighboring deserts. "That makes my work easier."

"Why, you don't need my help, Marshal Forrester." Delphine's voice is breathy, sweet. "You and your officers do a fine job."

"Thank you for saying so, ma'am." He taps his hat against his chest, cutting the sketch of a bow.

"I wish I could persuade you to share your golden touch with Tacoma," the man in the dark suit says. "We have a penchant for iniquity in my town, and we are in dire need of charitable souls such as yourself."

A Tacoma man. Alma studies him with closer interest. He looks to be about forty-five. Money aplenty, judging from his fancy getup and the thick silver rope of his watch chain.

"Mr. Pettygrove, if you bring me a project, I will assist you with it," Delphine says. "I'm afraid I know nothing about Tacoma or how my husband's estate can best be used to help there."

"Now, sir, don't be looking to claim the favors one of our town's most esteemed residents," Forrester says, and places one booted foot between Delphine's skirts and Pettygrove. "Mrs. Powell, when will the bethel open its doors?"

"Father Martin just visited." Delphine raises her chin, holding her space against the marshal's incursion. "He reports the rooms inside are almost ready, and the funds from today should help provide our first supplies—blankets and other bedding, basics for the kitchen."

"Wonderful." The marshal edges closer to Delphine, covering the movement by tucking his hat behind his back and adjusting his weight.

"Mr. Powell's memory could not be honored better, I believe," Hamilton says, looking at Forrester, and whatever was intended by the words seems to work: Forrester stiffens, pinches his lips under his mustache. Pettygrove fiddles with his watch chain, casting an eye back toward the food tables.

"My dear husband had a powerful call to do good works," Delphine says. "I pray for him every day. And I intend to apply his generosity wherever the town may have a need. And perhaps in your town, too, Mr. Pettygrove."

Alma's cigarette is finished, along with her patience for this conversation. Delphine has these men on the hook, that much is plain. The marshal needs to mind his manners. Otherwise, Delphine seems in full control of the situation. Alma admires the simplicity of her cover: a wealthy widow, living a subdued life, paying tribute to her late husband through charitable works. The last person anyone would expect to tie to an opium ring.

Alma nods farewell to her smoking companion. At the back, the trays of food are ravaged but still offer sweet rolls dotted with walnuts, ham sandwiches, cherry pies. She takes two ham sandwiches and a sugary turnover. It's full of raisins and currants. Eating sweet, then salty, in alternate bites, Alma wanders to a table, says hello to the men sitting there, slides onto the bench. A priest walks among the tables, speaking to the seamen. The periphery of the room is crowded with silks and furs. A ring of wealthy men and their wives, drawn back, whispering as they watch the hungry sailors devour lunch, like visitors taking in feeding time at the Lincoln Park Zoo.

She lets her gaze trickle over their faces until she finds someone staring back at her: a young man, black hair combed down in muttonchops to meet the ambitious beard he's cultivating. Black eyes. Silver shine at his collar, at his cuff links. She keeps her eyes on his. Takes a huge bite of ham sandwich, letting her eyes drift down his pearl-buttoned coat, slow, then back up to his face. He is still watching her. He undoes his coat, tucks the front panel of it aside to get at a vest pocket and pull out a watch, though he does not look at the time or let his coat droop back into place, displaying the fine dark fabric over his hip, his side body. Alma swallows. Winks at him.

Something about Jack Camp is just right for this town. She's not sure whether it's the people here, or whether it's her. She hasn't

lived this long as Camp before, only donned his clothes and mannerisms for a few fights, for a few nights at a time. To do more
was a risk in San Francisco, where too many people knew her as
Alma Rosales. She liked that way of moving through the world.
The satisfaction of it, especially on dark corners: toughs thinking
a black-clad small woman meant easy pickings, and the way their
faces would twist when she unsheathed her knife or wielded her
knuckles. The feel of wearing her own hair, long: the pleasure of
combing it out, of sitting naked in bed and rolling her neck, so
strands tickled over her rib cage, her shoulders, her low back. Molly,
the woman who sometimes warmed her nights; Angel, the man
who sometimes did the same.

Alma likes moving through Port Townsend as Camp, too. She's
had far more fun than she expected on the distant spit of land. And
these men who look at Camp. They intrigue her. A new kind of
game. Not as urgent as the one she's playing with Wheeler—he is
a special kind of gunpowder to her spark—but a rough one, a test of
her bound body, a performance that would go beyond the surface
and into the realm of touch, shadowed alleys, hot mouths.

The bearded gentleman puts his watch away. Points at the door
with a slow open-close of his eyes. She starts on the second ham
sandwich.

Then Delphine crosses her line of sight, shed of her attendants.
Watery daylight glosses her upswept hair. Alma tracks her progress
across the room, and not all the rich women on the other side are
smiling. Two in particular make no attempt to hide their faces as
they whisper. Alma lip-reads enough to take their meaning—she's
heard it before. Quadroon. Colored upstart. How dare she.

Delphine glides up to the woman in blue-striped silk, who Alma
first saw on the steps. The woman is willowy, flushed. She holds a
teacup and a silver spoon. *Ting, ting.*

"Thank you all for coming today, and for your contributions."
The woman's voice has a faint quaver. "And let's give a toast to
Mrs. Conrad Powell, whose generous donation made our luncheon
possible, and also made the bethel possible—this good woman is
doing the Lord's work and watching out for her neighbors."

Gloved applause from the Upper Town folk, hearty cheers from the sailors. Delphine smiles and nods to the room in general, lovely despite her somber clothes. Alma huzzahs along with her table. That is good work. The Lord, indeed.

Then the priest is beside the two women and starts yammering on about charity, and Delphine withdraws from the center of attention. Alma is getting restless, ready to leave. Kopp has already vanished—to start collecting five thousand dollars, she hopes. Hamilton stands with Pettygrove and a yellow-haired woman in a violet dress. Hamilton offers her a glass of some fizzy beverage as she leans on his arm, pale and limp as a wilting iris. The marshal is at the food tables, picking walnuts off a sweet roll. And Wheeler? He's nowhere to be seen, not in the corners or in the dwindling knots of gentlemen. Her fancy bearded fellow gone, too.

A punishing stretch of time while the priest leads a prayer and it will be too noticeable to slip out. Once he's sketching a benediction over the crowd, she slides off the bench, ambles to the door. Drooping daylilies crest over the lintel, heavy scented, morose. And there are Wheeler and Edmonds. Just outside, sharing a cigarette in the rain, which has thickened as the clouds dropped lower. Edmonds has been crying. Wheeler watches Alma walk past. With his eyes on her, Wheeler takes a long drag on the cigarette and offers it to the collector, whose thick black curls drip as he hangs his head.

Coming in from the purple hatbox hall. Nell's bedroom smells of lamp oil and her perfume, with an undertone of burnt hair. Gold strands tangled around the little iron by the hearth. Her blue dress laid out on the divan under the window.

"Sorry for the mess." Nell scoops a few pairs of stockings off the bed, her dressing gown clinging to her thighs, her hips. "I didn't know you'd be stopping by."

"I was in the neighborhood." Alma holds out a bunch of daisies, rain-dappled and dripping, her eyes on Nell's haunches. Restless after two hours of drinking overpriced gin at the Delmonico. Kopp sent his rich friends away without mentioning Wheeler, as he had promised, but she stayed to watch him booze and gamble and stumble upstairs, just to be safe.

"Jack, you're always in the neighborhood."

All of Lower Town is contained in nine blocks, so this is true enough. But the Delmonico is just around the corner. Nell's fingers brush hers as she collects the bouquet. Alma leans against the wall by the door while Nell dusts off a cut-glass cup and sets the daisies inside.

"Quite a change from tuberose." Nell sits at her dressing table, holds a few pins with her lips as she twists up and secures a curl by her ear. "Innocence, after yesterday?"

"Funny thing. The florist was fresh out of dogbane and winter cherry, despite the season."

Nell goes still, her arms raised, a lock of hair in her fingers. Her eyes wide on Alma's in the mirror. Nell turns around. One forearm drifts to bar across her chest, pull her gown closed.

"Don't look at me like that," Alma says.

"Why are you doing this?"

"I just want to know how much it paid. Fucking me."

"It didn't pay anything."

"Then why'd you do it?" Alma shrugs against her bandage, wanting a pain she can manage. She didn't know how much Nell's betrayal meant until now, standing here again. Her pride wounded. How naked she allowed herself to be. "What's he giving you. I know he's at The Captain's all the time. Is there something going on there?"

"You're not talking about Nathaniel."

"No. You gave him my name. My cover. After I was good to you. After I made you spend."

Nell's face goes pink, her throat. Fine eyebrows knotting. She stands from her chair.

"I didn't give your name to anyone," she says, and her voice is hard with anger. "You've made a mistake. So stop a moment—"

"Then how did he—"

"Stop a moment, Jack," Nell says. "You sound like you're working up to a froth, and I'll tell you, if you insult me, there's no taking it back. I do not accept mistreatment. And I do not accept apologies."

The weight of just those insults pressing at Alma's tongue, sugar

dishes and open thighs and all the rest of the ugliness that's jabbing at her, and for once, for once, she keeps them down. Leans
hard against the wall. Sharp exhale that almost sounds like a laugh.
She's starting to like Nell too much.

"Then how did he know?" she says, wrung out, quiet.

"What happened?"

"I can't tell you."

"I understand that. We're in the business of secrets." Nell
crosses the room, stands warm and near and sweet smelling. "How's
your arm?"

"Hurts like a son of a bitch."

"You took off your sling."

Closer. Alma shifts her feet wider, one small twitch of each boot,
and Nell comes between them. Silk gown slipping open, gauzy chemise underneath. Her nipples rising under its thin cloth.

"You did make me spend." Hot breath on Alma's ear, curled hair
brushing Alma's lips. "I was hoping to persuade you to do it again."

Alma's good hand sliding between silk and soft cloth, body heat,
the supple rise of Nell's hip bone. Wet mouth on Alma's neck. Nimble fingers on her belt buckle. She closes her eyes.

"I think that can be arranged," she says.

No one on the Quincy steps. The door locked. Snowflakes drift
over her outstretched sleeve, lamplight yellowing the denim. Hollers from Water Street. A bristle of nerves. She clumps down the
stairs, takes the long way around Adams, since Wheeler is so careful with his set of double entrances. Such a transparent precaution.
Yet it might have its uses—it's plenty to fool someone like Kopp.
The Clyde Imports window is dark. She knocks on the glass.

Nothing, nothing. Then a flare of light at the back. Her shoulders loosening so quick it jolts pain through her bad arm.

A dark shape weaves through the filing cabinets, crosses into the
band of streetlamp shine on the carpet inside, and it's Wheeler and
she's glad to see him. Rosales, you are going soft. Stand up straight.
Lock the jaw. Toughening up so much that when he opens the door,
she growls, pushes in.

"Where's Conaway?"

"At the warehouse." He locks the door, his nostrils flaring when he faces her. "It's just him and Fulton, and they each need a shift to sleep."

"Right," she says.

"Were you at Nell's?"

"Yeah." Her shirt smelling of perfume. Her hands licked clean, though musk lingers.

Wheeler stands angled toward the office's back door. A line of hearthlight from the jamb cuts sharp and red over his torso, his cheek. His jaw working. Crosshatched shadows at his forehead.

"What did you learn at the fund-raiser?" he says.

"I have a lot to tell you. And quick."

He waves at the inner door. The back office is warm, air vanilla-tinged. On the desk a cigar wafts smoke. Whiskey mellows beside it. He is such a creature of habit. Though Alma is pouring gin as she thinks this, and she has her own pathways cut, too: her usual chair, her usual drink, the usual urge to amble up to Wheeler and see if she can get his hackles up.

"Kopp was an hour away from selling your name to some water-front businessmen," she says, capping the decanter. Her hand steadier than yesterday. "I got him in time."

"To whom."

"A man called Weiss. And his friend—short, fattish, graying muttonchops. At the bar Weiss called him Richard."

Wheeler leans against the front edge of the desk, thumb tracing an arc along the side of his whiskey glass. One polished shoe twitching.

"Weiss's brother," he says. "A banker."

"Who are they?"

"Weiss is a competitor of mine," Wheeler says. "Runs an import business of his own. He'd see me ruined if he had the chance."

"Yet another man out to get you," Alma says. "Is this town un-usually cutthroat, or do you just have trouble making friends?"

This is too much, somehow—a throwaway jab that hits Wheeler hard. He stiffens, a flinch of motion. His eyes narrow. Alma doesn't want him angry, not now; she needs his cooperation.

"I told Kopp Benson's turned sour on him," she says. "That started him talking. It seems Benson was recommended to him by someone. Kopp was under the impression Benson could bring him into the business."

"And they've been at this for months?"

"It explains the missing tar. Benson was being careful, starting slow, and Kopp was getting impatient. He only just found out you're involved, he said—that's why he came here."

Wheeler isn't moving closer so she crosses the room to him. Sets her drink on the desk at his hip. Left hand clenching in and out of a fist, the pinkie finger slow to wake out of numbness.

"We have to shut him up," she says. "He's coming here on Monday. I don't think he should be allowed to leave."

Wheeler looks down at her left hand, its pulse of motion.

"Still giving me trouble," she says. "Kopp was the one who set up the Seattle side. He'll come here, give us the last missing piece. And then . . ."

"He knows too many people," Wheeler says. "If he was that close to selling my name to Weiss, maybe others, it will look bad for me if he turns up dead. My reputation is not completely sterling."

Alma thinks of Wheeler walking just behind Judge Hamilton. His touchiness about lacking friends. Maybe he's run into more problems with the trust.

"It's sterling if you're on the trust," she says. "Right?"

"I had hoped so."

So he won't confide in her. Fine. He twists back to reach for his cigar. Opening the strong midline of his body, a row of dyed-pearl buttons tracking down his vest to his belt buckle. Glint of silk thread in the seam of his trousers. He sees her looking. Straightens up. Takes a long pull on the cigar, embers in his eyes. The space between them waking. Not draped in Driscoll's shroud as it was the day before.

"Come on," she says. "You don't move up, I don't move up. It's time to take a risk. You play things too safe sometimes."

"I like to have a plan."

"Let's make one. I would have had Kopp come sooner, but I'm away to Tacoma tonight."

The boat leaves at eight o'clock. And she spent too much time at the Delmonico, too much time at Nell's. She has less than an hour and she still has to change into women's clothes, pin on her woman's hair. Shape herself for the morning's performance with the Pinkerton's agents.

"Tacoma?"

"On her business. I'll be back tomorrow afternoon," she says. "That gives us time to set something up."

"What do you propose?"

"You can't get your hands dirty. I understand that." Alma tips back the last of her gin, tries stretching her shoulder. The pain duller than this morning. "If we kill Kopp, we have to pin his murder on someone else. Sloan, if we can."

Wheeler exhales smoke. Tongues a flake of paper off his upper lip. It's as if he's baiting her now, with the powerful coil of his torso as he leans to tap the cigar into its dish, with the openness around his mouth.

"Put his body in Sloan's cannery?" he says.

"That'd be one way to do it. Or plant King Tye on him. Sloan's going to swing for that anyway."

Wheeler nods, a small noise of interest.

"Benson's got to be dealt with also," Alma says. "He's not set to meet with Kopp again until Tuesday. So it might pay to keep him on the line until then—he could still lead us to the Seattle contact, or to a rogue crewman."

"Yes. I want to smoke them all out," Wheeler says. "You don't steal from me and get away with it."

There's his fight, there's his steel, come out for the clash. The set of his chin hints at violence. She grins, drawn in a step.

"Now, that we can agree on," she says. "I've got Kopp bringing a lump of cash. He thinks he's buying in. His money will cover the stolen tar, and then some."

"How much."

"Five thousand."

"Good Christ."

"He's *borrowing* some of it from the railroad," Alma says, sneering.

"He has no loyalty at all," Wheeler says. "After the way they've lined his pockets."

She's close enough to catch the mingled scents of vanilla tobacco and whiskey on his breath. The edge of the desk ghosts against her hip. Conspiring with him, an agile mind to dance with, adds fuel to her thoughts.

"What if no one finds his body?" Alma's eyes narrow as she follows the thread of a new idea. "What if we get word out he's skipped town with the railroad's cash? Then you've got nothing to do with it. You're in the clear. Enough men would believe it—they've seen him at the gambling tables. They know he takes stupid risks when it comes to money."

"Quietly dump him in the bay," Wheeler says. "Yes."

A knock in the next room, at the Clyde Imports door. Alma's gut clenches. She backs away from Wheeler, away from the inner door, her hand on her gun. Did she call Kopp wrong? Think she had him hooked and the whole time he was playing dumb, waiting to have cause to show up with the law? Or maybe she spooked him after all, and he ran to Benson crying for help.

Wheeler is up off the desk, nothing sprawling in his posture now, his body tensed as he stalks to the inner door. He peers out toward the Clyde Imports window, keeping near the doorjamb.

"It's Benson," he says, without looking at Alma.

"Shit. Kopp might have gotten to him."

"He wouldn't come here, then," Wheeler says.

"Unless he's fixing to kill you."

Alma is breathing again, but fast, unsettled. This plan is still full of holes. Full of pitfalls she didn't think about when she was sneering at Kopp in the schoolyard. Now Benson's here. And she has to be on that Tacoma boat, or she'll miss the morning rendezvous.

"I can wait in the hall, in case you need me," she says.

"No. Stay," he says. "If he talked to Kopp, he'll come out swinging. But if he hasn't, he still thinks he's scared you quiet, and I'm in the dark. Act like it."

"Keep him on the line."

Wheeler nods, a tight, small motion, and walks into the shadows of Clyde Imports. Clicking of the lock. Alma ready with her gun in case Benson tries anything when he comes in off the street.

Tight, loose. Tight, loose. Her left hand almost back to where she needs it. The dizzy heave of blood loss subsiding once she'd filled herself with food, with sleep. When she gears up for Tacoma, she'll have to remove Nell's bandage. See the wound, seeping. Wrap thinner gauze around the gash and hope she can squeeze her arm into a narrow sleeve. All her dresses are already tight across the shoulders, across the ropy slant of her trapezius muscles.

"Is there a problem?" Wheeler says in the front office.

"Yes, sir."

Boots scraping. The door ticks shut.

"Scuffle by the Quincy warehouse," Benson says.

Footsteps closer. She holsters her gun. Then the big man is in the doorway, head cocking when his eyes meet Alma's. She scowls at him but lets her grimace waver, lets her gaze skip nervously to Wheeler as he walks into the room. Benson grins. Too much satisfaction in that grin for him to know Kopp has turned on him.

"Camp." He juts his chin at her.

"Sloan's boys?" Wheeler says, sitting at his desk.

"One of 'em," Benson says. "And one of ours. McManus."

"Tom isn't in town."

"Oh, he is. Sir, he just shot Loomis dead."

Alma bites back an oath.

"Out in front of Chain Locker," Benson says. "Lot of folks saw it. And he wouldn't say a word to me, or Clay. I don't know where he's got off to."

Wheeler stubs out his cigar. Keeping hold of himself with that deep reserve of composure that she both admires and resents. He takes a long drink of whiskey. Benson waits, thumbs in his belt loops, one bootheel jiggling. Not looking at Alma at all after she played nervous.

"Who's posted at the warehouse while you're here?"

"I got Lyle on it," Benson says. "He was at the bar."

"Get back," Wheeler tells him. "I'll take care of Tom."

Benson knuckles his cap. With his face turned away from Wheeler, he winks at Alma. He hasn't seen Kopp. Not if he's this jolly. His heavy footsteps clump away through Clyde Imports. Lintel bell tinkling after the slam. Only then does Alma move to the inner door—the Clyde Imports office empty, Benson's bulk heading up Washington, his buckskin jacket mustard-colored in the streetlamp glow.

"I've got to go." She shakes her head. "You have to lock McManus down. We can't lose Sloan's cooperation before the next handoff. We've almost got him."

"I know." Anger thick in Wheeler's voice now that they're alone. "God damn it."

"Benson seems clueless," she says. "At least that's something."

Wheeler pulls a key from his vest pocket. Unlocks one of the drawers and withdraws his pistol. Spinning clicks as he checks the cylinder.

"I'll be back tomorrow at four," she says. "Keep the peace."

His face pale. Eyes electric blue when they snap up to hers.

27

JANUARY 25, 1887

TRANSCRIPT OF INTERVIEW WITH SAMUEL REED

WHEREUPON THE FOLLOWING PROCEEDINGS WERE HAD IN THE JEFFERSON COUNTY JAIL, PORT TOWNSEND, WASHINGTON TERRITORY, ON JANUARY 25, 1887.

LAWMEN PRESENT: CITY MARSHAL GEORGE FORRESTER, OFFICER WAYLAN HUGHES

TRANSCRIPTION: EDWARD EDMONDS, ASSISTANT DEPUTY COLLECTOR, U.S. CUSTOMHOUSE

OFFICER HUGHES: You said Sloan was suspicious of everyone, even his own men. Do you mean someone in particular?

MR REED: Yeah. Lowry.

MARSHAL FORRESTER: Who's that?

MR REED: Another of Sloan's men. He came on before I got there. He lived at the boardinghouse, too, but I didn't talk to him much. He was usually with Sloan, and I stayed as far away from Sloan as I could.

OFFICER HUGHES: If they were so close, why was Sloan suspicious of him?

MR REED: Lowry was keeping company with Sugar.

MARSHAL FORRESTER: She must have been some woman.

MR REED: She was. Anyway, Sloan didn't like us to go out for girls. He said if we wanted one, he had plenty in-house. Only charged us half price. And of course, this wasn't just any girl. Sugar and Sloan had their bad blood. But Lowry met her at some point, started courting her. Sloan didn't take him to task over it at first . . . he was too busy dealing with the railroad man.

OFFICER HUGHES: The man he mentioned when he was knifing you?

MR REED: I think so. How many railroad men can there be?

MARSHAL FORRESTER: Too many, nowadays.

OFFICER HUGHES: Do you know the railroad man's name?

MR REED: Kopp. I remember it because I thought it was funny. I thought he was a cop, when I first heard Sloan talking about him. See? *Kopp* sounds like *cop*?

MARSHAL FORRESTER: You're slow as molasses, son.

OFFICER HUGHES: I've heard of this fellow.

MR REED: You don't think it's funny?

OFFICER HUGHES: When you say Sloan was too busy dealing with the man . . . do you mean Kopp is dead, too?

MR REED: No. No, he and Sloan were doing business together. For a while, Sloan thought Kopp was maybe spying on him. But like I said, he thought that about everybody. Soon they were partnered up. Kopp was buying dope off of Sloan.

MARSHAL FORRESTER: How do you know that?

MR REED: I was usually posted at the cannery with Loomis. Doing the dirty jobs he didn't want to do, cleaning up after each batch of men, the filth they left. So I saw opium crates. Some would come in, some would go out. Kopp visited a few times to check on them. Poked around with his walking stick, that door knocker of a gem on top enough to settle a man for life.

MARSHAL FORRESTER: It's fake.

MR REED: You know him?

MARSHAL FORRESTER: I know him enough to know it's fake.

MR REED: Oh.

MARSHAL FORRESTER: I've been keeping an eye on Kopp. Got a tip from his employers he's not to be trusted . . . as false as his cheap baubles. Sounds like it's time I pay him a visit.

MR REED: He's not here anymore, sir.

MARSHAL FORRESTER: What?

MR REED: He came by the boardinghouse yesterday morning. Told Sloan he'd borrowed some funds from the railroad and had to leave town.

MARSHAL FORRESTER: Son of a bitch.

MR REED: He gave some money to Sloan.

MARSHAL FORRESTER: I'm never going to hear the end of this, damn it.

OFFICER HUGHES: Sam, did you often see Sloan at the cannery? Or overhear his men talking there? You must have gotten an earful about his business. Things we need to know.

MARSHAL FORRESTER: Like where he's sourcing his tar, and where he's shipping it.

MR REED: Sloan didn't talk to me much, after that first time. I'd overhear the things he said to Loomis when he came to visit the cannery, and sometimes other conversations at the boardinghouse.

OFFICER HUGHES: What kind of conversations?

MR REED: Talk of men he knew, protection money, bribes.

OFFICER HUGHES: What men? From the waterfront?

MR REED: I didn't know any of the names.

OFFICER HUGHES: What about XXXXXX or XXXXXX? Did he mention them?

MARSHAL FORRESTER: Strike that, Edmonds. Strike those men's names.

E. EDMONDS: Yes, sir.

OFFICER HUGHES: But there's been talk—

MARSHAL FORRESTER: I won't see those men dragged through the mud. I won't have it.

OFFICER HUGHES: Listen, Marshal—

MARSHAL FORRESTER: If you don't settle down and start following my instructions, I'll have you put off this case and call Jackson in here. Do you want that? Do you want a junior officer pulling rank over you? Taking your spot in the smuggling bust of the decade? Your work finding and bringing Reed in this morning made obsolete? No?

OFFICER HUGHES: (inaudible)

MARSHAL FORRESTER: No. I didn't think so. You did good work

today, Hughes. Finding Reed based off those men's reports, linking him to the Calhoun woman's murder. If you want justice for her, for the others Sloan has killed or ruined, you follow my lead. Understood?

OFFICER HUGHES: Yes, sir.

MARSHAL FORRESTER: What else did you learn from Sloan's conversations?

MR REED: That's what I was saying. Not a lot. Not a lot I could follow, anyway. And I tried to avoid him. I didn't like to be in the same room. That room upstairs in the boardinghouse reminded me . . .

MARSHAL FORRESTER: Is that where he knifed you?

MR REED: Yes. I hated going in there. Loomis knew it, and he'd make me go fetch things from inside. Just to be a hard case about it. I hated that bastard.

MARSHAL FORRESTER: Didn't you say Loomis is dead?

MR REED: Yeah. He got into a fight on the docks. A stevedore shot him. That put an end to his bullying.

MARSHAL FORRESTER: Don't gloat too much.

MR REED: I have cause.

MARSHAL FORRESTER: It looks bad. Especially when there's no proof you didn't do it.

MR REED: Oh, there were plenty of witnesses. My hands are clean. But after Loomis died . . . Well, that's when Sloan started killing the others.

28

JANUARY 23, 1887

Tacoma is ripe with fish and sewage, iron and salt. Pounding rain drums the stench out of the waiting ships, the teeming docks. Alma chose lodgings right in the thick of things. Bustling waterfront commerce, swarms of longshoremen. The stevedores weave through heaps of crates and sacks and boxes that wait to be freighted east or sailed west—all those veins to pump full of tar. The railroad's industry plain in the men's crowded efforts as they move shoulder to shoulder, shifting cargo on this pier and the next, and the next, and the next, until the world smears into a blur behind the rain.

Alma steps off the boardinghouse's sloped veranda. Liking the look of her new stomping grounds. But she can't explore them properly just yet. Her damp skirt hems are thick around her legs. Her cloak heavy with rain. Camp's clothes weigh half as much as these, at least. At the end of the pier she hails a hansom cab, the horse blindered and thickset, the driver squinting against the wind. She rucks up her skirts to climb in. The seat is soaked, her folds of cloth ungainly.

"Victory Hotel," she shouts above the weather and the stevedores' calls and the long, low boom of a steamer as it churns toward its mooring.

The coach rattles over plankboards and then jars into mud. Rough roads, air bitter with charcoal. They climb the bluff that separates the waterfront from the main body of town. Tacoma is all bricks and pitted wood. Smokestacks knife into the sky to the south. The town has the same split-level setup as Port Townsend—industry on the water and houses up above—but Tacoma is bigger. Dirtier. More like a real city, full of useful nooks and crannies. The downside of this is, if the Pinkerton's agents aren't where they said they'll be, Alma will never find them. They could be moving across the Sound despite their promise to wait, despite their letter. They could have used it as a ruse to lure her out of town and take the glory of the strike themselves. She would expect as much if it were only her. But they believe she's working with Lowry, and it's unlikely they'll hang him out to dry. She's banking on that old-boy mentality.

The Victory is a tall, balconied building, new paint on the sign but otherwise grim. The lobby cluttered with dismal gray furniture where men smoke and thumb through newspapers. Alma looks for a pair of men—*We will be drinking coffee at the back*, the letter said, *and I will have a red scarf*—and finds the red scarf first, a swab of color in the thick-brushed shadows. A wash of relief. But she must make sure it's them. Then negotiate. And only after that, breathe easier.

She crosses the lobby, untying the knot of her cloak and folding it over so the wet cloth is inside, off her sleeve. Her corset tight over her belly. It reminds her how to move: how to walk leading with chest and chin, the tight bandage on her shoulder nipping into the skin under her dress. Always some sort of binding, some restriction.

"Good day, Cousin Alfred," she says at the little round table. "It's been too long."

The men look up at her, appraising. One is white-haired, with a salt-and-pepper mustache and sunken eyes. The other is a younger man, close to thirty. He has a watery complexion—hair, eyes, and skin all the same milky gray. The impression is that of a sickly man, but he has broad shoulders under the red loop of the scarf, sturdy long hands wrapped around his coffee cup.

"Cousin Polly," the younger man says, standing. "Five years, gone so quickly!"

She gave the correct opening; he gave the correct response. These are the Pinkerton's agents. Another pulse of relief, warm in her chest.

He takes her cloak. She sits in the chair next to his.

"This is Grove," he says, nodding at his older companion. Which makes him Kennedy.

"How do you do," she says.

Grove sits forward, clasping his hands between his knees.

"We're anxious for an update," he says. "Your letters have been . . . perplexing."

"I can't stay long," Alma says. "I need to get back on the eleven o'clock boat. I'm worried about Lowry."

"So are we," Grove says. "Who's this woman he's been seeing?"

"A workingwoman. She's harmless."

"Is she a distraction?"

"No," Alma says. "At our last meeting he said he was close to finishing his assignment."

"How often do you see him?" Kennedy says, taking out a silver case and tucking a cigarette into the corner of his mouth.

"Nearly every day."

"And the man who keeps the boardinghouse?"

"I've only seen him once," Alma says. "Youthful. Handsome. Not who I expected, given what he's up to."

"Illuminate the situation, as you see it." Grove sips his coffee. His teeth are long, laced with stains. "Don't bother being discreet— it's safe enough to talk here."

"Lowry has been at the boardinghouse for a few weeks now," she says. "Pretty soon after we arrived, he told me he'd gotten himself a spot on the man's crew."

"This is Sloan?"

Alma looks around as if nervous. She has decided to play it timid—the hanger-on in over her head, competent enough to act as an agent's assistant but worried about making mistakes. She has guessed what the men have heard about her at the Colorado office: a firecracker, once, but after that Yuma fuckup she's not to be trusted, not to be given too much to do.

"No one knows you here," Grove says, impatient.

"Yes—Sloan owns the boardinghouse. I told you as much in the letters."

"Just keeping the record straight," Kennedy says.

"That's where Lowry's been living," she says. "I meet him at a café on the other end of town. I go every day, in the morning, and if he has something to tell me, he comes, too."

This would have been their arrangement, or something like it, if Lowry weren't long dead in San Francisco. Alma would have met with him away from the opium smugglers, so he could pass along information without raising suspicions. His planned cover was a dockworker, and a man like that couldn't write his own letters— he wouldn't know how to write his own name.

"So what has he found?" Grove says. "Besides an entertaining woman?"

Alma smooths her skirts, her fingers catching on the damp gray twill.

"Sloan is moving product from Victoria using small boats, and girls," she says. "Lowry estimates about two tons per month. He's part of the wharf crew, so he's seen the crates come into Sloan's keeping. He thought the customhouse was helping at first, but they have other schemes keeping them busy. Now he believes this goes higher. That's why he needs time. He thinks the smugglers might be working with a wealthy railroad man, maybe some police. And he's near to getting proof."

Kennedy is nodding, the smoke from his cigarette rising in a jagged column. Grove finishes his coffee. Frowns.

"Most all of this was in the letters," Alma says, and there's no need to feign her annoyance. That ridiculous cipher took hours to piece together, each time.

"Like I said," Kennedy says, "we're just getting the facts straight."

"That's the bulk of what he's told me," she says. "Sloan has the girls bring product down from Canada in their dresses and their luggage. They're moving almost a third of his supply. He uses an old boat to send product through to Seattle. Lowry says he wants to expand to San Francisco next."

"I'm concerned about this woman," Grove says.

Maybe it was a mistake to mention a woman. Alma meant it merely as a detail, signifying how deeply Lowry had gotten himself undercover. But Grove keeps picking at it.

"When you say *workingwoman*, are you using a euphemism?" Kennedy says. "No need to be delicate."

"Lowry would get comfortable at a whorehouse," Grove snorts. "That dog."

"She dresses very fine," Alma says. "And she's often out with other pretty women. But if you're suggesting she's a brothel madam . . . Well, I don't know. I don't know anything else about her."

"Remember McParland, out in coal country." Grove is speaking more to Kennedy than to her—a blunt dismissal. "He near on had a wife when he decided to get out. And he near on decided not to get out, because of her."

"Lowry's only been there three weeks," Alma says. "Hardly the months-long campaign McParland made."

Grove sniffs, looking past her at the gray light of the windows. If he doesn't expect her to know about recent agency history, he's not going to expect her to know much else. Her hold on the situation is slipping. Kennedy seems willing enough to listen, but if Grove is in charge—and she can't get a read on the pair's pecking order—he might ride roughshod over her plea to wait. She needs three more days.

"You're both doing good work," Kennedy tells her. "But perhaps you need to remind Lowry to focus. I don't want to come rushing in and ruin the setup he's orchestrating—"

"If you did, they might kill him," Alma says. "He's seen two men go in the time he's been with Sloan. Both accused of peaching. And another man—Sloan had his throat opened. All the way to the spine. And his tongue cut out."

Pinning Beckett's death on Sloan will add to Sloan's reputation as a butcher, and clear any possible suspicion about Wheeler's involvement in the customhouse man's death.

"That is unsavory," Grove says.

He signals to the lobby attendant, holds up his empty coffee cup. Alma asks the attendant for a lemon cordial and soda water.

A vile drink, especially without liquor added, but it will sting her lips and keep her on her toes.

"Give him three more days," she says. "That's what he asked for. I'll tell him you'll be coming in on—what is that? January twenty-sixth—you'll be coming in on Wednesday, so he better be ready to get out."

"We can come to town and not disrupt him," Kennedy says. "That might spook Sloan into doing something ill-advised, showing his hand."

"I don't like that." Alma knots her fingers in her lap, stops speaking as the attendant returns with their drinks. The lemon cordial is too sweet. Its sickly fizz tickles her throat. "Lowry's been putting himself at terrible risk. It's taken a toll on him—I'd swear he's lost ten pounds since setting up at that boardinghouse."

"What the hell are we going to do in Tacoma for three more days?" Grove pulls at his earlobe. "All that nonsense with the stagecoach and now we're stuck in the mud here?"

"You volunteered for this," Kennedy tells him.

Alma watches the men over the lip of her glass, peering into the crack between them and trying to see its cause.

"It wasn't worth the pay raise," Grove says. "And I'm sick and tired of your company."

He stands, picks up his jacket. His coffee still steaming on the table as he walks toward the street.

"Where's he going?" Alma says, worried that he's headed right for the docks—Grove didn't want to listen to a thing she said, and if he doesn't need his partner's approval to move, he is a danger.

"Sulking again," Kennedy says. "He's been a trial since we passed through Snake River country. Fell off his horse; now he's afraid he's getting old."

Grove ducks through a smaller, inner doorway near the exit.

"Are you worried he'll do something rash?"

"If by something rash you mean get blazing drunk at the bar."

Kennedy leans forward, picks up the other man's coffee, takes a long sip. He winks at Alma over the edge of the mug, and it occurs to her to laugh—if he's going to be on her side with the help of a little flirting, she'll play whatever part he likes.

"You won't move too quick on Lowry?" she says, letting herself sound a little breathless. Letting her relief about Grove soften her voice.

"Sweet on him?" Kennedy says.

And all she has to do is blush. Sip her cordial.

"Don't worry," he says. "He can have his three days. It'll take that long for Grove to dry out after today, I suspect. But don't go setting yourself up for disappointment. Lowry has his pretty madam. She's probably blond, and pink, and plump. Hard for a girl like you to compete with that."

He nods at Alma's drab dress, the dirt on her knuckles she couldn't quite scrub clean. She didn't powder her face. Her thick-boned wrists knock together in her lap. Apart from her clothes and voice, she has made no efforts at female delicacy—and Kennedy is reading her plainness as desperation. As invitation.

"I know," she says.

"Now I, on the other hand . . ." Kennedy leans forward to set the coffee on the table, his pinkie finger brushing Alma's skirts. "I am all alone in Tacoma, with only a grumpy old drunk to keep me company."

"I have to get back," Alma says, fluttering her eyes wide. "I can't risk missing tomorrow's morning rendezvous with Lowry, to tell him about your plans."

"Take the evening boat."

Alma glances at the windows, as if she's considering it. Lets her cheeks heat. As if she'd be excited to have this drooping, pallid man touch her, and after he just called her ugly.

"Come on." Kennedy jostles his knee into hers. "I know you Women's Bureau girls are all the same. Unmarried. Lonely. Just wanting a bit of adventure. Eh?"

Alma holds her drink with both hands. Looks down at her lap. She is thinking of his leering mouth kicked full of mud. When she looks up again, she is smiling.

"I'm not opposed to adventure," she says. "But I want to finish the work first. I have a lot to prove, you know, after my dismissal. I want to show that I can do a good job."

He bends his leg away, puts his hand on her thigh. His palm warm through her skirts.

"I'll make sure to tell the boss you did a good job." He leans in, lowering his voice, breath fetid with smoke and coffee. His scarf smells like a dead sheep. "If you work hard. I like an eager woman."

"I will work hard," she says, and his fingers on her leg tighten. "Come on Wednesday."

"Yes."

"But not until then?"

"Right," he says. "Where should we meet?"

"The French Hotel," she says. "It's right across from Sloan's boardinghouse. A good spot for staging a raid—you can see the house from the bay-facing rooms."

"Wednesday. We'll be in on the first steamer."

He squeezes her thigh again. She stands, his hand falling away. Quick scan of the lobby, just in case, but there is no one familiar—no one sitting close enough to hear their conversation. On her way through the door she sees Grove at the bar, a little alcove through the low inner doorway, sipping a tumbler of amber liquid. Drink up.

Tacoma's a rough place. Maybe the two agents won't make it to Port Townsend at all. She could arrange it: pay some tough to find the men now that she knows their faces. Stage their run-ins with a knife. But she needs them alive. She needs them to come down hard on Sloan. Still, the temptation is difficult to shake. She keeps testing herself, to see if she'll really do it, until she's back on the Port Townsend–bound steamer, chilled again by the rain, grinning. She bought time enough to set her plan in motion.

Alma hurries through her boardinghouse lobby, cloak hood shading her face. It's unlikely anyone in the house has ever been sober enough to notice her comings and goings, other than the manager's coin-counting child. But she has been up and down these stairs for almost two weeks in Camp's clothes. There are a few curious glances—one staring sailor doesn't blink or track his eyes after her, perhaps he's dead—but no one stops her. She unlocks her door. Strips off all the wet garments, the twill and lace, slowed by her aching shoulder and its stiffness.

In the fading daylight she unwinds her last binding: a long curl of gauze that peels off her shoulder. No blood on it today, just a little clear seeping. Underneath, a pink band of flesh, marked with the pattern of the cloth. A four-inch furrow in her skin. Nell's neat stitching. No smell, no redness radiating from the wound. It's healing clean. Her body is strong. Pulsing with health. She loves it.

All bare, in the center of the room, Alma runs her hands over her skin. Callused palms catching on scars. The gash on her shoulder. The little nubs of scab on her arm and side from where she fell into glass. Her ribs and stomach imprinted with long red lines from the corset's boning. These marks crosshatched by the angry chafing left by her binding cloth, three inches above and three inches below her breasts. Old bruises fading to faint yellow stains on her rib cage, her legs. She lifts one breast, fingering the rawness underneath it, the stinging flesh. Just a day or two of wearing nothing. How would that feel? To float in a hot bath and dry on clean sheets and sleep. Wake. Stretch. And, maybe, turn to someone. Silk pillows. Warm brown skin under her fingers, under her lips. Quiet laughter. Companionship. That's how it was once.

She thinks of Delphine, holding her hand in Nell's shop, concern in her dark eyes. The way Delphine says her name. Maybe, in Tacoma, they can be lovers again. Share that body connection. That tenderness she hasn't seen Delphine offer to anyone else.

Candlelight bats upon the lamp's glass, flutters in the corners. Her body unclenches, not needing to hold any kind of pose. Rain taps on the window. Voices from the room next door, two men, groaning, a low pulse of sound. Satisfaction. All the strings she's been laying out, the threads of her plan, are knotting together like they should.

The light brightens from gray to orange. Alma raises her bowed head, her sense of time disrupted by the unexpected sun. She walks to the window. The sun hangs low on the horizon, showing clear in a gap between thick iron-colored clouds and the jutting rise of Upper Town's cliff. The light has no heat, but it stains her golden through the dirty glass—her arms outstretched to brace against the casing; her breasts small, nipples dark; the jagged forelock falling just over the edge of her right eye. A few breaths, leaning into the light, and then the sun dips below the cliff edge, leaving her body, the room, dim.

She dresses as Camp, quick. Already later than she said she would be for her meeting with Wheeler. He'd better have no news about Benson, and good news about McManus. After buying time from the Pinkerton's agents, after spending her boat ride coming up with a perfect trap, she'll be damned if McManus is going to be the breaking point.

It's full dark when she reaches his offices. No one on the back step, but the Quincy door is open. No one in the hall. It's too quiet. Something about her boots stamping mud into the carpet, that thick, lonely sound in the single lamp's light, makes her uneasy. She slides her knife from her vest. Sticks close to the wall as she walks, her hip gliding along the blue paper.

Around the dogleg, slow, to the last empty notch of hall. Wheeler's door is closed. Firelight gleams at its bottom seam. No voices. She nudges open the door enough to peer inside. Wheeler sits at his desk, eyes on hers. She waits, braced, for the lunge of motion as someone unseen slams into the door or steps into view with a ready pistol. But there are no sounds save the fire's snapping. Wheeler raises an eyebrow. Alma steps into the room.

"Why the theatrics?" he says.

"The Quincy door was open." Alma flips her knife, letting him see the flash of it in her hand. Shaking off her nerves. Grinning a little.

"I knew you were coming. You're late, by the way."

"It's been a long day," she says.

"Your business in Tacoma was concluded successfully?"

"Oh, yeah." She takes her usual chair, elbows on knees, right heel jiggling. "I have good news. But how are things here? What did I miss?"

"It's been strangely quiet." Wheeler sets down his pen. "Nothing unusual from Benson. Nothing from Kopp, no warnings that he's started rumors."

"Good. And McManus?"

Wheeler shakes his head.

"I don't know where Tom's got off to," he says. "And Sloan hasn't made his move yet. As I said, it's been strangely quiet."

"Maybe everyone knew I was out of town." Alma bobbles her knife from palm to palm. "Saving the fun stuff for me."

"What's your good news? I could use some."

"The Pinkerton's agents are coming," she says.

Wheeler stops, whiskey halfway to his mouth.

"Excuse me?"

"On Wednesday," she says. "Just in time."

"You're going to have to explain why this is good news."

So Delphine still hasn't told him. But she needs a keen set of
ears, a keen brain, to help her vet her plan. Which means Wheeler
needs to know everything about the situation. There's an element
of showmanship, too, in her urge to share—tell him all that she's
been juggling, let him see how she's tamed a beast of a problem.

"Remember how you thought I was with the law?" She walks
to the sideboard, pours herself a tall glass of gin. The blue wall going
fuzzed as liquor stings her eyes watery. She tests holding the glass
in her left hand. It's all right. Steady enough, her shoulder not wailing even though her elbow is crooked, bearing weight. She picks
up the silver-topped whiskey decanter and turns around.

Wheeler stands behind his desk, his pistol leveled at her. His
eyes ferocious.

"Jesus," she says, almost dropping the whiskey.

"Have you sold us out?"

"No. God damn it, it's a cover. It's a cover story. Put the fucking gun down."

"What do you mean?"

"I'm not talking to you until you point that somewhere else,"
she says.

He lowers the gun, slow. Lays it beside his glass. Not taking his
eyes off hers.

"All right," she says. "I used to be a Pinkerton's agent. My badge
got taken away after an . . . incident. And then the Women's Bureau
was disbanded altogether in '84."

Holding the decanter aloft, in a sign of peace, she approaches
the desk. Sets the heavy glass at its edge. He ignores it.

"I worked for a while as a private detective in San Francisco,
helping rich women catch their cheating spouses red-handed. I met
Delphine in the city," she says. "After she came up here, she got
in touch with me again. Had me start running jobs for her; for
the Families. Then, a few months back, she said she'd heard that

Pinkerton's agents were sniffing around the trade in Puget Sound. She asked me to use my old ties to the agency to get an in—figure out what was up, attach myself to the agent on assignment here, if possible. And that's what I did."

Daniel Lowry was the perfect mark: well-liked in San Francisco but a little crooked, often seen taking kickbacks at the central police station. He agreed to pitch her proposal to William Pinkerton— on the condition she help him fence a few stolen necklaces. "This is the last time," she told him, "I want to go straight." He got approval from Pinkerton for her assistance, received his dossier. Everything was going to plan until he informed Alma he'd be taking a young heiress with him instead. "It's just the adventure that will coax her away from her father," Lowry told Alma in his rented rooms. He said: "She'll learn the cipher easy enough, it's simple stuff." Alma let him finish his drink while she flipped through her options. Then she launched herself at him, gun out.

"You weren't here just to audit me," Wheeler says.

She comes around the side of the desk. Onto that patch of carpet two feet from him. He doesn't look pleased but his hands aren't ready for the gun anymore, either; one holds his whiskey, and he brings the other up to rub the back of his neck. The hard curve of his triceps taut against his shirtsleeve.

"That was part of it," Alma says. "She told me about the missing product, too, so I could be on the lookout. Happily, the business was waterproof under investigation. Except I think I found your weak spot."

He gives her the smallest twitch of a grin.

"The agents coming are the ones we're getting Sloan on the hook for," she says. "I met with them in Tacoma this morning. They're set to arrive on Wednesday. So we have to have Sloan, and Kopp, and Benson—and all the thorns in our sides—ready for them to hang. Just like she ordered."

"I suppose you have an elaborate plan to effect this."

"You know me so well."

"That is absolutely not true." He steps forward, collects the decanter. Doesn't step back. "I don't know a thing about you, as you've just demonstrated."

"You know I like to fight." She lets her eyes drop to his belt, crawl back up his body. "You know I like to fuck."

His mouth open. He sets his whiskey on the desk. Loosens his tie. Alma grins. Brings her gin to her lips, and her left hand spasms—too much movement, too much strain on her deltoid. The glass cracks to the floor. Liquor cold all down the front of her shirt and vest. She has to laugh, when she was going for flirtatious and ended up looking like a fool.

"This god damn hand," she says, stooping to collect the two halves of the glass. "Barely nicked by that bullet and it's causing me a world of hurt."

"Alma—"

"Camp." She glares up at him. "Don't make a habit of using that other name. It's wrong."

"Camp." His voice different for the different name, something staccato, more businesslike, in his pronunciation. "What's your plan?"

"Oh, it's good. It'll get everyone where we need them. Kopp is going to disappear with the railroad's money. Sloan is going to be arrested for murder and tar smuggling. A little mess of mine"—she means Lowry, but sees no need to tell Wheeler his name—"is going to be tidied. And Alma Rosales, disgraced Pinkerton's agent, is going to end up dead."

"That doesn't sound like a very good plan for you," Wheeler says, his head cocked.

"Don't worry about me," Alma says, grinning. "I always come out on top. But we'll need help getting everything into place."

She carries the glass pieces to the sideboard.

"Help from Nell," she says. "From your new friend Edmonds, and Delphine's friend the marshal. But I haven't worked out how to get Benson, or his partners in Seattle. They're loose ends."

"Don't use that name for her," Wheeler corrects, then pauses. "How do you know she's friendly with the marshal?"

"Didn't you see them at the fund-raiser?" Alma says. "Him and Hamilton falling all over her, along with that Tacoma swell. I used to earn my bread by following stray husbands. I'd say all three of those men are having impure thoughts where she's concerned."

"The Tacoma man—Jim Pettygrove?"

"That was his name, yes." She wipes her hands on her trousers.

"Pettygrove has a wife." Wheeler has gone withdrawn again, the interest she was teasing out of him tucked away. He looks worried.

"And Hamilton's wouldn't stand up in a strong breeze," Alma says. "Maybe they're looking for new ones."

"Maybe." Wheeler sits down at his desk. Thumbs through a ledger.

"Have you been pipped at the post?"

"What?" he says, distracted, pages still flipping under his fingers.

"Did Delphine promise to marry you? Is that your promotion? She's richer than God, it would be something."

"I could never marry her," he says. "It would cause too much of a scandal. She promised she'd get Harrison Doyle out of my way. Clearing my claim for a spot on the railroad trust. She promised me that. And I'm to be Hamilton's candidate for city treasurer, when he runs for mayor in the spring. He's served before, and Brooks is not planning to run. He'll be reelected."

It's so boring. A railroad trust and a thankless job. The treasurer. But then, it suits him. It suits him perfectly. He'll be in city government, helping the business. He'll be respectable.

"You'll have a sterling reputation," she says.

"Yes."

"You don't move up, I don't move up." She pours a replacement drink. Sets it on the edge of his desk and drags her chair close. "Here's my plan. Help me make it work."

Hustling down Water Street toward Nell's house, the rain paused but the mud ankle-deep and sucking, slowing her steps. Past the National Bank, the butcher's, the coffeehouse where Driscoll ran to get their steaming cups. Damn that kid. So full of life and then dropped by a bottle, Jesus. She's shaking her head over him, sick with it, with guilt, when two men step out of some nowhere shadow and flank her, take her arms, and nudge a gun into the small of her back, against her spine.

"What the fuck?" she says.

"Quiet," one tells her, gripping her arm just below her stitches so the raw skin is wrenched.

She doesn't know his voice. She doesn't know either of their faces.

They steer her the wrong way, back toward Quincy, then toward the water, and when she sees where they're going, there are two options—twist free to run and risk a crippling shot, or let herself be taken in to see what comes next. It might be another bullet. Or worse. What will she do? For a heartbeat more she is undecided, staring into the chaos on either side of the line, riding the parallel tracks before life bends off in different directions. Then she lets out a breath, drops her head. Lets them lead her into Sloan's cannery.

29

JANUARY 12, 1887

Eleven Days Earlier

"Mr. Sloan will see you now." The phrasing strangely at odds with the man's rough face, his ashy greatcoat.

"He did make me wait," Alma says, raising an eyebrow.

She stands from her chair with a thick rustle of skirts. Extra petticoats under the rich green silk trap the heat of her legs, her pelvis, so within all the gaudy wrappings she is sweating. There's an itch at the side of her left thigh she can't scratch. But she looks as fine as she ever has—curled russet wig bouncing at the edges of her eyes, French chalk cloying on her cheeks, carmine bitter on her mouth—and as she follows Sloan's man through the drowsy afternoon parlor, the sailors draped over couches or playing desultory games of cards all stop, blink, gape, as her boots press squeaks out of the boardinghouse floor.

Up a narrow stair, Sloan's man too close behind her. A tepid stench pulses from his body. Her skirts quiver as he brushes against them with each step. The brocade reticule looped over her wrist is heavy with her knife, her brass knuckles, but the close quarters make her jumpy. The big man herding her with his body makes her jumpy. This boardinghouse is built like a rattrap, and she's seen Sloan's women when they, twitching, venture out. He does not treat them well.

"End of that hall," the man says.

In the space after he speaks, the air at the back of her head shifts;

there is a distinct sniff. He is leaning over her. Smelling her powdered neck.

"You've been very helpful," she says coolly, not looking back at him.

"Pike!" he hollers, near her ear.

Alma flinches. A man steps out of a room down the hall. Something metal is in his fist—a blade. Alma dips her hand into her purse, taking hold of her own knife.

"You're wanted downstairs," the man, still too close behind her, says.

"Five minutes," Pike says, and goes back into his room.

Deep breath. Shoulders up. Start walking. The walls are pocked with narrow doorways. Closed; closed; open, a man dozing in a low cot, a bare-breasted woman curled beside him; open, the man called Pike, shaving in a tin mirror. Afternoon sun slants hard on the metal disk. She recognizes Pike from the warehouse on Madison Wharf—his left arm and hand are runneled with burn scars. Closed. Open, another sleeping man, spent opium pipe on the floor beside him. Jackpot.

Sloan's making this too easy for her. Pipes out in full view. His bawdy house on display. Alma's only seen twenty-four hours of his organization, and he's the picture of waterfront vice: crimps, girls, knockout drops. Tar. He's the man she needs to know. The man she'll replace. Delphine must be tired of working with such a low fellow, but maybe Sloan's all she could find out here in the sticks.

At the end of the hall a door is just open, leaking daylight. Alma pushes inside. The space is crowded with tables and stools. A man sits near the door, working his way through a spread of lunch: rye bread, cheese, pickles, salt fish. The room smells of his food— pungent oil, brine—and stale liquor.

"You asked for me?" he says.

So this is Sloan. He's younger than she expected, in his late twenties only. Lean. Long fingers, graceful hands, busy as he saws away at the cheese rind. A faint curl in his blond hair. Trimmed sideburns trending to auburn at his jawline. Thick brows. Cheekbones set high.

She can appreciate him, but he does not seem piqued by her.

His eyes barely trace over her powdered face, her winking paste jewelry. He does not stand or move to shrug on his jacket. He continues to trim cheese slices and lay them on a heel of bread, taking sips from a beer mug and dabbing foam from his mustache with a calico cloth. Ill-mannered. But he is also beautiful. Delphine likes beauty. And if Sloan is Delphine's deputy, he may be testing her—playacting, as Alma is, but to some other purpose.

"I intended to discuss a financial opportunity," she says. "But I can see this is a bad time."

"You've already interrupted my lunch," he says. "Go on and tell me why."

"I just arrived in town."

Alma saunters along the perimeter of the room. She stops in front of a glazed window, winter sunlight a bare warmth on the back of her neck. If he won't give her any advantage, she'll take those she can—use shadows to make her face hard to see, so he will have difficulty gauging how his insults land.

"I'm looking to set up shop on Water Street," she says. "If we're going to be neighbors, I thought we might arrange an understanding. Take it one step further and share interest in my enterprise."

Sloan takes a bite of his bread and cheese.

"I don't work with women," he says around the food.

"I hear you work with quite a few women, actually."

"They work for me," he says. "That's the key difference."

"I'm surprised to hear you're not interested in profit, Mr. Sloan."

Alma scents something here—something more than wharf gossip about Sloan offering tar on his bill of goods. His flat refusal to work with women seems like a good cover for Delphine's pulling of his strings; no one would expect her to be his boss, with his attitude toward the gentler sex. Now, the women working for him; Delphine would not like that. The only way to find out more is to get Sloan talking. But he is sucking clean a fish bone. Draining the last of his beer.

"I've got a boatload of young ladies en route from San Francisco," Alma says. "And if you don't want to be my partner, I'm afraid I'll have to consider you a competitor."

"A boatload, huh?" This heavy with sarcasm. "Listen, missus . . ."

"It's miss," Alma says. "Miss Sugar Calhoun."

"All right, Miss Calhoun." He wipes his hands, stands slow, so the legs of his chair drag over the floor. "I don't like competition. Choose someone else as your friendly neighbor—otherwise your girls might find themselves in some trouble."

He drops the calico cloth. Walks over to her at the window, so the light picks out the warm brown of his eyes, the red strands in his mustache. He is taller than her by too much; she does not like to be looked down on.

"You might find yourself in some trouble," he says. "Some would say you came looking for it, walking into my house dressed like that."

It's no good if she hurts him, it's no good if she loses her temper. But it is hard to not grip the loop of her little purse, heavy with weaponry, and slam it against the side of his skull. He steps a notch closer. Under the salt-fish stink, under the beery sourness on his breath: the hothouse scent of opium smoke.

"Well"—she doesn't flinch away from his crowding—"this has been a most disappointing afternoon. Not what I'd been expecting at all."

"What were you expecting?"

"Interest." She lifts her chin. "When I asked around to see who would be a good contact for this type of business, I was told to visit you."

"Told by whom?"

His leg is pressing into the front of her skirts. The shifts in the silk echo through the petticoats to her skin, the small hairs there, so he seems even closer. She smirks up at him, eyes narrowing, mouth closed, and he grabs her by the throat. Slams her head into the windowpane. The pins twisted into her wig jab the back of her skull.

"Told by whom?"

"A man at the French Hotel," Alma says, choosing the hotel closest to Sloan's boardinghouse, the clapboard-fronted lodgings just across the road. Blood collects heavy in her face, heavy at her jawline. "I can't recall his name."

Don't strike out even though it's hard to breathe. Not when he's got tar on him. When he's the best lead you've got. Her vision starts to pulse. Sloan's fingers will leave marks.

"Try," he says.

"I can't—it might be Jules?" Grasping at the first name that comes to mind, from her code book, because no one told her about Sloan. She found him herself. The thin reediness in her voice alarms her; if Sloan does not let go in the next few seconds, she will have to fight. "Or Julius. Short, thin. Dark hair. No good at faro."

"I don't know anyone named Jules."

Sloan loosens the vise of his fingers and Alma brings her own hand to her throat. Her skin fever-hot to the touch. Not much exaggeration called for as she blinks, catches at breath.

"I don't want to see you again," he says, stepping out of the window's light to the table. He wipes his hand with the calico cloth. "I hope you take that as the warning it's intended to be."

"I understand," she says, still leaning against the wall. Letting him think she's frightened. Her heart is thudding for other reasons. Sloan's deep into more than one dirty business, and she would bet his tar is no different. But she'll have to come at him another way. If he won't play with a lady, he might be inclined to deal with Jack Camp.

"You're a brute." She keeps her hand at her throat, where the powder has likely smudged off, a little tear in her disguise.

"No, Miss Calhoun." Sloan sits again, slices another wafer of cheese. "That was me being a lamb. Come back again and you'll find a lion."

It is hard to hold down her grin. She'll be back that night. With teeth of her own to bare. Already her plan is taking shape. The filthy hands. The stained work shirt. If he likes blood and beatings and throttled necks, she'll give him a show—walk right up to one of his boys at that Madison warehouse and knuckle him into a pulp. Then offer to take his spot. You need good fighters, Mr. Sloan. You need lions.

"I won't trouble you again," she says, and stalks out into the hall.

30

JANUARY 23, 1887

Inside, the cannery is a boxy space. High ceilings. Reek of piss and blood and moldy straw. Cut in two by a brick wall at its center. The stench of broken bodies everywhere, but there's just rusted canning-line machinery and empty crates, stacked tall, dim lamplight slitting through their boards. The men lead her around a corner and through an iron door, to the other side of the brick wall. Here a warren, more like Sloan's boardinghouse. One of the rooms lit by a single candle. Sloan sits inside, on a chair against the wall, wearing a gray vest. His shirtsleeves rolled up despite the chill. His hands empty.

"Camp," he says.

"Don't try nothing," the man with the gun at her back says.

She is nudged into the room. There is a twitch of movement to her left, at the door-side wall.

"Oh, Jesus," she says, voice tight.

It's McManus. Mouth bound with a rag. Elbows behind him, chained to a bar set into the brick. Eyes wide on hers. No blood on him but his bad leg is twisted under him at a sharp angle. Nothing the knee joint could withstand. She follows the low thread of sound in the room and it's coming from him, a patchy whine riding each of his inhales.

"What is this?" she says. "What the fuck is this?"

"I thought we had a deal," Sloan says, not looking at McManus, not rising out of his languid slump. " 'Civility'? I believe that's how you put it."

"And that was broken how?"

"When this one got trigger-happy and murdered my man Loomis," Sloan says. "He didn't even try to hide it. I'm shocked you didn't hear. He fed him a bullet right in front of Chain Locker."

"You know it's because Loomis killed one of ours."

"No, no." Sloan stands, so much taller than Alma, and behind her in the hall his two crimps are staying close, boots shuffling, metallic clicks as one shakes bullets from his pistol cylinder, reloads. "No spinning this. I was there."

He walks over to McManus. The wheezing quickens.

"You two," Sloan says. "You started it. Making trouble. Loomis didn't do a thing—he just wanted another gin. It must have been a dockworker with the bottle. Or a mill hand. Those lumber boys love a brawl."

"We're getting your product," Alma says. "I know you want it. Sixty pounds, best-quality King Tye. Give him to me, and I'll have it for you as scheduled, tomorrow night."

Damn it. She shouldn't have to be begging to sell him tar.

"I don't want to wait," Sloan says. "And I want it for free. This shipment and the next month's. To compensate for my loss."

She'd promise him sixty pounds free, sure. Six hundred, to get her and McManus out of here. But Sloan can't have the tar until tomorrow. It's got to be tomorrow, or their plan for Kopp doesn't work. Once Kopp is dead, everything hinges on the timing of the tar handoff to Sloan. The setup for the Pinkerton's agents. The setup for the internal mole that will plug the leak. All these pieces have to fit into place so that Wheeler's name is clear, Sloan takes the fall for everything, and Alma is positioned to feed the police the alibi of a lifetime.

If she trades McManus for the tar tonight, it will destroy the entire scheme.

"No," she says.

Sloan raises his eyebrows. Picks up one boot and sets it, light, on McManus's hard-bent leg, where the kneecap ought to be. McManus twitches.

"I don't have it yet," she says. "Just wait one day, why's that a problem?"

"Because I want it tonight," Sloan says. "And now I want the next three months free. Poor, dead Loomis."

"I don't have it yet."

Sloan's boot grinds down. McManus screams, a high animal sound muffled by the rag. Alma clenches, loosens, clenches her left hand. Waits for it to stop but it doesn't.

"Three months free, and tomorrow," she says, loud, over the shrieking.

"All right." Sloan takes his boot off McManus. "I appreciate that you're willing to bargain."

He comes toward her, all neat-tucked shirt and crisp trousers. Pleasant smile. That boyish twinkle in his eyes. Maybe she read him wrong, those first few times. He's not playing a breaker. He is one. Or it's something else she's seen before: a man playing a part so long, holding it so tight against him, that he's not playing anymore. The mask melded onto his face.

"Since we've started negotiations," he says, looking down at her, "let me lay out the butcher's bill."

He waves at McManus, who is slumped forward and heaving, wet darkening his gag, sweat running down his temples.

"This one, he's been a scourge upon me for years," Sloan says. "Shot the kneecaps out of three of my boys. Nearly broke the skull of the last one—he'll never walk proper again, and now he's slow, to boot. I assume he prepared your delivery of Pike's fingers, as well as dispatched Pike himself. Add Loomis to that tally and it is a bloody one."

"You're a pimp and a kidnapper," she says. "I don't buy that you were expecting a genteel tea party on the waterfront."

"Of course not. Only a little less carnage."

"He won't be much threat after this."

She nods at McManus, drooping so heavily he might have passed out. His chained elbows stretched taut behind him. Sloan keeps his eyes on her. He is two feet away, a distracted squint in his eyes, a tilt to his jaw.

"Oh, I'm sure of that," he says. "I've changed my request. Three months free and the delivery tomorrow, and you walk. If you want him to come with you, you bring back that delivery tonight."

"I don't have it. What fucking part of that do you not understand?"

Coldness in her gut. Sloan still peering at her, making her skin itch. The realization McManus can't be saved. He's already a dead man. It's just a question of how long Sloan will keep him breathing before making him stop.

"You remind me of a woman I met recently," Sloan says. "Something in your eyes."

Fist clench, so tight her shoulder spikes with pain. In the hall behind her the two men are talking, quiet. The scraping flare of a match.

"Are you trying to insult me?" she says, making her face as hard as she can, her voice, her shoulders. Her body slick with sweat. This is a bad spot like she's never seen. All exits blocked, guns everywhere, blood-scented air, and McManus shaking, making broken sounds, at the edge of her vision. The back of her throat burns.

"No," Sloan says. "It's just that the resemblance is striking."

"I'm walking," she says. Fighting to stay steady when every part of her throbs with the urge to escape. Get out.

"And the tar?"

She shouldn't look at McManus but she does. He is watching her, chest bellowing, dark hair spackled to his forehead. He knows she has it. He knows the night boat came in two days ago as scheduled, and anything they were set to trade with Sloan is waiting, boxed up and ready, in the Madison warehouse. Fifty yards away on the next wharf. McManus knows it, and while she looks at him, his face changes, the light dimming in his eyes. He knows she's not coming back.

"Tomorrow," she says.

"Suit yourself."

Alma's in the hall, shouldering past the two crimps, when the screaming starts again, louder, wilder. Through the brick wall. Through the warren of crates, and her throat stings with bile. Still walking. She vomits outside the cannery door. Steaming clumps on the bricks. Wet, cold night air sharp in her mouth. Still walking.

She wipes her chin on her sleeve and forces her legs faster, jogging toward the lights of Water Street.

Up one block, over, up another, over. At the corner of Washington and Taylor she stops, breathing ragged. Hunkers down beside a wide pile of planks. Her arm aching. Her head.

She had to. She had to. McManus was on the scales opposite Delphine's entire operation. She made the best choice for the business. But his eyes on hers, the light in them fading.

"Fuck."

She tilts her chin back, sucking in deep breaths. A thin shadow jabs into the star-flecked sky. A building crane. This is the corner where the crane's load fell; where the horses startled and trampled Harrison Doyle. Delphine arranged it, somehow. But not flawlessly. Doyle's widow is wrinkling the neat array of Delphine's promises to Wheeler. The railroad trust, uncertain. With Wheeler worried about Judge Hamilton, the treasurer position seems uncertain, too. And now McManus is being cracked open. All the things a body can feel. Too much. She thinks of him in the alley, Mary's soft hand on his body, giving him pleasure, slow. Sloan won't make it fast.

Focus.

She can't tell Wheeler. He needs to stay on top of Edmonds and Benson. They need to follow through with the plan.

Her pulse settles. No one has come tearing past in pursuit. She spits into the mud, sickly tang still on her breath. Waits another minute, two, her legs going stiff with crouching. When she's sure the street is quiet—no movement other than the flickering of lamps in the house across the road—she stands. Blinks hard. Walks the last block to Nell's.

Just to be safe, she goes around to the back, into the narrow alley. Pounds with the side of her fist. A light flares in the window opposite and she stops. There are footsteps inside.

"Who is it?"

"Camp," she says, quiet.

Nell opens the door, her derringer glinting in one fist.

"Why'd you come to this side?"

Alma pushes past, in a hurry to get into the house. Nell is in her dressing gown, its silk wrapped over her fine corset. The pale

heave of her breasts pressed high and plump by the shelved boning, deeply shadowed in the light of a single wall candle.

"I need to wash my face," Alma says, on her way to the kitchen.
She ladles water from the cistern into a coffee cup. Pulls open the
door to the courtyard and clumps down the steps. Wood creak.
Splashes in the dirt as she rinses her mouth, spits; rinses; and
again. She dumps the rest of the water over her face. A shock of
cold, dripping from her shorn hair, the good feeling of clean.

"Come back in, it's freezing," Nell says from the door.

Alma sheds her bile-streaked jacket as she climbs the stairs. She
closes the courtyard door. Drops the jacket and crowds into Nell,
pressing her against the kitchen wall. Their mouths connected.
Nell's breasts warm under her hands.

"Are you drunk?" Nell draws back. "You smell like you bathed
in gin."

"Honey, just kiss me." Wanting that body connection, that quick
pulse, while they are alive and whole and hungry. "And don't go
outside tonight."

"Your hands are like ice." Nell takes Alma's fingers from her
chest, folds them in her own. "Jack, I've got to go to work. I'm due
at The Captain's in half an hour."

"That's ages away."

Alma lifts her chin, licks at Nell's lower lip until she opens her
mouth. Tight tangle of her fingers in Alma's hair. Alma's thumb
tracing the seam where the corset edge presses into one heavy
breast.

"Come to bed," Alma says.

They bumble down the hall, Nell shouldering off her robe, Alma
shedding clothes in between mouthfuls of warm breath, warm skin.
Vest, shirt, boot, and boot. A haze of heat by the door as they pass
the brazier, its filigreed light on Nell's dangling corset laces. At the
bed Alma pushes Nell onto her back, pushes her ankles wide.

"Show me," Alma says, and undoes her belt, her other hand on
Nell's thigh, fingers dimpling the flesh.

After, Alma stands up, knees twinging. She wipes her face on
her discarded trousers. Smoky wool rough on her lips. In the bed
Nell is pink and languid, shifting over for Alma to lie beside her,

their skins scented with creamy musk. Soft nap of cotton sheets pulling at the small hairs on Alma's arms, her legs. All the things a body can feel. She closes her eyes. Nuzzles her face against Nell's breasts.

"Jack. Are you all right?"

"Better now," Alma says.

"I didn't think I'd see you today." Nell's hand tracing lines along the back of Alma's neck, so soft it aches.

"You getting greedy for my company?"

"Maybe."

"I like that." Alma curls down, moving her mouth from Nell's breasts to the warm softness of her belly. She looks up along the other woman's body, one ear at Nell's navel, which stirs with the long wavelike churn of breathing.

"Did you go to the fund-raiser yesterday?" Nell says. "I wish I'd been invited. I heard the food was nice."

"I did. The food was all right. No strawberry tarts, though."

"Oh! Damn."

"Now, ma'am," Alma says, thinking of the long food tables, the marshal picking at the last pastries. "That's no kind of language for a lady like you."

Nell laughs, her stomach rippling under Alma's cheek.

"Sometimes you sound just like a cowboy," she says. "Plenty of men out of the New Mexico Territory talked like that in the lumber camps. All chatter about branding and cay-yotes."

"I can keep you guessing all night, honey," Alma says, still patterning her sentences after the marshal's Southwestern drawl. Something she heard plenty of in Yuma, that shithole.

"Who else can you do?"

"Tell me a name," Alma says.

"Nathaniel."

"Now this is too bloody easy, you're making it no trouble at all."

"That's just like him!" Nell's eyes are bright with amusement. She hitches herself up, closer to sitting. Alma follows along, keeping her head in Nell's lap.

"Davy Benson," Nell says.

Nothing flinching about it, nothing about his name changing her delight in their game. She's not helping Benson steal from the business, no way. Alma still doesn't know how he found her out.

"This one's a bit harder, ma'am." Alma clears her throat. "Aw, tarnation, you'll pardon my mistakes, I hope."

Nell laughs, a throaty chuckle that moves her body against Alma's.

"Another."

"Don't go The Captain's," Alma says, and she has switched to an accent that feels bare, in this moment; the words bare, too. "*Quédate conmigo*. We can listen to the wind."

"Why, you sound like one of those Chilean sailors," Nell says, still taking Alma's words as play. "They come in sometimes on the packet ships, always wearing calico scarves."

To Alma's ear the Chilean accent is miles away from what she just used, but it's doubtful Nell knows a thing about *Californios* and *Norteños* and the countless other dialects and regions that can color spoken English.

"My father's Mexican," Alma says.

"You don't look it." Nell pushes Alma's bangs off her forehead, searches her face.

"I look just like him," she says, sharp. Old wounds itching. Old pride, protectiveness. As Camp, she does look like her father. Or she would, if she combed her hair properly. Put on a suit. Softened her eyes, her smile.

But Nell doesn't mean to insult. Her voice is kind. Her fingertips, soft as feathers, draw little circles near Alma's ear.

"My mother's people came from Scotland," Alma says. "They migrated to Kentucky, of all places, and then Los Angeles. When she married my father, her parents disowned her."

Nell's smile slips. She bites her lower lip. Her thighs shift, warm and supple under the back of Alma's neck.

"But my parents died," Alma says. "My mother at the start of the war, so I barely knew her, and my father after. An uncle took me in. My mother's brother. And he never let me forget what he thought of my father. Or my father's blood."

"Oh, Jack."

"I don't much remember my mother," she says. "But my father . . .

After every Sunday mass, he would pick a bougainvillea off the vine outside the church and tuck it in my hair. And he loved oranges. He would squeeze orange juice on everything, every damn piece of food that came onto his plate."

A line of wet trickles down Alma's cheek. Nell thumbs it away, and Alma reaches up to catch her hand, kiss her fingers, the knob of her wrist. Anything to stop her own mouth. She is talking too much. You're going fucking soft, Rosales.

"Time to get to work." Alma sits up. "You'll be late."

Nell watches from the bed as Alma steps into her trousers. Her left hand only a little slow on the buttons. Alma won't meet her eyes and goes into the hall to collect her other clothes. When she comes back into the bedroom, Nell is wearing her chemise, hands busy behind her back as she tightens her corset.

"Honey, Wheeler and I need a favor," Alma says, pulling on her boots.

"Oh, really." Laced tight, Nell sits at her dressing table, turns up the lamp. "And you think I'll say yes?"

She winks at Alma in the mirror.

"He says you know the city marshal."

"He's one of my gentleman friends," Nell says. "At The Captain's most every time I am. He ought to be there tonight."

"We need his help," Alma says. "And we need you to be the one to ask for it. He'll be sure to remember all the money Mr. Wheeler donated in the past, and Mr. Wheeler hasn't forgotten the marshal's fondness for Kentucky bourbon—there's a crate ready for him, as a gift."

"This must be some help."

"A man's going to be brought in to the jail on Tuesday." Alma buttons up her shirt. "Accused of murder. And he, in his defense, is going to accuse Barnaby Sloan of all sorts of mischief—smuggling, torture, killings. The marshal needs to make sure nothing too rough happens to this man, and that the conversation stays on Sloan as much as possible. If Wheeler's name is brought up, it should not be entertained for long."

"What are you up to?" Nell twists to face her, holding a bottle of perfume in one hand and its slender glass dipper in the other.

"Something big." Alma grins. "There's more. You got it so far?"
Nell nods.

"There's also going to be a man from the customhouse who wants to sit in on the interview, take notes. The marshal needs to let him."

"No roughhousing, keep it on Sloan, customhouse man."

"Yeah. And once the alibi's given, the marshal lets the man walk free and goes for Sloan," Alma says, over the clink of her belt buckle. "Last thing: Wheeler's guard Fulton is going to show up at the jail, and he needs to be left alone with Sloan in a cell, before they let Sloan talk. That's a lot. Do you have it? Can you get the marshal on board?"

"I've got it. And if you offer George Forrester a whole crate of bourbon, he'll let you do most anything." Nell powders her throat. "I'll make sure to lead with that particular incentive."

"All right, honey. Go get our lawman."

"Yes, sir." Nell knuckles her forehead in a salute, then tips her face back and taps drops of belladonna into her eyes.

"Come by the offices tomorrow night," Alma says. "To let us know how it went. And bring an extra dress. Nothing too fancy."

No sense in asking Nell to give up one of her best outfits when the dress is going right into the bay.

"Will I see you tomorrow?"

"Not until the offices." Alma shrugs on her jacket, leans down to kiss Nell's bare shoulder. "Be safe."

Alma lets herself out the back door, chill wind chasing Nell's warmth from her skin. Darkness crowds in, and worry. McManus's howls. Is he still screaming? Will his disappearance distract Wheeler? Or worse, will his corpse turn up on Wheeler's back steps, just when every part of this perfect plan is fitting into place? Sloan won't break McManus's body just for the sport of it. He'll want to show Wheeler what he's done. Maybe even tell Wheeler that Camp wouldn't make a deal to save McManus. Just to drive the knife in deeper.

Jesus. Alma drags her bile-soured sleeve across her mouth.

The only thing buying her time now is how long McManus holds out.

31

JANUARY 24, 1887

"I don't know who's in Seattle," Benson says.

Alma hits him in the soft meat over his liver, twisting into the punch. He coughs out an oath. Sags forward. She hits him again. Using her right arm only, but her left is tingling, wanting to snap out and back, jab and hook.

"God damn it." Benson's gray eyes are squeezed tight, pale against the red blaze of his face. "I can't give you a name I don't know."

"You're lying," Alma says.

"Kopp sold you out," Wheeler says, his arms folded over his chest. "Why protect his friends?"

Benson's breathing is pocked full of hitches. While he gasps, Alma shakes out her arm, her neck, a thin trickle of sweat ribboning down her temple. She shrugs off her jacket. Tosses it onto the desk. Wheeler sits in the chair behind it. Clay is in the corner, smoking, impassive. They're in the back office of Clay's boardinghouse. Muffled voices filter in from the lobby, but louder are the wavelets under the wharf, Benson's wheezing.

Alma tongues salt off the corner of her mouth as she folds up her sleeves to the elbow. Finally, Wheeler is watching her work. Watching her hammer punches home. She'd rather a standing opponent—a circling opponent, the trading of pain, the thrill of landing a fist just right, the total captivation of another's attention.

Whaling on Benson while he's tied to a chair feels cheap. But she owes him some blood. And she likes Wheeler's eyes on her, the narrowed heat of them over the rim of his whiskey glass.

"I ain't got shit else to say."

Alma rolls her neck. Eyes on Wheeler. The sweat-ripe bulk of Benson between them as she settles her breath, cracks her knuckles. That same current that connected them at the boxing match back in the air, smell of blood, of electricity. She gauges the bottom of Benson's sternum, then locks her gaze with Wheeler's as she slams her fist into the thin strip of bone. Her muscles hard, fast. Benson choking. Wheeler's lips peeling back from his teeth—oh, yeah, he's in the game, she wants Clay and Benson out so they are alone, they can knock bodies at last.

Benson starts laughing, a thready chuckle.

"Fuck you," he says. "You queer piece of—"

"Wheeler already knows," Alma says. "That won't buy you anything. Confine yourself to tar. And Kopp."

Now Benson is not laughing, his face starting to turn more gray than red, shifting against the ropes that hold his limbs, his torso, to the chair. Clay steps up to the desk. Lights a new cigarette with the end of his last and stubs the butt into an ashy tin dish. Benson is the cause for Peterson's troubles with the police and otherwise—the one who got the boatbuilder involved in the tar thefts and blackmailed him into cooperation. Clay told Wheeler as much when Wheeler assured him Benson was under control, and Wheeler arranged Clay's presence here as an olive branch: to make up for Peterson's suffering.

"You want to walk, you tell us who Kopp's working with," Wheeler says.

Alma hits Benson again in the sternum. Then in the meat of the throat. His eyes popping bloodshot as he gasps. A bubble of spit on his lower lip.

"I only knew Kopp. He arranged everything on the Seattle side," Benson says, voice rasping. "And there was Beckett, but he was damn useless."

"Beckett," Wheeler says.

"I saw him all the time at The Captain's." Benson curls forward, inhaling bad, and Alma fists his curly brown hair and hauls him upright, so he can't hide his eyes. "He was crazy for that dancer Kitty Jean. He's the one got me talking to Kopp."

That night in the Cosmopolitan's gambling parlor, when she was casing Dom Kopp, Beckett and Kopp argued over Beckett's reluctant friend. That friend was Benson. Reluctant to steal more opium too quickly. And after Kopp spoke of Benson, he mentioned Irondale.

"What's in Irondale?" Alma says.

Nothing in Benson's posture, his eyes, signaling surprise, but he's got a damn good poker face; he hadn't flinched in the street when she asked about Kopp. It's a shame Benson turned sour. With his size and his habit of playing dumb while keeping sly, he's a useful man to have around. She lets go of his hair. Wipes its oily residue on her trouser leg.

"Kopp's depot," Benson says. "And Peterson's boathouse."

Clay shifts in the corner, not making a sound, but his movement catches Alma's attention. His face blank. Cigarette sending a curl of smoke along his cheekbone.

"We kept a load of tar there once," Benson says. "I snagged it from the Madison warehouse, and Kopp was going to send it over to Seattle in a special crate. But he was too chickenshit to store the crate at his depot, even though it was mostly full of bricks. Why the fuck would you keep bricks in a boathouse?"

"Bricks." Alma clenches, loosens her restless left hand as she follows a thread of memory. "A crate full of bricks."

That foggy morning on the Seattle dock. Dockmen stacking crates heavy with bricks next to her. Next to Frank Elliot, who recognized her and told her he'd recently arrived in Puget Sound with his missus. Mrs. Loretta Elliot. Up to no good again, maybe.

"Did the crate have a name on it?" Alma says.

"I didn't look that close. It was weeks ago."

She steps away from him, pulls a torn envelope off Clay's desk, a charcoal pencil. Her hand jittery after the punches, but she traces out the lines well enough. The sunburst logo stamped on the Elliot & Co. crates stacked on the Seattle dock. The same logo she saw in the local paper, on Nell's kitchen table, advertising the best bricks and building supplies in the Sound.

"How about this?" She holds the paper up to Benson. "Was this on the crate?"

The spit on his lip is tinged red. His eyes tick between her and the sketch.

"Yeah," he says.

Loretta Elliot. Knowing her, she was perishing of boredom from the moment she stepped onto Seattle soil. In a rush to make friends in low places, as she likes to do. Maybe one of those friends told her how, using her husband's company's crates, she could move a lucrative amount of tar.

Loretta saw some of Alma's opium hauls down San Francisco way. And not three weeks ago, Frank Elliot told his wife Alma was in Puget Sound.

"Did the Seattle people give you my name?" she says to Benson.

He shrugs, ropes creaking, and she punches him in the stomach.

"They said look out for a woman named Rosales, from San Francisco," Benson says, breathing hard. "Who knows a thing or two about tar."

Damn it, Loretta. That was unfriendly. Though maybe it wasn't a warning, as Benson took it. Loretta needs all the help she can get—judging by the cut-rate price she put on the auctioned tar in Seattle, the woman has no idea what she's doing. Maybe she was just reaching out to someone else with contacts in the trade—trying to recruit Alma for her fledgling ring. Whatever her intentions, Loretta's proven to be one hell of a nuisance.

"You said you didn't bring a woman with you from the city," Benson says. "So I figured it was a dead end—until I stopped by your boardinghouse."

This explains his patter of questions about San Francisco, that rainy afternoon at the warehouse. And later, he was the one who went through her gear while she was out at Nell's. He saw the men's clothes mixed with women's and put two and two together. Clever, Benson. But not clever enough.

"Who's your man on the loading crew?" she says. "The one who swaps the bills?"

"I don't have one." Benson shakes his head. "Never tried the bill swap before—things were taken care of by a man in Seattle."

Alma sets the paper on the desk. Benson's talking easy enough now, so this might be the truth. Her left hand clenches, loosens. Its bones and skin itching for a throw. Bend, twist, drive from the hips—her shoulder yowling but a damn good hit in the fatty center of Benson's gut. She wants him too busy with trying to breathe to listen in on her and Wheeler.

Around the desk. Wheeler's body a magnet in the dim light, in the smoky kelp-tinged chill. She leans down to his ear. Clove aftershave in her nose, her mouth. Her hand at the back of the chair, thumb knuckle tracing the edge of his shoulder blade.

"I know who's behind this," she says, low. "A woman who's married to a former cop. A boring former cop, who won't be happy to hear how his wife is using his new business as a front for smugglers."

"So we have enough?" Wheeler says.

"Yes. We don't even have to ask Kopp."

Wheeler stands. Picks up his hat. Alma peels herself away from him, from his heat. She shakes out the bar rag at the edge of the desk and crams it into Benson's mouth. He tries to bite her but there's too much cloth between his teeth. His stretched cheeks shiny with sweat. McManus, gagged, comes back to her. The thin line between her and Sloan. It's a dirty game.

"He's all yours," Wheeler says to Clay.

Alma puts on her jacket, opens the door. Outside, a narrow alley, sun dropping straight down from overhead. A vicious wind tears between the boardinghouse wall and the clapboards of the oil and glass shop next door. The alley blocked from street view on all sides by the two buildings' angled stagger. Benson's muffled shouting is almost lost in the wind and erased entirely when Clay follows Alma and Wheeler out and shuts the door behind them.

"He won't come back?" Wheeler says.

"He won't even get on alive," Clay says. "No sense taking chances. Captain Patchett owes me a favor. He'll dump him quiet a few days into the crossing."

There will be no body to link back to Wheeler. And he and Clay will be on good terms again, so Wheeler doesn't lose his best source of waterfront information. Wheeler has structured this part of the plan neat as you please.

"Did you two enjoy yourselves?" Clay says.

Alma looks up from her cupped hands, the cigarette flaring between them. Clay's black eyes are narrowed against the sun, moving between her and Wheeler as they stand beside each other. Wheeler adjusts the collar of his coat, one eyebrow raised.

"What?" he says.

"I find it strange you'd blackmail me when you have a strapping young man of your own," Clay says, nodding at Alma.

"Careful," Wheeler tells him. "We've only just repaired relations."

Clay's mouth twists. He shrugs, gold earring catching the light, and goes back into his office. The splintered gray door clicking shut.

"It's that obvious," Alma says, grinning. She takes a step toward Wheeler. His coat still unbuttoned, catching the wind to flap against her knees. She slides a hand over his hip, bone ridge under fine-milled tweed, belt tracking along the top of her thumb. Finds the heat of his low belly.

"Not outside." He knocks her away, jaw tight.

"How much longer are you going to make me wait?" she says, not moving back.

"Not outside." He buttons his coat, blue scarf tucked close to the hard pulse in his throat, and stalks toward the street.

They emerge onto the foot of Quincy Wharf. Chain Locker is twenty yards away, on the pier. Sloan's cannery just opposite. Its brick walls cooling Alma's blood a touch. McManus is still in there, she hopes, and not on Wheeler's doorstep. Maybe dead by now. If he's lucky.

Up Quincy Street, pausing at the Water Street intersection by a wrought-iron lamppost. Early-afternoon crowds all around them so Alma can't stand as close as she wants. Playing businesslike, as though her body is not primed, wet at the armpits, wet between the thighs.

"Who are the Seattle people?" Wheeler says, quiet, his eyes tracking over the sidewalk opposite.

"Frank Elliot was a lawman in San Francisco," Alma says, also in an undertone. "Incorruptible and a bother because of it. But his wife—she's game. She's also the one who gave my name to Benson. Now Elliot's out of law enforcement and runs a brickmaking company in Seattle. If Loretta's using his product as a cover for tar, I ought to let him know. Straitlaced bastard like that, he'll turn his own wife in. It doesn't get us the missing tar back, but we've sure as hell plugged the leak."

"Telegraph him," Wheeler says. "Soon, before the post office closes."

"I will. The plan's still golden."

"It is." He looks at her, finally, and it jolts her good.

"I don't have to sleep," she says. "I can come back to the office now."

"If you don't rest, you'll never make it," he says. "You'll get sloppy. And I have to speak to Edmonds. Stick to the plan."

Alma laughs, her tongue ticking over her back teeth. How will she sleep, keyed up like this? Thinking of the slick underside of his belt against her thumb.

"You and your god damn plans. All right. I'll see you tonight."

She doesn't look back, walking south on Water Street, afternoon sun dripping off awnings in little sparks of bright, wind chilling the damp hairs at the back of her neck.

Down the boardinghouse stairs. That stain on the landing wall is shit—it's been there for three days and lets off a vicious stink. Alma shakes sleep out of her eyes, her head, drowsy but waking fast. Soft parcel tucked under her arm, her last note for the Pinkerton's agents in an envelope tucked into her vest. She wrote it sloppy, breaking out of the cipher halfway.

Agent in danger. Discovered. I am going into boardinghouse after him. This part in code, and not in code that makes a lick of sense—no cover as a real letter with real sentences, just a jumble of words that point to the right spots in the Verne book.

It is Monday night, January 24. Come quick. This part written straight. The temptation to spot the paper with ink, or tears, to add to the drama. She refrained.

Out of the lobby, into the cold. Hustling down Water Street, thinned crowds after ten o'clock, but Sailor Town's smoky bars are bustling, lit with fiddle music and shouting. She crosses Quincy—

the urge to turn toward the office enough to hitch her step—and continues to the French Hotel. Her collar turned up against Sloan's boardinghouse, opposite. Her new cap pulled low over her eyes. In the hotel lobby her boots ring on polished floorboards. The lamps are lowered for the evening, a muted golden glow. She waits by the door, studying the bill of fare for that week's suppers.

The desk clerk is alone, but a man in a pink gambler's shirt soon walks up to the desk. He leaves it just as quickly, whistling. No good.

Then a fur-coated man stomps down the back stairs, florid face, winking cuff links. While the clerk is dealing with him and his loud demands for hot water, she slips the envelope onto the counter.

"Please pass that along," she says, quiet.

The clerk barely looks at her, nods, and takes the letter, tucking it behind the desk and trying to get a word in edgewise as the fur-coated man works himself into a lather. How can he shave with cold water? God only knows.

And that's another piece in place. Back into the street, grinning, parcel squeezing soft under her arm as she strides up Quincy Street toward the offices.

Conaway is back at his post on the steps. Now that Wheeler knows who's coming, he's shuffled things to fit their scheme. Conaway's meaty face droops with tiredness. He was on the stevedore crew the night before, new to the work, learning how to replace Driscoll on a quiet shift with no shipment but plenty of innocent cargo to haul. Then given only a few hours' rest before being called to the office.

"Long night," Alma says as she climbs past him.

"You're telling me." He takes off his cap and rubs the heel of his hand over the space between his eyebrows.

Down the hall, and there is a bounce in her step, an expansive feeling of success. The plan is good. It's going to work. The Pinkerton's agents, distracted for a long while, barking up the wrong tree; Sloan, set up to fall; Kopp, disappeared; Benson and his Seattle friends smoked out. Alma and Wheeler satisfying Delphine's instructions to keep the business safe. The night stretches out before her in a slow unroll, each part of the scheme clicking into place. The next day will bring a fine piece of footwork she's looking forward to. It will keep her on her toes.

Then after, when they're all lying low and Alma's getting cozy in Tacoma, Delphine might finally come for a private visit to see how she's settling in.

But first. Wheeler's door. Wheeler waiting inside.

"You left the note?" he says when she slips into his office.

The room is warm with hearth heat. He sits at his desk, jacket off, cuffs rolled up. Watchful. When she locks the door behind her, his mouth twitches.

"I did."

She drops the parcel—her auburn wig, wrapped in brown paper—in the corner. Wheeler's chair creaks. He walks to the liquor board and she does, too, watching as he pours a whiskey. Alma reaches over, sleeve brushing his vest, and takes the glass. Has a long drink.

"So," she says, handing it back. "We're not outside."

His mouth on the glass where hers warmed it. Throat muscles rippling as he swallows.

"Why won't you let me call you Alma?" He plants his hands on the sideboard's marble. Jaw working.

"Because I like being Camp with you."

"I don't know what you want," he says, quiet. "I don't know how to see you. There's nothing gentle, watching you strike, but when we first—"

"Now, boss," she says. "I think I've made myself pretty clear."

She shifts, resting her left hip on the marble, not to make space but rather letting the movement bring her closer to Wheeler, her mouth a few inches from his ear. His nostrils flare.

"I want to fuck you," she says, and he tenses. "And not the other way around. And if you want to fight me, if you want to make it—"

Another inch closer to him.

"—hard, I don't mind that one bit."

Her breath speeding. Her collar tight. Finally. Wheeler is burning up beside her, ears red, neck red, close enough so the heat from his arm runs along the front of her body, close enough that his clove aftershave is all she can smell. And he is not moving away. Her left hand closes proper into a fist.

"Don't go easy," Alma says. "I'd be disappointed."

She reaches up, slow, and traces the backs of her fingers along his nape. He is tight-locked. Breathing fast. Ropy muscle in his neck. The rise of his shoulders knotted and firm.

She turns her hand over, opens her palm on his spine. Squeezes. The smallest reminder of danger, of her position in charge.

He grunts. Stands, quick, shaking her off. The shovel hook he sends up into her rib cage is a bonecrusher. Alma catches at the table, clumsy. The liquor bottles jangle. One tips, shatters, filling the air with the sharp scent of gin. Wheeler glowers at her. Fists at his sides. Erection pressing against the seam of his trousers.

Alma's side is pain-bloomed and throbbing, her body is throbbing, and this is good. This is going to be good. She licks at the corner of her mouth. Sheds her gray coat.

"Get ready for me," she says.

He lowers his chin, teeth bared in a feral smile, and that calls Alma forward. She feints, watches how he withdraws—quick on his feet, but those shiny shoes won't help him keep his balance—dips back and lunges in again. Jab to the jaw, her left arm still waking so the strike is too short. He weaves sideways. Her cross connects with his cheekbone, thumb knuckle brushing the side of his mustache. He comes in anyway, growling. She slips his jab, his fist stinging her ear, and that would have been a bad one to take in the jaw, he's not holding back. Just like she wanted. There's weight behind his punches she can't manage, and though she is faster, he is stronger, bigger. A challenge.

Hook to his ribs. It knocks a grunt out of him, but he catches her with a low uppercut while she's changing levels, a snap of pain in her teeth.

"Is that the best you've got?" Wheeler says, and she moves in again before she's ready, goaded by his sneer. Foolish. He hits her square in the diaphragm—so well aimed she'd admire it more if she could breathe, or see—and as she folds forward, he catches her by the collar, hauls her upright. Slams her against the blue-papered wall.

"Looks like I'm going to fuck you, after all," he says.

She is still fighting for air, her stomach hollowed, her collar cutting into her throat. His hand moves between them, rough against the stinging flesh of her belly, her belt buckle clinking. Blood hot and salty on her lip. Sweet ache between her thighs. This fight's not over. Then he palms her sex and she thinks maybe it is. His fingers pushing into her. Wheeler bites at her neck, growling, teeth and mustache scratching her skin. Thrusts hard against her thigh. A hitched groan sounds in her ears before she realizes it came from her own mouth.

There's a knock in the Clyde Imports office.

Wheeler's teeth, his fingers, go still.

Two more knocks.

"God damn it," Alma says.

It's Dom Kopp. Here early for his big chance to buy into the trade. For their plan to work, for everything to be set in motion, they need him to come inside. He can't be kept waiting and get spooked. He can't walk away.

"Tomorrow," Wheeler says, twisting her face toward his. "Before you leave town."

His fingers still curling inside her. Eyes burning, cheek red from her knuckles. He is a beauty.

Alma nods, as much as she can with his fist still at her throat. He pulls his hand from her trousers. Steps back. She is breathing hard, angry at the interruption, excited by the promise to pick up where they're leaving off. She watches him smooth himself out, hoping for a glimpse of bare flesh. He adjusts his trousers, still buttoned; fixes his tie; tugs at his cuffs. Alma straightens her collar and belt, not bothering with the rest. Wheeler has to look the part of a gentleman. If she is rumpled and bloody, sharp-toothed, it will only help them get Kopp where they want.

Wheeler leaves her at the liquor board, goes into the Clyde Imports office. The sound of his footsteps, another triple knock—Kopp's getting nervous out there, the fool—and the clicking of the lock.

"Mr. Kopp. Come in."

Alma tosses back the rest of the whiskey. It is tinted with juniper, the sides of the glass wet with liquor that slopped out when she fell against the table. Her body aches, in good and better ways, a twinge at the back of her jaw the only pain that she could do without. How is it going to be tomorrow? More sparring. Then falling onto Wheeler's desk, or into his chair. She doesn't want to wait. His eyes on hers as he touched her. Her scent on his fingers.

Focus.

It's time to get to work.

32

JANUARY 24, 1887

"I've kept quiet, like you wanted," Kopp says.

"Did you bring the money?"

Alma comes into the office as Kopp is pulling a fat envelope out of his jacket pocket. He flinches when he sees her. She stares at him flatly, nodding a mute greeting.

"Anyone else going to come sneaking up on us?" Kopp says to Wheeler, not letting go of the envelope.

"No," Wheeler says. "How much do you have?"

"Five thousand," Kopp says. "I only had three, but I borrowed more from my railroad contact. He doesn't know why, of course. I understand discretion."

Alma tongues her sore back molars. This is better than she'd hoped. A huge sum of money, yes. But more than that, Kopp just received yet another cash infusion from the railroad. If he were going to skip town and steal the railroad's money, getting away with as much as he could carry, this would be the time to do it.

Wheeler holds out his hand. Kopp hesitates, bobbing the envelope like a fishing lure.

"What does this get me, exactly?" he says.

"A fifth of our trade," Wheeler tells him. "We need a new cutter, and this is going to finance it. You can expect to recoup your investment in six months' time and make money from there. Does that math suit you?"

"Add it up for me, man." Kopp waves a hand dismissively. "In terms of profit."

"Ten thousand a year, once you've bought in," Wheeler says.

Alma is glad Kopp is ignoring her, facing away, so she can roll her eyes at this number. Wheeler's coming in a little high—it verges on farce—but he knows Kopp's illusions about the trade. And there is sense in promising so much so soon. If Wheeler told Kopp it would take three years to make his money back, the greedy bastard might take his envelope of cash and leave before they're ready.

"And what else must I do?"

"Nothing," Wheeler says. "That's the beauty of being an investor."

Kopp hands him the envelope. Wheeler doesn't even look at it, only tosses it to Alma as though it's stuffed with garbage. She cracks the seal. United States Notes, not local-bank bills—the good stuff. Kopp may be a fool, but he knows how things work in the world of under-the-table dealings. She sifts through the notes, pulls one out and holds it up against the single lamp's hazy light. Sniffs its bank freshness, crisp paper and hot ink.

"Clean money." She counts it twice. "All here."

"Excellent," Wheeler says.

He shakes Kopp's hand. It's Alma's turn to speak up.

"He wanted to see some product, sir," she says. "I told him you might allow it."

"Don't trust our quality?" Wheeler says, his tone sharp.

"I'm curious." Kopp taps his walking stick on the carpet, imperious once again now that he's paid to play. "Never seen the stuff."

"All right, Mr. Kopp," Wheeler says, leaning against a desk and folding his arms over his chest. "I'm going to give you very clear instructions. Go into the Union Hotel's bar across the street. Get one drink. Enjoy it. Then come back along Quincy. There's a recessed doorway between a tailor's and a paint shop. A little back way to storage space. I'll meet you there. Try to be inconspicuous."

Kopp nods, sees himself out. Alma and Wheeler are left alone again. She gives Wheeler the envelope, but now that things are in motion, he doesn't let his eyes stay on hers for more than a moment.

"Five thousand," he says, thumbing through the notes.

"And there's Kopp," she says. "Wandering around Sailor Town with it burning a hole in his pocket."

"Put out the lamp."

Wheeler locks the front door. She snuffs the flame, so the room is lit only by the hearth glow spilling from the back office. In the dark she is intensely aware of his body moving before hers. The muted shine of his eyes, the weight in his footsteps. They walk into the inner room. Wheeler locks that door, too. When he turns around and catches sight of the gin-spattered sideboard, his face flickers.

"There's time enough before he comes back," Alma says, close beside him.

"No. You clean that up." He nods at the cracked decanter, the dripping marble. "I'm going to speak to Conaway."

"You don't like how I clean."

"I don't like how you do most things." Wheeler throws the money on his desk. "This was your plan. Stick to it, why don't you."

"Your plan, too," she says, ambling to the liquor board and righting the broken glass. "It's possible to work and have fun at the same time, you know."

"I rarely find that to be true."

He goes out into the hall. Alma shakes her head, laughing quietly. He's as cranky as a mule now that they've gotten started. Maybe he's nervous.

There's nowhere to put the broken decanter but into the hearth. The bottle is mostly empty, all that bitter juniper leaking out through seamed cracks in the sides. She throws it against the chimney bricks, liking the smash of the glass, the way the flames leap and flare under the spattering of liquor. Little shards of glass tick down through the firewood, snapping in the heat.

Once the broken bottle is cleaned up, Alma shrugs at the board—still dripping, a few other bottles askew—and leaves it to sit at Wheeler's desk. She draws the envelope of cash toward her. Takes out six hundred-dollar bills. Most of Kopp's money is going to Delphine, to cover the loss of the four stolen batches of tar. But Alma needs six hundred dollars to cover Sloan's King Tye purchase, since he's not paying for it and she doesn't want Wheeler to know why: how she had to leave McManus to die and give Sloan the tar for free, to buy time. Sloan has not yet brought out McManus's body. That means there might still be a way to keep Wheeler from finding out how Alma abandoned him.

She folds the notes into a tight square. Tucks it into her inner vest pocket and leans back into the rich creak of leather, propping her boots up. Pulling a coiled length of cord from her pocket, she spools it around her fingers, lets her head fall back. She's never looked at the ceiling in this room. It is plastered neatly, but smoke stains crawl up the walls and onto the molding over each bracketed lamp. The cord slithers around her knuckles. She dips her thoughts into the future, that deep, icy unknown, a place she does not like to tread, though at this moment it seems almost inviting. The picture of another evening like this, except the office is in Tacoma. Wheeler might visit. In his gray coat, with a new gold tiepin she can pluck out, toss to the carpet. Or Delphine. Draped in a blue velvet cloak. Wearing a gown, like she used to. Saffron silk, or bloodred. She might sit by the fire. There might be diamonds in her hair. And Alma might offer her a drink. Didn't I tell you I'd make you happy, Rosales? she might say. Yeah. You did.

Footsteps in the hall. Voices. Alma unknots her hands from the cord, puts it in her pocket as she stands out of the chair. And here are Wheeler and Kopp. That was a fast drink. Kopp's face is sharp and eager. He has no idea.

"I thought I told you to clean that up," Wheeler says to Alma.

"It's clean." She walks toward them. "Mostly."

"Unfortunately, you have another mess to deal with," he says.

Wheeler shoves Kopp at her and she is ready, catching the startled man by the shoulders and driving her knee into his gut. He sags, wheezing. She grabs him by the hair, twisting his flashy jacket to trap his arms and letting him drop to his knees. Once he's down, she's on him, a boot in his back sending him face-first to the carpet. He squirms but there's no strength in him, all slack muscles and flopping, no breath deep enough even to scream. She sits atop his pinned shoulders. Loops the cord around his neck. Whining. Twitching arms. The cord bites into her hands and she bears down, glad she can't see his eyes, and soon it's over, piss stink rising from under the body.

"Hardly seems fair when they don't put up a fight," she says, flexing life back into her fingers.

"Roll him over." Wheeler's face is stony. "He'll ruin my carpet."

"Oh, my apologies," Alma says, sharp. "Jesus Christ. Come help me, don't just stand there."

She tugs at the body, not lingering on the purple face, the jut of swollen tongue. She picks apart the knot of Kopp's tie. There's a bit of blood at his throat, where cord cut into skin.

Wheeler crouches on the other side of Kopp. He twists the man's vest buttons free as Alma pulls open his tie. There is no talking now. They barely look at each other. Alma's handled bodies before and she's sure Wheeler has, too, but this stripping of the corpse bothers her more than it did to strangle him—that was force, a necessity, while this feels invasive, perversely intimate. She glances up at Wheeler and he is pale, scowling, working open Kopp's shirt with grim determination.

There's a rap at the door. Alma pauses, the still-warm weight of Kopp's arm heavy in her hands as she tugs off his sleeve.

From the hall: "It's Nell."

Wheeler stands, looking eager enough to get his fingers away from Kopp's belt buckle, and wipes his hands on his trousers.

"Come in," he says.

Nell steps through the door, a paper-wrapped bundle under one arm. She inhales sharply when her eyes catch on the body on the floor, on Alma's dogged yanks to remove the arm from the sleeve. But she recovers just as quick. Alma admires that.

"I brought the dress," Nell says. "Though now I don't know if I'm going to get it back."

"You're too damn smart, Nell," Alma tells her, as Kopp's bare arm flops to the carpet. "And I hope you're not squeamish—Wheeler might need some help getting those trousers off him."

"Jack. Marshal Forrester wasn't at the dance hall."

Alma lets go of Kopp's undershirt. Sits back on her haunches, her chest tight. Wheeler is frowning.

"Wasn't he supposed to be?" Alma says. "What about last night?"

"Not then, either. He might still show, but I don't know when."

"Damn it."

There's no plan if Forrester's not brought in. He has to play his part at the police station tomorrow, so he has to be briefed by Nell tonight.

"I'll go back," Nell says. "What should I do if he doesn't come by?"

"Go to his house," Wheeler says, at the sideboard, taking his time pouring a whiskey. "It's not far from yours. Just up the hill on Tyler."

"I don't want her to do that," Alma says. Nell is not supposed to be in any trouble, not doing anything out of the ordinary.

"He doesn't have a wife," Wheeler says, straightening his shirt cuffs. "He won't mind."

"Fuck you," Alma says. "She's not going to go whore herself to the marshal."

"I'll pay him a call," Nell says to Wheeler. And to Alma, icy: "I've been there before. And I don't appreciate you speaking about me as if I'm not standing right here."

"Fine," Alma says.

She pulls out her knife, frustrated by the struggle to peel off Kopp's layers of clothing, frustrated by the hitch in the plan. She grips a handful of trouser over Kopp's meager thigh and sticks the knife in, cutting open the cloth from pubic bone to ankle. Nell shouldn't have to go to the marshal. And it stings that she's siding with Wheeler. For weeks, Alma has been thinking about the three of them in the office, but it's never been good in real time: first she was bleeding out and puking, now a piss-drenched corpse is on the floor. Nell agreeing with Wheeler and snapping at Alma, to boot. It's a letdown.

"Good luck to you," Alma mutters.

She doesn't look up when Nell leaves, too busy cutting and ripping cloth. The tearing sounds set her teeth on edge. Kopp's pale body is covered in faint downy hair. When this brushes her skin, she grimaces.

"This is going to take all night unless you lend a hand," she tells Wheeler. "Where's your razor?"

He sets down his whiskey. Takes a leather bag from the armoire.

"Remind me why I thought this was a good plan," he says.

"It is a good plan." She cuts free the last bit of trousers, so Kopp lies there in a tattered nest of cloth, bare except his for damp smallclothes, socks, and left boot. "As long as Forrester doesn't fall through."

"We both know Nell's powers of persuasion."

Alma glares at Wheeler. He kneels at Kopp's head, one swipe of his razor taking off half the dead man's yellowish mustache. They finish preparing the body in silence.

Hoop & Barrow's woodshed lets in knifing wind. No sleet yet but the air tastes of it, metallic and frosty. Alma waits atop two crates of opium: the second transfer to Sloan. It had better be a smooth one. The night has only just begun.

Just before the hour, two men come slouching up to the shed. Alma recognizes one of them from last week; the other is new, young, with a scarred forehead and nervous fingers.

"Where's the tar?" the first man says.

"It's all yours," she says, standing from the boxes.

She takes out a cigarette case, matches. Offers the case to the young man first, then his glowering companion. Only the young man takes one, match flare catching in the scar across his forehead as he leans forward to draw life into the tobacco. Wind kicking hair into his eyes. The first patter of hail sounding on the pier boards.

"Can I borrow you for a minute?" Alma says to the young man. "I need to move some gear to the head of the wharf."

He looks at his mate, who shrugs and takes Alma's seat on the opium crates.

"What's your name?" she says as she leads the young man to the back of the shed. A few boxes are stacked in the shadows, and a large burlap sack.

"Evans."

"If you can manage those, I'll haul this along," she says, nodding at the sack.

"Yes, sir."

Evans is compact but strong. He squats and lifts the three stacked crates all at once, grunting, his cigarette flickering red in the sleet. Alma takes the bag by two corners and drags it backward, bumping heavily over the plankboards. When they come out of the deep shadows, two men are outside Hoop & Barrow, staring at them. The paid witnesses: waterfront men given five dollars apiece to watch what happens on the pier that night and then go tell the cops about it. Alma stops, lets go of the bag. Takes off her cap to wipe her forehead. Beside her, Evans stops, too. Sets down his load.

"You like working for Sloan?" she asks him, drawing deep on the cigarette, so the flare of it lights her face. The men by the saloon are still watching.

"He pays all right," the boy says, working on his own smoke. "Always lots of girls around."

"Good times."

She picks up the edges of the bag. Nods at him to start walking. It takes them a few minutes to reach the wharf's southern edge.

"I'll manage from here," she says. "And if you get tired of Sloan, you come talk to me. All right?"

The boy shakes her hand, slouches back toward the woodshed and his companion. Alma squints into the sleet, sees a muted, flashing light. The scow's dark lantern. Barker is ready and waiting.

She checks the wharf is empty, save for those two pairs of eyes by the saloon, who've now come closer. They're getting a good look. Stooping, she unties the top of the bag. Her own auburn wig spills out, let loose and wild, half covering Kopp's face. His mustache shaved, his eyes slivered white at the bottoms. The wig is cold in her fingers. She pulls the bag down farther, so Kopp's shoulders are visible, pale against the green frills of Nell's dress. In plain view of the witnesses, she stands over the body. Lights another cigarette. Ice chips collect in the darkly curled wig, in the lined grooves of Kopp's throat, in the flower-decked neckline of the dress.

"Goodbye, Mr. Kopp," she says, around her cigarette. "Or should I call you Miss Calhoun?"

She takes a deep lungful of smoke. Imagines Grove and Kennedy, in two days' time. Piecing together how things went down, after they collect the note she left them at the French Hotel and read through Samuel Reed's transcribed confession. Their subsequent report to Pinkerton: a high body count and a river of illegal tar, all linked to Port Townsend's smuggling kingpin, Barnaby Sloan.

Alma flicks her cigarette into the water. Picks up the body by the waist, so the head flops over her shoulder, the curls trailing down her back. It was a nice touch, to disguise Kopp this way: one of Wheeler's additions to the plan. Not only will it conceal Kopp's murder, but it adds a woman to Sloan's list of victims. The police will take Sugar Calhoun's slaying as the height of barbarity. They'll think Sloan is a monster. Hanging will be too good for him.

The scow, with Barker at the helm, bumps against the dock. It's a macabre dance over to the pier's edge. Alma steps down into the boat—a moment of lost balance, her weight altered perilously by the body—and then she's laying Kopp into the stern sheets, green dress dark against the sailcloth.

She covers the body with a loose edge of tarp. Tucks the six hundred dollars into one stiff palm, where Barker knows to look for it.

"All yours," she whispers, and Barker, a dark shape at the tiller, grunts his understanding.

Alma climbs back onto the dock. Walks past the crates Evans carried; they're unmarked, mere props, full of old rope ends. A whiskey double is waiting for her at Chain Locker. She'll need it—she's got to stay awake until the morning, stay warm outside the bar, so she can be there, frowsy and red eyed, when the cops show up looking for the gray-capped, gray-coated man who was last seen loading a woman's body into a boat on Union Wharf.

33

JANUARY 25, 1887

TRANSCRIPT OF INTERVIEW WITH SAMUEL REED

WHEREUPON THE FOLLOWING PROCEEDINGS WERE HAD IN THE JEFFERSON COUNTY JAIL, PORT TOWNSEND, WASHINGTON TERRITORY, ON JANUARY 25, 1887.

LAWMEN PRESENT: CITY MARSHAL GEORGE FORRESTER, OFFICER WAYLAN HUGHES

TRANSCRIPTION: EDWARD EDMONDS, ASSISTANT DEPUTY COLLECTOR, U.S. CUSTOMHOUSE

OFFICER HUGHES: What is it? Come in, Jackson. Hurry up.

OFFICER JACKSON: Nothing on Samuel Reed from the Chicago bureau, Marshal.

MARSHAL FORRESTER: I'll be damned.

OFFICER HUGHES: All right, very good, Jackson. Close the door, won't you.

MR REED: I told you. I'm not a bad man.

MARSHAL FORRESTER: You were just roped into working for one.

MR REED: That's right.

MARSHAL FORRESTER: And you didn't find it in yourself to break away.

MR REED: . . . No.

MARSHAL FORRESTER: So you're a weak man.

MR REED: That's not . . . fine. Yes. Yes, I am.

MARSHAL FORRESTER: Honest at last.

MR REED: I said I would be.

OFFICER HUGHES: Enough! You said after Loomis died, Sloan started killing the others? What others? What are you talking about? Who were these people?

MR REED: It started with the stevedore who shot Loomis. Sloan tortured and killed him as revenge. At the cannery. I was there. It was . . . it was god-awful, sir.

OFFICER HUGHES: And the other man you mentioned . . . Lowry? What was the trouble with him? Did Sloan go after him, too?

MR REED: Like I said, Lowry was courting Sugar. And Sloan didn't like that. Sloan told Lowry to knock it off. After all, she was the competition for his cathouse, with her own girls, and Sloan didn't trust her.

OFFICER HUGHES: And Lowry stopped seeing her, after he was warned?

MR REED: No.

MARSHAL FORRESTER: Something tells me all this didn't work out well for Lowry.

MR REED: Sloan was angry with him, but Sloan needed him. Lowry had come up from San Francisco, at the beginning of the year. He used to work with dope down south, I heard, and talk was that he was helping Sloan set up a line to there.

MARSHAL FORRESTER: Maybe Sloan will lead us to some other scum down California way.

MR REED: Maybe. Anyhow, after Sloan killed the stevedore, Lowry came to me. In my room at the boardinghouse. He said Sugar had told him I might help their cause. That's right—their cause! She'd convinced him to betray Sloan. I couldn't believe it. He seemed like a more levelheaded man than that.

OFFICER HUGHES: So Lowry and Miss Calhoun joined forces against Sloan?

MR REED: Yes. Lowry told me he was in love with Sugar. He said she was scared, after the stevedore's death, that Sloan would come after her next. Lowry said he'd protect her. He'd die protecting her.

MARSHAL FORRESTER: What did he want you to do?

MR REED: He wanted my help to get Sloan arrested. The same thing Sugar had asked of me, a few days before. He said he'd go with me to the police so we could testify.

OFFICER HUGHES: About Sloan's opium?

MR REED: About everything. The opium, the shanghaied men, the murdered stevedore. Lowry said Sugar told him I might still have a conscience, even though I'd turned my back on her. That I might still care for her, a little, after the old times . . . care enough to help her and her girls stay safe.

MARSHAL FORRESTER: But you didn't care.

MR REED: I did. I do.

OFFICER HUGHES: Did you agree to help?

MR REED: . . . No. But it was lucky I didn't start agreeing. During our chat Sloan passed by, real quiet, and stopped outside the doorway. He heard what Lowry was saying.

OFFICER HUGHES: You didn't warn Lowry to stop talking?

MR REED: What could I say? What could I say, god damn it? Sloan nearly bled me to death and there was no getting away from him! Kept me in his damned house, on his damned crew, for weeks! And he just stood there in the shadows by the door, staring at me like the god damn reaper, while Lowry whispered his own death sentence! I knew Lowry was finished. I wasn't going to hang myself, too. Not after seeing what Sloan did to that stevedore. He kept that man alive for ten hours in the cannery. Ten hours, just screaming. I can't get it out of my mind. God help me.

MARSHAL FORRESTER: All right, Reed.

MR REED: (crying, inaudible)

OFFICER HUGHES: Sir. We've got to move on Sloan. This is insanity.

MARSHAL FORRESTER: Reed. Reed. What happened to Lowry?

MR REED: . . . He's dead.

OFFICER HUGHES: When was he killed?

MR REED: Yesterday. I wasn't there. I heard about it from one of Sloan's men while I was drinking at Chain Locker.

MARSHAL FORRESTER: What happened?

MR REED: Sloan took him and his cousin out into the strait. Chained them and tossed them overboard.

OFFICER HUGHES: His cousin?

MR REED: Lowry had a cousin. They came to town together. It was sweet . . . they'd meet every day at a café to see each other. My guess is Lowry didn't show yesterday, so she went to Sloan's boardinghouse looking for him. At the worst possible time.

OFFICER HUGHES: She? This cousin was a woman? Sloan drowned another innocent woman?

MR REED: Yes. Lowry told me her name, once . . . Anna? Alma? I can't remember. Poor soul. Her and Sugar . . . I should have done something. I know it. I know I should have done something.

OFFICER HUGHES: My God.

MARSHAL FORRESTER: All right, Hughes. I've heard enough. I want Sloan in shackles and confessing within the hour.

OFFICER HUGHES: Yes, sir.

MARSHAL FORRESTER: I'm looking forward to this. Aren't you?

OFFICER HUGHES: I look forward to justice, sir. Properly served.

MARSHAL FORRESTER: Then you'll just have to look away while I enjoy dispensing it.

MR REED: Please. Can't you let me out of here? I told you everything.

OFFICER HUGHES: No. You're a key witness. The key witness.

MARSHAL FORRESTER: We've got to have you on the stand, son.

MR REED: He'll kill me. Oh, he'll kill me, just like he killed Sugar and Lowry and Lowry's cousin . . . They turned on him and now they're dead. He'll never let me walk out of here after ratting on him. Please.

MARSHAL FORRESTER: Make sure you put on your good uniform before we leave. You'll want to look sharp for the papers.

OFFICER HUGHES: The papers?

MARSHAL FORRESTER: We'll be on the front page for weeks. Maybe even in Peoria.

MR REED: Please! You've got to let me walk.

MARSHAL FORRESTER: That's enough. Edmonds, we're done here.

34

JANUARY 25, 1887

Forrester hauls Alma up by her jacket. Gray oilcloth pulling hard on her bad shoulder, her tensed neck muscles. She's not wearing as many layers as she would like over her binding cloth. But to yank her collar sideways enough to show the cops her wounded deltoid, she needed to go without a vest. Her legs are shaky, cramped from sitting in the splintered chair after spending the night in a sleet-filled gutter. She leans on the table as blood seeps back to places it ought to be. The light creeping through the barred window is soft and blue.

"Jackson! Get that new cell two open."

Forrester's hoarse bellow pummels her eardrum. He must be thirsty for his bourbon with the way he played his part today. Almost too farcical. But he followed Nell's instructions to the letter. In the corner Edmonds is packing his things away, straightening the thick stack of papers covered in shorthand. His fingers dark with ink. A splotch on his doughy jaw, too. He was the natural choice to record Reed's confession: locked down hard by Wheeler's blackmail; handy with pen and ink; his transcript imbued with authority because, as a customhouse man, he's a federal government employee. Hughes is rising from his chair, shaking his head, his blond shock of hair stiff and bristled as wheat chaff.

Alma raises her shackled hands, knuckles bleariness out of her eyes. Her lashes are sticky with tears. She didn't have to dig deep when performing Reed's final breakdown. Guilt, more regret than she expected, twists in her gut at the thought of McManus. How she left him to be taken apart. And Driscoll: she thought of him, too, while crying, and had to stop before she lost control of her act.

"You've got to let me go," she says to Forrester, swallowing hard. "Sloan sees me here and I'm a dead man."

Fist still locked in her jacket, he steers her toward the door. His big, rangy body smells of raw leather. Fucking cowboys. Most of the Pinkerton's agents out West are his brethren, loose limbs, loose drawls, lips tobacco-fattened. Happy to take all kinds of liberties with their policing, especially when it comes to nonwhite bodies. He jostles Alma and she bites back a sneer.

Into the hall and they are alone. A short passage lit by a high window and a partially open door at the middle, before a dogleg turn. The jamb is sunset lit, facing west—the door leads to Washington Street. Alma glances up at Forrester. Starts to tense for when he lets her run.

"Jackson!" he yells.

And he's still walking, pulling her past the open door and toward the dogleg turn.

"Forrester," she says, quiet. "Forrester, you have to let me walk."

"Shut up."

He shakes her, hard. A spike of pain in her shoulder. A cold squeeze in her gut. He's got to let her walk. That's the plan. Fulton won't come in until he sees her leave. If she can't get out on time, Sloan will be dragged in, and god damn it, if he sees her, he'll start yelling Jack Camp and Wheeler this and Wheeler that, and it's all over. Her performance as Samuel Reed, ruined. Wheeler's name tarnished. All gone to hell, when they're a half inch from everything working just so, in tune with the perfect plan.

Jackson comes around the bend, fuzz faced, staring. He curls a soft hand through her elbow, taking her from Forrester. Taking her toward the stairs down to the cells. No.

"Marshal—"

"I hear another god damn word, I'll put Sloan in with you when he arrives," Forrester says. "What do you think about that?"

"No," she says, voice raw, face clenching, and there's no feigning here. If Forrester's gone bad, it is over. It is over. They are
fucked.

Jackson guides her down the wooden steps, their boots rattling
the boards, and in the damp lower level she could push him, bash
his head against the wall and make a run for it. Samuel Reed is a
wanted man anyhow. The open door five yards away. But they are
just reaching the stone floor at the bottom, she is readying her
fists, her balance, when more boots sound on the stairs. It's Hughes.
One hand on his gun, a squinched focus in his eyes, his lined forehead. He watches as Jackson removes her shackles and puts her
into a cell. Clicks shut the padlock.

"Please, he'll kill me," she says, the iron bars cold and rough
under her palms.

"We won't let that happen." Hughes shakes his head, taking the
keys from the younger officer.

"You've got to let me walk. You've got to let me walk!"

Her voice rising into a shout as the men climb the stairs, a fraying
shout because what went wrong with the plan? It was so good, it
was airtight, and someone put a hole in it. Wheeler? No. Delphine?
Why? Nell? She did have to prep the marshal, who played it perfect until the end. But she wouldn't . . .

Gut heave, forehead pressed to cold iron. Spin of faces. Betrayals.
You trust them, and then they can fuck you.

Boots on the stairs.

Alma reins in her breathing. Scuffed leather boots appear. Long
legs. A silver-etched belt buckle. It's Forrester.

"You lied," he says.

He walks to her cell, boots clicking on stone. Flicks something
small toward her. Metal glint. Metal tinkle on the floor.

She kneels to collect it. A lockpick. Her lungs unfold.

"You are a safecracker. We missed that when we frisked you,"
Forrester says, quiet, nodding at the pick. "The hall door's open
for another five minutes while Hughes shifts uniforms—then we
head out for Sloan's, and the night watchman arrives. He'll put your
man Fulton in here. I'll leave Sloan in Fulton's keeping, once we
bring him in."

"You scared the shit out of me," she says, already reaching around to fit the pick into the padlock.

"How was I supposed to let you walk after that?" Forrester says. "Come in here telling a list of sins a mile long and then you think you can just move out?"

The padlock clicks open. Alma keeps her hands on it, her eyes on Forrester.

"I *can* just move out," she says. "That was the deal. Now remember, no wanted posters for Reed. Persuade eager young Officer Hughes that it's not worth the trouble."

"Fine." Forrester's thin mouth is tight with distaste. He doesn't like dealing with her.

"Blame Sloan's murder on me," Alma says. "Fulton knows that's the plan; he'll leave quiet when you come back and find Sloan dead. Say I murdered Sloan and then escaped. You'll still be a hero, what with catching Sloan and putting an end to his crime spree."

"I don't know what you and Miss Roberts are up to," Forrester says. "But your friend Wheeler is in a bad spot. If you go through all this trouble just to hang, I don't give a good god damn, but don't string her up. She's a fine woman."

"What do you mean about Wheeler?"

"This isn't the first time his name's come up lately," Forrester says, knuckling his nose. "And most conversations can't be redacted."

He climbs the stairs. Alma waits for him to clear the top. Maybe Kopp did squawk. Maybe she didn't catch him quick enough at the fund-raiser or watch him close enough that evening at the Delmonico. The padlock drops heavy into her palm. She opens the cell door and rebolts it, the pick gleaming on the floor inside. Another fire to put out. But the plan moves on. They can see to Wheeler's damage control after Sloan is trussed for slaughter.

Up the stairs, careful, treading at the boards' edges. No squeaks. The hall is empty. She hurries around the corner. Golden light seeps through the cracked door. The handle is cold under her fingers, the sky free and open and cloudless. Orange in the west, haloing Upper Town, but dark is rolling in fast over the bay. Alma pulls her cap from her back pocket. Works it on as she passes under the crude wood of the back entryway. In the street the wind is strong, the air fresh with salt and iron. Snow is coming. She takes a deep breath.

At the corner of Washington and Madison she pauses, lights a cigarette. Turns toward the arranged corner, where the half-built building that will house the Electric Light Works sits. And there's Fulton. Watching her from the bricked stoop. He nods. He's ready to go in, ready to wait in the jail cell's dark corner and take Sloan by surprise. Fulton's old, but still quick with his knife, and he told Wheeler his plan: throat, heart, then upper lung, just to be sure. Sloan will be dead in under a minute—and a corpse can't testify. Only Samuel Reed's account will remain: an account that paints Sloan as a crimp, an opium smuggler, and a murderer. The most vicious criminal Port Townsend's ever seen.

Alma walks on. Two blocks away from the jail and she is smiling, a tight grin of triumph, cold wind stinging her teeth.

At Nell's house she doesn't even knock, just grips the tailor's shop latch expecting it to be open and barging inside. The shop itself is empty, though the brazier's coals are rosy, still releasing heat. Alma's vest and knife and holstered pistol are on the sewing table. She shrugs off her jacket, slips on the vest. She wants some time alone with Nell to celebrate. Then it's off to Wheeler's office, to celebrate more. She's going to make her last evening in Port Townsend a damn good one.

"Nell!" Back through the open hall door, her weapons in hand. The bedroom is dark, quiet, its square window draining of light. "Nell?"

The kitchen, too, is empty. Now a seam of worry opens in Alma's stomach. She loops on her shoulder holster, unsheathes her knife. Walks slower, waiting for a sound, a footfall not her own. At the end of the hall, in the little silk-draped parlor, a candle is burning. A fizz of unease raises the hairs on her arms, her neck.

Just inside the door she stops. Exhales hard, not quite a laugh, her shoulders going soft with relief.

"You had me worried as hell," she says, shaking her head.

Delphine is sitting on the cushioned divan, smiling. She wears a touch of cosmetics, carmine on her lips and a flush in her cheeks. A red rose is set in her hair.

"Nathaniel told me about the plan," she says. "How did it go?"

"It was good." Alma leans against the doorjamb. "Edmonds got the whole confession down, so it's all on record for the Pinkerton's agents when they arrive tomorrow. No mention of Wheeler. Everything pinned on Sloan: the smuggling, the murders. A quick knifing when Sloan's brought into the jail and that'll be the end of him. He's the man to hang for all our sins—that's what you wanted, yes?"

"It's exactly what I wanted," Delphine says. "And our moles snared, too."

"A small concern in Seattle," Alma says. "Nipped in the bud. And Benson's not going to thieve again. He's not going to breathe again, I'm sorry to report. He'll have a proper burial at sea."

"I must say I am impressed."

"You look beautiful." Alma is warm under the sun of Delphine's compliment, her unexpected presence. Here they are, alone, in this room with all its finery. "What's the occasion?"

"I remembered you wanted to see me in one of my old gowns," Delphine says. "There's no escaping my widow's weeds here, but I thought I'd spruce myself up as best I could."

Alma's heart is speeding as she does the possible math of why Nell's away and Delphine is here. Usually that would mean a scolding. But there's a better, more enticing option. Alma takes off her cap. Tosses it onto the little round table, where the teapot's steam smells of licorice and aniseed.

"Sit down," Delphine says. "You must be tired after all that."

Alma sinks into the armchair opposite. Once her body is folded onto the soft upholstery, the knot of nerves in her stomach loosens. She could sleep right here. She could eat. But most of all she could use a touch, a skin-to-skin connection.

"It's been a long day," Alma says. "And I'm not quite done. I've got to debrief Wheeler, then make the night boat to Tacoma."

The last piece of the plan: Alma has to disappear. According to Reed's confession, Alma Rosales is dead. And she can't remain in Port Townsend as Jack Camp, either. She wore Camp's clothes while playing the part of Samuel Reed. Now the police know Reed as an accomplice to Sloan's crimes, an escapee from jail, and the man who killed Sloan. Reed can't be found—and he certainly can't

be seen hanging around Clyde Imports. The Reed alibi was constructed to keep Wheeler, and the business he runs for Delphine,
spotless. So Jack Camp has to disappear, too.

"Dear Rosales," Delphine says. "It has been a long day. But
there's one more thing I need to ask of you."

"What's that?"

Delphine rises out of her chair. As she crosses the room, skirts
whispering, Alma swallows hard. She wants the moment to rush
faster—Delphine leaning into her, their mouths meeting, the strong
wet press of tongues, her hands on Delphine's hips—but also slow,
so she can remain in anticipation, all thrumming pulse, all wanting.

Alma parts her legs to allow the other woman closer. Delphine
leans forward, skirt silk catching along trouser twill, and reaches for
Alma's chest. Her touch trails sparks along the top edge of Alma's
binding cloth to her inner arm, the side of her bound breast. Then
her fingers leave Alma's skin. Close around the butt of her pistol.
She pulls the weapon free, slow, the metal catching against Alma's
shirtsleeve. Alma laughs, soundless, disbelieving.

"Delphine—"

Her dark eyes fixed on Alma's. She nestles the pistol grip into
Alma's hand, her fingers warm.

"He's in his offices," Delphine says, quiet.

And then Alma understands.

The heat leaves her in a rush. Her skin prickles, at once too tight
and too loose on her body. She shakes her head. It doesn't make
sense, the contortions they went through, the way Sloan has been
set up to swing—none of it makes sense if Wheeler is going to fall.

"Why?" she says.

Delphine pushes away from the chair, her skirts dragging over
Alma's knees. She pours tea into the cup on the table. Her brow is
knotted. She picks up the teacup, sets it down without taking a sip.

"Why kill him?" Alma says, still stunned. "He's been nothing
but loyal."

"He has been loyal. And a good tutor for you," Delphine says.
"But things here have gotten complicated. We're shifting shop."

"We?" Alma holsters her gun, its heavy gleam wiring her jaw
tight, so her teeth ache.

"I'm going to Tacoma, too," Delphine says. "Port Townsend is losing its shine. At first we had the best spot in the Sound, right under the customhouse men's noses. But their help is starting to draw too much attention. And Port Townsend is on the Pinkerton's agents' minds. Tacoma is safer. Bigger. It's more than five times this size. A growing city for our growing enterprise. And a new friend there."

"Jim Pettygrove." The man who was fawning over Delphine at the fund-raiser, along with the judge and Marshal Forrester.

"Yes."

If Delphine is surprised at Alma's good guess, she doesn't show it. She sips her tea, tapping her nails on the table, her eyes fixed on the glitter of her ruby ring. Alma has never seen her so uneasy.

"Pettygrove owns a steamboat company," Delphine says. "And I've just purchased a large share. No more skulking around in a cutter, wary of the revenue boats. No more delays and bribes on the Red Line. Pettygrove's boats will carry our product full-time. And you'll be positioned to link deliveries between docks and trains."

"You still haven't told me why Wheeler has to go. What about business here?"

"It's falling apart." Delphine sets down her tea, sharp clink of china. "You see it. Conall Driscoll, a guard, deceased. Davy Benson, a thief, deceased. Tom McManus, gone missing after murdering a man in full public view. Nathaniel Wheeler . . . well, Nathaniel is up to you."

"I don't think we should kill him." Alma comes out of her chair. "He's a valuable man. This plan was part his. He's smart, Delphine."

"Smart, yes. I know. But smart or not, there have been too many rumors about him lately," Delphine says. "I will not allow his troubles to link back to the business and bring us all down."

"Kopp was spreading those rumors, and he's dead," Alma says. "Wheeler can put out any other fires."

"Judge Hamilton is nervous. But still, the situation might have been saved, until last night."

Delphine pushes a thick strand of hair from her cheek, the fine bones in her wrist shifting.

"What happened last night?" Alma says.

"Hamilton and Mayor Brooks received telegraphs from a Mr. Frank Elliot."

Alma's lungs squeeze. She closes her eyes.

"Shit."

"It seems he used to be a lawman in San Francisco," Delphine says. "He claims he has proof Nathaniel's been smuggling product through Seattle using his company goods and is preparing to press charges."

God damn it. Elliot has turned crooked and has his claws out. Or else Loretta Elliot intercepted Alma's telegraph to him and wrote back herself. Either way, the plan to lock down the leak in Seattle has backfired. Badly. And how did the Elliots know to go after Wheeler? Kopp. Kopp must have told them who was running Port Townsend's opium trade—as soon as he learned Wheeler's name. As soon as he came to the office wanting to buy in. Almost a week ago.

"That's my fault," Alma says. "Let me fix it."

"I'm afraid it's too late for fixing," Delphine says. "As you well know, the Pinkerton's agents are coming tomorrow. In search of opium smugglers. And now Judge Hamilton and the mayor have damning evidence linking Nathaniel to opium."

Alma closes her eyes. This is what Forrester was talking about, at the jail. The conversation that couldn't be redacted. He meant Elliot's telegraphs to the judge and the mayor. Those telegraphs came in last night. Last night, when Alma and Wheeler were waiting for Kopp to show up at the office so they could kick off their plan. But the plan was doomed from the start. Elliot's trap closing around Wheeler as Alma worked to close her trap around Sloan.

After the long stretch of yesterday, after the hours spent performing as Reed, this is almost too much to absorb. She is so tired. Delphine's skirts rustle; her footsteps, slow, approach. Her dress nudges Alma's shins, then her hands settle on Alma's shoulders.

"Today Judge Hamilton made an effort to protect Nathaniel," Delphine says, and Alma listens with her eyes shut. "Spare him, as a gentleman, and a friend. But the mayor has never favored him, and in the end the mayor won out. He will have Nathaniel arrested tomorrow. He wants to drag him through the muck as an example to other thieves."

Alma understands what Delphine is implying. She shakes her head. Delphine's fingers tighten on her shoulders, prompting her to speak.

"He'd be a loose end." Alma says the obvious. "If he ended up in jail."

"I don't want to kill him," Delphine says. "We've worked together for years. But that strong bond is also a weakness: he knows far too much about my business. I can't afford for him to be arrested. He might talk. So he must disappear tonight."

Alma looks up. Carmine glistens on Delphine's lips as she leans close. There's a strong pulse in her neck. Her perfume clouds Alma's head.

"Disappear him, then." Alma is spinning through their options, dizzy with it all. "There's got to be another way. I'll take him to Tacoma, quiet."

"And you think he'd run?" Delphine says. "Knowing him, do you think he'd play the coward?"

"If it meant staying alive," Alma says. But she's not sure.

"Then what?" The red rose in Delphine's hair is blood bright, pulsing at the edge of Alma's vision. "He can't be seen with me, in Tacoma. And if you're my deputy there, you are linked to me, so he can't be seen with you. Wheeler is tainted with tar. The scent of it will follow him, after these accusations—especially if he disappears, the guilty man's last resort. We cannot be tainted with tar, Rosales. I survive by keeping my hands clean."

"Damn it." Alma understands the logic, the cords tight-coiled around Wheeler, around both of them. "If he went somewhere else—"

"Nathaniel Wheeler is no Samuel Reed." Delphine's voice is clipped; she is growing impatient, but the somberness remains in her dark eyes. "Able to vanish without a trace. His face and name are well-known here. Even if he took a boat to China, he'd be a wanted man, and wanted men can talk if they're captured. This is how it must be."

Alma releases a long breath. She sees the fatality of it. And if Delphine—with that knifing intelligence Alma prizes—if Delphine can't see another way, Wheeler is finished.

She reaches out to curve her palms over Delphine's tensed

waist. Warm lace, warm silk, knobbed corset boning. Smooth skin waiting underneath. Touching Delphine brings back the night Alma first had her, when they twined and panted in a canopied bed, on the top floor of the Nob Hill house, high above the glittering city. It was the first time Alma held a woman, and the most painfully sweet. She was young enough. She still believed in love.

"I came here to celebrate your success," Delphine says, her body softening toward Alma's. "I only found out about Elliot's telegraphs and the mayor's plans an hour ago, when I ran into Judge Hamilton on my way through town."

She places one palm on Alma's chest, just above her heart. Through the vest and shirt and binding cloth, a pressure, warmth.

Alma has missed holding her. She pulls her closer, and Delphine does not resist. Their mouths connect, slightly open. Delphine's breath is sweet with licorice tea. Her lips faintly bitter with carmine. A current zings through Alma despite the grim task ahead.

"This is a hell of a thing to ask of me," Alma says, when they shift apart.

Delphine nods, her eyes on Alma's.

"If you can't do it, I'll send Joe," she says.

"I'll do it." Alma reaches between them to her shoulder, adjusting the leather holster there. Bearing up under its weight. This is how it must be. "If Joe shows up, Wheeler might get spooked. But he's expecting me."

"Be careful, Rosales. And be quick. I'll see you in Tacoma within the week."

"All right," Alma says.

35

JANUARY 25, 1887

Up the narrow steps. Through the blue hall. Wheeler's door is ajar. She knocks as she pushes it open.

He is at his desk, pen in hand but eyes flickering up to her.

Alma closes the door. Leans against it. He puts down his pen.

Now's the time to do it. His gun is on the desk but too far to reach quickly.

"It's done," she says.

"And they bought it?"

"Hook, line, and sinker."

Wheeler's eyes are hard on her, his shoulders stiff. Almost suspicious, but how could he be—she was blindsided, expecting a celebration and getting an execution order. Unless McManus has been found. Wheeler lifts his whiskey. Takes a long drink.

"The marshal's out picking up Sloan right now." She reaches into her jacket. He flinches a hair fraction, knuckles flaring white around the tumbler, but she pulls out her cigarettes, a matchbox. "I signaled to Fulton. He's ready."

"Good," Wheeler says. "He looks slow, but he's opened his share of throats."

She does not move from the door as she lights her cigarette.

"Didn't see Conaway," she says.

"He's out to get supper." Wheeler is starting to breathe faster, his gaze dropping to Alma's boots, then crawling back up her body. He hasn't heard about McManus.

"So we're alone?" she says.

Now's the time to do it. No witnesses, his trigger hand full of liquid and glass.

"Yes."

She drops her free hand to the lock. Twists it shut. Stubs her cigarette out on the bottom of her boot. She can't tell if she's just killing time, or if she's about to change her mind.

"Get up," she says.

He does, and she is crossing the carpet, shrugging off her jacket, her holster, shucking her knife. This will be fists only. Bone and flesh, while they still have it to sling. She rolls up her sleeves to the elbow. Cracks a knot out of her neck.

Wheeler comes around the desk and Alma walks toward him, popping her shoulder forward to deliver a cross to his mouth. He ducks under it, returns with one of his own, and Alma tilts her face so it glances off her jaw, stinging her nerves awake. She trips back toward the wall, playing clumsy, and when Wheeler follows—he is overeager, coming at her too fast, too reckless—she spins and lunges up. Bars a forearm across his throat, slams him into the wall. Her left shoulder roaring as she muscles him against the blue paper. In the clinch she pounds short punches into his ribs, his stomach, and the wall is not the ropes—he has no room to wind up and return the blows.

When he jerks to the side, she lets him twist away, leaning on the wall herself to catch her breath. There's pain and then there's pain, and she doesn't want him too distracted, too bruised to come back at her the way she's hoping. He's no spring chicken, after all. Alma laughs at this, her face slipping against the sweat of her bare forearm on the wall, and that's when he comes close again, grips her by the back of the shirt and throws her to the ground.

Rolling out of range, she slams into the desk, hard, using it for leverage to launch herself up to standing. She leans over the wood, using her smaller size to her advantage—letting him think he's got her struggling when she's only just gotten started. His hand on her shoulder and she skips out from under him, kicking the back of his knee so he falls against the desk, and here is where she wants him, off-balance, swearing.

Alma shoves into place behind him, and he's only half fighting now. One hand wrenches tight his collar, fist against knobbed vertebrae. Her other unbuttons his trousers, fumbling inside, clutching hard, hot, his shoulders tight as she muscles him against the desk, thighs set into the backs of his, knuckles tapping the wood as she works her wrist fast, his breath fast.

Now's the time to do it. When he's faced away and panting, sweat gathering at his nape. When his hands are open and empty, flexing white against the white-paper-littered surface of the desk.

But he feels good, he smells good, clove aftershave and salt and musk, she's been waiting for this for so long, she is whispering filth in his ear—"You like it when I fuck you, you like it when I've got you hard and aching, you like it, tell me you like it, tell me you want more"—and he is groaning, little guttural blurs of noise that draw a thread of heat tight between her thighs.

"God damn it," he says, and the hitch in his voice has her growling, shoving him harder into the desk.

"Tell me." She slows her fingers. Squeezes.

"More," he says, bucking into her hand.

"What?"

"More. I said more, Camp."

And that's what she wanted, her name in his voice when it sounds like this, when it's torn open and rough like this. She presses her face into the back of his neck and bites at the slick skin.

He throws her off with a shudder and she blunders into his chair, that second of lost footing made slower when he turns and her eyes catch on his sex, thick veined and weeping. Her mouth opens, hungry, but he is not waiting for play—he grabs her by the hair and slings her facedown over the desk, the full strength of his arms apparent in the force of it, the bruising way the wood bites into her thighs. She reaches down to her belt and he lets her undo the buckle, then whips the belt from her trousers and catches her hands, twisting them behind her back, looping the leather strap around them. Her muscles protest, her bad shoulder searing, but there is chill air on her thighs, fingers on her bare hips, pressure, slickness, and then he is fucking her, grunting, papers crinkling under her cheek as her body throbs.

He grabs a handful of vest and shirt, just between her shoulder blades. Yanks her up a few inches and slams her rib cage down, knocking the breath out of her. Thrusting hard as she gasps for air, for more.

"You don't make me beg," he says, but she did, she did, and heat coils in her, her hip bones jolting into the desk, it is good, it is what she wanted, and it's the last god damn time. No. It doesn't have to be. But Delphine—

"Fuck," Alma says, hissing when he pulls out of her, leaving her cold.

He undoes the belt, hands unsteady on the buckle. Alma shakes free her arms, wincing at a spasm in her left shoulder. She flips over on the desk. Kicks off her boots, kicks down her trousers, Wheeler watching her and stroking himself, slow, his hand glossed with wet.

"Your arm," he says, quiet, breathing fast. "I forgot."

"It's fine."

She doesn't want him to be gentle, not now. Legs bare, pulling him back to her by his loosened tie, locking her thighs around his hips, and this angle is good, "Harder," she is saying, she slips her hand between their stomachs down to slick heat. Bites at his neck, all tensed muscle, all salt. Her fingers working her body to a tingling fever. His mouth at her ear, thick breaths, "Oh, God," he is saying, "Oh, God."

After, Wheeler peels his body from hers, their skins sticky where he rucked up shirts and vests. He is still breathing hard. He wipes sweat from his temple.

"Get me a drink." Alma levers up onto her elbows. Ledgers and scribbled notes stick to the damp skin of her low back, her haunches.

Wheeler pauses. Shirt half-tucked into his trousers. Eyebrow raised. A pale patch of skin, a dark thatch of hair, are visible under the white edge of his shirttail. Alma licks salt off the side of her mouth. He follows her gaze, gives a small huff of a laugh.

"A gin," she says, staring until he is buttoned up. She draws on her trousers, her boots.

At the sideboard he lines up two glasses. The broad strength of his shoulders made plain by the clinging of his damp shirt. Belt looped over powerful hips. That fighter's body.

Now's the time to do it. Now. Before she changes her mind.

Alma walks around the desk to her usual chair. Sits down, groaning, her body bruised and pummeled, small muscles and big infused with sensation, with fresh blood. She lowers her arm into the muddle of jacket and holster beside the chair. Her pistol is cold. Heavy. She watches Wheeler pour the gin and cap the decanter as she gentles back the hammer, brings him into the sight. Her hands smell of their bodies, their mingled sweat and fluids.

"Once Fulton is done, there are more of Sloan's men I want to go after," he says, pulling the stopper off the whiskey. "Some to recruit. Some to shut up."

Turn around, god damn it.

"We can pay them a visit tomorrow."

He half turns, bottle in one hand, empty glass in the other, and sees the pistol leveled at his chest. His face goes tight. His neck throbs so that Alma can almost hear his pulse.

"Alma."

She shakes her head. She won't tell him about McManus. It's a gift to him, that not knowing.

"Are you going to go down swinging?" she says, her body still burning from the warmth of his. "It's the only thing a man can do."

Heat sparking in his eyes, his mouth peeling into a grimace, she keeps that look and its intensity to remember always, his moment of glory before he throws the whiskey bottle at her and lunges forward and she ducks, glass smashing into the desk beside her as she keeps her aim true.

Now's the time to do it.

She pulls the trigger.

AUTHOR'S NOTE

While Alma, Delphine, Wheeler, and company are fictional, Port Townsend's history as a smuggling hot spot is fact. In the 1880s, Port Townsend was a powerhouse in sea trade, vying with San Francisco as the busiest American seaport on the West Coast. The Port Townsend customhouse was famed for corruption, and with help from the customs officials, smugglers were making fortunes by dodging the import tax on opium, which could be as high as six dollars per pound. Newspapers speculated that the opium smuggling was a centralized effort; the *San Francisco Chronicle* published a piece on the purported "great smuggling ring" in November 1893:

> The opium ring of the Northwest is a fearful, shadowy, impalpable something; shadowy in form, but most substantial in fact. It makes its presence known, yet is itself unknown. The subordinate members obey a system . . . [directed by] some prominent citizen whose reputation in the commercial and social world is untainted . . . [U.S. government agents] are baffled and, watch as they will, they cannot find evidence enough to bring this man to justice.

This quote, of course, helped inspire Delphine: the woman—not man—in charge. Many of the ring's import methods and its connections to other Puget Sound cities are based on documented cases of opium smuggling. And in one famous bust (reported extensively by Tacoma's *Daily Ledger*), where the *Haytian Republic* steamship was seized on suspicion of untaxed opium aboard, the smugglers were using an imports and shipping business to cover their activities.

The following texts and resources were foundational to my research for this book: *Port Townsend: An Illustrated History of Shanghaiing, Shipwrecks, Soiled Doves and Sundry Souls* by Thomas W. Camfield; *Shanghaiing Days* by Richard H. Dillon; *Pinkerton's Great Detective* by Beau Riffenburgh; *The Napoleon of Crime* by Ben Macintyre; the Chinese in Northwest America Research Committee; the historical newspaper collection, especially the *Daily Ledger* archives, at the Tacoma Public Library; the Jefferson County Historical Society; and the Maritime Museum of British Columbia. Thank you to Stephen Li for the Taishanese transliteration.

ACKNOWLEDGMENTS

Thank you to Jeff: you were there from the beginning, and I'm so glad we're family. To my *mamá*, Lily, for encouraging me to read, write, and dream. To Kelly, for your friendship and for being the very best companion on this writing journey. To Gladys and Ivory, for always making time to visit. Thank you to my agent, Stacia Decker, for believing in this book and being its champion. Thank you to Daphne Durham, my editor, and her assistant, Sara Birmingham: your enthusiasm and keen questions made the revision process a joy, and I'm in awe of how you've made my words shine. To Carrie Callaghan, for a suggestion that made a tremendous difference. I am deeply grateful to Yaddo, where I wrote much of this book; my time in residence there was a gift of inestimable value. Thank you to Blue Mountain Center, where I learned so much from the wonderful community of artists and activists. To the Jentel Artist Residency Program, and Sara, Maeve, Vanessa, Helen, Thad, and Lynn. To George, Marilee, and Emma, for offering a beautiful place to work. And to Katy, Connor, and Jamón, with love.

A NOTE ABOUT THE AUTHOR

Katrina Carrasco holds an M.F.A. in fiction from Portland
State University, where she received the Tom and Phyllis
Burnam Graduate Fiction Scholarship and the Tom Doulis
Graduate Fiction Writing Award. Her short stories have
appeared in *Witness*, *Post Road*, *Quaint Magazine*, and other
journals, and her nonfiction can be found at Autostraddle.
She is the recipient of a Grants for Artist Projects award
from Artist Trust. She lives in Seattle. *The Best Bad Things*
is her first novel.